ONE MIND'S EYE

Books by the Author

Shivering World

Crystal Witness

One Mind's Eye

Star Wars Novels

The Truce at Bakura

Balance Point

Firebird Novels

Firebird

Fusion Fire

Crown of Fire

Wind and Shadow

Daystar

Non-Fiction

Writing Deep Viewpoint

Grace Like a River: an Autobiography
with Christopher Parkening

Exploring the Northern Rockies

ONEMIND'SEYE

KATHY TYERS

A
NOVEL

To **Cheryl,**

For suffering my need to compete and control,
sharing my worst wounds,
sharpening my wits,
sheltering me,
shouldering my tears.

01

Air streams whispered out of ducts and vents, masking murmurs and quiet footsteps. On the third floor of the Nuris University library, sound seemed smothered under a weight of wisdom and recirculated air.

Llyn Torfinn stood at an i-net station, listening nervously. The wall at the end of her aisle was opaque blue glass, and it glistened like a gigantic opal. Closer by, head-high racks displayed information printouts, data spools, and ancient-looking scrolls and books. Her brother Niklo had explained them as replicas, dignifying the library with the appearance of Earth-date antiquity.

Clasping her thin left arm with her right hand, she glanced over her shoulder. Fortunately, there was still no sight or sound of Karine—Niklo's natural mother, who had adopted Llyn despite her baffling history. Karine had brought Llyn down to Nuris University to attend a choral festival. She'd ordered Llyn and Niklo to report to one of her professor friends for a tour of the campus.

As if Niklo needed a tour! He lived here now.

Instead, Niklo had agreed to help Llyn run this search. Karine should be busy at the governmental pyramid for at least half an hour, and here in the library, data could be accessed that was not available over normal channels.

Llyn, especially, couldn't have looked for this information at Karine's residential clinic, because she was officially a patient there. Karine, a well-known clinician and a genetic empath, had locked that i-net branch.

So Niklo hunched over the dedicated terminal, hurriedly searching the Concord's medical network for families compatible with Llyn's DNA. Karine had always claimed that Llyn was related to no one.

But even tube babies had genetic parents. Llyn desperately hoped to find the kin she could not remember. If they hadn't forgotten her, they might take her home.

"Huh." Niklo pushed his chair back.

"Did you find them?" Llyn asked, encouraged by his tone of voice. "My parents?"

"No. I found you."

"Oh?" Llyn leaned over his shoulder. A wisp of black hair fell into her field of vision.

He pointed at the screen. "I accessed our clinic records with my family code. At the home terminal, that doesn't get me in. But look. Here it did."

Llyn peered at the screen. The file looked like a medical log.

Patient #721: Llyn (matername not in thought stream). Address of origin: unknown. Mass: 34 kg. Height: 1.46 meters. Physical condition: poor. Mental condition: total dysfunction. Preliminary brain scan confirms hypertrophy of the temporal lobe, particularly the dorsal region that governs hearing.

Llyn nodded. Nothing about her background had ever made sense. Five years ago—just a few days before Karine logged that entry—Concord authorities had found Llyn hardwired into an artificial reality unit, floating limply in an unlicensed laboratory's AR tank, unable to speak, terrified by her rescuers. Her personal locator chip transmitted on a frequency that did not appear on Concord records. Her gene typing matched no strain on Antar's med-net.

The authorities had ordered Karine to rehabilitate her.

She glanced around again. "Are you sure this terminal's secure?"

"You're worried about Mother?" Niklo had always been subliminally sensitive to body functions, including Llyn's tension. He stared at the screen through his fringe of brown hair and touched it at a control point. "I've got this under a security lock. She won't find us."

Llyn didn't trust security locks to keep the empathic Karine out of net searches. After five years as Karine's patient, she always assumed someone was watching.

She returned to Karine's old notes and read quickly, skipping technical sections. Maybe something in this journal would unlock her memory.

> *Admission: Subject has been placed in another clinical float tank with motion frame. Remains unresponsive, except to immersive first-person artificial reality. She seems content with the projection helmet and gaze-tracker I programmed, but confused to find that the images do not obey her. She must learn that she does not control the real world.*

I learned, Llyn reflected bitterly. Her oldest memories glimmered: dim color washes, brilliant three-dimensional grid lines, a universe that obeyed her whims. Simple melodies that Llyn had composed as she wafted along had moved the small images of her life.

She remembered nothing before the AR. Still, according to Karine's medical specialists, she couldn't have been there since birth. Neural pathways had kicked in as Karine trained her. She'd relearned human language.

No one knew where she'd mastered it before.

She assumed she'd been kidnapped, probably from some other Concord planet, but she couldn't guess why. Why would anyone lock a child's mind into a different universe and abandon it there?

She vividly remembered being wrested out. A huge moving form had stripped off the transducer helmet, and darkness garroted her vision. She'd flailed in all directions, robbed of direct brain input, struggling to find up and down axes in a gridless world. She'd tried to sing up an image. Any image.

> *Preliminary diagnosis: This subject may never live "normally," but perhaps she can contribute something to society. It will take years to readjust her.*

"Sounds like Mother," Niklo muttered.

"Yes." Llyn understood this world better now. In the unlicensed tank on an inadequate motion frame, her muscles had atrophied, and she'd missed her growth spurt. She'd been child-sized when they found her. They'd guessed her age at eleven. She'd only grown a few centimeters since then. Karine had eventually revised the admission estimate up to thirteen, but to this day, no one was sure how old she was. Probably seventeen. Possibly eighteen—or sixteen.

Her family would know.

She skimmed another section. Karine predicted a long struggle with verbal and written language. Then Llyn's eye caught the word "adoption."

> *I have begun legal adoption proceedings. I would hate to lose custody of this unique subject.*

Llyn pointed at the words, which looked as hard and cold as the screen. "Unique subject." Niklo snorted. "You're more than that."

"To you." Feeling as if she'd been slapped, Llyn read on. The next section described her lagging tactile development. Whoever put her in the tank had inserted a biochip in her upper spine, blocking all sensations except those transmitted through the AR. She still had trouble differentiating hot and cold, rough and smooth, sharp and blunt.

> *Plus zero point five years: Morphing of "Mother" agent to match my face accomplished. Subject should accept discipline now. She has resisted each infinitesimal change in imagery and is keenly aware of geometric proportions. Insists on attempting to control objects by croaking, despite repeated failures over six months. I will not be controlled.*

A chill settled on Llyn's shoulders. She skipped far ahead.

> *Plus one point nine years: Subject stood upright with aid of walker. I drained the float tank to celebrate. Subject became violent. Confined her to padded room. Kicking and wall striking will accelerate muscular and tactile development.*

Niklo whispered, "Nasty."

"Me?"

"Of course not you. Mother."

Llyn skimmed at a furious pace, looking for an incident she remembered vividly. Minutes were ticking away, and Karine would certainly find them if she started looking. Campus Security could track their PL chips to the library, and Karine would search them out one floor at a time by the scent of their mental activity. It was no use running from an empath.

> *Plus two point eight five years: Subject evidenced a deep, unaccountable catatonic state.*

There it was!

> *Plus two point eight six years: Second catatonic episode. Evidently, something in clinical environment is overloading area 41 of the gyrus of Herschel or some other brain center. Sound recognition depends on so many cortical zones.*

> *Plus two point eight seven years: Catatonic-state stimulus identified as auditory tones that relate to each other within the unmusical tonality of her former artificial reality. She perceives the tonal sequences as "control music." I have banned music from clinic grounds and removed all metal and glass objects, potential producers of musical tones, from the subject's environment.*

Llyn sighed. To her, those "episodes" had been heart-healing flights back to the only home she remembered, where broad sweeps of color danced through the stable grid. Abstract shapes sang there, shaped by rhythm and pitch. Many nights she had lain awake at the clinic letting faint remembered melodies feather the back of her mind. The music's haunting, pure light cast dim shadows on reality's dull backdrop.

Karine had hired a music therapy specialist to analyze output from the AR transducer. He'd finally made Karine understand that the AR music divided each octave into seventeen fractional steps, instead of the "standard" twelve half steps of most cultures. Llyn remembered his visit. He'd played the seventeen-tone scale on a portable synthesizer, and she'd slipped away. Instantly, joyously.

> *Plus three point five years: Subject has passed several grade levels at my satellite classroom. Fine mind, although social development still juvenile. Tactile sense lags on. Stubborn outbursts continue. Attempting to discipline consistently by stimulating pain sense with electroshock.*

Llyn pursed her lips. To this day, Karine rarely praised her. She'd always felt slow and stupid. It was startling to read that Karine thought otherwise.

The most recent entry was six months old and surprisingly personal.

> *Plus four point five years: Subject insists she is ready for independence. Her resilience is admirable, but she is gravely mistaken. She will never be able to live alone. Before we give children freedom, we must equip them to use it.*

> *Llyn will always need me.*

"She hopes," Niklo muttered. "I think she needs you worse than you need her."

Llyn considered. For all Karine's genetic empathy, she seemed not to care how often or how badly she hurt Llyn.

As if supernaturally responding to her critical thought, the floor shook. Llyn didn't so much feel the quake as hear it rumble beneath ground level. Hearing still was her dominant sense.

She glanced up to see what she stood under, then aside for the nearest reinforcement. Falling objects had killed Karine's husband eight years ago, and Karine had never remarried.

She was married to the clinic.

Niklo swatted her arm. "Hey." His tone was blasé. "The University buildings and sky domes are quakeproof."

So was the dome over Poulenc, supposedly, where Karine's husband died. Llyn steadied herself with one hand against a shelf. There'd been no worry of self-preservation in her other world, no bony body to pummel toward strength. It was a world that still wanted to reclaim her, and every moment she must resist. This world could kill her the way it killed Niklo's father, if she didn't pay attention.

"Well." Niklo pointed at a control over the terminal. "That was informative, but it wasn't what we wanted. I'll try the Genetics department."

"Thank you." Llyn glanced up the aisle again. At a terminal along the opaline wall, three women sat in quiet conversation. Racial variety persisted on all nine Concord worlds, even after centuries of intermarriage. Most people still chose mates who looked rather like themselves.

Hair and clothing identified these women as offworlders. One wore the archaic garments of the Tdega system—embarrassingly snug to Llyn, who daily pulled on full gathered culottes and a loose tunic top, the garb of both sexes here on hot, humid Antar. The other two women wore their hair in ornate topknots that marked them as Unukalhaians.

"It's getting unusual to see Tdegans at Nuris U," Niklo murmured, looking up. "Everyone was talking about it last term."

"Maybe they're here for the festival?" Llyn eyed them, envying their freedom.

"No. They're students. They keep to themselves these days."

Llyn squinted and made herself really see them. Karine rarely mentioned other Concord worlds, and she didn't encourage Llyn to follow i-net news, but maybe—could it be?—she was Tdegan. She did have black hair and a long, oval face, like many Tdegans. She envisioned how she would look wearing snug, warm garments. Skinny, she decided. Or from Unukalhai: would her hair knot that way if she grew it longer?

Maybe she'd been born at an even more distant Concord world, such as Kocab. She'd never be able to afford to send i-net search calls that far, unless she disproved Karine's gloomy predictions and found a way to earn her own living.

She would! She would live independently someday. She was not Karine Torfinn's property.

She tapped Niklo's shoulder. "Genetics department. Good idea."

He leaned down again.

02

The seismic rumble echoed westward, and Karine Torfinn paused while ascending the governmental pyramid's main stairs. High above her, Nuris University's fiberglass dome was pale blue. Its framework, a honeycomb of metal-composite arches, distributed stresses from the constant ground movement. The pyramid, too, had been built for stability under seismic strain. Antar was a planet that rarely slept quietly.

Karine had been reluctant to bring Llyn down to the city domes, for fear she might have a catatonic episode in public. Still, she wanted Llyn and Niklo to glimpse the most powerful man in the Concord star cluster, Head Regent Anton Salbari. Today's choral festival celebrated his birthday.

Taking Llyn to a musical event would be risky, but Llyn had started to push for independence. Karine had been promised seats in a private theater box. This would provide an excellent opportunity to show Llyn how vulnerable she still was.

Up the pyramid's main corridor and left, Karine stepped into the Empath Order's Nuris office. As a trained empath, Karine could—with minimal effort—sense other minds' electromagnetic wavelengths. Some empaths could shift a subject's frequency, altering moods or emotions. Others, like Niklo, were sensitive to localized neural wavelengths.

Niklo would have made an excellent Physician Interface for some settlement, but he refused to develop his gifts. Karine suspected that he had enrolled in NU's seismic geology program to escape his calling. Still, he was legally an adult now. Her parenting duties had ended.

Except for Llyn.

A young man slouched at the corner desk overlooking the main entrance. The pyramid's sloping interior walls reflected bright daylight onto twenty workstations, all of them occupied. Karine didn't recognize this young receptionist, but that didn't surprise her. With a twenty-patient resident load, she rarely escaped the 200K to the city. Her staff might insist they could care for patients without her, but she didn't trust them. She barely trusted Niklo to chaperon Llyn today.

She caught the receptionist's attention. "Any news?" she asked. "Has the *Aliki* exited Tdega Gate?" That consular ship had been launched on a critical mission sixteen days ago. Planet-to-Gate, Gate-to-Gate, and planet-to-planet travel times for ships and transmissions within the settled Concord were too complex for guesswork.

The man looked up from his handheld reader. He shot her a pinched expression. Karine listened for his shallow-level mental frequency and synchronized hers to it. Instantly she felt his worry. "Not that we've heard," he said. "It vanished through Antar Gate on schedule, seven days after launch. It should have spent six days in relay. Once it arrived at Tdega Gate, its commtechs would transmit back to Antar. That word could arrive in two point six additional days. Today.

"We should not have sent that ship," he added.

Karine lowered her eyebrows at him. He looked even younger than she'd thought at first glance. Probably part-time student help. "Why not?"

"We're risking two hundred of the Concord's best people. The Casimir family isn't stable. Ask anyone. They're likely to—"

"That," Karine said firmly, "is why we sent top negotiators. Even the Casimir family wouldn't dare move against them." Everything she heard about those people made her despise them.

"I hope you're right, Medic Torfinn."

"There could have been a delay at one Gate or the other. Or, Creator forbid, an accident." Such an event would behead the Concord's power structure, not to mention the Empath Order. Athis Pallaton, the Order's revered statesman, led the mission. Representatives from seven other worlds' University families were also on board.

Karine strode to the office's main multinet projector, just a few meters away. She selected i-net for information and waited momentarily while the system approved her voiceprint. Then she requested a private projector. Dark letters on the main screen directed her to an alcove on a windowless wall.

She took the cubicle and caught up on Order business. Like so much else, it could not be accessed off campus. There'd been a promising birth in the Torfinn family—a distant cousin's first daughter, whose prenatal testing had shown she would carry the empath mutation. A training group was due to start in three months. One death, which she'd already known about. The census stood at 158 genetic empaths, five up from last year. Seventy-eight had taken training. The rest were young, marginal, or secretive.

With that completed, she switched over to c-net for communication. Using the large terminal instead of her small personal reader, she asked for Yfanna Ruskin's home line.

Professor Ruskin, Karine's old college friend and mentor, had promised to look after the children while Karine caught up on clinic and Order business. Professor Ruskin had taken Karine in, too, years ago while Karine attended University. Those had been good days, her first taste of freedom.

Karine slid her view-glasses out of a tunic pocket, wanting to see threespace imagery over the terminal site. A virtual desktop sprang into existence, invisible to anyone not wearing the glasses.

Professor Ruskin's voice sounded alongside her left ear, where the glasses' earpiece projected it. "Hello, Karine. Welcome back to the city." The professor's image did not appear, so she must be answering from her remote unit.

"Thank you for taking the children on tour. How is it going?"

Professor Ruskin hesitated. "I haven't seen them yet. Perhaps they decided to tour on their own. I can hardly believe your young Niklo is already studying here. He must be quite a young man now. I'll bet you're proud of him."

Not at this moment. Karine balled a fist down at her side. Niklo *knew* that Llyn must not be taken out in public. What would he do if she had a catatonic episode? "I'm terribly sorry. You probably waited some time for them to come."

"Not really. I'm out in my little garden, and time goes quickly when I have dirt on my hands. Don't worry about the young people. I'm sure they're fine."

"I'm not."

"I seem to remember a young woman who changed housing stacks twice to stop her own mother's daily checking in."

Karine flinched. Her mother had insisted that she was only "interested" in Karine's college life, but that had been an entirely different situation. "Llyn has a debilitating medical condition."

"I'm sorry to hear that."

"She's making a slow but steady recovery."

"Does your mother still try to change your plans whenever you tell her ahead of time?" Professor Ruskin chuckled.

"I'm afraid so," Karine answered in the same light tone. She and her mother had not communicated in decades.

"Well, don't worry about the young people. Just let me know if you need help locating them."

"I shouldn't."

Karine cut the connection and scowled. Niklo! Llyn! Such behavior could not be tolerated. Temporarily doubling Llyn's workouts would be appropriate punishment. The girl hated to exercise.

She had felt uneasy about bringing Llyn here from Lengle township, but Second Regent Filip Salbari—Head Regent Anton Salbari's oldest son, and an empath like herself—had asked to meet Llyn. Karine had never been able to refuse Filip a reasonable request. Filip had offered concert seats in his private box.

She plunged back into the Empath Order database and accessed Campus Security. Searching twenty-six buildings for PL transmissions could take a few minutes—

But it spotted them in seconds. Using a security clearance even Niklo didn't know she had, she scanned the library multinet system. Niklo's ID had been logged in on the third floor, at a dedicated i-net terminal. Frowning, Karine noted he was using a security lock. Her clearance let her leech his line anyway. Genetic information scrolled across her remote unit's virtual desktop.

Again? She grimaced. Llyn's preoccupation with her genetics embarrassed Karine. *She* was Llyn's mother. She had painstakingly restored Llyn's ability to function in real-world, real-time fourspace. She was not jealous. She merely wanted to be loved as she loved Llyn, and she didn't want relatives turning up, claiming prior guardianship.

She frowned. Furthermore, Niklo knew that searching the topic was forbidden. It would be a long time before she trusted him again. She had given him a generous allowance for his first year at university. He was about to experience a drop in funds.

The University library, full of strangers and odd stimuli, was incredibly unsafe. Hurrying, Karine pointed at the c-net microphone to activate it. She recited Niklo's call number.

He did not answer. He must have chosen a terminal with a message mute, the kind that stored calls in the order received.

She did not bother to leave a message.

If Niklo was unreachable, she had backup. Her clinical aides, Elroy and Tamsina, had also come to Nuris this morning, wedged into the family charge car. She had enjoyed the trip across open country.

She called Tamsina.

Within seconds, Tamsina's face appeared over the c-net board. Tamsina wore her black hair short, framing a chocolate-brown face. Tamsina had to be at a terminal, too, which was not unusual. Many Concord citizens spent a quarter of their waking lives sitting or standing at some net station. "Yes, Medic Torfinn?"

"Niklo and Llyn are on the third floor of the library. I want to talk to them."

"You want me to sign off, go find them, and then call you back?" Tamsina's voice sounded slightly strained.

"Exactly."

"May I finish what I'm doing? It'll take just a few minutes."

"Now, please."

Tamsina's face vanished.

Karine pointed back over to the local channel. There should be time for a final routine check she ran whenever clinic business brought her to

NU. On this secure terminal, she could request other information that wasn't passed uphill to the clinic in Lengle township. She always made certain that no one else ever asked for information on the laboratory where Llyn was found.

She had first seen Llyn floating in a two-meter tank in central Nuris, and the memory lingered. Optical cables had connected a state-of-the-art artificial reality processor to motion sensors in the girl's black gelskin garment. She looked tiny and gaunt, almost skeletal. Her masked, helmeted head seemed like a huge mismatch for her body. Straight, oily black hair flowed out from under the helmet and trailed into the float solution.

Karine frowned. She had no sympathy for the escapists who frequented Nuris's ARcade. To impose artificial reality on a helpless child was unforgivable. Llyn was still helpless in many ways, and still a child.

Another mystery: if Llyn had been immersed without a motion frame for years, as her mental state suggested, she should have been even more severely crippled. Someone must have moved her into that particular tank shortly before authorities found her.

RAKAYA SHASRUUD LABORATORY, she keyed in. The unlicensed "researcher" had suicided before Antaran enforcement officers could get any insights from her. As usual, the screen lit with old information—

She peered closer. No. This time, it wasn't all old.

She clenched her hands. Someone had begun stripping the net for information about Llyn. He or she had used various clearance codes to avoid a trace, but the requests on this worldwide net started only last week. The inquirer must have just arrived on Antar from one of the other Concord systems.

And since Llyn and Niklo had also requested background data on Llyn less than an hour ago, that unknown person might be alerted the moment he or she came back online.

Karine blinked at the screen. She'd dreaded this. For five years it had been touch-and-go, with Llyn fighting her help, resisting it, and then submitting—but a real struggle for Llyn might begin now, today. Someone else might want custody.

Stupid, careless children! Karine shut down her terminal. She could reach the library before Elroy and Tamsina, if Tamsina was determined to stall.

Niklo rocked his chair. "I don't know," he murmured. "I'm not finding anyone who matches even ten percent of your genetic parameters."

"It was worth a try." Llyn tried not to sound as disappointed as she felt. Her chromosomal parents were probably dead. "To me, anyway."

"Maybe Mother knows something she's not telling us. I'll set this to continue searching and file any report that comes up on my dorm terminal."

"But that could cost—"

"I'll put it on Mother's clinic account. The numbers people don't bother her unless there's a shortfall." He waved his hands and stood up.

"But—"

Niklo grasped the back of her neck and kneaded. "Your muscles are in knots. Want to go for a walk? We could check in with Professor Ruskin, so we can tell Mother honestly we did it."

"Well, yes." It was just like her brother to realize without being told that she ached all over. "A walk sounds good."

Silky fabric swished between her legs as they walked up the library aisle. Her new deep-blue outfit sparkled where iridescent threads had been woven into its fabric. It was a special purchase for this afternoon's concert. She had programmed fabrics and styles into the clinic multi-net, then scrutinized hypothetical outfits. Karine ordered the resultant ensemble from Nuris instead of home-synthesizing it. Llyn had never felt so beautiful.

Nor so fretful. Nuris University was one more environment she couldn't control. She missed the inner world's safety. Its beauty. Its privacy.

They had almost reached the huge main stairwell when a feminine voice filtered down from an overhead speaker. "Niklo Reece, please contact the main desk. Niklo Reece, please contact the main desk."

That wasn't Karine's voice, but she must have arrived at the library. Llyn halted beside a glass door. "How did she find us?"

Niklo shook his head, grimacing. "I don't know. I really thought … Llyn, I'm sorry."

"Don't worry for me." Llyn shrugged, but they both knew that any consequences would fall more heavily on her. Glumly, she followed him downstairs.

The library processing area surrounded a green open space. Evergreen saplings, imported from fertile Tdega and planted in painstakingly reprocessed soil, flourished under lights. One mammoth pine grazed the third balcony. It was marvelous.

She spotted Elroy and Tamsina near a circular processing desk at one edge of the grove, close to the foot of the stairs' lowest course. Elroy stood with his broad back to the stairwell and leaned over a desk. Slender Tamsina, watching the stairs, elbowed her big partner. He turned around, rotating slowly like a small planet. They both walked forward.

"Is Mother headed over?" Niklo asked.

Tamsina wrinkled her nose. More Afro than most of the Concord's racially mingled settlers, she had a smooth complexion Llyn envied. "Probably. She called from the pyramid. If there's still a back door, we might get out before she arrives. Give her time to cool down before you have to look her in the face."

Niklo pointed toward a half flight of steps that led down and away from the main stairwell. "That way."

Llyn darted toward the stairs, grateful that Elroy and Tamsina wanted to defuse any potential parental fireworks.

Automatic glass doors let them through. They stepped onto a triangular porch that pointed away from the pyramid. "Where are we going?" Llyn quickstepped along a sidewalk lined with young trees. Everything seemed to grow inside the University dome. Traveling here from the clinic, klicks and klicks of centuries-dead trees and bushes had depressed her.

"Remember, you're supposed to rendezvous with Filip Salbari before the concert." Elroy clumped along, taking one stride for Tamsina's two. "We'll head for his campus office."

Llyn nodded as she hustled. Regent Salbari had a reputation as a peacemaker. The walkway curved away from the library between soft, fragrant lawns and stone buildings.

"How do you two know so much about NU?" Niklo glanced at Tamsina.

"You're not the first person to go to school here," she said. "Elroy and I graduated ten years apart."

Karine's assistants led them to an unmarked stone building. It had no porch, only a broad sliding door. Tamsina beckoned. "This way." Once indoors, she turned right and trotted up a flight of stone steps.

This was it. The real seat of power, the information-flow gate for every settlement on Antar.

Llyn followed.

Inside the main doors, a long mural displayed highlights of Concord history. Hidden from Earth-based view by a cloud of dust and dark matter, the Concord star cluster had been spotted by outbound probes: eight F- and G-class suns and a hot blue oddball. The first wall panel showed the flotilla of colony ships that had been launched less than a decade later—not to scale, of course, but nothing drawn to scale could fairly represent stellar distances. Llyn knew it was the fourth generation—fed hydroponically, since carbon-based nanotech was so vulnerable to cosmic radiation—that made landfall six hundred years ago.

Shipboard, a political hierarchy had evolved out of the information-flow controllers. They had arranged the star cluster's exploration, terraforming, and settlement. Some wit had named the settlement committees "Universities" and their controllers "Regents." The names had stuck. The political structure survived.

Nuris University was the Concord's finest hard copy repository and its most complex i-net archive. Just standing here gave Llyn a pleasant shiver.

And these painted panels were magnificently proportioned. The next panel naturally depicted a huge metal frame. The settlers had found nine such frames—now called Gates—in the nine Concord cluster systems, obviously abandoned by some previous civilization. Objects hurled at the Gates emerged days or even weeks later, light-years away, through other Concord Gates.

The third panel displayed two worlds, one verdant and one brown. Lush Tdega, already possessed of terrestrial atmosphere and plant life, had been slated for first settlement. But marginal Antar was closest to its Gate. By settler consensus, Antar became the Concord's capital.

Llyn stared upward as she plodded upstairs. Really, the building itself was a fourth exhibit. Three of the Concord's most powerful University

Regent families lived here in Nuris, on Antar. The Salbari and Sheliak patriarchies and the Tourelle matriarchy had risen to power two hundred years ago, when during the Devastator crisis they downloaded and saved much of the Concord's culture and technology. Now they administered Nuris University, and so they governed Antar—and therefore, the Concord.

She paused on a landing. Her legs ached. The sprint had really drained her. Day after day, she exercised to exhaustion. She still wasn't muscular enough to suit Karine, nor big-boned enough, even though Elroy regularly injected her with a calcium- and hormone-laced growth solution. The injections should have made her scream but didn't.

Maybe someday, Karine would stop overstimulating her and try gentleness.

She finally rounded the last corner. Niklo stood in the upper hallway, waving her forward. "Come on, Llyn. He's here, and he's anxious to meet you." He ducked through the door.

Llyn paused, puffing. This hallway's carpet looked like the same deep shade of green as the clinic's. She wondered whether Karine had deliberately chosen that shade, or if she had unconsciously duplicated Regent Salbari's environment. She certainly talked about him enough.

She turned left through the open door.

The man who stood behind the broad desk wasn't tall, but he was magnificently dressed in long black culottes and a silken pale-green tunic. His collar stood up alongside his throat, displaying a pair of red blood-stones, the Empath Order garnets. Karine also wore a garnet on formal occasions. Owning two of them meant this man had been specially honored by the Order. Apparently, his hair had been blond years ago. Yellow now and streaked with gray, it waved alongside his face.

"Good afternoon, sir," Llyn said, remembering Karine's coaching in social interactions. "May I assume you are Regent Salbari?"

"I am. You are obviously Llyn. I am delighted to meet you."

Llyn still learned more from people's voices than from their faces, and she liked Regent Salbari's mellow baritone. Stepping closer, she offered her hand. He clasped it momentarily and drew Llyn toward a small, curly-haired woman who stood on his right. "This is Vananda Hadley, Llyn. She is my wife's sister, a colleague of mine and your mother's."

"It is good to make your acquaintance, Gen'n Hadley." Since Karine had allowed this trip in the name of Llyn's social education, she took a stab at greeting the stranger. The woman didn't correct her, so evidently she didn't have an extra title as Regent Salbari did. Simple "Gen'n" sufficed.

Llyn looked Second Regent Filip Salbari up and down. It felt strange seeing him in the flesh, since Karine quoted him constantly. This wasn't even a hologram. He still looked handsome in a warm, fatherly way.

He waved her toward a seat in his office. Niklo, Tamsina, and Elroy had already sat down. Niklo actually swung a leg, looking comfortable and casual.

"You must excuse me for a few minutes." Regent Salbari gestured toward a terminal at one end of his desk. "We're expecting a report momentarily on the *Aliki*. It should have reached Tdega Gate three days ago."

Llyn mostly understood the *Aliki's* mission, because Karine had taken pains to explain it. For two hundred years, since the alien Devastators attacked the Concord without warning, Concord worlds had been scrambling to repair atmospheric damage and reestablish food production.

Humans had escaped the attack in anything they could launch: trade ships, freighters, pleasure craft. Antar had been fully resettled for just fifty years since then, and recently, Tdega had begun to charge stiff prices for food. Its production templates had survived there, undamaged—protected, evidently, by atmosphere and concrete—but Tdega had never shared those templates.

So Nuris University had sent the *Aliki,* carrying the Concord's most honorable and persuasive negotiators and staff, in a diplomatic effort to renegotiate food aid and Tdega's special position in the Concord.

After all, food could be grown out in the open on Tdega. Production templates would be better used elsewhere. Concord worlds must cooperate, because if the Devastators had also found Earth and its other colonies, the Concord settlers might be all that remained of humankind.

All that remained. Llyn shivered.

Regent Filip Salbari stared at a projection console in a corner of his office behind the desktop. Llyn was impressed. He hadn't put on viewglasses. He must have implants.

"Llyn." Vananda Hadley stared at Llyn with intense green eyes. Her voice seemed oddly birdlike. "I'm pleased to meet you. Are things going well with Karine?"

A tumble of feelings spun through Llyn: her respectful gratitude, her growing discontent, and her frustrated longing to find her origins. "Yes," she began. "I have made great progress—"

"Thank you." Smiling, Gen'n Hadley leaned back in her chair. "You don't have to go into any more detail."

Llyn blinked.

Niklo chuckled from the chair on Llyn's right. "Checking on Mother, Gen'n Hadley?"

Vananda Hadley inclined her head toward Niklo. "You and Llyn are flourishing, under the circumstances."

Llyn understood less than half of this conversation. She shot her brother a questioning look.

He steepled his fingers. "Vananda is the Order's strongest living listener. She has known Mother longer than we have."

Llyn felt her cheeks heat. "Gen'n, I mean no disrespect to—"

"I'm not the strongest," Vananda said softly. "Father is on that ship bound for Tdega."

Was Vananda Hadley the famous Athis Pallaton's daughter? Now Llyn was really impressed. According to Karine, Regent Pallaton's ability to synch rapidly with a succession of speakers and his impeccably honest reputation would ensure clean negotiations.

Regent Salbari rotated his chair toward the desktop again. Evidently his screen had not shown him what he wanted to see. "The Order asked him to go."

"Father volunteered." Vananda Hadley's tone became deep and sincere. "Just as Jahn did when he entered service." Concern flooded her voice when she spoke that name, *Jahn*. "You're not responsible for his welfare, Filip. We don't know there's been a mishap."

Llyn wondered who Jahn was and why Vananda Hadley loved him so openly. Husband? Son?

Elroy stretched his long legs into the center of Regent Salbari's forest-green carpeting. "Where do you suppose Karine is?"

Vananda Hadley shut her eyes momentarily and announced, "On the stairwell. Headed up here."

Niklo sprang up.

"Sit down, son." Regent Salbari rested his forearms on the desktop. "We knew she was coming. She asked me to alert her if you arrived."

Llyn crossed her knees and stared at her feet. Maybe in this office, Karine wouldn't explode.

She appeared in the doorway half a minute later. Her rigid shoulders made a stiff platform for her long tunic. Her brown hair, cut chin-length in a businesslike sweep, hung forward. A dark expression clouded her eyes. "There you are," she said. "Professor Ruskin had no idea where you had gone. This is not responsible behavior—"

Vananda Hadley stood. "Good afternoon, Karine. Welcome back to Nuris. We've missed you."

Karine glanced at the smaller woman, raising an eyebrow. She hated to be interrupted, particularly in the middle of correcting someone. "Hello, Vananda."

"Won't you sit down?" Regent Salbari glanced at the vacant office chair.

Karine sank into it, but Llyn recognized a glower that meant she would hear more later. "Anything from Tdega Gate?" Karine asked Regent Salbari. Her vocal rhythm sounded strained.

"There should be, momentarily." Regent Salbari glanced over his shoulder. "Karine, you and your family would be welcome to join us for tea after the concert."

Karine's frown lines smoothed away. Communal eating was a deeply emotional holdover from shipboard days, when people often met in person. "Thank you." Her sincere speaking voice sounded as if she'd rather sing. "We would be honored. I will see you at your box. First, though, I need to speak with my children."

Llyn shrank inwardly. She hadn't escaped after all. Vananda Hadley, sitting out of Karine's line of sight, firmed her lips.

"Llyn?" Karine glanced at the door. "Niklo?"

Llyn stood up, suddenly weary. Now that it was too late, she also remembered a favor she'd wanted to ask Regent Salbari.

It would have to wait. Maybe during the concert, maybe afterward.

Elroy slipped out of the office, and Llyn followed slowly.

03

Llyn walked beside Karine, whose black culottes also swished as she walked. "This has nothing to do with right and wrong, and everything to do with your safety," Karine said. She paused on the sidewalk and laid a hand on Llyn's shoulder. Llyn barely felt it. Elroy and Tamsina walked a step ahead with Niklo, and then they halted, too.

"You aren't like other people." Karine kept her voice low. "There are things you will never be able to do. I'm protecting you from potential danger. You were foolish to go to the library."

Llyn answered cautiously, not daring to provoke her further. "I didn't go alone. I have sense enough not to do that."

Faint compression lines appeared around Karine's lips. She didn't respond until another group of foreign students passed them. Llyn had never seen so many human beings in the flesh.

Not that she recalled, anyway.

"Listen." Karine fingered her garnet pendant. "I always check current records of the Rakaya Shasruud Laboratory when I come into Nuris. That information is only available on secured terminals in the city."

Llyn glanced up at the dome's blue underside and the honeycomb pattern of braces that held it in place. They fascinated her, but she had no memory of Rakaya Shasruud. "I know you do," she murmured.

Karine stepped closer. "My terminals also record incoming activity. Someone else has been stripping the net for information on you—not today, but in a random pattern over the last week."

Llyn smiled slightly. Maybe she was less alone in this world than she'd thought. "Someone else knows about me?"

Karine pointed at Niklo. "There, you see? She's that naïve! You can't expect her to know what is dangerous."

Dangerous?

Niklo shrugged. "She tries to be careful. We all do."

Karine squeezed Llyn's shoulder, and now Llyn felt it clearly. "I don't think anyone would look for you with generous motives. You could be in danger. We are going straight home."

"Home?" Llyn cried. "What about the concert? Wasn't that supposed to be part of my social lesson? We have Regent Salbari's personal invitation."

Elroy cleared his throat and bent his head down toward Karine. "Regent Salbari did ask us to attend. His private box should be the safest place there."

"I would like to hear the choir," Tamsina put in. "I sang in it when I came up for University."

"It'll start in just a few minutes." Niklo pointed west across the lawn. Karine had led them several degrees off the direct course. "They've opened the auditorium."

Llyn tried not to beg with her eyes. Karine tended to punish that pleading expression.

Karine frowned. "All right. We will go straight to the auditorium and wait there."

Mentally, Llyn blessed Niklo, Elroy, and Tamsina. Aloud, she murmured to Karine, "Thank you, Mother."

Tamsina led across the grassy campus at a stroll that spared Llyn's energy. They approached a tall building that was almost square, except that Llyn's eye for geometry picked up asymmetries in its roofline.

Karine had explained that this afternoon's concert was not as formal as an evening affair would have been, but she'd specially ordered Llyn the silky outfit, so Llyn expected to see other people's finery. Nor was she disappointed. Many men walking up the tall auditorium's steps wore black culottes with white tunics, the height of formality. Some women belted their tunics over their culottes. Others let both garments hang loose and blend into a long line. Body scents mingled and clashed in the foyer. A hubbub of voices baffled her keen hearing. She could distinguish only snatches of other groups' conversations.

"...new composition by Elex Hale ..."

"...never been any navigational problems ..."

"...but it wasn't on the final exam ..."

Llyn tried not to worry that she might experience a flashback. It had been several weeks since her last one. Any pair of musical notes, if they related to each other in the tonality of that lost inner world, could render her helpless. In a way, Karine was right. Attending this concert was inviting disaster.

But what pageantry! Chandeliers spiraled overhead. Concertgoers crowded a food and drink station, and uniformed ushers stood at all doors. She spotted three black-haired people who looked predominantly neo-Asian, a blend of oriental and Native American families who'd banded together on one of the generation ships.

Karine steered the group through the foyer toward a curved, shining staircase at its right. Llyn hadn't a guess what choral music might sound like, but the idea intrigued her. Many voices together ought to communicate more deeply than a single individual. It seemed logical.

At the foot of the stairs, two ushers watched the throng. Their black uniforms looked exactly alike, right down to the metal woven into their belts.

Karine stepped up to the woman. "I'm Medic Torfinn," she said. "Party of five, to join Filip Salbari's group."

The usher raised a personal reader. "Yes. Box three is at the top of the stairs on your left. Go on up."

Karine beckoned to Llyn and led the way. The stairs were carved from black stone flecked with red, white, and gray. Llyn wondered how this enormous building had been reinforced against quakes. The staircase was much quieter than the lobby below. She followed Karine toward a doorway and paused there, winded. Karine strode through.

Niklo stopped beside Llyn's shoulder. "Are you all right?"

"There's been a lot of climbing today." Llyn straightened her shoulders, loosened her hands at her sides, and walked in.

The hubbub that had assaulted her down below boomed up here, too. Regent Filip Salbari stood two stair steps below her. Beyond and below him, a large window opened over the auditorium. Regent Salbari reached for her hand and presented it to another elegant woman, whose curly brown hair sparkled with tiny white flecks. She wore a brilliant green velvet tunic over her culottes. "Llyn, this is my wife, Favia Hadley. Favia, Llyn Torfinn."

Vananda's sister would be another daughter of the famous Athis Pallaton—right? Aware of Karine's scrutiny, Llyn glanced down respectfully. For the past year, Karine had drilled her in public-place poise. Chin forward, eyes moving. Hands loose at your sides, ready to reach out for balance, gifts, or handclasps.

The woman's bright eyes were brown, not green like her sister's. Favia looked older than Karine, maybe forty-five or fifty. One of her eyebrows was raised. Didn't that suggest amusement? "I hope you enjoy the concert, Llyn. Karine, may I compliment you on your daughter?"

Llyn warmed from her shoulders to the top of her scalp. Favia Hadley's voice accepted both Llyn and Karine.

Karine backed up to stand beside Llyn. "She is a good student." Karine smiled toward Regent Salbari.

The adults turned aside to converse, so Llyn pivoted and took a look around. Regent Salbari's box, walled on three sides but open to the enormous room below, overlooked the stage from one side. Studying the angles of stage, ceiling, walls, and floors, she abruptly realized she could follow the paths that sound waves were meant to travel once they left the stage. Voices babbled down in the hall, creating discordant chaos.

As if he'd perceived her thought, Regent Salbari touched a button on the wall. A transparent panel slid down from the ceiling and shut off the din.

That might come in handy later, if she blacked out and the party wanted privacy to revive her. Karine had warned her to anticipate this.

Karine was always predicting disasters.

Llyn stepped to the edge of the box and stared down. From up here, she primarily saw hair colors, mostly brown like Karine's, with many darker and a few lighter. On well-dressed bodies, fabrics flowed loosely, some brilliant and some pastel. Distant mouths moved, but with the transparent panel in place, she couldn't hear their speech.

Tamsina joined her at the balcony's edge, resting a manicured hand on the back of a plush seat. "Don't look down," she said. "Look across at the other boxes. That's where things are really interesting. Straight ahead—see those three boxes? That's the Tourelle matriarchy. They own half the manufacturing on Antar."

Llyn peered across the hall. Five women, four men, and three small children had taken seats in the opposite box. Another dozen people milled in boxes to its left and right.

"Left from them," Tamsina said, "are two Sheliak boxes. That's a paterline like this one. They're short a few today. Two of them went to Tdega to represent us in the talks."

Even from this distance, Llyn could see one woman's necklace sparkle. The jewelry must be massive.

"One more box left, you can just see … there, see the man wearing all black? That's Head Regent Anton Salbari."

Llyn straightened and stared. There stood Regent Filip Salbari's father, the most powerful man in the Concord. Other than his all-black academic attire, from this distance he looked like an ordinary man of sixty or seventy.

"Did you say Anton Salbari?" Niklo stepped down behind them. "Where?"

Abruptly Karine turned her head and looked down the steps. "Llyn," she exclaimed, "get away from that window."

Llyn backed around Niklo. "Why? What's wrong?"

"Someone might see you. Someone who was looking for you on the net—"

It was tempting to step forward again anyway, but Regent Salbari spoke up. "It's time we were seated. Llyn, you're here." He motioned her to the center seat in the front row. To her delight, he sat down beside her. His seat had exceptionally wide armrests. He fingered one of them, and the window reopened. Below, the hubbub quieted.

This was her chance. If she blacked out during the concert, she might not see Regent Salbari again. "Sir?" She bent close to his shoulder. "May I ask you a favor?"

Out of one corner of her eye she saw Karine cock her head, eavesdropping.

"Certainly," Regent Salbari said, "within reason."

She plunged forward. "There'll be an on-site class offered next week up in Lengle. It's on Antaran history. I'd like to take it."

Karine leaned across Llyn toward Regent Salbari. "Llyn, we've discussed that several times. It's not a good idea, because—"

Regent Salbari lifted a hand. "Wait a moment, Karine. Llyn, why would you want to take it in person? You have terminals at the clinic."

"I'm always at the clinic. Sir," she added.

"Yes. She takes satellite classes," Karine said. "She sees other people."

"But not in person." He nodded at Llyn. "It's lonely for you, isn't it?"

He understood! Karine understood, too—she had to, she was an empath—but she did nothing about it. Llyn nodded. "I want to broaden my boundaries, sir. It's important to me."

Regent Salbari glanced at Karine. "That's normal for a person your age. But be aware that you can broaden them too far. Things can go out of control inside them. Your pets can get into your garden."

Karine nudged Llyn.

"On the other hand," he continued, lowering his voice to a whisper as the audience silenced, "the scars that you suffer in life often prepare you for your greatest accomplishments. Your pets' fresh droppings may burn today's plants, but in time those spots become the most fertile."

"Interesting thought," Karine muttered.

Llyn's cheeks warmed. If she'd made that sort of biological observation, she'd have been instantly disciplined.

Regent Salbari folded his hands in his lap and whispered, "Let's see how she does tonight, Karine. Her social development probably does need accelerating."

"I disagree. Social development is not necessary for survival in this world."

After all Karine's coaching, how could she say such a thing? Llyn opened her mouth to argue.

Regent Salbari crossed his legs and smoothed his culottes. "Karine, in the struggle for human dignity, there is always a cost. Sometimes you must make difficult choices—"

Another man all in black stepped onto the stage. Regent Salbari lifted his hand again, ending the conversation.

Llyn sat back. At least Regent Salbari wanted to give her a chance.

Now it was imperative that she not have a flashback. There was something at stake.

The man in black talked for several minutes about Nuris University, the excellence of its programs, and Antar's centrality to the Concord. He praised Head Regent Anton Salbari at length.

Llyn stifled a yawn.

Abruptly the opaque panel on stage vanished. Llyn knew she was supposed to be quiet, so she didn't gasp, but she'd never seen a wall do that in this world. Was this a flashback?

No. Four rows of ordinary people, most of them only a little older than Niklo, stood on steps that curved toward the downstairs audience. At first, they looked as if all their tunics and culottes matched, until Llyn realized they wore electric-blue robes. A woman wearing a matching robe paraded to center stage. Everyone in the theater clapped their hands together, so Llyn joined in. She found she could vary the sound by angling or cupping her palms. When hundreds of people did it, it made a soft, high-pitched roar. She liked it.

Karine sat with her lips pressed tightly together, her stare darting from Llyn to the stage. Llyn braced in her seat. At any moment she would probably waft away. Always before, she had enjoyed—deeply—what she couldn't control. This time she must squelch it. If her mind flashed back this time, Karine might lock her up. For good.

"...one of the oldest poems recorded among Earth's Irish population," the robed woman continued, "credited to Ireland's patron saint, Patrick. 'The Deer's Cry.'" She turned and raised her arms. Without any visible cue for pitch, a hundred mouths opened. Llyn sat breathless as they sang, hypnotized by a new and complex harmony.

> *"I arise today*
> *Through the strength of heaven:*
> *Light of sun,*
> *Radiance of moon,*
> *Splendor of fire,*
> *Speed of lightning,*
> *Swiftness of wind,*
> *Depth of sea,*

Stability of earth,
Firmness of rock."

She had never heard anything so beautiful. Voices grouped by timbre echoed each other in an intricate rhythmic and harmonic chase.

"I arise today
Through a mighty strength, the invocation of the Trinity,
Through belief in the threeness,
Through confession of the oneness
Of the Creator of creation."

Karine had called her triangular garnet pendant "Creator's Blood." She had taught Llyn more about the empaths' religion, but she hadn't demanded that Llyn follow it. If Karine had presented it this way, she'd have found Llyn a willing convert!

Abruptly Llyn realized she'd remained seated in her chair, pulled down by stodgy and unimaginative gravity. Only the overhead lights glimmered. No grid lines measured the universe, no geometries enticed her. Instead, lyrics leaped like deer off the stage, up to the box, into her mind. She stared straight ahead. She would not look at Karine. She would act like a normal person.

Involved in the song, she recognized a string of words she'd already heard. She'd read poems that had refrains. The melody, too, sounded familiar here.

The third time it happened, Llyn murmured along under her breath. "I arise today through a mighty strength …" This time, she glanced aside. Karine had turned fully toward her, ignoring the choir.

Llyn stopped. Was she doing something unacceptable?

Karine shook both hands in an encouraging gesture. Llyn whispered along with the refrain's last line. Regent Salbari also watched, and she thought his slight smile looked kindly.

Llyn faced forward, closed her mouth, shut her eyes, and relaxed in the deep, soft chair. The music flowed on, a choral multitude in perfectly pitched harmony. The universe felt right.

"I arise today
Through a mighty strength, the invocation of the Trinity,
Through belief in the threeness,
Through confession of the oneness
Of the Creator of creation."

The song ended. Momentarily grieved, Llyn joined thunderous applause. She gathered her culottes to stand up.

The woman onstage caught the robed people's attention again. Llyn held her breath. Would there be more?

The choir began another song. Llyn relaxed, bathing in a sense of power. Just for tonight, the universe made sense and she could control herself in it. She'd never felt so happy in this dull, gridless world. For the first time she could remember, a deep sense of loss and homesickness dropped away.

If reality could always be this wonderful, she might actually prefer it to her sweet geometric memories. She might stop caring who had conceived her. She might reach out to the future.

The choir had finished its third song when Regent Salbari reached for his right armrest. Llyn saw only a few colored buttons, but Regent Salbari stared into the air over them. Lines deepened on his forehead and between his eyes. He grasped Favia Hadley's hand, bent close to her sparkling hair, and whispered into her ear. Llyn was too inexperienced to interpret strangers' faces, but she thought Gen'n Favia's wide eyes and slightly open lips meant shock.

Almost immediately, a plainclothed man walked out into the center of the stage and interrupted the robed woman, who had been reciting an introduction Llyn hadn't heard. He grasped the woman's arm and spoke to her softly, then stepped to the center of the stage. "Gens and Gen'ns, I apologize for interrupting this concert. We will conclude with the next anthem. There is bad news. A sensor sweep of space near Tdega Gate has positively identified an expanding cluster of debris as wreckage from the Antaran consular ship *Aliki* and the Tdegan *Pride of Lions*. We have no word yet as to how they were destroyed, and an investigation will begin immediately. But first, let us observe a moment of silence in memory of those courageous passengers and crews." He bowed to the robed woman.

She clasped her hands and stood without moving for several seconds.

A shipload of the Concord's best people? Two shiploads? Stunned, Llyn glanced left. Head Regent Anton Salbari's booth window had already dropped and darkened. Across from where she sat, the other boxes' occupants had kept their windows open, but people were already hurrying up their short staircases to leave.

Filip Salbari stood. "Excuse me," he murmured to Llyn and Karine. "Thank you for attending." He kept one hand at his wife's waist, and they hustled up to the box door.

Gen'n Favia Hadley's father was among the dead, wasn't he?

How horrible.

Karine looked dazed, her stare glassy.

"Are you all right?" Llyn whispered.

Niklo bent across Regent Salbari's empty chair. "Do you think Tdega destroyed them?"

"Surely not." Karine's lips moved, but her gaze was fixed straight ahead. The choir started singing again. "Sh," Karine said.

Llyn straightened in her chair. Terrible visions of a spaceship's last moments sprang into her mind, fueled by historical dramas she'd seen. She heard little of the choir's final anthem.

Even Elroy and Tamsina remained silent as Karine led back to the open area where she had parked the family car for recharging. Niklo kissed his mother perfunctorily and strode off toward his tall, concrete housing stack, probably eager to turn on his e-net for developments.

The car had no viewing screens. Llyn took one more uneasy glance up at the honeycomb braces supporting the dome and then slid onto the back bench with Tamsina. Elroy took the driver's seat.

From the other front seat, Karine switched on nonvisual news. The reader was finishing a grim catalogue of debris that the survey ship had found, chiefly metal shards and expanding gases. Their composition seemed to support a theory of space-warp destruction, possibly caused by a long-dreaded malfunction finally developing in the Gate system. Concord settlers still did not understand how they worked or where the energy came from to operate them.

The i-net reader went on to reiterate why the Concord had sent the *Aliki*. Concord representatives had been ordered to promise naturally fertile Tdega all their own planets' future resources at drastically reduced trade rates, if only Tdega delivered the templates. Everything from faulty silica to weak welding had been blamed for the food shortages.

Karine snapped off the speaker. "That's all we'll hear for a while."

"The real reason for shortages," Elroy said, "is that the Tdegan government won't release those nanotech templates."

"The real reason," Tamsina insisted, "is that nano-machines couldn't be programmed to fix themselves." The microscopic technology had proved so fussy to maintain, in fact, that it had only been economically successful for food production and locator chips.

The car sped out of the huge University dome and into a dim inner pipeway, where two-way traffic felt claustrophobic under pale yellow lamps. The next open area, green with grass and shrubbery, was flooded by filtered sunlight and lined with shop-and-domicile stacks. Llyn glanced up at another sky-blue city dome.

She had heard that Nuris was a sizeable network of domes and pipeways. Now she knew.

Two ships. Maybe four hundred people. Poof.

One more pipeway took them into the final dome southward. Llyn stared up longingly, determined to remember this scene as part of her day at Nuris University. This dome's ceiling seemed even farther away. An air liberation factory, where oxygen was chemically released from pulverized surface rock, thrust tall stacks toward the dome's underside. Inside this dome complex, the artificial atmosphere was thick enough to support indefinite outdoor activity. Outside, thanks to constant efforts at atmospheric renewal, people could survive without supplemental oxygen—but Antarans carried breath masks if they planned to work outdoors.

Nuris's southernmost arch loomed overhead and passed behind, and they emerged into the open. As usual, heavy clouds shrouded a sullen sky. To Llyn's surprise, Antar's red double star peeped through near the horizon. It was a monthly event, at most. A seeder plane swooped out of the clouds to land alongside the cluster of city domes. Nuris University was still re-cooling Antar's upper atmosphere after the Devastators' crippling attack, precipitating out water as quickly as possible, seeding the clouds with algal spores. More free water would support more oxygen-producing algae on the planet's surface—and would itself absorb carbon dioxide, a buffer effect that the Devastators had destroyed when they boiled off so much of Antar's old ocean. Fertilizing the algae with iron also helped absorb greenhouse carbon dioxide.

The Devastators had bombarded planetary oceans, raising vast thermal storms that almost turned the Concord worlds into clones of Earth's sister Venus. Seven systems' settlers were wiped out. Only the Tdegan and Antaran flotillas had escaped detection.

The car swerved around a geothermal area. Outside Llyn's bubble window, volcanic plains sped by. Much of Antar was virtually featureless, except to geologists interested in the composition of lava flows.

Between broad algae paddies, they passed evidence of Antar's pre-Devastator past. A ghost forest of brush and scrub, brittle stems and twigs two hundred years dead, stood unrotted. The terraformers still called Antar's environment "bacteriologically impoverished." Antaran survivors had risked their lives, returning to thwart a runaway greenhouse barely in time.

Llyn curled up in her seat and watched the volcanic plains flow past. In her memory, the refrain of that first terribly sweet anthem thundered again, its melody matched by torrential chords:

> *"I arise today*
> *Through a mighty strength, the invocation of the Trinity ..."*

Two ships. Destroyed. Had the Devastators come back?

Another car pulled up beside theirs. Evidently it was fuel-powered, because its engine droned noisily over the charge car's soft hum. As it accelerated and sped past, the pitch of its engine changed.

The bubble window over her head shimmered and collapsed. A glimmering grid appeared, defining space-time with a slow, dignified sweep. Against a blue background, brilliant geometric shapes coalesced.

Old friends! Leaving her weak, skinny body droopy-eyed in the car, Llyn sang herself upward. Grid lines dropped as she rose, free of dependence, free of confinement, with a blessed sweep of harmony flooding her perception.

She floated, rejoicing. A softly colored choir sang songs of the universe. The very stars vibrated, overjoyed to exist. Exalted to the depth of her spirit, Llyn vibrated out a melody with them, singing her own line to the stars' accompaniment. It was a song she didn't remember, yet somehow she knew it by heart. It was her own song, a gift from the true Composer. She was not required to sing anyone else's line: not Karine's, Niklo's, or Filip Salbari's. Only Llyn's. If every star sang its own melody, the result would be magnificent.

Utterly contented, singing this new gift of song, she wafted effortlessly into a glimmering opal sky.

"Oh, no. Medic Torfinn!"

Karine turned toward Tamsina's exclamation. Llyn had slumped in the seat, staring up at the bubble dome, wearing a rapt smile.

Karine had learned to hate that smile.

"She did it again." Tamsina reached into her pocket for the penlight she always carried. "I'll—"

"What else is wrong?" Karine demanded. Why was Tamsina hesitating?

Tamsina bent over and rummaged on the seat. "I can't find my penlight. I must have lost it somewhere. I—I was looking down at the floor during the concert. I must have set it aside."

Stupid! The easiest way to recapture Llyn would be to force open one eye and whisk a bright light back and forth in front of it, but Karine had left her light at the clinic, depending on Tamsina. "Elroy?"

The big man shook his head.

Several years ago, Karine had implanted a white-noise generator in Llyn's left ear, trying to prevent these episodes. It hadn't helped. They'd had to remove it. "You'll have to do it the hard way," Karine said.

Llyn grinned idiotically as Tamsina reached for her forearm.

Bitter pain shot through Llyn, high in a shimmering sky. Pain in her arm...

What was an arm?

Irrelevant. She wafted on, singing as she flew. A splendid green pyramid appeared near her horizon. She sang herself toward it.

Pain continued to nag at her. Hazy fog descended over her shimmering world. Her green playmate blurred at its edges. Annoyed, Llyn twisted and spun around a Z-axis marker. She tried to sing color back into fading grid lines.

Her playmate wilted, turning dreary and brown. All around her, beautiful harmonies faded. The world was ending, dying …

Her arm hurt.

Arm. Llyn remembered the shape of an arm. It was part of that other world. The world that hurt. Rumbled. Frightened.

Maybe she could escape. She poured on speed. Grid lines whizzed beneath her. Vainly she tried to sing color back into her beloved inner realm, but it kept darkening. The grid lines vanished. Like thousands of candles snuffed simultaneously, her choir winked out. *No,* she mourned. *Not again.* She sped on in a black vacuum.

Someone out there—hopefully Tamsina—had been pinching her. They would watch as Llyn's body convulsed in rigid seizure.

She knew what she ought to do, but she hesitated, reflecting on the oddity of what had just happened. Choral music had no effect on her equilibrium, but let a single note change pitch, and that left her helpless. How could this be?

"Llyn!" Karine's voice thundered. "Come back!"

Karine doubtless sensed that her "unique subject" was making no effort.

Hurt and angry, Llyn huddled in her dark cocoon a few moments longer. All of the stars had sung together, and she had sung with them. She never wanted to forget that. She must not feel humiliated when Karine demanded to analyze and criticize her sweet flashback. It had been *right.* The universe might collapse, but that music had held meaning.

"Llyn, you will begin returning or I will cancel that on-site class regardless of Regent Salbari's permission."

Resigned to bitter reality, Llyn gathered herself for the long climb back out. She thought about tightness. Thought herself tight. Tightness.

Instantly the pain snapped off.

Tamsina's work was done. Now Llyn's must begin.

She owned a mouth. She had lungs and vocal cords—her own, not some other creature's. Her will was not a parasite on this thin human body, but its rightful soul. She drew a deep breath and worked her mouth, lungs, and vocal cords. A faint tone, ugly and harsh compared to the inner world's harmonies, resonated through her skull into physical ears.

Reluctantly, she opened her eyes. She rubbed her sore arm. She would have a glorious bruise. It took abusive force to make her feel anything. Why hadn't Tamsina used her penlight?

Karine's face peered over the front seat, eyes narrow. "What happened?"

Llyn tried to remember. Something about … engine noises? Outside her bubble window, the road wound uphill under darkening clouds. A craggy chain of new mountains, still growing by centimeters each day, glowered down. The car had nearly reached Lengle township and the Torfinn-Reece clinic.

"I don't remember much." She glanced aside at Tamsina. The other woman looked apologetic, bowing her head and clasping both hands in her lap. Tamsina knew what must follow. For an hour or more, Llyn would be even more sensitive than usual to melody—to any melody, even as short as two notes, if they related to each other in her private world's tonality.

She would also be vulnerable to the sensations Karine used to discipline her.

Llyn ignored Karine's stare, looking out at Antar's landscape instead. The South River valley glowed a soft, fertile green by twilight. Mosses, ferns, and other plants grew here, genetically engineered for quick spread on a hot, humid planet that was returning to life under the terraformers' guidance.

Elroy steered off the main road at a bend of the river and followed its blue-white course one more kilometer upstream. Between a windbreak of fastpine and a fiberglass half-dome that enclosed Karine's small orchard, airtight stone walls constituted the clinic enclave. Llyn tried not to think of it as her prison, although that sense had been growing over the past months.

She wondered whether Karine would deal first with the flashback, demanding to empathically "see" everything Llyn had just experienced, or if she would first punish Llyn for escaping with Niklo to the library.

Did she dare to hope that Karine, caught up in concern for that destroyed consular ship, might skip directly to dinner?

Probably not. As Karine often said, hope was cheap.

Elroy parked in a low stone garage. They walked silently through a glass walkway full of narrow-leafed, oxygenating plants to the clinic's main entry. Up here in the mountains, prevailing winds piled the clouds that formed over Mare Novus, the world's largest sea. The clouds rose and cooled and dropped rain here, and greenery grew along warm rivers. Despite Lengle's altitude, those winds made the air here slightly better than at Nuris. People could comfortably walk short distances outdoors.

Inside the main entry, Llyn took a quick look up the spacious, carpeted hallways toward staff housing and the therapy area. Muffled laughter—as much noise as she ever heard in this building—suggested a help group meeting behind a closed door. She didn't see anyone in either direction, although Karine might sense more than Llyn perceived.

"This way." Karine walked up the right hallway and stopped in front of a room Llyn had come to dread.

"I didn't do anything wrong." Llyn tried not to plead, but she couldn't help it.

"I think you know differently." Karine slid the door open. A light switched on automatically.

Llyn spotted the electrical console, the patient monitor, and the examining table. In here, Karine punished Llyn—and occasionally other patients—using mild electrical shocks she called "tactile response therapy."

"I'm too old to be spanked, Mother."

"You were acting like a child, and this isn't a spanking. It hurts me as much as you. Literally."

True, if Karine chose to synch. Karine would monitor Llyn's sensations and emotions until she sensed a repentant attitude. Resisting only prolonged the punishments.

Llyn hesitated, digging one heel into the hall carpet. She could just stand here, but Karine only had to touch a button to call Elroy. And as kindhearted as he was, he worked for Karine. Once, he had given Llyn bruises wrestling her onto the table—and had avoided her eyes for days afterward.

She felt fire in her cheeks as she walked through the door.

Half an hour later, Llyn quickstepped back into the hallway with her shoulders and arms stinging. Around the corner past the broad lobby, two stair steps dropped down into a plainly furnished dining area. She smelled poultry roasting. Tissue-cloned meat was a rare treat at the clinic. Apparently someone on staff felt sorry for her.

Karine followed closely. Llyn halted at the door of her supposedly private bedroom, which was located for Karine's convenience close to her office, therapy rooms, and the dining area. "It's too early for dinner," Karine said. "You have time to exercise."

Llyn frowned. She'd managed enough "proper attitude" to stop Karine's therapy session within a few minutes, but she couldn't hold that emotional pose forever. "I have two exams tomorrow, one in math and one in ecology. I'd like to study."

"No. You're full of adrenaline. Go spend some time in a gym." Karine gripped her arm. "I think I can understand why you wanted to visit the library, but you must trust me. I'll help you look for your genetic parents when the time is right."

Llyn almost gagged. Karine didn't simply punish infractions. She wanted to reshape Llyn's soul. The declared goal was Llyn's independence, but Llyn couldn't imagine Karine releasing her from the clinic if she lived to be a hundred.

"All right," she mumbled. "I'll work out."

"That's my girl."

Llyn slipped into her room. Gritting her teeth, she eased the door shut. *I'm not your girl,* she wanted to scream. She would give so much to be normal. Whole. To have only one mind's eye.

She slipped out of her festive blue outfit and into old exercise clothes.

04

Jahn Emlin had traveled from Antar through Tdega Gate four months ago in a fast tenpod drop ship. Fresh out of empath training and unburdened by dependents, Jahn had volunteered to work undercover—partly because no Antaran who studied a three-dimensional representation of the Tdega system, with that crazily skewed orbiting artifact, could say with assurance that the alien threat had ended.

And there were weightier reasons for accepting this assignment. Antar's requests for duplicate food-production templates had been ignored for years. Besides performing surveillance, Jahn hoped to report the master templates' location.

For all he knew, he was the only Antaran operative on Tdega. If others existed, he could not betray their presence. He did hope there were others. Antar's future was too much for one young man to carry, no matter how well he'd learned his job.

Today, he was ready to move into position.

He braked a Tdegan maglev near the employees' approach to the Casimir Residence alongside a smooth sweep of lawn. As the maglev's hum dropped in pitch, a lifetime of whispers and sidelong glances rose out of his memory.

"Of course he did well in training. His mother coached him from preschool on."

"Vananda was impossible to live with. Jerone Emlin went south to Pawson with a younger woman and became a seeder pilot."

"The first time Jahn hits trouble, he'll either fall flat or run away, like Jerone did."

He silenced the mental whisperers. Second Regent Filip Salbari had asked Jahn to travel alone to Tdega, establish deep cover, and seek employment with the Tdegan government. That was what mattered. Most of the espionage equipment he'd been issued was back at his apartment, but not all of it. Today he carried two personal locator chips, which was highly illegal. All Concord citizens were injected at birth with one—just one—in the shoulder muscle.

He also carried one in a ring.

Approaching the palatial Casimir Residence, which occupied Bkellan city's northwestern edge, Jahn guided his maglev up a grooved ramp. A tall metal gate, crested with the Tdegan emblem—a nine-pointed gold star ringed in black—stood shut. A guard stepped out of a stone blockhouse.

Jahn lowered his window. He handed out his ID and a folded slip of printout.

The guard scrutinized them. He eyed Jahn.

Jahn looked away. Antar's best intelligence operatives had given him a new persona that included a new history. They had cross-matched his DNA to a registered Tdegan strain that was similar to his genetic parameters, so random detection of the insertion was unlikely. When he first arrived, his immediate task had been to insert his physical data in relevant streams of Tdega's main i-net. He'd done the insertion himself, using the best information-flow training Antar could give him, a system leech unit, and a net code stolen by a previous Antaran agent. While inside the net, he'd also tried—unsuccessfully—to find out where those food templates were stored.

A chemical implant had turned his fair skin olive and his auburn hair black. He had sheared the front of his hair and grown out the lower back. This morning, he'd caught it at the nape and braided it in a long, thin queue, like most Tdegan men.

The guard's shirt fit closely like Jahn's, but Jahn's was a nondescript pale blue while the guard's was such a dark shade of red that it looked almost purple, with brass bars and stripes.

Jahn rubbed the smooth reddish agate in the ring that concealed his second, illegal PL chip. He could afford a nervous gesture today. This was his first day at a new job. Anyone might be edgy.

He altered his awareness slightly, as if turning a corner. The mental gesture came automatically, and he silently thanked the Antaran women and men who had trained him—including his mother and grandfather, Vananda Hadley and Athis Pallaton.

His grandfather was dead, his ashes scattered in space. Grandfather Pallaton had been a logical negotiator for Antar to send, and Jahn had hoped to see him from a distance. Last night's news, announcing the destruction of both consular ships, had stunned him.

The gate guard felt alert but not alarmed, a professional peacekeeper. He slipped Jahn's ID into a reader slot.

Jahn stared at the Residence. He'd checked that ID card against every kind of reader in Bkellan. If it did not scan unimpeachably, his career in Tdegan government would be short. Treason and espionage carried the death penalty here. Jahn Emlin would be no exception.

Jahn *Korsakov,* he corrected himself. He couldn't afford to think of himself as Antaran anymore. He was Jahn Korsakov, perhaps for the rest of his life.

Still waiting, he sniffed the air through his open window. He'd lived on fertile Tdega for four months, but he still cherished its cool, dry breezes and blue sky. This morning he'd awakened to a heady new scent, clover fields starting to bloom. Tdega's axial tilt produced deeper seasons than Antar's. Summer was ripening the southern hemisphere, and Bkellan city twinkled with flower gardens.

On the minus ledger, Tdega's gravity was about twenty-five percent stronger—and it had taken him two weeks to build up enough endurance to work through a Tdegan day. Tdega's daily cycle consisted of thirty-two local "hours" and encompassed two planetary rotations, with two sunrises and two sunsets per working day.

At least the Tdegan week had just six of these cycles.

The guard handed back Jahn's card and printout. "Park up there." He waved north of the pale concrete Residence. "Your office is on the second floor, north."

Relieved, Jahn closed his hands on the steering yoke and waited while the guard backed into his stone cubicle. A few moments later the metal gate swung upward, and he re-extended the drive magnets.

He was in.

From up close, the Casimir Residence seemed to sprawl. Ornate stone cornices decorated the old west wing. This edifice officially housed the ninety-nine-year-old Head Regent, Donson Casimir, but with Donson's son the Vice Regent dead on board the *Pride of Lions,* real power had shifted to another generation. The Head Regent's grandson, Gamal Casimir, would be strengthening his grip on the government.

Jahn found the north entry without difficulty and rode an elevator to the Residence's information-flow office. He stepped through an open door into a foyer that looked universally Tdegan: more wood furniture, technology smaller, flashier, and more advanced than Antaran equivalents. Voices buzzed, and soft electronic tones beat odd rhythms around him. A woman wearing narrow green view-glasses sat at a desktop that slanted toward an ion-green multinet terminal. He spotted several doors and three open carrels behind her. A man sat at one carrel, pointing and sweeping his index fingers in midair while he mumbled, moving data as he processed it.

"May I help you?" the nearest woman asked blandly.

"Jahn Korsakov." He presented his printout and card. "I'm your new information-flow person—"

"There you are!"

Jahn spun around. A huge man with round, ruddy cheeks stood beside another desk. "It is Korsakov, isn't it?" The man's boisterous baritone filled the office. His body bulged inside tight Tdegan clothing, and fleshy folds made his trousers bunch over his knees.

Jahn presented his hand palm up, in the Tdegan manner of greeting a superior. The big man covered it with his own hand and rotated their palms into a handclasp between equals.

"You're Mr. Vayilis?" Again Jahn shifted his awareness, synching his inner frequency to the other's mind. The big man was sincerely glad to get more office help.

"That's right, Arne Vayilis. I'll be your supervisor."

"I'm hoping you'll show me the net lines."

"Of course. Excellent, your credentials, by the way."

"Thank you." Now, of course, Vayilis would grill him. Jahn had memorized pages of information to cover his alleged work experience. He'd supposedly trained as an information-flow condenser here on Tdega, using in-home programs offered through Bkellan University. His made-up parents farmed rock maize north of Bkellan.

Actually, he'd studied Tdegan geography and customs with the best tutors at Nuris University. He knew every centimeter of that Tdegan rock-maize farm from a planetary imaging system.

But instead of questioning him, Vayilis walked to a vacant carrel and grasped the back of its wooden chair. "This'll be your stable for now. We're so shorthanded that I have to monitor in-flo as well as personnel in the other wing, so you'll probably get your own office soon. Our in-flo condenser is an important team member. We have to keep up with an incredible volume of news and surveillance. Deciding what needs to go uphill to the chief is going to be your job."

Jahn eyed the closed doors on either side of his carrel. Shorthanded? That explained how he'd been hired—or so taunted the scornful whisperers. But why were they shorthanded?

He smiled up at Arne Vayilis. "I'm sure I've got plenty to learn."

"We have three more hours of daylight. What if I showed you the rest of the office wing now, then settled you down with your tutorials?"

Jahn couldn't have hoped for more, and he said so.

The tour covered most of an elongated Tdegan hour and more than the office wing, because Arne Vayilis also had access through the western guard station. Vayilis took him into the function area that separated the west wing from the genuine residential area.

"Meeting rooms," Vayilis said.

Jahn walked toward one of the smaller doors. "May I look in?"

"Ah, not that one. That's the Oak Room. It's being set up."

Jahn spotted a server's station outside the huge wooden door, with several chutes opening over its length. He imagined a system for sending food directly from Residence kitchens.

"I wish you could see it, though. Inlaid table, parquetry floor. All oak.

Check this one." Vayilis walked on to another door. He touched a black panel at shoulder height and spoke his name. The broad door slid open.

They stepped into a massive grand hall with a vaulted ceiling. Tiers of light rods ascended like a huge candelabra and vanished into the ceiling. Jahn whistled in admiration.

Vayilis poked a rod at floor level. "Actually, they're built smaller as they get closer to the ceiling. Creates an illusion of greater distance."

"I'm impressed." No harm admitting it.

"One more, then." Arne Vayilis led up the grand hall to an open door. Two decorative guards in dark red uniforms stood in front of it, but neither spoke to Vayilis, whom they apparently knew. He probably authorized their salary deposits in Central Credit.

Vayilis beckoned Jahn into a room large enough to serve as a spacecraft hangar. Jahn's childhood residence dome, near a mountain geothermal complex, would have fit between these walls—and this room smelled of greenery instead of sulphur. Vayilis's footsteps echoed.

Jahn stepped out onto the floor and almost jumped back. Polished planks of glossy, straight-grained wood lay underfoot. Tdega hadn't lost its forests to the Devastators. No wonder the first human settlement groups had had to divide the nine systems by lot. Each group had wanted Tdega, fertile and Earth-like except for its short rotational day.

But Antar had built its own wealth of culture, knowledge, and history. Also, on Antar, the new races—empaths, gillies, and seers—were not persecuted.

And Antar was the official capital.

"I thought you'd like to see part of what you'll be working to uphold." Arne Vayilis grinned. "Once you go on duty, you're expected to keep to the west wing unless someone invites you out here."

"I understand." Jahn continued to stare. This gilded, wood-trimmed palace was Donson Casimir's home.

Yet legally, it was also the property of every Tdegan. This might be a relevant insight into the Tdegan outlook. Compared with Tdega, Antar was a cloud-enveloped desert punctuated by spartan resettlements.

Yet those resettlements were monuments to human fortitude. Jahn followed Vayilis back up the grand hall. Pausing in front of a door, he glanced at his reflection. He'd applied dark toner to his temples and chin, de-emphasizing the square lines of his face. Even so, the reflection didn't look satisfyingly Tdegan.

During their shipboard exile, Tdegan scientists had developed computer-randomized DNA to protect themselves against inbreeding and mutations. From that stock had come the uniformly oval facial type. Most Tdegans resembled the DNA stock's chief developer.

"Will there be many changes in staff with Regent Casimir's death?" Jahn asked. Vice Regent Aeternum Casimir had been a formidable leader.

Vayilis shook his head. "I doubt it. We're busy these days. My personnel people won't want to waste hours headhunting."

"Where has everyone gone?"

"Oh, mostly to Lahoma."

"Really." Jahn wanted to ask questions, but Vayilis's tone of voice hinted that "Lahoma" was a place he should know about.

"The plant's Vice Regent Gamal's baby. They hope to bring it up to capacity within a few weeks."

Plant? Baby? Jahn synched and probed hastily. Vayilis radiated a sense of adventure. Jahn had caught it from others here in Bkellan. In Vayilis, it felt concrete, with inner reasons supporting it.

Vayilis grinned. "First ships should come off the line in just a few months."

Shipbuilding! Filip Salbari had warned Jahn that Tdega might be turning toward seceding from the Concord, even though the other worlds urgently needed its resources. This could be proof on a platter.

Jahn maintained a light conversation with Vayilis until they returned to the office. Then, as Vayilis lingered with the man in the next carrel and while Jahn slipped on a pair of view-glasses, Jahn reached out again with his inner sense. Hesitantly, he ascertained which mental frequency Vayilis was using, and then he gradually matched his own to the Tdegan's. He winced as he approached deep synchrony, when his mind's electromagnetic waves almost matched Vayilis's. They reinforced and then canceled, creating weird troughs and valleys.

At last Vayilis's thoughts focused. His second son and the other man's nephew had been hired at the Lahoma plant, reprogramming line androids. Within weeks, Lahoma would hire another flood of workers. Vice Regent Gamal Casimir had already put mines and smelters on double schedule. Something big was afoot, and Arne Vayilis couldn't wait to see it.

Jahn wished Arne Vayilis would think more about the Lahoma plant, but he'd focused on his son and the economic stimulus of …

A wartime economy?

Startled, Jahn clung to that mental frequency. He rode tightly, but the big man walked away. The sensation faded. Jahn couldn't feel certain that he'd touched knowledge instead of fantasy. To the mind, they felt identical.

Exhaling hard, Jahn opened his eyes. He'd already been awake for twelve Antaran hours. He needed a few seconds to focus his mind into his own sphere of thought.

His desk had appeared, projected in exquisite detail above the terminal. He should attend to business. Still, he couldn't keep his thoughts on office work. War was being noised in Bkellan city—no peaceful secession, but ancient-style aggression. More people might die, an abstract possibility he had thought he understood until unexplained tragedy killed his grandfather.

Antar needed intelligence now more than ever. Whatever it took, even though he'd worked here less than a day, he must develop higher contacts in the Residence power structure—quickly. If he meant to serve Antar, he must penetrate the inner circle of the new Tdegan Vice Regent, Gamal Casimir.

Would his cover hold?

A serving woman filled Gamal Casimir's wine goblet. One wall of the Oak Room displayed a constantly changing aerial view of the Residence. Flower beds side-lit by the setting sun, a shadowy hedge maze, breeding kennels, and darkening fruit groves appeared in random order.

Gamal Casimir eyed the image. To him, it looked like a genuine window. He'd been injured as a child and needed microsurgery to restore vision in one eye, and a secondary neural infection had recently robbed him of that eye's vision again. His eyes looked normal, but he had no depth perception.

He was content that way for the present. He had his reasons.

His Security Chief, Osun Zavijavah, sat on the farthest end of the table with the best view of the display wall. "Fill his glass, too," Gamal ordered.

The serving woman shuffled toward Zavijavah's end, past the ringed-star emblem inlaid on the table.

Gamal's nephew Bellik sat closer to him. Some people outside the family called Bellik Casimir the family buffoon—lanky and formal, vertical in all his features, and notorious for making superlative declarations. For today's midday meal, he wore his charcoal-gray military uniform with a new Commander's half-moon on each shoulder.

The woman filled Bellik's goblet without needing to be told, then backed out of the Oak Room.

Gamal stood. "A toast. To my father's memory."

"Aeternum Casimir." Bellik raised his glass. "He brought Tdega to the threshold of greatness."

At the table's other end, Security Chief Zavijavah also lifted a goblet. Thin-queued with a drooping mustache, he returned Gamal Casimir's gaze through a handsome pair of wraparound dark glasses. "We honor him."

Gamal savored the upcountry vintage. Bellik drank deeply. Zavijavah, on duty, barely tasted. Immediately he turned back to the security wall.

"Well." Bellik set down his glass with a clunk and wiped his narrow mouth. "Aeternum gave me a job, and I did it. I hope he's happy now, wherever he is."

"Speak respectfully of the dead," Gamal said. "You owe my father a debt."

"I do." Bellik picked up his glass again. This time, he drained it.

Determined to nullify the Antaran show of force, Aeternum Casimir had ordered young Bellik to destroy the *Aliki* as it emerged through Tdega Gate. When news arrived that Athis Pallaton would head the Antaran delegation, Aeternum had decided to go out on the warship *Pride of Lions* and observe the catastrophe.

That night, Bellik had approached his uncle Gamal. He had volunteered to destroy both ships, handing power to Gamal while negating the Antaran power play.

Gamal Casimir had survived numerous family plots by defending himself at long range. Others might take direct risks. He rarely encouraged them, but if he stood to gain, he never forbade them.

Aeternum—on the other hand—had brought Tdega to the brink of supremacy and balked.

"Was it difficult?" Gamal asked.

Bellik leaned back in his chair and stared up at the Oak Room's beamed ceiling. He shook his head. "As soon as the Antaran ship emerged from our Gate, I signaled my robot on board the *Pride*. The transmission lag in both directions gave the ships time to dock."

Gamal stared at his nephew. A hooked nose made Bellik's face look even longer, with close-set eyes and a small mouth. Even his ears were long and narrow. "You'll see to it that the investigating team explains the incident satisfactorily."

Bellik nodded. "Tdega will miss him," he added piously.

Bellik probably wondered whether his uncle would make him heir right away, bypassing Gamal's son Siah. But Gamal must keep Bellik from playing a similar trick on himself—or Siah—one day. Siah was a fool, but he deserved a chance to demonstrate his abilities. "Yes. It will miss him greatly," Gamal answered. Then he changed the subject. "Antar will eventually send another ship. They won't give up yet."

Bellik cupped his long hands around an imaginary object on the tabletop. "Our team will announce that unidentified malfunctions killed the *Aliki,* and that its wreckage rammed the *Pride of Lions.* That will also erode Antar's confidence in its ships."

"Good. The Concord's fleet is aging." Gamal nodded. Still, he disliked letting Antar think there'd been an accident.

Bellik wrinkled his nose. "Its leadership is aging, too. They've got too many mass-produced fifty-year-olds."

Gamal, too, was almost fifty, although he hadn't been conceived in a tube rack. Antar's first *in vitro* generation, created immediately after resettlement, included two of its current Regents. The same situation existed on several other resettled worlds, where they had hurried to repopulate after the Devastator crisis. By contrast, Tdegan policy kept population regrowth steady and slow.

Feeding the rest of the Concord was an unjust weight on this world.

"So much the better," Gamal said. "The test tube children don't think originally. Antar should have reestablished its own food production years ago." Hydroponics had fed the first colonists. According to Bkellan University, it ought to be feeding Antar and the other systems—almost.

Bellik stared into his wineglass. "After any global disaster, the first industries to recover generally involve simple raw materials. And small items for local markets, the kind of items the Concord is trying to steal from Tdega."

"Who are you quoting?" Gamal asked, amused.

Bellik shrugged. "I don't remember."

"Whoever it was, he talked sense. What else did he say?"

Bellik furrowed his high forehead and dropped his voice. "Heavy industries take longer to establish. The Concord also depends on Tdegan technology for robotic and military hardware that would keep the Devastators at bay if they returned."

Gamal no longer flinched when he thought about the Devastators. No human had ever spoken with a Devastator and lived to describe it, but Bkellan University's archives contained unconfirmed speculations. The most popular theory described them as large, dexterous arachnids from a low-gravity world. They allegedly possessed a hive mind and had little respect for individuals of any species, even their own.

As for their abortive attack on humankind, they had supposedly struck the Concord a side blow, barely related to their real war. They had been fighting a race they feared so terribly that they'd tried to sterilize the Concord cluster just to keep those enemies from taking it.

After a lifetime of quietly searching, Gamal Casimir had found answers.

But he had not gone to the Devastators.

He had located their enemies. And those enemies might save Tdega from any future threat, either from outside the Concord or from greedy worlds inside.

"So," he said, "do you think the Concord will let us secede, or must we prove that we're serious? We'll let them get hungry if we have to, but there's no point starving them. And they're too fearful to fight."

Bellik chuckled. "We have thirty percent of the cluster's population and its newest technology. I don't see that Antar has a choice."

Secession would lead, in time, to realignment of the cluster around

Tdega. The Devastators' ancient enemies would help Gamal weaken Antaran leadership from the inside. His father had known Tdega must leave the Concord for a while. He just hadn't put teeth into taking the next step.

Bellik didn't yet know about the new alien contacts.

Gamal eyed Osun Zavijavah over his shoulder. Zavijavah sat rubbing his left temple.

Zavijavah knew.

Gamal raised his wineglass. "Where will your bombers be, real-time?"

Bellik glanced at his reader, which lay on the table next to his goblet. "Halfway in from Antar and Ilzar Gates, crawling like Kocaban haulers. I've taped and transmitted my speeches. All we need now is your signal."

Gamal folded his hands. He shut his eyes. Enormous power lay in three simple words. He wanted to savor speaking them.

He imagined his bomber captains listening eagerly.

"Send the signal," he said.

05

Jahn Korsakov's two-room apartment had come with a small working desk, a table, and a cot. He'd added a small potted plant. He didn't know what it was called, but his mother had lovingly nursed a bed of these exotic, feathery yellow blossoms back on Antar. They grew wild here on Tdega, seeding into crop fields via tiny, parachuted seeds.

He touched a bloom and yawned. He'd heard on the streets that it was easy to spot newcomers on Tdega. Just look for the bags under their eyes. That joke contained more than a grain of truth. Sleepiness was his enemy, and any hint of suspicion at work could block him from promotion—or worse.

So instead of lying down to catch up on sleep, he set a dedicated burst transmitter on his desktop. It was small enough to conceal in his personal luggage. The coding console looked like his reader, but it was thicker and made of virtually indestructible black metal.

From a stash in his closet behind three pairs of shoes, he lifted a set of forearm-sized cylindrical units for storing and retrieving information: empaths' mnemes, including a tiny concealable remote. Shutting his eyes, he pitched his electromagnetic inner sense to his personal coding frequency. A cluster of soft clicks indicated that the mnemes had unlocked simultaneously. Setting the first unit next to his transmitter, he keyed the mneme to transfer data into the transmitter's storage circuits. While the first unit ran, he preset the second and third.

The empath mutation had arisen shipboard, among Antaran survivors of the Devastator sweep. According to geneticists, it resulted from a latent gene that had lost its suppression mechanism: all humans might have been empaths, but for an ancient change in the genome that his sect linked with the Fall. All living empaths traced their ancestry to a baby born shipboard, whose parents had been alert enough to realize that his giftedness was no ordinary intelligence.

Other Antaran mutants, the seers and gillies, had scattered to resettle the eight devastated systems. But the empaths remained together, drawn to a common religious group. The Sphere sect, an offshoot of historical Christianity, had become dominated by their descendants.

His Grandfather Pallaton, born before Antar was resettled, had helped establish the Order. After a century of hiding the empaths' existence, no mean trick shipboard, Grandfather Pallaton had revealed himself to Anton Salbari's father. Empath tradition said that Grandfather Pallaton spoke with passionate, intelligent reserve to the three new Regency families. Instead of liquidating the empaths shipboard—as they could have done, since any group with unusual abilities threatened the status quo— the new Regents offered service positions to any empaths who came forward. Pallaton had urged the Order to keep detailed records and learn to regulate their abilities. Jahn remembered him clearly—

He rubbed his eyes. Mustn't drift off. Food would help. He walked out to the main room and across the carpet to his dining station, where he ordered dinner. The building's main kitchen had already run out of the best options, leaving the most expensive entrée and the cheapest. He chose the inexpensive grain with vegetables and sent down his order.

Back in the bedroom, on the desk across from his cot, lights blinked on top of the first three mnemes. He keyed the next three and checked his burst transmitter to make sure the information had been stored, then wedged the first three units back into place behind his shoes, beside the variable frequency transponder he would use for lock-and-alarm breaking when he started hunting inside the Residence.

A soft chime from the kitchen announced his dinner's arrival. He pulled it from the chute and ate quickly, with short pauses to key the other mnemes. Soon the transmission was ready to send, all but his newest information. Using a voice-to-data recorder program, he dictated a quick but detailed evaluation of the post-*Aliki* situation as he understood it, ending, "It appears that a military buildup is underway. Defensive posture strongly recommended." He tagged that message to transmit first at Tdega Gate and Antar Gate, hardened it separately from the other information, and rechecked his work. All according to training, all on the first try. His teachers would be pleased.

No, not pleased. Satisfied. Over eight years, they'd repeatedly raised the standards they expected him to meet, although some empaths still whispered that he'd ridden his mother's coattails.

He had come off his work shift at second dawn, and he wanted to transmit under the cover of second darkness, so he must wait at least six more elongated hours. Now he could sleep awhile.

At work tomorrow, he must start looking for promotion possibilities. Personnel didn't want to waste work hours head-hunting. By pre-checking daily, he would spot any potential east-wing opening before Arne Vayilis tried to fill it. He must get work in the east wing.

He skimmed his news before undressing for bed. According to i-net services, Gamal Casimir had claimed jurisdiction over the Tdegan Outwatch base in Bkellan. The Outwatch maintained bases on all nine settled worlds and eighteen beacons scattered around Concord space, watching for signs that the Devastators might return. Technically, it was based on Antar.

Jahn shook his head, and his queue tickled the back of his neck. Casimir's cutting of the Tdegan Outwatch's link with Antar took Tdega out of coordinated protection. Coming right after the *Aliki's* destruction, this action also suggested sinister possibilities.

He must not worry about it for the moment. He must rest. Yawning again, he climbed into bed.

Shutting down his mental undercurrents took time. Again he hoped that Anton Salbari had planted other agents in Bkellan.

…And that he hadn't. Tdega was becoming dangerous. Without Jahn's report, Tdega might have risen to full wartime footing before Antar guessed that more was afoot than a purely political plunge toward isolationism. Even if he transmitted successfully tonight, it would take his information two and a half days to cross the relay between Tdega Gate and Antar Gate.

And what about the *Aliki?*

Surely that wasn't an act of war. Aeternum Casimir had also died in the … Jahn did hesitate to call the incident an accident. It had boosted Gamal Casimir into power all too smoothly.

If he thought about that, he'd never sleep. He fluffed his feather pillow, a Tdegan nicety, and resolved not to think about Tdega at all.

He thought of home instead. He remembered his father Jerone as a shadowy red-bearded figure who had always frowned at family meals. Jahn had been three when his father left. His mother's family had drawn Jahn in, imprinting its strong tradition of serving society. In that sense, he felt more like a Hadley than an Emlin. His father *had* been his mother's second cousin. During the shipboard exile, the ancient prohibition against marrying cousins had fallen, as human gene-fixing became even more vital than modifying the terraforming stock.

Radiation-caused mutations had arisen anyway. Some were severe—those babies had died—and some were trivial, such as the dominant gene for reddish hair. Others had the potential to change life and society.

Jahn didn't mind being empathic. He did mind the whispers. He'd worked hard, preparing during his adolescence for a mission that might make his life exceptional. Most of his Hadley and Pallaton relatives had government positions of minimal risk: information tracking, political mediation, and mental and physical healing. Jahn's empathic ability, like his mother's, was to synch and listen. His skills would not settle in at mature levels for five to ten more years. Only chance had made him the empath at the right age, at the right stage of training, to work undercover now.

Within two or three years he might take a Tdegan wife—terrifying thought today, but he might adjust to Tdegan ways. Tdegan women did develop shapely legs in stronger gravity.

That was the thought of a man who needed sleep.

He finally drifted off as the sun fell past second noon. In his dreams he was a Tdegan soldier. He sat on board a huge spherical spaceship—

His alarm woke him an hour after second sunset. Most of Tdega would sleep seven more hours. He had caught three. He'd make it through the next day if he drank enough coffee. He stumbled across the room into his small personal. There he splashed his face with cold water, staring into the mirror at an olive-skinned, black-haired stranger, who wore an agate ring instead of an Empath Order garnet. He turned his head and eyed the queue dangling at the nape of his neck. That much of the dream was real. He looked almost Tdegan.

Packing his transmitter, he paused with his hand on its cold surface. This would be his first attempt to transmit after four months of silence. Pod One had landed him midcontinent. He'd sent two pods to confirm his arrival and check the transmitter. He had eight pods left in orbit.

He murmured a prayer, finishing in a spontaneous whisper. "Help. Please."

Then he slipped his transmitter into a blue fabric case, slung the strap over his shoulder, and walked down to the garage.

The better Tdegan maglevs had retractable wheel gear and backup combustion engines for rural operation, and Jahn had leased a good vehicle. Around Bkellan's elegantly laid-out, grooved road system, the country turned rural immediately. He made the bumpy transition in a slowdown area designed into the road system. From there, it took less than ten minutes to reach open farmland.

Even in the dark, it was easy to identify fragrant clover fields. Tdegan farmers grew clover for honey production and livestock fodder, taking agricultural diversity for granted. Barren Antar had a sugar synthesis plant and marginal tissue-cloning operations.

He drove six more kilometers up an unpaved boundary road before he felt isolated enough. Then he connected his transmitter to the car's power point at the center of his gearing dial, stretched out the cable, and set the small burst transmitter on his car roof. He ran a handheld sterilizer over the transmitter to destroy biodebris, a precaution in case he ever had to abandon the unit.

The night looked likely to remain cool and dry. He glanced around again, orienting himself by the magnificent stars. Two of them, almost brilliant enough to mimic the unwinking gleam of Tdega's sister planets, stood almost ninety degrees apart. They had to be Sunsis and Ilzar, Tdega's nearest neighbor stars. Antar, a brilliant red double, lay below the horizon tonight.

His stealth-shielded drop ship remained in synchronous orbit south of Bkellan, within transmission range from groundside. He couldn't transmit to the Tdega Gate relay from here. The pod he launched tonight would boost half a day Gateward, transmit, and self-destruct. Antaran stealth shielding was excellent and the launch burn would be short, but when each pod left orbit, there'd be some risk of detection. That risk would grow every time he sent a pod. Pod ships had been used as couriers for decades, so this one—smaller and more powerful than some—might not be traced to him even if detected. But if Tdega destroyed it, his usefulness to Antar ended.

He laid a precurved parabolic wire along the ground, aimed it to transmit toward the drop ship and minimize atmospheric scatter, and sterilized that, too.

"Pod three," he instructed the transmitter. "Receive. Five-five-nine -seven-two-four-four."

A green light appeared on the transmitter.

"Pod three," he murmured again. "Bolt system. Eight-one-two-six-zero-one." An explosive bolt would separate pod three from the core and the seven remaining pods. He drew a deep breath. "Pod three. Launch. Code four-one-six." The green light blinked three times and extinguished.

All thirty coordinate sets had been programmed into his subconscious by Grandfather Pallaton, information too precious and confidential to risk on printout or even in circuitry.

Jahn restarted his car, climbed back out, and touched the burst transmitter's orange activation key. The car's engine dropped more than an octave in pitch.

This was the dangerous moment, if he'd been monitored. He unhooked uplink, antenna, and transmitter and flung them with his cables into the passenger compartment. He accelerated along the country road and around the next three corners. Odds of anyone intercepting that burst might be astronomically slim, but he had only one life to lose.

And Tdega was considering war on the rest of the Concord.

He drove back toward Bkellan city by a circuitous route.

If Antar ever received his ninth pod, it would send another tenpod if it could, and he was expected to find his own way home if necessary. He'd also been given tools and weapons to help him stow away on an outbound ship, if that proved necessary.

Neither would be easy.

He approached Bkellan city from the south. Ahead, low over the horizon, lay the shining menace the Outwatch feared: the alien space station orbiting Tdega's red sun. No life had been detected on board since it arrived two centuries ago, while terrified humanity huddled in its inadequate fleets. From the far reaches of the Tdega system, human survivors had launched a probe at the menacing station as soon as it arrived. Some unknown, inbuilt weaponry had vaporized the probe on approach. And the next probe. And the next.

But it never attacked. Over the next two hundred years, it periodically corrected its orbit with awe-inspiring matter/antimatter bursts. That orbit, skewed eighty degrees from the planetary ecliptic, took it far north of Tdega, then slightly south. At present, it was approaching perihelion.

A widespread theory that the Devastators left it in orbit to destroy life on Tdega, but that it malfunctioned, made as much sense to Jahn as anything.

Had it caused the *Aliki/Pride* catastrophe?

06

Llyn laced her fingers and stared at the ceiling. The windowless room was absolutely silent. She could hear nothing but her pulse, and she felt as if she were swimming in Karine's padded recliner. Heavy external headphones mashed her ears. Karine leaned forward on a nearby chair, crossing her ankles against its frame.

Llyn amended the imagery. She wasn't swimming in this recliner, but floating downstream while Karine tried to climb onto her back. Into her mind, actually.

"Llyn." Karine's voice crooned, mildly reproving, through the headphones. "Show me that episode."

Karine punished resistance, though she didn't always call it punishment. She had experimented—once—with a disciplinary AR sequence. It so terrified Llyn that even Karine panicked … and Llyn had remained catatonic for days, or so Tamsina told her. Llyn didn't recall either the sequence or its aftermath.

An inpatient crisis had kept Karine busy around the clock after their trip to Nuris University, and then she'd needed rest, so Llyn had enjoyed the unusual privilege of relaxing and reflecting for two days. The choral concert had deeply affected her. So had the flashback that followed, with its unique gift of song. She yearned to repeat them.

Karine mustn't know that.

Gathered white culottes made Karine look heavy. She would squash Llyn—or sink her—if she sat on her much longer.

"Llyn?" Karine said quietly. "Your thoughts are wandering."

Llyn resigned herself to the usual ordeal. "All right."

Karine's hand tightened on her remote unit. White noise drilled into Llyn's head. Hesitantly at first, and then with better focus, she recalled the sweet sense of floating. Once again in memory, she swam lazy somersaults around the bright grid lines. The flirtatious green geometric appeared, plainly communicating playfulness. The white noise kept her from fully reentering the inner world. For some reason, this worked—although using the noise to ward off unanticipated flashbacks never did. She'd spun into the inner world only once from this chair, despite Karine's white noise, and she'd flung off a set of lightweight featherphones. Now Karine clamped these monsters onto her ears.

"Why did you find the green pyramid enticing?" Karine's voice reverberated left of center inside Llyn's skull.

This was the most humiliating aftermath of her episodes, exposing her beloved inner world to Karine's scrutiny. "The way it moved, I think."

"How so?"

Llyn sifted her memory. "Its—its points waved at me."

"Did you choose to wear green today because of the pyramid?"

Llyn glanced down. She'd chosen spring green for her tunic, forest for her culottes. "I don't think so." She wished she, too, were an empath. She'd heard they could block synch by rapidly modulating their inner frequency—

"Llyn, where is your mind?"

Anger surged through her, then regret. Hurriedly she thought about something pleasant—Regent Salbari's kindness, Niklo's attempt to help her—but by the time she'd shut off her resentment and opened her eyes, Karine stood wiggling her fingers over control surfaces on the sound generator.

Sighing, Llyn pulled off the headphones. "Sorry," she mumbled. "I didn't mean to hit you."

"Anger is a normal human reaction."

But no one liked to feel it aimed at themselves. Maybe Karine wouldn't discipline her, but there would be consequences. How Karine felt about her determined the freedoms she withheld.

"What do you want to do now?" Llyn laid the headphones on the stand beside her.

"Talk." Karine settled back onto her chair.

At least she'd stopped halfway through the flashback. "What about?"

"Your trip to the library. Refusing to go straight to Professor Ruskin's home, the way I told you to."

"I've lived here for five years," Llyn said. "I'm ready for more independence."

"You're not going to earn it that way."

"I'm not a child."

"Not physically." Karine raised an eyebrow. "But in many ways, you are."

"No, I'm—"

"You lost two years of development at a crucial point of your life, and you remember nothing before that."

"I grew and learned. In the inner world."

"That doesn't count in this world. We are battling a severe addiction. Where did you have your previous episode?"

Llyn thought back several weeks. "Out in the orchard." Karine kept twelve fruit trees under fiberglass. They clung to life in Antar's hot, humid environment.

"Why?"

"I was listening to the stream down below the hill."

"That is correct. And the time before that?"

How could she forget? "I was walking past the kitchen. The staff was clanking dishes." She'd crumpled in front of the whole clinic population, less than fifteen minutes after Tamsina complimented her on her poise.

Karine nodded. "It only takes two notes, if you're in a relaxed, vulnerable mood."

"Then I won't be vulnerable anymore. I'll never relax." Llyn compressed her lips. The inner world was sweet, but if she ever hoped to escape Karine, she must leave it alone.

Still, stress also made her vulnerable. If only she could convince Karine!

"Good idea." Karine glanced over Llyn's shoulder, probably at a clock. Llyn hoped this session had gone long enough to satisfy her. "The apples are ripe," Karine said in a bland but probably insincere voice. "Go pick a gallon or so."

Freedom! Llyn swung her legs around and sat upright.

"Freedom?" Karine asked.

Llyn froze. She had thought Karine had finished synching. She should've known better.

"You can be perfectly free at any time." Karine crossed her arms.

That sounded too good to be true. "Yes?"

"But only within strictly defined limits. Think of children playing on a steep-sided mesa. Frightened, they stay in the very center. But if someone erects a strong fence, they're free to play at the very edge of the cliff. You are safe only within fences, Llyn."

Prison walls, Llyn corrected her silently.

Karine lowered her voice. "I wish you'd stop thinking like an adolescent."

That was progress. Generally she accused Llyn of thinking like a child.

The wall intercom beeped four times. Karine had received a message from someone on her priority list. "Think about what I told you," she said as she strode out.

Llyn rubbed the back of one hand with her other thumb. She could almost feel it. Almost. If she could regain her sense of touch, maybe that would help her hold on to the real world when a flashback threatened.

Feathers would help her more than electric shocks. Didn't Karine understand?

She slipped back into her shoes and walked down the hall, out a door on the other side of the hillside clinic, then down toward the small grove under the inflated fiberglass half-dome. Elroy stood steadying a ladder for a patient who stood dropping red fruits into a box. They both waved.

Squeak, the clinic's pet dedo, dashed uphill toward her, wagging his whip-like tail. Llyn bent to pet him. Purring, he rubbed his huge black-and-white head against her thigh. She barely felt the pressure, but his throaty purr was irresistible.

It had been bred into dedoes for exactly that reason. Named for an ancient gargoyle they supposedly resembled, they had been genengineered by an unorthodox animal advocate in Vatsya Habitat. Utterly unintelligent, unable to register pain, and totally omnivorous, dedoes had surprised humankind by thriving. They'd been equipped with several stomachs and such a wide range of intestinal bacteria that they could subsist on compost.

Even more vitally, they satisfied the hab-confined Vatsyans' need to care for other creatures. "Biophilia," Karine called it. Their value to medical patients was so well established that most clinics kept a dedo or two.

Squeak was getting fat. The patients loved his purr so much that they often slipped scraps to him, despite Karine's orders.

Llyn scratched Squeak's flop-eared, leonine head. He pushed it higher into her hand. A dedo's main instinct was to snuggle. Squeak could nestle against a cinder block and purr about it.

Llyn had been told that she couldn't feel much more pain than Squeak did. Since she hoped to live independently someday, to her it was a liability. "That's enough, gargoyle." She gave Squeak a final pat. "I need to pick apples."

Without her to lean on, Squeak toppled. He purred and scrambled back up onto short, muscular legs.

As Llyn propped a ladder against one tree's stoutest branch, a cloud seeder plane flew over, its engine buzzing steadily. With one more load of sky seeds, one more half ton of moisture would be precipitated out of the cloud cover. Besides undoing the Devastators' damages by thinning that perpetual shroud, they were watering and widening the algae paddies.

She climbed up, poked her head between branches, and started picking. She liked garden work. It gave her time to think. After today's class (if Karine let her attend it), this evening would be the clinic's biweekly Patient Social Encounter. Karine scrutinized her behavior at these "parties" and critiqued every word, stance, and gesture. She punished casual behavior with bland food, extra time on the sweat machines, or cutbacks on her net privileges.

Where was it all leading? Llyn didn't want Karine's answer. She didn't want to be marginally self-sufficient. Somewhere was a job only she could do.

She set a red-streaked yellow apple into her box and reached for another.

Karine checked the clinic's central multinet terminal near the kitchen. A call request had been logged from Vice Regent Filip Salbari. Delighted, she turned on one foot and hurried to her private office. When she sat at this wood-toned fiberglass data desk, she could look out the window on her right, or left into the hallway, or over the multinet at a stereo portrait of her late husband. She sat down, recited Filip Salbari's NU access code, and slid on her view-glasses.

His face appeared immediately. She thought she saw more gray in his hair than two days ago, but it could've been a poor transmission.

"I'm returning your call, Filip. Have you heard any more on the *Aliki?*" He must be carrying more stress than usual.

He shook his head. "Nothing. Our lives and our work go on. I wanted to know if Llyn survived the trip back from Nuris without another episode."

"Sadly, no." Karine detailed the return-trip incident.

Filip's expression sobered. "There have been several more attempts at stripping the net for information about her."

"In two days?"

He nodded. "There appears to be special emphasis on locating her. Please keep a close eye on her. Two eyes, if you can spare them."

"I shall." So, her reluctance to take Llyn to town had been justified. Someone had seen her at the concert.

"You should also know that Nuris University has been anonymously threatened with violence if she isn't brought forward."

"What?" Karine straightened her glasses. "That's ludicrous!" Empaths feared violence even more desperately than most Antarans. A victim could broadcast anguish and pain at astonishing range. That disciplinary AR episode had been her single real mistake on Llyn's behalf. "Do you see any connection with the previous stripping attempts?"

"It would be difficult not to."

"Then I assume that the on-site class is out of the question."

"Absolutely not. If we protect Llyn so closely that no risk is ever involved, she will never learn to be human. Besides, the class will be held up there in Lengle, not Nuris. Our mysterious observer should not see her there."

"I don't like the idea."

He shook his head. "Llyn is no child. I synched with her for some time at the concert. She is extremely mature in some ways—"

"And an infant in others. Don't say she doesn't need—"

"I am asking you to send her to the on-site class at Lengle. When does it begin?"

"This afternoon," Karine snapped. "It's too late."

"I'll have my staff register her. Get her dressed and get her there."

"Is that an order, Filip?"

"Yes. It is."

Filip Salbari rotated his chair away from the office terminal. Vananda and Favia sat side by side in deep chairs along the other wall, near an open window. His wife Favia, taller and older, had the darker hair, but both sisters wore curls, and both had put on deep rose-colored tunics this morning. They'd spent the last two days planning a private memorial service for their father.

"She fought it," Vananda observed.

"Hard." Filip straightened a stack of printouts that a colleague had dropped on his desk.

Vananda, his fellow empath, shook her head. "Karine is a fine clinician and she has always been considered an excellent caregiver, but this relationship is becoming toxic."

"It seems incongruous." Favia's fresh grief showed in her swollen eyes. "How could she err like this? Someone of her profession should know better."

"The best of us develop blind spots," Filip said. "And there was nothing toxic when the adoption was approved."

"She lost Namron years ago." Favia looked off into space. "She is losing Niklo. She is determined not to lose Llyn. Controlling Llyn has become a vital part of her happiness."

Vananda raised her head. "Could we have an attempted enmeshment case here, Filip?" she asked.

He pursed his lips. Attempting enmeshment was a serious accusation among empaths, a real risk to personhood. "I am not sure. It should be checked, though." He straightened. "Do you have any suggestions? You've both relinquished grown children."

"So have you," Vananda said. "Trust your instincts."

"There are differences between fatherly instincts and motherly ones."

Favia smiled back at him. He shallow-synched with her and mentally splashed in his wife's affectionate warmth. "If I think of anything more," she said, "I'll suggest it."

"My hands are tied." Filip raised them, separated. "Unless Karine commits a legal offense, she has jurisdiction over Llyn for another full year unless she declares Llyn competent."

"She may never do that," Vananda said.

"Someday she will see what is under her nose." Filip glanced out his office window, across the city. Ground traffic looked slow today. "Anything else to accomplish before we head out?" The memorial service was planned for the family estate, northwest of Nuris. His pioneering grandparents had rebelliously sunk roots far from the new power center.

"Only a few things," Favia said. "I'll be ready in three or four hours." The sisters embraced. Vananda slipped out.

Favia paused at the door. "Shall I meet you at the town house?"

"That will be fine." As her footsteps receded, Filip dictated a message to his staff: enroll Llyn Torfinn in that Antaran history class at Lengle townsite. "You have only an hour," he finished it. "Please act immediately."

Llyn tried to stroll casually into the classroom, as if she did this every day. Tables and chairs surrounded an empty stretch of tile flooring, like the spokes of a wheel. Most of the chairs were occupied, and to Llyn's satisfaction, a few students looked almost as old as she was. Normal children, raised in warm, caring families. She'd bypassed the upper-primary children in her first satellite group, plus two midgrade classes beyond them. She felt stupid in some ways (she'd been told that mathematics would always be closed to her—something about arrested development of one of her brain connections), yet she excelled in most other subjects. What would she have been, what might she have accomplished, if she'd been allowed to live normally?

At any rate, she already knew Basic Antaran History. Insisting on this class was her own contribution to her social education. She wanted to rub shoulders with other young people.

She had also hoped to escape Karine for two hours each day—for three weeks—but Karine stalked beside her, clutching the shoulder strap of a large purse. She probably carried a medical arsenal.

A thin, mustached man waved them to a table. Karine remained standing and caught his attention. "Have they all been told?"

Llyn flushed. She guessed she knew what was coming.

"No," the man said. "I thought I would wait until everyone arrived."

"That will be fine," Karine said.

Not with me. No one consulted me. Llyn sat down and stared at the tabletop, fighting anger. Thanks to Karine, her fellow students would never consider her normal. Still, if she coped with this situation, maybe another class—another group—would accept her friendship.

Several early-teen children murmured and looked back at the door. Another girl entered, staring straight ahead. Balanced on her shoulders was a black object shaped like a fat letter C. The girl was a gillie, one of the other recent throwback mutations. The black object was her prosthesis, a water tank fitted to her neck. Oxygen from a second tank that she wore like a backpack bubbled through the clear black gill-tank, letting her breathe.

Once all seats had filled, the mustached man gestured to Karine, who introduced herself and announced, "I am here supervising Llyn Torfinn, who has a rare brain disorder. If she hears music, she could collapse. That might endanger her or any of you, so for the duration of this course—or as long as Llyn stays with you—I must ask you all to refrain from singing, whistling, letting metal objects clink against each other, or playing instruments. Any sounds that her subconscious could construe as music will be strictly forbidden. Do you all understand?"

Llyn wished she could slide under the table. She clenched her hands on the tabletop and examined her fingernails. When she finally dared to look up, she saw the gillie's blue eyes. Llyn returned her shy smile. Compared to that girl, she looked normal.

Antarans accepted the gillies—and empaths—as easily as the thousands of artificially conceived children, because their souls and minds remained human. But one evening, brooding about Niklo's rebelliousness,

Karine had wondered aloud whether Llyn's soul was damaged by spending so much time in the AR.

Distracted by that black thought, Llyn lost track of the instructor's narrative until Karine pinched her arm and pointed. The instructor was twirling an ethereal red-gray ball in the air in front of him.

"Evidently," he said, "those same previous inhabitants of the Concord cluster moved our planet to its orbit. Our binary star's gravitational tides prevented planets from forming within its habitable zone. Vatsya, though, is the only B-class sun in the middle of a 'burp' of otherwise uniform star formation. It emits too much high-energy radiation to allow life, but our planet formed there. We don't know who moved it, or when. Or, more vitally, how they generated enough energy to do it."

A sharp-chinned boy of eleven or twelve sat behind the gillie, running a finger around the back of her tank. He looked like trouble. Llyn hoped he didn't decide to whistle just to see what her episodes looked like.

"Why did they move it?" a girl near the gillie asked.

"We can't even guess." The instructor shrugged his narrow shoulders. "Because this system is central to the cluster—that's what we've always assumed. The Concord cluster has obviously been desirable real estate for millennia.

"The first human settlers did know what they were approaching. They had full data on all nine systems, two generations before landing. They knew, for example, that Miatrix was deficient in radiational wavelengths necessary for growing any plants that terrestrial herbivores could eat. They also spotted the Gates, although they didn't know what—"

Another girl spoke up. Blond and soft-faced, she had a precocious tone to her voice. "Do you know what happened to Earth?"

The instructor didn't seem to mind being interrupted. This must be his day for covering groundwork. "The Devastators probably sterilized it. If Earth has been resurrected, we haven't heard, and we haven't got the technology to go back there and see what happened."

Llyn decided to try speaking up. "But we haven't picked up any messages. Not even modulated radio waves."

The mischievous boy tapped the gillie's tank. She leaned away and gave him a dark look. The boy stared blandly at the instructor. Llyn watched, fascinated. He was getting away with it! "I heard," he said as if he'd done nothing wrong, "Antar's orbit is unstable. We're going to crash into one of the suns."

"It's possible." The instructor sounded unconcerned. "Evidently the civilization that placed Antar had the tech to correct its orbit if necessary, but we don't. Our world could crash into a sun in a mere twenty or thirty thousand years. Or it could be slung out of orbit into deep space. In either case, I don't expect to be here. Do you?"

Two of the younger children tittered.

The sharp-chinned boy finally looked serious. "But why didn't the Devastators use nuclear weapons? That would've sterilized Antar forever."

"We honestly don't know. Maybe it gives us a clue to their mindset. They seem to have been driven by fears—"

The ground rumbled underfoot. The instructor glanced up and smiled at his students. "These tables are reinforced, of course, in case we ever have a Big One—"

The ground shook again. Llyn looked from the instructor to Karine, who raised an eyebrow. "Just a moment," the instructor said. "Let's see if—"

The floor heaved, tossing children and chairs.

Llyn dove under her table, where she nearly collided with Karine. Dodging Karine, she butted heads with another student. The ground shook again. Windows rattled. Llyn slowly counted to ten. The rolling subsided.

Her stomach hurt.

"Stay where you are." The instructor's voice shook. "I'm going to contact Nuris for an epicenter. It looks as if we'll study geology today."

Llyn huddled in her place, trying not to shiver. "That was the biggest rattle in five years," she murmured to Karine. "Wasn't it?"

"Yes," Karine muttered. Llyn heard pain in her voice. Sweat beaded on her forehead.

Someone within Karine's sensing range must've been badly hurt. Maybe even killed. Llyn didn't say it out loud for fear of frightening the children. "Do you want to lie down?" she asked. "Put your head in my lap? You don't look good."

"Just for a moment." Karine nodded. "The teacher might need me."

The ground rumbled again. "Aftershock," an older boy announced. His voice squeaked.

Staccato footsteps pounded back to the classroom. The instructor reappeared. "Everybody follow me!"

Llyn's classmates surged after him, older boys first, then the younger children. The older girls hung back. That was a social behavior she'd have to ask Karine about. She found herself jogging in step with the gillie, culottes flapping as they trailed the others. "What is it?" Llyn asked.

"I don't know. This is scary. I don't like it."

"Me neither."

Llyn glanced at Karine. Her tunic's collar looked dark. Maybe wet.

The instructor herded them down a flight of stairs into a dark, echoing storage area thronged by other teacher-student groups. "Your parents have been called. You'll all go home as soon as they come for you. Apologies, Medic Torfinn. I should have just sent you and Llyn away."

"You had other children to worry about." Karine's voice came out thick and cloudy.

"What's up?" The sharp-chinned boy had an equally sharp shouting voice. Several others echoed him.

The instructor motioned them to stand closer. He bent down and lowered his voice. "Please keep this quiet," he said softly. "There are younger children nearby and we cannot panic them. But Nuris University has been bombed."

Karine clutched Llyn's hand. The boy turned whiter than Karine did. "Bombed?" he asked. "Who did it? What's going on?"

"I don't know yet," the instructor said. "I don't know if anyone knows."

Karine sat motionless, staring horrified—at Llyn.

07

A thin wind whistled around the Torfinn-Reece Clinic's main entry, and Llyn paused outside the hillside entry. Downhill below the clinic, pale fabric clung unusually close to the fruit trees.

Elroy squinted up at roiling gray clouds and waved Llyn toward the glassed entryway. "Come on," he cried.

Llyn plunged indoors. Karine and Elroy followed.

"Any idea what happened?" Karine paused just inside the front door, and Llyn stopped, too. Karine had tried again to tune in the i-net all the way home, growing frantic as they careened up the hill road. All they heard was static and short, garbled transmissions. An explosion that shook Lengle township, 200K from Nuris, was no small bombing.

"No idea." Elroy's voice dropped to a lower pitch. "We closed off all streamside windows and deflated the orchard cover to treetop level. Everyone's in the lower story. I told them we'd stay down until we got an unambiguous all-clear."

"Good work. Go on down, and take Llyn with you. I'm going to call Filip."

Llyn had to admire Karine's self-control and Elroy's quick response. It felt weirdly good to be safely home.

Elroy grasped her shoulder. "Come on, come on."

Karine dropped onto the stool next to the clinic's main multinet terminal. She recited Filip's communication code. Nothing happened.

Bombed! What would they do if c-net was down? There used to be emergency generators ...

She tried again. Then again. She stood up, walked a lap around the dining area, and demanded Filip's number once more. When those generators came back online, she must be the first caller through.

After several minutes, the unit hummed. She jabbed her REPEAT key. There was an odd delay of five or six seconds. A stranger's face appeared over her terminal.

"I'm calling for Filip Salbari," Karine said before he could speak. "Is he—"

"Regent Salbari is not available," the man said. "How may I help you?"

He couldn't be dead! "This is Medic Karine Torfinn." She steadied her voice. "Is Filip alive? Do you know—"

"He was traveling from Nuris to the family estate for the funeral when the attack occurred. He is safe, and he is extremely busy. How else may I help you?"

Some of the tension melted out of her shoulders. She swallowed hard and pushed out more words. "My son, Niklo Reece, lives in western student housing. Is there any word out from the University?"

"Very little." The man frowned, shaking his head. "I can tell you that West Housing was destroyed."

Karine gasped. The edges of her vision darkened. "Maybe Niklo wasn't there."

"I hope not, Medic Torfinn. Sincerely."

She hardly knew what to ask. "What happened? Who bombed the University?"

"Nuris University and the Outwatch base were both targeted by intersystem warships."

He'd said it so calmly that she wondered whether she heard him right. "Warships? I thought—"

"They came through Antar Gate a week ago, identifying themselves as Kocaban cargo haulers. Antar Outwatch was about to insert them into a standard parking orbit when they accelerated, dove, and launched two clusters of missiles. They are headed back toward Antar Gate. Fast."

Her pulse pounded. Had the Devastators returned? They had never bothered with anything so small as a university. They wasted whole planets. But no human would willfully damage a life-supporting world. "Are we pursuing?"

"Antar has no Outwatch ships left."

"We're … grounded?" She felt almost dizzy. Anton Salbari must call Tdega for a rescue. No—wait—Anton Salbari had been at the University. "Wait." Her voice shook. "Who were they—the ships?"

"Judging by their escape velocity, they are new and advanced. If they were built inside Concord space, they have to Tdegan."

Tdega, the world that must keep Antar from starving? She frowned. "That's only a supposition. They could be alien. Is Anton Salbari alive?"

"We don't know. He was at the University. We have positive whereabouts on three other Regents, but the worst destruction is centered in the upper residential cluster."

That elegant cluster housed the Tourelle and Sheliak families, as well as several of the Salbaris' other relatives. Someone had tried to lop off Nuris's headship. She'd first thought that the bombing and those mysterious searches for Llyn were related. Now … perhaps not.

"Will someone notify me if Niklo checks in?" she whispered. She'd had no sense of his death or injury, and today, her listening sense was so acute she felt raw. Surely she would have known if Niklo were gone.

"Yes, we will. But he must remain in the Nuris area. We have declared emergency wartime footing. All private transport is banned. How secure is your dwelling?"

Somehow she would spirit Niklo out of the city, but for the moment, she concentrated on the small question that she could answer. "It's quakeproof. Rad resistant, or so I'm told. We've never had to test it."

"Agreed. Not in fifty years." Stress lines darkened the man's face. He would have a long night.

So would she.

"Call if you need assistance, Medic Torfinn."

"If I'm needed, I will be here."

"Oh. Yes. There will probably be hundreds of survivors who require your services. But not today. Thank you. Keep us in your prayers." The face vanished.

Karine slid off her view-glasses. "No!" she whispered, covering her face with achingly empty hands. "Not Niklo!"

———

A Residence Security guard swung open the main door of Gamal Casimir's favorite upstairs lounge, the fire room. Gamal squinted his good eye. His only surviving son walked up the carpet, carrying a sheaf of printouts. Siah, the shortest and heaviest of his generation, had piggy eyes in the middle of a round, petulant face. He took after his mother, who'd died trying to birth Gamal's third daughter.

Gamal sat in a cushioned, carved wooden chair with the hearth on his right. Beyond the flickering fire, Osun Zavijavah stood staring into its heart. Eerie orange reflections wavered on his black wraparound glasses as he stroked his drooping mustache.

The sun stood just past second noon, late evening by Tdegan clocks. If the Casimir family meant to present a unified front, then tonight—before the public reacted to the Antar attack—he must interview his son Siah and then his other nephew, Bellik's brother Alun. Gamal's own first son and eldest daughter had been executed nine years ago, convicted of assassinating Gamal's older brother. After the tragic triple loss, Gamal had agreed to raise his nephews—Bellik, then seventeen, and Alun, only ten—alongside his surviving children.

Tonight, the family would likely split again.

Siah stopped in front of the hearth and puffed for breath. "You called me in, sir? I have the new export figures." He waved the printouts. "Do you want them after all? Is that why you called me?"

"Are those negotiation figures?" Gamal asked.

Siah nodded. When he blinked, his little eyes almost disappeared.

The fire popped. Gamal's grandfather Donson, sitting in a corner chair, woke up and sipped from his wineglass. Gamal had asked the old Head Regent to sit in with him this evening for appearance's sake.

"Antar's attempt to impose its pricing on Tdega is now a dead issue," Gamal said.

Siah had favored going along with the Concord power play. "Is it, Father?"

"If Antar took that step, what assurance do we have that their controls would ever be revoked?"

"We have their word—"

Gamal interrupted. "Treaties have been broken throughout history, particularly when there are regime changes. Essentially, there is no reason for Antar to dominate the Concord."

"Antar is geometrically central—"

"And only slightly closer to its Gate than Tdega is to ours. What is the real point of maintaining a central government?"

"Tradition." Siah shrugged slightly. "And Nuris University."

"Correct," Gamal said. "If certain people hadn't salvaged centuries of data for Antar, Bkellan University would have become the Concord's information treasury by default."

"Obviously."

Gamal steepled his fingers and watched Siah's face. "Our forces struck Antar this morning."

Siah's topmost chin quivered for an instant. "What do you mean? Attacked?"

"Yes. The primary target was Nuris University."

Siah blinked with his mouth half open.

"I am realigning the Concord, Siah. Antar wants to keep us from rising, but we won't be kept down. Once we rule ourselves, the smaller worlds will look to us for goods and protection. Can you support that position?"

"I ..."

Security Chief Zavijavah's head turned. Behind those glasses, he eyed Siah.

"Sir." Siah tossed his printouts toward the fire grate. They fluttered onto the carpet. "I cannot condone attacking Antar, but I will not stand in your way. If I leave Bkellan with my family and stay quiet, will you pledge that we won't be ... harassed?"

Rotund little Siah would've made some other family a good son. He showed common sense. "Make no statement opposing my actions, and you will be fine." Gamal laced his fingers.

"Agreed. I promise."

"Then I pledge your safety. You are an intelligent man, Siah. Take care of my grandchildren."

"Are Bellik and Alun with you in this?"

Siah *would* wonder where his cousins stood. "That is Bellik's and Alun's business. Not yours."

Siah hurried away.

Gamal watched his son leave. Maybe Siah was smarter than he looked, letting Gamal take the risk and getting ready to jump to whatever side won.

"Any orders?" Osun Zavijavah stared at the fire.

"Not yet." Gamal raised a hand. "But if Siah is still in residence tomorrow morning, notify me."

A voice creaked out of the corner. "Where is Siah going?"

Gamal turned around. His father Aeternum had kept Grandfather Donson alive for an extra decade, despite astronomical medical expenses, partly out of gratitude—a smooth transition of power had made Aeternum a Vice Regent at forty-five—and partly because the aged Head Regent made such a good scapegoat. Whenever one of Aeternum's governmental experiments went wrong, the family blamed Donson's advice. Gamal agreed with his late father: Donson was worth his declining weight in geriatric medications.

Obviously confused, Donson waved at the door as it shut behind Siah. "Is he looking for Aeternum?"

Not yet, if he behaved. "He's gone away," Gamal said, "for a while."

Osun Zavijavah turned away from the fire. Gamal asked him, "Has Alun been called?"

"He should be here in four minutes."

The fire hissed.

"How are you feeling?" Gamal recrossed his legs.

Zavijavah thumbed his left temple. "It's becoming a distraction again."

"I'm sorry to hear that."

The door opened, and Bellik's younger brother Alun paused at the other end of the carpet. He glanced around the room. Lanky like Bellik, nineteen-year-old Alun had attended Nuris University for a year before he was called home. He had gone queueless while away, growing out his glossy black hair in the Antaran style. He attended Bkellan University now, but he still wore his hair unconventionally.

At least he hadn't come back wearing culottes.

"Good evening," Alun said crisply. "I'm glad you called me in. I've been wanting to ask about several changes of curriculum. I want to take my degree from a university, sir. Not a military academy."

"It will remain a university." Gamal bristled. He'd known Alun might be trouble. "It will soon be the best in Concord space. We are adding a few courses more relevant to the time."

"Plasma Weaponry? Underground Shelter Reinforcement? A Historical Overview of Interplanetary Warfare?" Alun shook his head. "The Tdegan military will not make Bkellan the best in Concord space."

Ah, but it already had. "Maybe our secession will."

"You can't secede without public debate. Give the Tdegan people a choice in the matter."

Gamal studied Alun through slitted eyes. There was no room in the family for obstructionists. Obviously, he didn't need to ask how Alun felt about striking Nuris University. "Siah is about to leave town." Might as well say it bluntly. "Do you want to leave, too? Or simply change your mind?"

"Neither, Uncle." Alun strode to the corner. "Hello, Great-granddad." He gripped and raised the old man's hand.

Donson smiled and mouthed the air.

Zavijavah watched them.

Alun turned back to Gamal. "Is that all, sir?"

"I wished to know how you felt about secession. Now I know."

"Yes, sir. You do. Please reconsider about the University, Uncle."

"Very well. Good night."

Alun walked out.

Zavijavah stepped across the hearth. Plucking at a gold band on his dark red coat sleeve, he frowned down at Gamal. "He's out, isn't he?"

"I'm afraid so."

"Rider is interested in Alun," Zavijavah said, developing an odd atonal lilt to his voice.

"That is understandable." Gamal thought he understood. "But Alun is likely to make trouble."

"That can be taken care of." Zavijavah paused as if listening to someone, then added, "He only needs to be kept quiet until Rider needs him. That won't be for awhile yet—"

Gamal raised a hand. He preferred not to talk about Rider in the old man's presence. Donson already looked asleep again, but sometimes he only catnapped. "Then we will not send Alun away." Gamal eyed his Security Chief. "Do what you must, but don't leave traces."

Zavijavah nodded and left the fire room. Gamal called for a servant to wheel Donson down to bed.

He, Bellik, and Security Chief Zavijavah would guide Tdega through this transition. Mentally dismissing Siah and Alun, he walked to a wall cabinet. He wanted to check something Zavijavah had told him.

He drew out an irregular round object, bleached white. It stared up at him with large, empty eyes: his brother Hutton's skull. Father of Bellik and Alun, Hutton had been Gamal's rival and tormentor, ruthlessly suspicious of Gamal, eventually poisoned by Gamal's children. Gamal had recently reclaimed Hutton's skull from the family vault. It would remind him of what he must do—and why—if he meant to lead Tdega toward peace and power.

He returned to his chair, crossed his legs, and dangled a foot over the hearth before he raised the skull and stroked its dome. It felt like silk, even where tiny fingerlike protrusions joined one plate to another. Thick and rigid, it had housed a human's ultimate possession—one that he never fully utilized.

Gamal saw no resemblance between Hutton's arrogant face and the empty-eyed object in front of him. The skull looked friendlier.

He contemplated the tiny hole behind one ocular orbit. An optic nerve had passed through that hole to the brain.

Now he saw clearly what Osun Zavijavah had tried to explain. The ear and mouth apertures gave better access to gray matter. Bone surrounded the eyes, preventing a foreign object's penetration.

It mattered greatly to Zavijavah, because Zavijavah carried an alien ambassador inside his skull.

As Gamal understood it, his new allies the Chaethe had arisen as intelligent symbiotes to a non-intelligent carrier species. "Riding" other species however it suited them, they had tried to invade a nearby system—and they incited a war that exploded outward, involving every habitable world that the terrified Devastators could reach. It had been the Devastators who depopulated the Concord star cluster.

And now, the Chaethe parasites were settling the Concord's rim, quietly absorbing the Sunsis system's human population and controlling travel through its Gate. They waited at Sunsis, as Zavijavah's Rider had put it to Gamal, to see whether humans knew how to fight. They still lived in terror of the Devastators. On their own, they were incapable of defending themselves or their offspring. They needed strong allies, bodies they could move. To fight back.

Gamal wanted leverage over the other Concord worlds, but he also needed power to protect Tdega against the Devastators if they returned. Tdega was the most fertile world in human-settled space, and its environment must not be destroyed. He could not really secede from the Concord without destroying all of the Gates, so the decision was simple. He needed the Chaethe as allies. That would tumble the Concord's power balances in Tdega's favor, if Antar decided to fight.

But Rider was very alien. Sometimes it made statements Gamal could not comprehend. Gamal had experimented, years ago when the ambassador first came to Tdega, with ways to communicate. Safe within a host's skull, a Chaethe preserved the host's natural speech centers. However, Rider insisted they had additional levels of intelligence that humans could not comprehend. Rider refused to give any other information.

Since Gamal needed that power balance, his experimentation continued privately between Gamal and Rider—via Zavijavah.

Gamal upended the skull and thrust his finger through an ear hole. Wiggling inside the brain cavity, it looked wormlike.

An ear hole was large enough, too. So was the gap at the base of the skull.

He wondered why Chaethe preferred penetrating through the human mouth.

Alun Casimir strode into his cousin Siah's Residence suite and let the hall door slide shut. Before he could speak, Siah's wife dashed out of the side bedroom, chasing a chubby-legged boy. "Hinton, stop that. Put your coat on!" They vanished behind Siah into the main bedroom.

Siah stood beside the main entry access panel, across from a group of still-life paintings. A head and a half smaller than Alun, Siah obviously enjoyed Residence food. Still, deep honesty showed in his face, and his shrewd eyes were steady. Siah was the only relative whom Alun trusted.

His untucked casual shirt looked like he'd thrown it on. "Father called you in, too?"

Alun nodded and braced for an argument. "I just came from the fire room."

"We're heading out in fifteen minutes. Come with us. The kids are thrilled to be taking a surprise vacation."

Alun rubbed his chin. "I'm not leaving. You shouldn't, either. That's cowardly."

Siah pointed a fleshy finger at him. "I'm old enough to remember my sister Danza and my brother Gonsalve. Someone in this family doesn't make exceptions."

Alun shook his head. "Then send Fidele and the children away. But together, maybe we could do something."

Siah spread his hands. "Alun, running away is the first line of defense. Sometimes taking a stand is the right thing to do, but you're going to do it prematurely. Don't push yet. He's not ready to listen."

Siah rarely missed the point so completely. "Uncle Gamal has no idea that he's taking things too far," Alun said. "He won't find out, either, unless someone tells him so. Somebody has to ring the alarm buzzer."

"And get flattened."

"I probably will, unless you stand with me." Alun grimaced. "I shouldn't be the only one to speak up. You're hiding behind your own family."

"When you have a family, you'll understand," Siah murmured. "Either that, or you'll make their lives miserable, ringing your alarm buzzers."

Alun thrust his hands into his pockets. "Not the family I'm going to have."

"Nobody's perfect, Alun. Fidele is the gentlest, most intelligent woman I know, but we've had arguments. Sometimes she's right."

"So?"

"So I don't cut her down when we disagree. We're going to stand together. But we're going to stand elsewhere.

"Maybe," he added softly, "Father will eventually do himself in. That's why I think you're challenging him too soon. I've made arrangements with Bkellan University to set up a secured link. Not even Father will know about it. That's my right as a Regent. Wherever we travel, we'll be able to keep track of what's going on here."

"Good idea." Alun rubbed his face. "But …" There didn't seem to be much else to say.

"You won't go with us?"

"You won't stay?"

"Well." Siah exhaled and pursed his lips. "We're obviously not going to convince each other. Good luck, Alun. If all else fails, go to the Antaran embassy. The Ambassador's a good man. He has offered us all asylum."

Alun clasped his cousin's hand and left the suite. Neither of Siah's offers tempted him. He was doing the right thing.

Somebody had to.

Osun Zavijavah took a late dinner in his apartment on the east wing's ground floor.

He lived in a single room, carpeted with minimal furniture: one bed, one table, one chair. No shelves. Clutter made him uneasy. He always kept his closet door open so he could see inside.

He did not mourn Aeternum Casimir. Aeternum had hired him, but Gamal Casimir brought him into his own bitter inner circle. Zavijavah's job was to oversee Residence guards and make sure that information lines remained secure.

His five senses were sharper, if anything, than before Rider infested his life. He took excellent care of his body these days. He had no choice. It was valuable to Rider. He'd never been this meticulous with diet and exercise.

He sat at the small table in his darkened room. Tonight he missed his family. He'd spoken with them two days ago, so he must wait four more days to call them again. They were safer on Tdega's far side. Safer from any Concord counterattack, safer from the Casimirs' notorious infighting, and safer from anything Rider might pressure him to do.

Gamal Casimir had long threatened to punish Zavijavah's family if his service ever slipped. If Zavijavah did not give Casimir—and Rider—full cooperation, Casimir had promised Zavijavah's family Riders of their own. So far, they knew nothing about the alien parasite. He would rather die than let any of them become carriers. But Casimir kept him on several chains, controlling Zavijavah's fate as dispassionately as if he were one of the brutes in the kennel out back.

Zavijavah ate mechanically. His menu rarely varied: beef liver, dark green vegetables, puddings that tasted metallic and left dark smears in his mustache. His jaw popped as he chewed, aching clear up to his temples. He laid down his fork and pulled off the dark glasses that hid his eyes from the world. He rubbed his temples with both hands.

He had been born a seer, a mutant with enormous eyes that gathered tremendous amounts of light. His Vatsyan mother had applied for one of the few immigrant visas Tdega offered each year—rather than have the abortion her parents demanded—when she learned she was pregnant by a seer. She'd schooled Osun at home, and he'd found nighttime security work in which his unnatural eyes were useful.

They had also attracted Rider's attention. Rider perceived the physical world through its carrier's senses, and it found sensory enhancements fascinating.

Without preamble, its thin voice spoke inside Zavijavah's head. "Get Alun Casimir ready. I don't want him sent away."

No one else ever heard Rider's voice. "Let me finish eating." Since they were alone, Zavijavah answered out loud. That helped him separate his own voice from the parasite's. Rider seemed to check in and out of Zavijavah's consciousness, spending little time eavesdropping. Zavijavah wondered what else occupied its attention.

"You have orders. Take care of Alun."

"I will. But first, I'm eating this garbage for you." Bitterly, Zavijavah cut another bite of liver. "I'd prefer it warm."

An unearthly wail echoed between his ears. "Now," Rider shrieked. The reedy voice had not lost patience. It was simply enforcing an order.

Zavijavah dropped his knife and fork. He bowed his head and shut his eyes. When he couldn't see, *it* couldn't. Shutting down his vision was the only way he could get back at it. "Let me catch my breath," he muttered.

"Breathe deeply."

"Listen to me," Zavijavah said. "Alun lives in Residence. I've asked my staff to inform me when he falls asleep. I don't want a confrontation tonight. I have a headache. You know why."

The wailing faded.

He finished his dinner, chewing around the aches and pops of his sprung jaw. Rider needed this iron-rich diet so that Zavijavah's body would lay down a thick sheath around each of its offspring spores. Soon it would enter a reproductive period. With its second spore mature, and before a third started to form, Zavijavah must help it infest a new host. He'd been through that already. He dreaded doing it again.

After he finished eating, he went to his terminal and pulled on a pair of shaded view-glasses. From his net menu he considered several ways to render young Alun harmless without damaging his senses or dexterity. Rider had told him that it found human intelligence extraneous. Still, Zavijavah had more sympathy for a fellow human than an alien parasite. He didn't want to leave Alun mindless.

Something untraceable …

A binary poison. The first dose would bind to cells in Alun's limbic system deep inside the brain. The second dose would react with the first, liberating a tiny dose of free radicals in that single target zone … and then vanish from the body.

He keyed for delivery of the reagents he needed, then lay down on the bed. His head hurt. Hoping to lull Rider, he remembered …

He'd been wheeled onto the Residence lift nine years ago, drugged and strapped to a medical gurney. Gamal Casimir, acting alone, had propped him up on his side, pulled off his dark glasses, and switched on a brilliant light. He had attached a metal frame to Zavijavah's head, shoulders, and mouth. Squinting through tears, Zavijavah had seen the similarly anchored head of another man.

He would have screamed if he could have breathed, as Casimir—then only an Assistant Vice Regent—forced back his head, opening his mouth almost 180 degrees. He had screamed when something shot between his teeth and up through the roof of his mouth. He'd thought he was dead.

Casimir had flicked ash from a cigarillo and released both hinges of the jaw vise. Zavijavah swallowed blood.

Then it began, an audible hissing as Rider entangled itself, refreshing its genetic material with its new host's nucleotides, creating itself a new body out of Zavijavah's intracranial cells.

He shook his head and dismissed the hideous memory. An odd sense of pleasure winked out. Rider apparently enjoyed reliving its "liberation." It generally launched offspring spores this way, remaining inside its carrier host. That time, it had abandoned another host to take Zavijavah. It often stroked Zavijavah's pleasure sense when he pleased it by remembering.

A voice drifted out of the wall next to his bed. "Your subject is asleep, sir." Several minutes later, the voice spoke again. "Delivery on its way."

Zavijavah got up. He washed his face and slipped his dark glasses back on, then his uniform coat. By the time he finished straightening it, his entry alarm rang. He touched the ADMIT light, and the door slid aside. One of his employees stood outside, holding a tray.

He took it and dismissed her. On the tray lay three numbered ampules, a syringe, and an absorbent cloth.

How simple the implements humans used to destroy one another.

He slipped the items into his coat pocket and rode the lift to the second floor. He strode past the guard station, where he saluted but did not name his destination.

When he thumbed the security panel outside Alun Casimir's suite, the door slid aside. He drew off his dark glasses.

He found Alun sleeping on his back, easy to identify by his unshorn hair. Relieved that the job would be easy, Zavijavah opened the first ampule and doused the cloth. Gingerly he lowered it toward Alun's face.

He checked the time. Thirty seconds would ensure that Alun slept through the rest of the treatment.

He knew why Rider wanted Alun Casimir. Alun would eventually give one of Rider's spore offspring a voice on Bkellan University's Board of Regents. Gamal Casimir had agreed to take Zavijavah across space to Sunsis when Rider's next spores matured, along with Alun and one other new victim. At Sunsis A, the warmer of two habitable planets, other Chaethe carriers maintained a "liberation" facility where transmitting hosts could be medicated and receiving hosts given good care.

Zavijavah would remain a carrier for the rest of his life. Every four and a half Tdegan years, he would need to return to Sunsis to liberate two spores. Casimir could have taken him to Sunsis when one had matured. Casimir was still experimenting. And he'd heard that a Chaethe could leave or enter an uncooperative host in even grislier ways—

Thirty seconds. A false sense of pleasure trickled through his nerves, rewarding him. He removed the cloth and pressed the second ampule into the syringe.

He disliked what he was doing. He disliked what he was becoming. But he could not endure Rider's wails inside his head.

He rarely resisted now.

08

Llyn perched on a cargo box and stared at the cellar's stone floor. Shelves loaded with multicolored crates lined the walls, shimmed to lean against the concrete. With all windows closed and lamps burning overhead, the air smelled slightly stale. Squeak lay on Llyn's feet, grooming his black-and-white fur—and her shoes—with his absurdly long, black tongue. Most of Karine's patients assembled at mealtimes, so Llyn knew most of the faces and voices that surrounded her, but two middle-aged women she'd never seen before sat close by, each talking to herself with Tamsina seated between them. A man who sat alone in one corner had not moved since she spotted him. A child lay on the floor, sobbing.

Watching them as she waited for further news of this afternoon's bombing, Llyn realized how disabled she'd been when Karine first brought her home. She'd covered a lot of ground.

She wished Karine saw it that way.

The basement mostly held raw materials used for in-home manufacturing, but Llyn had spotted a pair of crates labeled "LLYN/transducer." They surely contained Rakaya Shasruud's AR unit, with the gelskin and connectors that once linked Llyn to it. Llyn couldn't believe Karine had kept it. Nor could she guess why. It was tempting to open those crates and peer inside.

The elevator door opened, and Karine stepped through. She called several names, Llyn's among them. "Please step into the elevator."

Llyn crowded in with the rest of them.

Karine didn't activate the lift. Evidently she simply wanted privacy to speak with a few relatively stable patients. "Here's the story," she said. "Several spaceships came through Antar Gate last week. We know now that they were not the Kocaban haulers their markings indicated. Today, they dropped missiles on the University and the Outwatch base and then headed for Antar Gate. We are on an emergency wartime footing." She glared at Llyn. "We still don't know if Niklo was at the University when it was hit."

Niklo! Llyn clenched a fist.

"I need full cooperation. You might as well know that my fuse is going to be very short until we find out if Niklo is all right."

"Of course." Elroy filled the corner behind Karine. She craned her neck to look back at him. "Anytime you want to lie down and let us take over," he said, "just tell us."

Karine shook her head. "There hasn't been an all-clear. We're staying down here until we get one. We will keep busy. I'm going to divide staff and residents into three groups. We are going to restack—"

"Karine." Elroy took a stern tone. "Don't you think there will be an all-clear soon if those ships are already on their way out of the system?"

Karine shot him a look that would have withered one of her apple trees. "Until I have heard an all-clear, we will assume that there won't be one. As I was saying, we will restack all of the cargo crates into three long piles mid-room. We'll create four large areas, then partition one area with three smaller piles. In case we end up living down here, I need to isolate certain patients and segregate everyone else by sex."

It sounded as if Karine needed to keep busy.

"Llyn. You're with me."

Of course.

Llyn walked to her assigned spot on the cellar's stone floor. A woman on her left passed her cargo crates by their handles. Llyn handed them to a woman on her right. After slinging only four crates, Llyn could barely grip the fifth crate's handles. She flung it along and begged, "Wait. Please. I've got to rest."

Karine glowered from her position near a concrete wall. "You think you're ready for independence? How can you help yourself if you have to quit after only this long? Have you been slacking on the exercise machines?"

Llyn flinched. "Just a little break. That was all I needed. I'm ready to go again."

The conveyor line restarted. Llyn pushed herself, determined to keep up.

"Oops," Elroy's voice sang from one end of the cellar. "Sorry, Squeak." There'd been no yelp, of course.

Karine turned around. The woman on Llyn's left stepped in front of her and handed a crate directly to the woman on her right. "Thanks," Llyn whispered, "but you shouldn't—"

"Shh." Fifteen centimeters taller than Llyn, the woman looked as if she could handle crates two at a time. Llyn didn't protest again.

The third time it happened, Karine caught the big woman in mid-pass. "Llyn!" Karine cried. "Get back in your place, and—"

The downstairs intercom buzzed. Karine lunged for it.

I was in my place! Llyn would've shrieked if she'd dared. Her nerves were as frazzled as anyone's. Couldn't Karine, the great medical psiologist, understand that?

The big woman dropped her crate. Llyn sat down on it. The big woman sat down behind Llyn and leaned against Llyn's back. The warmth felt good. The cellar smelled mustier than ever, and the rearranged crates now dampened its acoustics. Her coworkers murmured to each other. Not one group kept working. Llyn could no longer find the crates marked "transducer," to her disappointment.

Karine spoke into the headset. When she hung up, she looked somber. "That was an all-clear," she announced. "No further attack looks imminent. The travel ban will remain in place, but that doesn't concern us today. Stand up, everyone. We're going to put the crates back."

Somebody groaned.

Karine ignored him. "Kitchen crew, you're excused to go upstairs. We'll need dinner."

By nightfall, it was clear to Llyn that Karine hadn't simply developed a short fuse. She was ready to blow. From Tamsina's head-shaking shrugs, Llyn knew she wasn't the only one who noticed.

Karine hovered near the main multinet terminal by the kitchen doors, looking frightened—until she spotted Llyn looking back. Then her brow furrowed. She stared with an expression Llyn couldn't interpret.

Near midnight, Llyn spied Tamsina strolling past her open bedroom door. "Tamsina," she hiss-whispered. "Come in for a minute. Please."

The brown woman slipped into Llyn's room, followed by Squeak. He seemed as blissful as ever. How lovely to be that stupid, sometimes. Tamsina slid the door shut behind her.

"What's wrong with Karine?" Llyn asked. "Has she gone crazy?"

"Well." Tamsina sat down on the bed. "She's worried, of course."

"She's angry with me or something. Is it because I didn't work hard enough down in the cellar?"

"No, she's not angry." Tamsina folded her arms. "At least, not that she knows. I think she feels guilty about the time that she spent on you over the last few years, instead of with her son—"

"I tried to get more time to myself—"

"I know, I know." Tamsina shook her head. "Niklo wanted to escape, too. He told me he needed to do a few things imperfectly."

Usually, Llyn understood too little of others' comments to laugh at appropriate times. This time, she understood. She chuckled.

Tamsina spread her hands. "I think Karine wants to blame someone for her tragedy. I don't think she'll stick you with it for long, though. She's too good a clinician not to notice her own symptoms."

"Will we go back to a regular schedule tomorrow?"

"I'm arranging reduced shifts. I think that you—and the patients who are closest to getting release certification—should keep to your rooms, stay out of her way, and do something productive. You've got studies, haven't you?"

"Always. Not to mention exercises." Ruefully, she rubbed her thin arms. They actually hurt after all that work downstairs. She'd never been able to exercise that long before.

Time alone, though? Lovely! She had surreptitiously set her personal terminal to download a collection of Nuris University Chorale recordings, back this morning when the world had seemed normal, before she and

Karine left for the classroom and war arrived on Antar. Nuris University Chorale had recorded three collections a year for forty-eight years. Before going to bed, she'd checked to see if any recordings had transferred onto her console before the invaders' attack knocked down the net. Three years' worth of music, nine collections, already were hers to enjoy.

Tamsina and Squeak left. Llyn snuck out of bed and retitled the choral collections as schoolwork. Then she slipped back into her bed, feeling ashamed … not about hiding her music from Karine, but ashamed that she could feel so delighted about the possibility of lying on her bed tomorrow, listening to music. There had been a disaster. Hundreds of people might have been killed, and more might die. *She* might die before she really learned to live.

What a time to be growing up.

Filip Salbari smoothed hair back from his face two-handed, rubbed his eyes, and stared at his net board. Damage reports still poured in from Nuris and outlying areas. One of his staff had flown down this morning, returning to the rural Salbari estate with another grim count of seventeen students found dead under dormitory rubble. A list of names followed. Antar's badly stretched police force, supplemented by Outwatchers, was already notifying next of kin.

Half of the victims' next of kin were probably victims as well. The private memorial that had been planned for this afternoon must honor many more victims than Athis Pallaton, even if it only commemorated Regents and other empaths.

Filip felt dazed, angry, and old. Tdega still had not claimed responsibility for the *Aliki's* destruction, but after yesterday's attack, it was difficult to see the loss of the *Aliki* as anything but another act of war. The hope of malfunction was almost universally gone. The *Aliki* was now considered a target, like Nuris University, of an attack. Filip had already transmitted to Ilzar and Unukalhai, the two other Concord worlds nearest their Gates, for assistance.

Meanwhile, a transmission had arrived from Jahn Emlin in Bkellan. It warned of military preparations in addition to the stockpiling that Antar's official Ambassador had already reported. Emlin was too young to carry so much responsibility, yet Antar needed him now more than ever.

If only that warning had arrived one day earlier—

No. The Regents never would have evacuated Nuris on the basis of Jahn Emlin's warning. Who would have believed that civilized humans could do this? Attacking a ship offworld was despicable, but striking a habitable planet went beyond comprehension.

Why? Creator, how could they?

Filip blinked. Another total had appeared on the screen. He had never felt this complex of emotions, hatred among them, except when empathically counseling extremely troubled individuals. He tried to subdue his feelings. He must not distract the other two empaths working in his estate's nerve center: his younger brother Alcotte, and Alcotte's twenty-year-old daughter, Rena Tourelle. Rena sat at a map board, calling and keying in data, looking pale. She was strongly gifted, already one of the best nexus empaths on Antar. Among other things, nexus allowed one person to link two, even three others.

Five years back, Filip had been secretly asked by a vote of empaths to head the Order, but not for any grand effusion of psychic ability. The Order had always feared that public announcement of its headship would make the post seem glamorous or cause competition for it. Actually, it was a spiritual leadership that called for restraint and humility. Today Filip felt glad that he was not as gifted as his niece Rena—or as his daughter Stasia, the family rebel. Those young women were suffering. Stasia sat alone in her room this morning, ostensibly angry that she couldn't work in the nerve center along with her father, Uncle Alcotte, and Cousin Rena.

Another total appeared. This couldn't be happening in his lifetime: humans slaughtering humans. Antar must respond appropriately, and the responsibility was Filip Salbari's. His parents' bodies had been found just after midnight. The deaths down at Nuris elevated him to Head Regency of Nuris University, effectively head of the Concord.

He was trained to administer a learning center.

Antar had no ships to strike back with, and striking Tdega would be wrong. The entire Concord needed Tdega's produce to survive. If the situation that inspired the Concord to send the *Aliki* had been ominous, it was critical now. Tens of thousands would starve, here and elsewhere, if the Tdegans cut supply lines.

And why hadn't they done that—instead of attacking? He couldn't guess.

The Concord would meet here at the Salbari estate, in Conclave, as soon as the other worlds' emissaries—those who survived here, plus those deputized to represent the attack victims—could assemble.

Have mercy.

A touch on his shoulder brought him upright. His brother Alcotte stood at his side. "Are you all right?" Alcotte murmured. His brother's short, neat red beard was gray at the sides, and though his eyes normally twinkled, this morning they looked dull. Filip and Alcotte were now the nearest generation to the grave. Alcotte had confessed that he felt as vulnerable about that as Filip did.

On the other hand, there was someone willing to take that burden off Filip's shoulders. Filip cast a glance across the estate's nerve center. Their Uncle Boaden, their father Anton's younger brother, had heavy cheeks that became jowls at his chin line. Boaden had merely protested last year when Nuris University made Anton Salbari's son Filip—not his brother Boaden—Second Regent. Boaden should have had plenty of time to contest the confirmation. Now the power shift was a *fait accompli*. Boaden must either remain content as a Vice Regent or else try to have Filip reduced from the Head Regency during a crisis.

Filip reached up to his shoulder and covered Alcotte's hand. "I'm all right. But I need to talk to Uncle Boaden."

Alcotte dropped his hand to Filip's upper arm and squeezed. "I understand." He backed away, smoothing his beard.

Filip crossed the busy nerve center, where six multinet terminals surrounded a dead, ceiling-mounted main projector. I-net was still offline. Net administrators had scrambled to cover the gap with c-net. That frequency cluster excelled at carrying casual conversations, but it barely sufficed for today's data flood.

Boaden stood speaking with a commtech at a terminal. As they finished, Filip caught Boaden's glance. "Could we talk?"

"Certainly," Boaden said stiffly. He followed Filip toward the center's main doors. Motion sensors retracted the doors into stone-lined walls.

Filip turned right. Paved with gray tile, the elongated porch surrounded a sky-lit courtyard edged by tall, fragrant flowers. Roses and jonquils nodded on long stems around a smooth green lawn. Several orchard trees dangled immature fruits. The courtyard flooded the estate's central halls with natural oxygen, and in here, Filip felt at peace.

A half wall separated lawn and garden from the stone porch, and carved stone pillars stretched up from its top to support the roof. High above, a sheer air dome grew darker and brighter with variations in cloud cover. As soon as he passed the second pillar, Filip clasped his hands behind his back. "I need to know that I can count on your help and advice, Uncle. We both know I'm not ready."

"We both know you have a reputation as a pacifist," Boaden answered in a mild voice.

Filip watched his feet swing across lines of tile. "That's true."

"The more you long for peace, the more vulnerable you become. Loving peace is no protection unless you back it up with the equipment for war. No one in his right mind *wants* war."

Relieved that they could agree on that point, Filip pursed his lips. "And we both know you want to retaliate."

"Justice is justice. No one attacks my people without learning that he shouldn't."

Filip shook his head, but he understood. In twenty years, dozens of empaths had approached him for personal counseling. Empaths understood others' viewpoints with exquisite clarity, and many struggled to maintain personal boundaries. They entangled themselves in others' difficulties and forgot to care for themselves.

Boaden, who was no empath and did not know about the other official load Filip already carried, was asking him to extend that wisdom to a planetary scale. Antar's boundaries had been execrably violated. Justice required retribution. "I respect your experience," Filip told him.

Boaden stepped in front of Filip. "And I respect your compassion. No one will accuse you of jumping into war unprovoked. You must *lead* the Concord, though. Decisions will be made in Conclave, and the Conclave requires a strong head. Can you function that way? If not, step aside and let someone lead us who can."

"I will try," Filip promised.

"Not good enough."

Filip looked back over his shoulder toward the bright lights of the estate nerve center. With NU gone, that was Antar's war room. "I will lead," he said. "But I need your help."

"I'll be behind, pushing."

"Thank you."

"And once the crisis passes, I will protest your elevation to Head Regent."

"I understand."

Boaden had made no secret of the fact he wanted the Head Regency to pass to his own child. Boaden's oldest son was admittedly more stable, at present, than Filip's untrained daughter Stasia. Filip had been too lenient with her, Boaden claimed, and Boaden was probably right.

But Stasia would outgrow this stage, and as soon as the crisis ended, Filip must step down from one office. "All I ask is that we work together for the present."

"We will do that." Boaden firmed the jowly line of his chin. Then he strode back toward the nerve center's lights. They silhouetted his back as he walked.

Filip lingered on the pavement. He inhaled, replacing stuffy, fear-tinged air with courtyard springtime. He planted both hands on the low wall, sprang up, and twisted sideways to sit. There he perched, balanced between pavement and grass, and pulled up his feet. On one side lay heirloom flower beds and some of Antar's finest pre-Devastator statuary. On the other side, the long stone porch receded like a study in perspective. Together they created an illusion of stability.

He bowed his head and let grief flood out of the pockets in his mind where he had hidden it. He'd just found out how impermanent human habitations still were. In 250 years without Devastator visitations, including fifty years of resettlement, they'd begun to pretend otherwise.

Truly, Nuris University had looked permanent and stable yesterday morning. According to grim maps and virtual projections, two-thirds of the city was rubble. Much of its elderly population, those who had not died in the initial attack, had gone into respiratory failure with the dome ripped away. Those had been souls born shipboard, resettled on a planetary surface they'd hoped to turn back into paradise. They had made incredible adjustments simply to live in a way Filip's generation called normal.

What would his father have done?

Filip could no longer ask. And Alcotte's wife Gladwyn, five months pregnant with a surprise fourth child, lay in bed here at the estate, agonizing over the loss of both parents, her sisters, and several young nieces and nephews. She'd begged Favia and Vananda to sit with her, now and at this afternoon's service. Filip wanted his wife Favia at the nerve center, but hammer blows of Gladwyn's grief bludgeoned Filip and the other empaths at frequencies no one else felt. He had to let the Hadley sisters calm her. They worked well together, even though Favia was not genetically empathic.

Up the pavement, the nerve center's door swept open. Bluish artificial light shone even brighter as young Rena rushed out onto the long porch. Rena kept her brilliant red hair ridiculously short, but she had such a sweet, vulnerable-looking face that longer hair might have kept people from taking her seriously as an empath. So she claimed. "Uncle Filip," she cried, "there's a message coming through. It's from a Tdegan ship."

Filip sprang down. Rena spun in place, and he followed her back through the sliding doors.

Distortion caused by distance cast shadows through the image hovering over the crowd, but Filip made out a black-haired stranger's long face. His front hair was cropped short, almost shaven, in the Tdegan style.

Filip edged closer to Alcotte, who stood near the image's edge. From this angle, Filip saw the Tdegan's queue. "Who?" Filip murmured.

"Bellik Casimir. This is a general broadcast. We put it on ten-second delay so you could get here."

Filip nodded. Bellik Casimir had been considered a long shot to succeed Aeternum. Why was *he* transmitting?

Bellik's image unfroze. His upper lip curled when he spoke. "...the indignity of nationalization. For five decades you have taken the best we could produce. Now you ask to pay even less? If your treatment were not so heinous, it would be laughable. You think you are so strong and that we should feel honored to serve you.

"What is your strength? Numbers? We outnumber you. Knowledge?

Our University was already better. Technology? We both know better than to think that.

"Now you see we are determined to end this domination charade. Since you cannot treat us fairly, we withdraw from the Concord."

Rena gasped. Alcotte tried to lay an arm across her shoulders. She drew away, shaking her head.

Filip took a deep, calming breath.

The image pulled back to display Bellik Casimir's dark gray military uniform. Two men in black versions of the same tunic and trousers stood at attention behind him.

Bellik Casimir folded his arms. "As of today, Tdega has seceded. Our neighbor systems, Ilzar and Sunsis, have chosen to leave with us. In case you harbor any doubts as to how seriously we take this, let me show you." The formal grouping blanked out.

As of today? There was a minimum two-and-a-half-day broadcast delay between Antar and Tdega. The message might have been transmitted from a ship retreating to Antar Gate. Or, if Bellik Casimir were not on board, it could be a recording.

Was Ilzar truly seceding? Its transmissions via Gate relay arrived a day faster than Tdega's. The Empath Order had an operative on Ilzar, at Zjadel. She would send her own report soon.

Filip recognized the golden brown globe that appeared in holo. It was Ilzar, in the system almost directly between Antar and Tdega, scanned through its cloud cover—but two unfamiliar black craters blistered its main continent's western seacoast. Rena gasped again. This time, she let Alcotte draw her close in fatherly comfort.

The voice intoned, "The city councils of Zjadel and Thark declared yesterday that they would not stand with Syyke in support of secession. Zjadel and Thark were given five hours to evacuate. Then they were targeted."

The satellite picture zoomed closer. The scene practically smoked at its edges. As Bellik Casimir had claimed, nothing remained of Zjadel but cinders. Filip recalled it as a center of arts and learning. Lives, cities—atmospheric catastrophe—what had this attack cost Ilzar? And had Jay Li Waverly escaped?

"Is that real?" Alcotte whispered. "Tdega has a planetary imaging AR system—"

"Now you see that we are far ahead of your defense technology. We could have used these weapons against Antar. We will, if you attempt to control us. Your day is finished."

The image faded into a star-and-ring projection that blanked immediately. Two shaken Antaran broadcasters appeared to perform the inevitable recap and analysis. Planetary imaging—and the vital difference between realism and truth—was the first theory they raised and dismissed.

Filip called, "Turn it down." He backed away from the huddle as Alcotte squeezed into it. Many people stayed, drawing comfort from touching each other while the broadcasters attempted to make sense of the violence.

Over the press, Filip caught another glimpse of Boaden. His uncle frowned and looked away.

Filip rubbed his chin. Tdega had broadcast that ultimatum over public channels. It must have wanted to ensure that the Antaran populace saw it at the same time as its surviving leadership. Discord would favor Tdega. Panic could make any other Concord world's secession almost inevitable.

Obviously, the Concord had been mistaken in trying to nationalize Tdega's resources. Yet that had seemed like the sensible request. Concord representatives had believed that compassion and the long view would prevail on Tdega.

Alcotte emerged alone from the press. "All recorded," he said. "Now we know what they meant to do with those ordnance stockpiles."

Filip nodded. Should he recall Antar's ambassador from Bkellan city? And what about Jahn Emlin, undercover? "What about Ilzar?" he asked Alcotte. "I don't believe that story about two cities refusing to cooperate. It sounds like Tdega browbeat a system it had to count on for mined goods."

Alcotte nodded. "The city of Syyke has Ilzar's major ore extractor. It wasn't destroyed."

"I noticed. Then our next step should be contacting Ilzar."

"And Sunsis?" Alcotte suggested.

It was time to make up his mind. Choose a course of action. Set it in motion. "Ilzar first," he said. The Conclave of University families—from

Antar and other Concord worlds that remained—would meet soon, and he would not declare war by himself. Other worlds, whose residents also died at Nuris University, would add their Outwatch forces to whatever remained on Antar. Ancient training and indoctrination devices—and the conversion of surviving Outwatch ships from other Concord systems—would build numbers rapidly if he started recruiting today.

Truly, striking Tdega was out of the question. But emancipating Ilzar seemed possible, even necessary.

Were Gamal and Bellik Casimir laying another trap for the Concord's aging Outwatch fleet? What would emancipation cost Ilzar's biosphere? He needed more information from Jay Li on Ilzar, and from Jahn Emlin on Tdega.

Alcotte laid a hand on his shoulder. "Are you all right, Filip?"

"Yes." *Creator, please. Give me wisdom. Not just for my own sake, but for too many others.* "Yes. We will do what we must."

09

Llyn lay on her bed with the featherweight speakers draped over her head. Three days had passed since the attack, and tremors still grumbled through the ground. There'd been no further sign of Kocaban haulers—or Tdegan attack ships—but according to Karine, who sat magnetized to that multinet terminal near the kitchen, magma was moving upward under the remains of the Nuris domes. They lay open to the sky, totally wrecked. Steady rainfall hampered searchers' efforts to locate survivors and bodies.

Llyn had stared at the first images out: half of the pyramid crumbled, beautiful library flattened, housing stacks collapsed. People downwind of the city had to stay indoors for fear of ashfall and possible radioactivity. Equally outrageous to the Antarans, an electromagnetic pulse had been discharged directly over Nuris University. It had flooded the i-net, reverberating outward in concentric circles of informational destruction, a calculated attempt to destroy not only the will but also the memory of the Concord. Of human civilization!

Llyn felt slightly vindicated about the recordings she'd dubbed. She had saved nine collections of choral music. Eventually, NU would reconstruct its archival system. For now, Antarans were waking up to the priority of simply surviving.

She adjusted the featherweight speakers and stared at a new crack in her room's off-white ceiling. Her favorite of the nine choral recordings resounded between her ears. Its lyrics sang of a spiritual yearning beyond life, death, or time. She felt exactly that way. What was the purpose of all this struggle?

While the music played, she poked her left hand with a pair of metal staples. On her palm, she could distinctly feel two pinpricks when she held them a centimeter apart, but no closer. On her forearm, the distance was two centimeters. She was working on it, though. Really working. For her own sake, not for Karine.

There was still no word from Niklo. Karine had sat at the terminal and let Elroy and Tamsina run the clinic. Llyn had heard her crying.

Llyn didn't think Niklo was dead, but she couldn't have said why. Determined to use the time while waiting for word, she'd worked on her studies and her senses. She'd convinced Tamsina to supervise a quick experiment, in which she listened to small musical groups. Evidently trio music was safe, but the moment she put on an instrumental duet, it dropped her into a trance. Tamsina brought her back with a penlight.

She was closing on one small element of control over her life.

Above her bed, a streak of light appeared on the ceiling. Karine stalked in, hunched over as if she had doubled her age in three days. Alarmed, Llyn whipped off the featherphones. "Oh no," she exclaimed. "I'm sorry I missed lunch. I lost track of time."

Karine bore down on her. Llyn had always felt like a mouse living in a hawk's nest, unable to leave. Today, the hawk meant to strike. "What are you doing?" Karine emphasized every word.

She wouldn't be able to hear the music, but she could sense Llyn's mental state. "These are recordings from the University. Choral concerts from other years. I helped save the University archive—"

"There is no—music—allowed at this clinic." Karine sounded as if she wanted to hit something. Llyn was obviously headed for tactile therapy.

"But I thought—I hoped—that after that concert, when it didn't affect me—"

"You hoped you wouldn't get caught, that's all." Karine blinked her puffy eyes. "There are rules in this clinic."

Llyn's insides roiled. She'd trespassed. She'd broken a rule. She certainly was guilty, but was the rule warranted? Was it reasonable? She couldn't think of a way to ask either question without infuriating Karine.

She could only spread her hands and say, "I didn't get those recordings because they were *wrong*. I got them because they were excellent. And—"

Karine stalked to Llyn's console and pointed at several buttons.

"What are you doing?" Llyn cried.

"Erasing."

"No!" She sprang off the bed. "You can't! They're irreplaceable!"

"It is not your job to preserve them." Karine backed away from the console and whirled to face Llyn. "We will talk about this later. Right now I'm too angry to decide how to punish you. I came here to tell you something else."

Karine's tone of voice demanded a reply. Llyn wanted to shut her eyes, go limp, and wish the world away, but she'd tried that once. Karine had shattered her withdrawal with tactile therapy of the worst kind. "Oh?" she managed.

"When you and Niklo searched the Nuris University library for genetic data, he left the search running. Concord-wide. On my bill."

She had forgotten! "Was it still running when—"

"It finished before the Tdegan attack. The results were reported to Niklo's mailbox. He did not claim them at the end of two days, so they were printed and filed. The printout arrived here this morning. So did several of Niklo's other possessions."

Llyn didn't dare ask what else the searchers had found, either online or in the rubble of Niklo's dormitory. Plainly, this delivery had sparked Karine's foul mood.

Karine moved only her mouth. "You are a strong genetic match to the generalized Tdegan ancestor strain."

Tdegan? She was one of those? Or was this an invention, an outlet for Karine's agony? "I didn't have anything to do with the attack, K—Mother."

"You are certainly deceitful enough." The hissing syllables plunged like knives thrown to kill.

"I didn't do it." It sounded like whimpering, even to Llyn.

Karine blinked red eyes. "And now you want me to leave the room. Don't you?"

How could she answer that? "No," she lied desperately. She did want Karine to leave, but Karine was her only source of comfort.

"I have always tried to do what was best for you." Karine rushed to the door. "I am leaving."

Karine sat rocking on the bedside. What had she done? What had she—

Tdegan?

Hours later, Llyn rolled off her bed and pulled on her nightrobe. She stumbled out into the hallway toward the kitchen for a glass of warm vanilla milk. As hard as she'd tried, she remembered nothing of Tdega. Only Antar and the inner world. It could not be true.

She nearly bumped Elroy, who was walking out of the kitchen area carrying a large, limp load. As he passed her, she realized that Karine lay over his shoulder. "Is she all right?" Llyn whispered.

Elroy nodded. "She finally fell asleep in front of the terminal," he murmured. "She hasn't slept since the attack. I'm taking her downstairs."

No sleep in four days? That helped explain Karine's outburst, though it didn't excuse it. "I'll take messages for the next couple of hours," Llyn said. At least she wouldn't have Karine bursting in on her. She needed time to lick her emotional wounds, and to rehearse what she should have said, and to think. Mostly think.

Elroy's smile looked grateful. Llyn took the console stool, sipped from her mug, and stared through her view-glasses. Information trickling down the c-net had all but dried up. Somewhere on Antar, people were preparing to defend against further attacks. Others hoped to negotiate. But nothing moved here at the clinic except the knives turning inside Llyn's heart—and Squeak, who lay licking and kneading a blue pillow at one corner of the tiled kitchen.

She had almost fallen asleep when the red message light blinked. The speaker beeped four times.

She shoved her view-glasses back into position. A face with lank brown hair and heavy eyebrows appeared over the projector. Niklo! He looked disheveled and stressed, but excited. His image actually bounced. "Llyn," he exclaimed. "Where's Mother?"

So relieved that she momentarily forgot what just happened, Llyn edged off the stool but kept her face in pickup range. "She was right here at the kitchen center. She's been here around the clock for four days. She just fell asleep. Wait a minute. I'll run downstairs and get her."

"No, don't. I've only got a few seconds. There are fifty guys lined up behind me, and I'd rather talk to you anyway." His head hung over the console at a ten-degree tilt, and one side of his face blurred. His c-net transmitter must have been damaged. "We were off campus on a geology field trip. We saw the warships dive in. They were huge. One of them blew up our transport. We were half a mile away from it, so we laid low and waited for the dust to settle. Then we started walking."

"Oh, I'm glad!" Her heart sang. "Where are you now?"

"Temporary housing, outskirts of Nuris. They banned travel, so I can't get home."

Lucky Niklo. "I know."

"Tell Mother I'm okay. Tell her the med facility was totally destroyed, though, and those kids don't take field trips."

"She knows that. She's been on top of all the news out."

"I should've guessed. Listen, kid. I survived because I set my own goals and I wasn't a med student. You do the same. Then live with the consequences. Even if the first consequence means Mother yells at you."

If only he knew. "Sounds good to me." She tried not to sound bitter.

"What's wrong?"

I'm Tdegan. If this hadn't been a public line, if he hadn't mentioned fifty guys waiting to use it, she would've said so. She ached to talk about it. To apologize, to explain to someone. Niklo had always treated her like a real sister, so far as she could judge. "We're okay. A few cracks in the ceiling, but nothing serious."

"All right. I'd better free the line. Love to everybody."

"You too."

She dashed down the hallway. It had been wonderful to talk with someone who was somewhere else. Like breathing thicker air.

Karine's room was dark. Llyn hesitated, then waved at the wall rheostat. The light came up. Karine didn't move. Llyn hesitated. She shook Karine's shoulder. "Wake up. Please, wake up. Niklo called."

It took a minute of shaking before Karine opened an eye. "What are you doing here?"

"Niklo called." Surely Karine would forget to be angry. She'd be so glad to hear this that she would forgive Llyn anything. "He's alive. He's all right. His geology group was off campus. They had to walk back."

"Niklo?" Karine sat up, a thin, white form in blue pajamas. Tamsina must have dressed her for the night. "What were you doing at the console?"

"You fell asleep there. Elroy put you to bed. He—"

"First you try to deceive me. Then you let me sleep through Niklo calling in. What kind of a daughter are you?"

Llyn stared, stricken again. She spun around and dashed back out through Karine's door, up the dim hallway, and into her bedroom. She shut the door hard. Tamsina would open it when she made her next round, but Llyn would get up and shut it again.

She would be awake.

Karine threw herself into her job the next morning. Now that she knew Niklo was safe, she must get back to work, and Tamsina had let the clinic slip onto a shockingly lax schedule.

She sipped her coffee in the dining hall overlooking the stream. Thumping noises traveled through the floor tiles. Llyn had started her workout.

Listening to Llyn raised her resentment level. The girl had smuggled music into the clinic, knowing it could harm her. What else was in her room that Karine wouldn't want to find?

She would search it as soon as she finished her coffee. For every illicit object she found, she would require Llyn to work an extra hour on the exercise machines. Anyone who couldn't pass four cargo crates from one side to the other needed more work, not less.

The door alarm sounded, startling her in the middle of planning a new schedule. She sprang up and met Tamsina in the carpeted hall. Her employee stood talking with two men and a woman wearing Outwatch blue-gray. "What is it?" Karine demanded.

Tamsina passed her a sealed printout. "Sign first, Medic Torfinn," the smaller Outwatch man said.

Karine had taken government orders before, signing for new patients. The first of her war victims probably waited outside in their vehicle.

Mentally grumbling—she didn't have time for one more patient—she traced her signature. Then she sliced the seal on the printout.

"From the Antaran government," she told Tamsina. Not from Filip, unfortunately. "We're to ..." She trailed off, reading too rapidly to explain aloud. She was ordered to surrender Llyn to a facility for Tdegan aliens. The Outwatch personnel had been sent to transport her.

Goose bumps rose on Karine's forearms. This was no time to relinquish Llyn to anyone. They had unfinished business to settle. And the unknown searcher for Llyn, if not dead at NU, was still at large. "Llyn is not an alien." Karine glared at the Outwatch man. "I legally adopted her five years ago."

The Outwatcher shifted his feet, looking uncomfortable. "If you'd like to call in and double-check, we'll wait outside."

Karine peered between bushes, out through the glassed entryway. A government charge van sat in the driveway. It looked legitimate.

But papers could be falsified, vans repainted. "Do that." She let them out, shut the glass door, and scowled at Tamsina. "Something is not right."

Tamsina waved the printout and shrugged. "This looks official. But Llyn isn't Tdegan. Why would they say this?"

Karine grimaced. "Niklo put in a genetic trace. I got the report this morning. If he hadn't sneaked away to the library, the Outwatch wouldn't have known about this." She snatched back the printout. "They wouldn't have even guessed." She stalked up the hall, wondering whether this really was the Outwatch.

She had actually suspected years ago that Llyn might be Tdegan, but she had shut it out of her mind. The face was right, though. The hair—and the behavior.

"Who're you going to check with?" Tamsina's voice faded behind her. "Filip."

She called from her upstairs office. While waiting, she studied the stereo portrait of Namron, her husband. Far too young to have died, he'd had soft black hair and a studious expression. She wondered what Nam would have thought of Llyn's behavior. Nam hadn't had Filip's assets or expectations, but he'd respected Karine's intelligence and self-discipline. He would have supported her now, even against the Outwatch, if Poulenc's dome inspectors had done their job years ago—if he'd assisted with patient evaluations instead of driving off to that seminar, going against Karine's wishes just that once—

Filip appeared online. He'd aged several more years, just like his staffer. "I've got people claiming to be Outwatchers in my driveway," she snapped. "They want to take Llyn away."

"Wait," he said. "Slow down. What is happening?"

She spoke slowly and distinctly, using short words. "Three people just arrived at the clinic. They are dressed as Outwatchers. They have a document. They say it entitles them to take Llyn. To place her in a facility for Tdegan aliens. They—"

"Is it the Rift Station facility?"

Karine scanned the printout. We request ... five changes of clothing ... Rift Station ... "Yes."

"Llyn is listed on my Rift Station documents as well. I've had my staff inspect the facility. It looks more comfortable than many homes, and it is certainly secure. Llyn will be fine there. Perhaps you would like a break from the pressures of—"

"She would not be fine there! I'm the only one who knows how to care for her." She had invested five years—five long years!—in the wretched girl's well-being.

"Commit your instructions to printout. Facility staff is handpicked. She will do well at Rift Station."

"I can't see her doing well without me. At any rate, she's in danger."

"We've had no more attempts to get information on her since the attack."

"Of course not. No one can travel, and the archives are destroyed. No one can access any information." It wasn't quite true, but Filip didn't argue.

He glanced aside, spoke to someone, and faced the monitor again. "I can't dictate your therapy, particularly with this girl that you cared enough about to adopt. But if you would allow me to advise you, I'd suggest you release her to internment supervisors without hesitation. They will be compassionate. They'll help Llyn avoid temptation back to her old addiction."

"You're wrong. You were wrong to expose her to the concert, too. She has been flouting my restrictions ever since."

"Wait." His voice turned stern. "Llyn needs protection. But some restrictions affect important liberties. Llyn is practically an adult. She must develop and exercise her Creator-given free will. Exercising any ability strengthens it. Llyn is a mature individual who needs—"

"I have already given Llyn the greatest possible liberty. Freedom from an electronic mind-set that locked her into an internal world." She intended to keep that processor crated in her basement until Llyn finally outgrew her need to be supervised. Then she would research and document its programming, comparing that information against volumes of notes she'd taken while training Llyn—

"There is a greater sphere, Karine. The law of liberty is not an oxymoron—"

"Filip, I'm warning you—"

"Karine." He lowered his eyebrows. "You will be in violation of wartime codes if you do not surrender Llyn to authorities. Since they have her on their list, they must have decided she's old enough to be taken from you."

She felt stunned to incoherence. "I … cannot … believe that our government is breaking families."

"Eighteen is old enough for many adult rights."

"Seventeen. And she's handicapped. Mentally, she's far younger."

"Not in all ways. Now that I've seen her, I believe she is mature enough for adult treatment. You will admit that she is more mature in some aspects than some people twice her age."

"I will not." Karine couldn't believe what she was hearing. Llyn could barely sense pain, and she lacked practical experience. She could sustain terrible injuries before realizing she was in danger. Karine's protective strategies had always revolved around Llyn's highest good.

Abruptly she thought of another way to solve the dilemma. Niklo couldn't come home, and Tamsina and Elroy were competent to run the clinic, provided Karine cared for Llyn. So— "Can you get me into the Rift Station facility?"

"It is already staffed."

"I mean with Llyn."

"As a resident?" Those lowered eyebrows shot up. "This is not a facility you can check into and out of. It is well appointed, but it is an internment center."

"If Llyn is mature enough to expand her horizons," Karine declared, "I am mature enough to limit mine for her sake."

"You have other patients. Would you—"

"None of them needs me the way Llyn does."

Filip frowned. "Obviously, you have not bonded to them in the same way that you have enmeshed yourself in Llyn's life."

Karine set her chin and ignored his accusation. She was not enmeshed. She cared.

"Would Namron want you to leave the clinic you founded together?"

He didn't need to mention poor Nam. "Namron homesteaded the land. I was always the clinician, and I am the mother. I must stay with my child."

"There is a time for letting go. The physical parent-child bond is not intended to be permanent."

"Llyn—needs—me."

"Karine," he said softly, "your reputation as a clinician is peerless. You have treated and released dozens of patients who were considered almost without hope. Do you mean to throw this away?"

She glared. "Not at all."

He looked down. In her mind, she saw him working a keyboard on the edge of his desktop. "I am issuing you a permit to enter internment as Llyn's special guardian, but I think it is a mistake. Your choice will carry its own consequences."

"All choices do." Karine yanked off her glasses. She felt betrayed. She clenched a hand on her desktop while letters appeared on the top sheet in her printout tray. When the permit finished printing, she seized it and waved the console off.

She walked to the exercise room, then through it into the ladies' personal, where Llyn was stepping out of the shower tunnel. Wide-eyed, Llyn wrapped a towel around her bony body.

"We're leaving," Karine said. "Pack five changes of comfortable clothes."

"Where are we—"

Karine backed out of the personal without answering. She hurried back to the entry and joined the Outwatchers in the glassed entry porch. "Fifteen minutes." She batted a fern frond out of her way. "You will be transporting two of us."

The small man stepped closer. "You should have had her ready ten minutes ago. Wait. Two of you?"

Karine handed him her printout. "Two," she repeated. "I am not giving my child to you people unaccompanied."

"Eighteen? That's no child."

"Seventeen. I've demolished that argument already. Read the printout."

"I did." The small man passed it to his partners. "Come with us, then, Medic Torfinn."

"We are not packed. I will come as soon as Llyn gets ready. She tends to be slow."

10

Jahn locked down his maglev and sauntered toward the fence that enclosed Bkellan's Outwatch base. Danger signs were posted on the wire every few meters, warning passersby not to touch. Two rows of new barracks stood behind it. Past them, according to Residence rumors, the launch area had been expanded.

Yesterday evening, as Jahn had struggled against overwhelming shock—the attack on Antar had been publicly lauded—to complete another day's work at "commendation" level, word had reached his office that Gamal Casimir wanted a private tutor for his nephew Alun. Alun had apparently suffered a devastating two-story fall. His injuries included a wrenched shoulder and multiple bruises, but also head trauma that caused a loss of mental capacity. Gamal Casimir was determined that Alun recover. He still could rise to the Board of Regents in less than two years.

To Jahn, this information was pure gold. The Casimir family had a reputation for turbulence, even violence, but Alun's new tutor would move immediately into Alun's second-floor suite in the east wing. Gamal Casimir had named Commander Bellik Casimir, Alun's older brother, as temporary guardian. Commander Bellik was running a war—a one-sided, unprovoked war that promised to be short—so, after quietly and unsuccessfully trying to contact the Antaran Ambassador in Bkellan, Jahn had come to the base this morning to apply for the job.

Behind the security fence, Bkellan Base teemed with activity.

Propaganda had already prepared the populace to enjoy the prospect of war, as if wholesale death were a major athletic event. Casimir had announced the formation of a new Tdegan Hegemony, incorporating Ilzar and Sunsis.

A guard stopped him at the main gate under a new ringed-star flag. Jahn presented his Residence ID. "I called ahead to speak with Commander Casimir about a job opening."

The guard checked a small reader. "Building straight ahead," he said. "Left door. Straight up the hall, to the last door."

The former Outwatch Headquarters building seemed bare but bustling, with small round windows along the corridor's left wall. The last door stood open. A willowy young woman sat at the data desk inside. Jahn presented his credentials again and was ushered through an inner door.

Straight ahead, a massive black swivel chair faced a floor-to-ceiling window that overlooked the base. "Come in," a voice said out of the chair's depth. "Come around."

Jahn circled the chair. Outside, three massive cranes were constructing a gantry. The window also overlooked a broad launch pit. It looked deeper than conventional craters, large enough for the enormous X-class shuttles that the Casimirs had announced they would soon build. Glazed with a smooth, reflective surface, by sunset light it looked like a bowl full of blood.

Commander Bellik Casimir's massive chair had two data terminals on each arm. From Jahn's angle, without view-glasses, he could not see either display. Bellik's dark gray uniform accentuated his lean build, his thin face, and his prominently hooked nose.

"Commander," Jahn said, "you are busy, so I'll be brief. I'm an information-flow specialist at the Residence. The new position tutoring your brother would fit my line of training. I would like to be considered."

Bellik frowned. Jahn had prepared carefully for this interview, rebraiding his queue, applying toner to narrow the appearance of his forehead and chin, and dressing in an unassertive, professional gray shirt that he tucked into snug black pants. He had also made another data insertion.

"You are already in service to the family?" Bellik raised an eyebrow.

"Yes."

"Hm." Bellik's hand moved on an armrest. Now would come the credentials check. While Bellik stared, Jahn listened. Bellik's mental frequency was steady and strong. Jahn could only spare enough attention to synch shallowly. He must remain alert. If he got this job, opportunities to probe Bellik would follow.

Bellik seemed irritated by the unexpected distraction, obviously. But as soon as he hired a competent tutor, he could get back to work.

Exactly.

"You did online study through Bkellan University." Bellik glanced up. "Not on campus. Why not?"

"On-campus was too expensive for my family." That was his official answer. "Economics kept me out of medical school."

"But you took strong grades in biology and education." Bellik's finger swept a control surface. "Arne Vayilis likes your work. You're going to insult him if you leave after only a week."

Evidently the faked University records had survived scrutiny. As for Vayilis—"Yes, but I've been collecting commendations. He'll vouch for my habits. You'll notice that I held a tutoring position before." He'd inserted that record last night. It would be the easiest fake to detect. He listened hard. He had some skill at nexus, which enabled empaths to link and listen together, or to tug another individual's inner frequency toward one's own.

Indeed, Bellik became slightly agitated. Jahn pushed back, trying to calm him. The effort knotted his shoulder muscles.

Abruptly the suspicious agitation snapped off. Bellik waved a hand. "Alun will need to be kept abreast of our war effort and internal affairs. You would receive relevant information on Residence lines and condense it into terms Alun could understand."

Jahn nodded soberly. On the inside, he squashed a temptation to celebrate.

"I would also want you to move into Alun's suite. He needs nurse-maiding. Any objections?" Again, Bellik raised an eyebrow.

Obviously Bellik expected him to hesitate, so he paused. Not only was the situation ideal, but he would enjoy nurturing an injured soul. Jahn needed to fight a hardening that had begun in his spirit since coming to Tdega.

"No," he said. "No objections."

Bellik shrugged. "You look qualified. Report to Personnel that I've filled the position. And don't bother me with details or reports."

Jahn exulted straight-faced. "I understand, Commander. You're extremely busy."

Bellik smiled, a slight twist of his narrow mouth. "Look out there." He pointed behind Jahn.

Jahn pivoted and faced the window. Near the left edge of that launch pit, a crane lowered a long boom.

Bellik stood. Lifting a triangular reader, he strutted closer to the glass. He was half a head taller than Jahn, but so lanky that Jahn probably outweighed him. "It amazes me," Bellik said, "how little war matériel the Outwatch thought it needed to defend us against a terrifying alien menace."

"You're right," Jahn said. It needed to sound like a casual comment.

"We'll keep that pit well slagged." Bellik sounded as pompous as gossip portrayed him. But Jahn didn't laugh. Bellik was Gamal Casimir's present choice of successor. The son, Siah Casimir, had recently moved with his wife and small children to the southern continent's rural heartland. Plainly, Gamal was cleaning house, disposing of potential heirs who might oppose his new war policies.

Bellik smiled out the window. His fingers roamed the reader's display.

Jahn wondered if Bellik knew about the *Aliki*. Since Bellik seemed distracted by the action outdoors, Jahn probed deeply. He should be able to detect thoughts that crossed Bellik's conscious mind—

Staggered by what he discovered, he plunged off synch. Bellik had personally destroyed both ships, and the memory resonated in his mind as he looked out at further military preparations. Bellik had assassinated his own grandfather—and Jahn's—with Gamal Casimir's blessing, using that exact triangular reader to trigger a remote robot. The memory grew vivid as he fondled the reader.

"We'll maintain twenty to thirty capital ships as soon as we can build them," Bellik said, interrupting Jahn's loathing. "I anticipate making at least one follow-up attack within one or two months, just in case Antar thinks we've expended our resources. As soon as this is made public knowledge, Alun should be kept abreast."

"Very well." —No! Antar would never strike back. There was no need for Bellik to order … he must send off another pod ship immediately … he must …

He must focus. His hands trembled. He was so angry that he wanted to attack Bellik bare-handed, but that would be no better than Bellik's actions. Bellik deserved to be brought to public, personal justice. "You've done well, Commander," Jahn said in a calm tone that it hurt to maintain. "You have many concerns besides your younger brother."

Bellik laughed. "Isn't that the truth." Synching almost against his will, Jahn felt Bellik's disdain and swagger, but only a trace of suspicion.

"One last thing," Bellik said. "Come with me."

Puzzled and on his guard once again, Jahn followed back into the hallway and two doors down. Bellik pressed his thumb to a recognition panel and spoke. "Casimir."

The door slid open.

A man wearing gray coveralls and a high, silver engineer's helmet sat behind a short desk. Another man sat on the desk's corner. Jahn knew the second man by appearance, although they had never officially met. It was Security Chief Osun Zavijavah, of Gamal Casimir's inner circle. Zavijavah wore large, dark-lensed glasses that wrapped his eyes and temples. His drooping mustache gave his otherwise youthful face a fierce aspect.

Zavijavah slipped down off the desk and faced Bellik. "Yes, Commander?"

Bellik posed in front of the seated engineer with his hands at his sides. "Well," he said, "are you ready to retract?"

"I said nothing disloyal." The engineer's helmet plate read KAI OLDION. "I do not believe Antar poses a threat. Secession will go forward easily, so there's no need to funnel any more of our resources into refurbishing this base. Though it pains me to say so," he added, shrugging. He had a long-nosed, good-humored face.

Jahn stood perfectly still. Oldion sounded like one voice of reason on a world clamoring for insanity. What an odd place to hear it.

He synched shallowly. Oldion, although pleased with his new promotion, hoped to rein in the Casimirs' aggressiveness. He disliked destruction. He had friends on Antar.

Bellik stepped out of his stiff pose. He pointed at the engineer. "Go home. Stay there. Your severance pay will be credited. Korsakov, this is the way out."

Oldion flinched. Following Bellik away, Jahn reached backward in his inner sense. Near Oldion's pained confusion, he caught an exotic sensation. An odd frequency ebbed and flowed, creating an irregular rhythm. It rose above Oldion's and one other human frequency, then vanished.

The other inner frequency was obviously Security Chief Zavijavah. What was the third sensation?

Jahn lurched off his listening stance in time to hear Bellik say, "There will be none of that sort of thing with my brother. No contradictions of official policy. You could be fired just as suddenly."

Or worse. "I understand," Jahn said aloud. *You swaggering murderer,* he added silently. Bellik had probably planned the attack on Nuris, too.

Jahn could believe in the abstract that Nuris was a ruined city, but not in his heart. His memories of Nuris were as vivid as yesterday. He had studied at NU, first the five-year general civilization degree and then his specialized training under Order empaths.

Bellik turned back up the hallway toward his office. Jahn remained outside the engineer's door, listening hard. Most empaths couldn't hear inner frequencies at this distance, but by pushing himself, he picked out the faint hum of mental activity. Two persons, plus that eerie overlay.

He must create an opportunity to listen deeply to Osun Zavijavah as soon as possible, although it would be dangerous. As Gamal Casimir's Security Chief, Zavijavah was the likeliest man in the Residence to sniff out a double identity.

Jahn drove back, explained his new position to Arne Vayilis, and stood through a four-minute lecture on loyalty. Then Vayilis slapped his shoulder and grinned. "You'll still be doing in-flo condensing, eh? You'll just be doing it for one person instead of a whole staff of hotheads. Anything unfinished down here?"

Jahn shook his head. "I finished yesterday's input last night."

"Then you probably want to get packing. When the Casimirs say 'immediately,' they don't give you slack time." He offered his hand straight up and down, to an equal. Jahn clasped it and hurried out.

Before driving back to his apartment stack, he walked past the function rooms to the east wing. "I've been asked to move into Alun Casimir's suite," he told the ground-floor guard. "I'd like to look it over before I decide how many of my belongings to pack."

The guard checked his credentials and provided directions. Jahn rode a lift up one story, and he emerged in an opulent environment. Subtle traces of wall color, mostly oranges and golds, shifted as he walked along a deep carpet. Alun apparently had the suite on the right at the hall's north end. As the guard promised, another man wearing dark Security reds stood waiting to admit him. Jahn presented his ID again.

"We'll record your security specs when you come back," the guard said. "Stop down at the office later." He touched an electronic key to the recognition panel.

Jahn breathed a quick prayer for guidance and stepped into an entry room nearly as large as his apartment. Through it and straight ahead were a large window and a broad bed with a textured brown cover. A door on his right opened into a smaller room.

As the main door shut, a young man peered around the inner arch. Only his head showed. "Hello," he said in a slightly comical singsong. "Who are you?"

"My name is Jahn. Are you Alun?"

"Uh-huh."

"Come out where I can see you, Alun."

"Bellik isn't with you, is he?"

Alun's droll manner drew a tease out of Jahn. He slapped his sides and said, "Let me check my pockets. Ah … no. He's not here."

Grinning, Alun stepped into the arch. The tall, thin youth vaguely resembled Bellik, but he lacked Bellik's exaggerated vertical features. He wore a blue bathrobe. "I look funny, don't I? But my shoulder still hurts when I pull on shirts. I fell out a window."

"Did you?"

"I guess so. Everybody tells me so. I don't remember."

Jahn took a moment to listen deeply. The young man was pleased to see an unfamiliar face. Evidently he feared the familiar ones. "What do you remember?"

"Looking up at an open window."

"Nothing just before that?"

"No." Alun pointed at his ear. "I guess I landed on my head. Nice to hit something soft."

"Sit down. Let me look at it."

Alun took a chair. His hair was shorn, with the back barely grown out. Jahn recognized the look. He'd gone through this stage before his hair grew long enough to catch in a queue.

Carefully he ran a hand over Alun's scalp. He found a slight bruise on one side, but no sign of massive trauma. He touched Alun's right shoulder.

"Ouch," Alun exclaimed.

"Sorry. Do you have pain medicine?" The injuries looked odd, almost as if he were already limp when he landed.

"Medic Jackson comes up. He gives me pills I need."

"I'll probably take over that duty." Jahn stepped away. "For now, I need to go back to my other apartment and pack. I've been told …" It seemed best not to mention Bellik by name. "I'm going to move into your extra bedroom. I hope that's all right."

"Oh, yes. I would like to have a friend here."

"I'll be your friend and your teacher."

Alun screwed up his face as if he were trying to look studious. "That's good," he said. "I think I've forgotten a lot."

That week passed quickly. Jahn had to wait three days before sending off his next information pod, including a request for revised orders, but he drove without incident into the countryside, completed his transmission, and returned to Alun's suite without being challenged.

His medical training was sketchy, but he felt certain that Alun's injuries resulted from a fall when unconscious, probably drugged. Landing squarely on his head would have caused more external bruising. Also, drugs—or some subsequent treatment, including the medicines he took now—could create loss of brain function.

He looked into Alun's files and found evaluations from a year at Nuris

University on Antar, and—even more telling—a recent likeness, long-haired with no queue.

Concord sympathies?

At the next opportunity, he synched deeply with Alun. Weird skips in Alun's inner frequency confirmed physical brain damage, not an ongoing drug dose. Still, the skips followed a suspiciously regular pattern. Jahn had synched with a brain-injured patient as part of his training. That time, the skips had felt random.

So apparently Alun had been silenced. Why not killed?

Jahn frowned and switched over to the day's data flow proposed for lessons. Alun had walked down to the hunting kennels. His favorite retriever bitch, Bear, had delivered a litter of puppies yesterday.

Alun's absence left Jahn time to play in the data pool. He'd already rejected eight daily shuttle flights to orbit as extraneous data for Alun to know but filed the information in his memory. Evidently Uncle Gamal didn't intend to favor Alun with information on what materials those shuttles carried or what was being built up there. Bellik had projected twenty to thirty capital ships. There were many classes of capital ships, though. Who would know?

Kai Oldion, perhaps? Jahn recited the personnel codes, pointed to the appropriate file, and scanned the roster. He found an address for depositing Oldion's severance pay, jotted it onto a printout scrap, and slipped it into his pocket.

Alun returned several minutes later, flushed and smiling. "Six puppies," he announced. "Fat and healthy and fighting for teat space."

"Bear must be a good mother."

"She's wonderful." Alun didn't seem brain-damaged when he talked about animals. Jahn had also wondered if his head had been shaved for scanning, but when he'd checked with Medic Jackson, he'd learned that the Residence didn't perform brain scans. There wasn't one scanner, conventional or handheld, in the Residence clinic.

So Alun's survival remained mysterious. Maybe Gamal felt there'd been too many deaths in the family and had decided to reshape young Alun.

"Get your shower and breakfast," Jahn said. "I've had mine. Then we have about three hours' worth of current events to go over."

Alun sighed heavily, gave Jahn a lopsided smile, and shuffled off toward the personal.

After a solid morning's work and the midshift dinner, Jahn left Alun at the first-floor clinic for tests as per Medic Logan Jackson's instruction. "Will I have time to go down into the city for two hours?" Jahn asked.

Jackson had light brown hair, an astonishingly square face, and three chins. "Mm," he said, "make it an hour and a half. Alun doesn't like being left alone."

"I'll come back for him here." Jahn hurried out to the parking area. Brilliant stars shone overhead. Human clocks might claim "afternoon," but Tdega's sky insisted "midnight." As he left Residence grounds, he thumbed a switch on a card he kept in an inside pocket, turning off his PL transmitter.

He found a public data terminal in the midtown business district. After squeezing into the booth, he touched in Kai Oldion's electronic code and keyed for a street address. Armed with that data, he drove first to a convenience market and then across town. Within ten minutes, he stood in the fifth-floor hall of a housing stack one class better than the one he'd recently left. He touched the entry alarm.

Half a minute later, a voice spoke from a sounding surface on the wall. "Who is it?"

"Jahn Korsakov," he said quietly. "I'm Alun Casimir's new tutor, but I wanted to talk to you about something else."

A scanner tilted in the middle of the door.

"I'm alone." Jahn barely smiled. "I really only want to talk." He raised the bag he'd picked up at the convenience store. "I brought a six-pack of Jerry's Better Bitters."

"Just a minute."

Footsteps approached inside the door. It slid aside. Jahn remembered the engineer wearing a high silver helmet. Bareheaded, he showed chin-length black hair, none of it braided, and a guileless face. "Come in," he said.

Jahn took a seat in the small living area left of the doorway, pulled the six-pack out of its insulating bag, and peeled off a bottle. "Good brand for the money."

Oldion nodded and took it. "I like your taste."

Jahn peeled off another for himself.

"What do you really want?" Oldion sat down in the middle of the room on the other wicker chair.

Jahn stared at Oldion while he synched again. Oldion seemed worried. Something about … Outwatch. Maybe there was better information to be had here than cargo manifests.

"I want to get a message to one of the Outwatch supervisors who left. Did you know any of them?" Jahn always had difficulty speaking while maintaining synchrony. The effort made him slightly dizzy.

Oldion raised both eyebrows. "I did help build the base, but—"

He plainly wasn't the kind to report Jahn, so Jahn interrupted, struggling to synch a little longer. "I'm not trying to trap you. I don't think it was wise to cut off the Tdegan Outwatch. I've always been nervous about the Devastator artifact."

Oldion calmed slightly. "Casimir's building two dozen ships," he murmured, "but not one is appropriate for watching the artifact."

"Exactly." Jahn drank from his bottle. Now, if ever, was the time to ask what class those ships were.

Or he could press a personal inquiry. "I'm getting a little nervous about staying on Tdega."

Calmer yet, now. "Brother, that makes two of us. We don't need to attack Antar to find trouble. It's orbiting our own sun."

Jahn relaxed out of the contact. For the first time in six weeks, he could almost let down his guard. Still, he couldn't bring Oldion into his confidence. Every friendship on Tdega carried the potential for betrayal.

Yet he craved company. Alun seemed friendly, but Alun wasn't all there. "Is there ever any way to get off-planet?" he asked softly. "I'd like to leave."

"Seriously?"

Jahn nodded. "But not right away."

Oldion stared into his bottle. "Not often," he said. "It's never been easy or cheap. But I've wondered the same thing. Jobs might be better elsewhere."

Especially after Oldion had been fired. "I'll make you a deal," Jahn said. "If you ever hear of a way to get off Tdega, invite me over for a brew after work. If I hear of a way out of here, I'll leave you the same invitation."

Oldion looked up. "Why did you come here?"

"I felt bad about your being fired. And the circumstances. You seemed like the most sensible person I've met"—*Since I got here*, he wanted to say—"in a long time."

"War's ugly." Oldion grunted the words. "It's brutal. I'm well out of it."

Jahn remembered hearing Filip Salbari call warfare *the machinery of death*. "What are you going to do?"

Oldion shrugged. "There's work in the factories. Lubricating line robots. I won't starve."

"I wish I could help you."

"I don't want to work at the Rez."

"Don't blame you." Jahn glanced at his wrist. He'd been gone almost an hour. "I should get back. Let me record my address for you."

Oldion pointed at his terminal, which sat on a corner table with its hibernation light blinking.

"What file do you want it on?" Jahn asked.

Oldion tilted his head and looked at him intently. "You aren't from around here."

Jahn's pulse took a skip. He thought he'd understood Tdegan customs, personal and online. How had he slipped, something about filing? Or was Oldion already on guard? Of course. That was it. "My family farmed," he offered.

Oldion hesitated. Jahn hastily synched. Oldion's inner frequency had accelerated toward fright. Evidently he had somehow deduced that Jahn might be a spy. Also that if Jahn were caught, and Oldion were connected with him, Oldion wouldn't live long. "We farmed," Jahn repeated. He tried the nexus tug toward calm instead of probing to see how he'd betrayed himself. Another time, though, he'd better know what not to say.

"I see." Oldion seemed to gather courage. He walked to the console and called out a file number. "There," he said. "Key it in."

This unit wouldn't respond to his voice, so Jahn pecked out his address code. "That'll get you my mailbox. I check it daily. Most of the time, I'm busy with Alun."

"What really happened to him?"

Jahn looked into Oldion's darkly compassionate eyes. "I don't know," he said. "I don't think it was a fall. I don't think it would be healthy for me if I found out. Or for you, if I knew and I told you."

"I agree. Please leave. I wish we could talk longer, but—"

"I agree," Jahn interrupted. "Things get nasty during wartime." He offered Oldion his hand, palm up.

Oldion clasped it and rotated their hands all the way over, leaving Jahn's hand on top when he let go.

11

Llyn had fretted when Director Graybill of the Rift Station Internment Facility called her into his office. She'd been the first inmate of her age group to drop out of the ongoing Z-ball tournament, and the athletic director predicted dire consequences.

As she walked down a long, echoing hall to be chastised, she marveled that she'd only been here two weeks. Station routines already felt natural. An Outwatcher had informed the inmates that their incarceration served two purposes: it underscored Antaran security while preventing violence against Tdegans living on Antar. There had already been three unpublicized incidents. Built as a boarding school, the Rift Station facility lay far south of Lengle inside the Rift city dome. Llyn found herself living with several hundred mostly long-faced, black-haired strangers who wore odd, snug clothing. She'd gotten used to their appearance in an amazingly short time. Now she surreptitiously stitched tucks into her culottes when Karine left the room. Karine hadn't commented—yet.

Llyn sat down in Director Graybill's office and braced herself, but Director Graybill didn't allude to the Z-ball tournament. He asked instead about her room, her bed, and her reaction to Rift Station food. "So you're reasonably comfortable?" he asked, leaning away from his monitor.

No noise penetrated this office. Llyn wondered if it had been soundproofed. On a sturdy metal table at one end of Director Graybill's desk, bubbles cascaded upward in a reverse waterfall at the back of a long aquarium. Colorful fish swam laps around bulbous plants. Watching them was oddly calming.

She shrugged. "If I had one wish …"

"Yes?"

She felt as if she were blushing. "It's just that my … mother has nothing to do but supervise me. One hundred percent of the time." She wondered how Niklo was coping in his temporary housing on the outskirts of Nuris's ruins. He probably had found work rebuilding the city.

"Let's talk about your mother." The supervisor swung a leg. "How is she coping with life here?"

"Well," Llyn said, "she's used to running a clinic. She calls up to Lengle every day. She checks on her patients, authorizes prescriptions, and gives Elroy orders—he's her assistant—but that doesn't take much time."

"The sheepdog has lost her flock."

Llyn knew that fable. She smiled.

"I understand that she covers her clinic business when you are in class."

"Yes, or down at the gym." Those were the only two places Karine never followed. Llyn had made friends, despite her standout clothing and natural shyness. Last week, standing along sidelines watching stronger, more talented and dexterous kids impress each other at three-dimensional Z-ball, Llyn had found Ilke and Tana. Before the war, she, Ilke, and Tana would have had little in common. Here, they were fellow outcasts, bonded by the others' disdain and a few common interests.

Z-ball had too many rules, and it required too much strength and speed. Any time the coach had rotated Llyn into the game, an opposing team member "accidentally" grazed her with the shimmering ball. That stung. Her skills improved quickly, and she'd learned to find satisfaction in that instead of the competitive element, but she'd decided that she preferred the familiar exercise machines over last-place honors in team sports. Immediately after she quit, Ilke and Tana quit, too.

She shrugged at Director Graybill.

"You were complimented on the record by your history instructor yesterday," he said. "Did he forward the printout?"

Llyn stared at the floor, a complex geometric mosaic that repeated three and a half times per meter. "Yes." She'd helped smooth an argument between two other students.

"You don't look happy about it."

"Oh, it was nice." She had so few possessions here. That printout would've carried her spirits for a while. "But Karine put it down the recycle chute."

He uncrossed his legs. "I don't believe that."

She probably shouldn't say this, but she couldn't resist. "Then you don't know Karine. Every time I get praised by someone else, she makes sure that I understand it doesn't count."

The director didn't answer immediately. Like Karine's, his face was shorter and more square than most of the inmates'—including her own.

"Maybe I don't," he said, "but I think she overstepped. That note was yours, not hers. I would be glad to ask your instructor to write you another."

"Not necessary." Llyn sighed. "But thank you."

Another long pause settled.

"Our schedule is different from what you're accustomed to." Director Graybill leaned back against his desk chair. Obviously, he was trying to draw her out. Get her talking. She wondered what he was up to, really.

"I'm learning the lines."

"Tell me about your classmates." His vocal tone changed from compassionate to administrative.

Oh. He wanted information. Would her new friends call her an informer? Yet her loyalty lay with Antar, not Tdega. And neither Ilke nor Tana was a subversive. "Well," she said, "living with an empath, I've learned to be honest about my own feelings. This is the first place I've had to deal with emotional waffling."

"Oh?"

"Take Carmine."

He shook his head, but he leaned slightly toward her.

"Seventeen. Slender. Popular. I don't know her mater—wait. All Tdegans have paternames." Antaran women carried their mothers' names, men their fathers' names.

"Slender ... oh, yes. Her."

"She feels terribly inferior. She's trying to cover it with social conquests. She has half the boys panting after her."

He barely smiled. "Are you an empath, Llyn?"

"Of course not." She bristled. "But I see and hear. I read people's voices very well."

"Hm." Director Graybill steepled his fingers. "Medic Torfinn tells me you're socially immature. How is it that you see and hear so much?"

"Hearing is my gift. It's all I had for years. And Karine doesn't see that I've grown up."

"She is your legal guardian for one more year." His tone sounded … disdainful? Cautionary? "That may be why Regent Salbari approved her request to come with you."

"I wish he hadn't. Don't tell her so. Please." Was she saying too much?

"We have had other communication with Regent Salbari regarding Medic Torfinn." That tone was definitely amused. "I will not say more."

"You'd better not. She'll know if you do."

"I know." He eyed her and added, "What is it like, living with an empath?"

Disarmed, she dropped her defenses. "This is the first time I've lived with ordinary people. I like them."

He smiled sadly.

Dismissed by Director Graybill, Llyn was directed to return to the room she shared with Karine. She walked back up a long hallway with windows on one side and classroom doors on the other.

Voices echoed behind her. "Llyn! Wait!"

She spun around and saw her two friends—what a beautiful sight! Ilke grinned under a set of bangs that almost covered her eyes. Tana wore a long, black braid over her shoulder, and even her shouting voice was sweet and lyrical. Both were younger than Llyn, but each had a tangible sparkle. Llyn liked being around happy people.

"Let's get something to sip on," Ilke puffed. "You can tell us what the Big Man called you out of class for."

Llyn twisted her mouth sideways. "He just wanted to know what it was like, living with Karine. So he said."

Tana wrinkled her nose. "I bet you told him plenty."

"Enough. But I still have to live with her."

Classes had ended ten minutes ago, and the crowded cafeteria hummed with conversations. Llyn and her friends helped themselves to bottled synthetic juice. Roughened baffles along two cafeteria walls and its ceiling were obviously designed to deaden sound, but the huge room also had two walls made of glass. One overlooked station grounds, and the other lined the long hallway. Sound waves bounced around in here almost as freely as in the inner world.

Silverware and glasses clinked without affecting her. Llyn had suspected that Karine made too much of environmental noises. Now she was certain. The flashbacks, she guessed, had been partly due to her consciousness of "control music"—and partly her involuntary attempts to escape the constant stresses that Karine piled on her.

So in a way, Karine was right. If she ruled Llyn's environment, there could be no music in it.

But Karine's unlimited time to supervise was the only unbearable thing about this glorified prison. Rift Station's food gave Llyn a dozen new pleasures to anticipate, and although others complained there was too little to eat, Llyn had gained weight. She also enjoyed the classrooms, theater, and potentially endless conversations.

Llyn's group was just claiming a corner table, far from the in-group's social games, when Karine hustled through a door close to the serving area. Llyn groaned. "How does she know?"

"What is it?" Ilke spun on her bench to face the door. "Oh. Mind-mama."

Llyn gulped her juice.

"Wonder what she wants." Tana flung her braid over her shoulder.

"She probably found out from the Director that our interview was over." Karine was always spiriting Llyn away from her friends.

But that gave them one more common enemy. Karine rounded out a set that took in Director Graybill, several hall monitors, and—especially—the food service supervisor, a stereotypically overweight woman who bossed the inmates' weekly duty shifts as if she really thought they were prisoners.

Karine walked directly to the girls' table, picking Llyn out of the crowd as easily as if she wore a projector. "Hello," she said to Ilke and Tana. "Llyn, come with me. Quickly."

"Is something wrong?"

"Come with me. I'll explain as we go."

Sighing, and then smiling at herself for picking up the younger girls' mannerisms, Llyn slid off the bench. She followed Karine up the hallway.

Karine held open the double door at the women's wing. "What is it?" Llyn asked.

"Come on." Karine didn't decelerate until their room door closed behind them. They'd been assigned a standard bedroom-and-personal unit far down the hallway. Outside their two windows were broad plains and a tall metal fence. Karine had claimed the bed near the windows, promising to trade eventually. The beds were mounted to metal corner posts and could be raised almost to ceiling level. At the moment, Karine's was up but Llyn's was still down. She sat on it.

Karine flicked the portable multinet terminal she'd been granted by Director Graybill. "I had a communication from Regent Salbari." Her tone reminded Llyn of the clinic at Lengle: Karine Torfinn, in charge. Karine Torfinn, passing down vital information.

Llyn leaned back on both arms. She had been awed to learn that kindly Regent Salbari had abruptly become the most powerful man in Concord space. She hadn't told Ilke or Tana she'd met him. The Tdegan girls called him a monster, and Llyn kept her mouth shut when they did, although it made her feel guilty. "What did he say?"

"He sends greetings—"

"Of course."

Karine glowered. "And an update on the current situation, if you'd like to hear it."

"I'm sorry. I interrupted." Karine rarely passed on snippets of inside information anymore. Whenever she did, Llyn assumed that she needed to feel superior, like a giver of good gifts.

"Regent Salbari tried to contact Ilzar and offer the Concord's aid, but they're not responding. Using Gate beacons, they could have called back ten days ago."

"From that, we assume they don't want to answer."

"Incorrect. We assume that they can't. Regent Salbari suspects that Tdega landed a military occupation force there. He also tried contacting Sunsis A. There's a settlement at each pole. Neither responded."

"What's he going to do?"

"There's a Conclave in two days." Karine stood rearranging toiletries on her desktop. Llyn had seen her do that under pressure.

"What was the rush to get back here?" Llyn asked.

Karine turned around and sat down on the edge of the student desk. "Over my orders," she said, "they're going to run Jink Band in the hallways."

Llyn had heard about that program from Ilke. Jink Band was a three-dimensional music vid. It occupied space—you could dance with a projected partner or sing with the band, as you chose—without view-glasses. E-net service was marginal since the attack, but enough programs had been recorded on private sets to reconstruct almost a year's worth of programming. This was according to Ilke.

"Oh?" Llyn asked. She didn't hope Karine would let her participate, since AR and music both were forbidden.

"Evidently the staff is concerned about those rowdy young people who like to lounge in the cafeteria. They've chosen three children to select episodes and two teachers to screen them. They're also going to play soft-tonal almost constantly in all bedrooms."

Ilke didn't think much of soft-tonal. She'd called it a relaxation channel for old folks. "Well?" Llyn glanced dubiously at a black membrane speaker mounted high on a wall. "Will our speakers—"

"They're more worried about controlling Tdegan troublemakers than they are concerned with your mental health. You're obviously not a troublemaker. So those are turned off. For your sake, of course."

Llyn had to speak up. "But you know I experimented while Niklo was missing. If more than two parts are playing, somehow it doesn't—"

"They are off," Karine repeated, "and they're going to stay off. And unfortunately, this means that you and I must stay in."

"In?" Startled, Llyn stared at her not-mother. "You don't mean in this room, do you?"

"Meals will be sent down."

Seriously? Had Director Graybill known this was coming? Was this why he'd wanted to interview her today—to find out how she had adjusted to previous circumstances? "That's not fair!" Llyn exclaimed. "No classes? No workouts?"

Karine shook her head. "We are temporary residents, and you're vulnerable during an episode. There are people at this facility who might take unfair advantage of you. You're already a target because of your clothing."

She had friends out there. How would she survive without them? "I could change my clothing. This isn't fair."

"We can do floor exercises together in here. We'll raise the beds—"

Llyn groaned. Karine was going to suffocate her!

"All right," Karine snapped. "You can turn back into a stick. You were starting to build a little muscle."

Karine had never complimented her on working out. Only now, when she could turn it into criticism, did she acknowledge that she had even noticed.

"Maybe we won't have to stay in here." Llyn said it aloud, since Karine would know what she was planning anyway. She sat down at her desk, put on her view-glasses, and dictated a message to Director Graybill. "Wish to protest confinement," she told the VTT recorder. "Have experimented. Harmonized music seems okay." She added a few details and pushed the SEND button.

Karine went on straightening her toiletries. "He's expecting to hear from you," she said mildly. "You'll get a quick answer."

This meant Karine had already spoken with him. Before or after her own interview?

Llyn was turning away when her answer appeared: "Karine is in charge of your welfare, Llyn. I'm sorry."

Llyn stared at the screen, feeling heavy and old. She couldn't bear to turn around and see satisfaction in Karine's narrow eyes.

Late that night, she lay thinking. Learning she was Tdegan hadn't settled her yearning for significance. She needed to know who she was, not who her parents had been.

Abruptly, she sat up with a chill realization. The more miserable Llyn became at Rift Station, the sooner Karine might expect Filip Salbari to release them out of compassion. Consciously or unconsciously, Karine was pushing Llyn into the most intolerable situation she could create.

What if Head Regent Salbari didn't do what Karine Torfinn wanted? How much more miserable could Karine make her?

"What is it?" Karine mumbled out of the darkness.

138 | KATHY TYERS

"Nothing." Startled and indignant—not even her thoughts were private with Karine this close!—Llyn tried to blank her mind and stifle her frustration. "Nothing," she repeated. "Go back to sleep."

12

Delays made Jahn nervous. After five days, Salbari had had time to respond—not only to Tdega's strike and Jahn's too-late warning, but also to Jahn's retransmission after securing his position with Alun. New orders could be waiting at the Antaran embassy, but the embassy was surrounded by electronic interference.

So Jahn drove over on the sixth morning, wearing Residence Security reds snatched from a third-floor storeroom. This morning's regular side-door embassy guard had fallen ill. It was nothing serious, merely a dose from Jahn's emergency supplies that would mimic a twenty-four-hour virus. Jahn had then arranged a two-point substitution on Personnel's files that left two employees each thinking the other had covered the regular man's sick leave.

Alun had gone down to the kennels. Jahn had given him the morning off, supposedly so Jahn could travel upcountry—because his invented father needed temporary help on the farm. It was thin cover, but it would stand middle-security scrutiny, because Jahn had sent in a summons from off Residence grounds late last night.

He hoped to return in four hours, at first sunset, and erase all evidence of his alibis.

Retracting the maglev's drive magnets, he parked it in a small lot alongside a stately white three-story building. The Ambassador and his staff remained indoors, imprisoned but provided with amenities, including an honor guard.

He strode to the side door, snapped off a salute to the Tdegan night watchman, and touched his ID to the other man's reader. A green flash okayed the change of guard. Jahn pivoted into the man's place. The watchman departed in his own maglev.

Now for the hard part. This guard post was watched. He couldn't simply walk in. He reached inside the building with his inner sense and listened.

Outside on the street, bright morning light agreed with his time sense. This was the one time daily when it did. Mature deciduous trees lined the avenue. Three birds flitted around a nearby branch, squawking. The odor of someone's breakfast drifted up the street.

He kept listening.

His vigil lasted twenty minutes. Finally, someone approached inside. Jahn recognized the Ambassador himself, passing the side door on his way down an inner stairway. Shutting his eyes, Jahn pushed himself fully alert. He got a nexus grip on the Ambassador and tried to panic him.

It worked. The white door flew open, and a tall man with a full head of silvery-gray hair appeared in the doorway. Jahn felt the Ambassador recognize him, and the other man kept his wits admirably. "Please come inside for a moment. My aide is choking," the Ambassador exclaimed.

Jahn pushed through the door. The Ambassador shut it. Jahn stood on a landing in the middle of a flight of wooden stairs.

"Emlin," the Ambassador whispered. "No, Korsakov. Are you all right?"

How strange to hear that name. "Yes. Are you?"

"For the moment."

"I found work inside the Residence. Do I have new orders? Is there anything I can do for you?"

"I and my staff are secure for the moment. We received a tightbeam transmission, but we've had no way to contact you—"

"I know. Have you mnemed or printed it? I can only stay inside for a minute. Mnemed would be safer."

The Ambassador trotted away downstairs and returned quickly. "Here," he said, panting.

Jahn pocketed a portable mneme and hurried out to finish his shift.

Safely back inside Alun's suite, after filing an online report on the "choking" incident under another employee's name, he relaxed on his bed and keyed the mneme for playback. His new orders would've been programmed by another empath onto Jahn's inner frequency of deepest relaxation, modulated for Gate-to-Gate transmission, and then transcribed by the embassy's powerful transceivers back to their original format. As Jahn lay listening, he did not hear words. He simply understood new information.

The Concord requested specs for the ships under construction in orbit, which came as no surprise. He already had some data.

Salbari also requested any information that might turn public opinion—on Antar, Tdega, and the other worlds—against Gamal Casimir's drive toward dissolving the Concord. Analysts interpreted Gamal's actions as early steps toward subverting other worlds into his new Tdegan Hegemony.

The Concord also needed background information on any members of the Casimir family who might inherit power if Gamal and Bellik fell.

Was he being set up as an assassin? That had never been part of his assignment, but all the rules had changed when Tdega opened war. Jahn hoped that he never received such an order, but he might save many other lives—possibly including his own family's—by carrying it out if it came.

More new thoughts drifted into his mind. He should keep working with Alun, nurturing Alun's regrowth back into old mental patterns. Alun had shown promise, signs of cooperating with the Concord. Salbari suggested a medication that regenerated damaged nerve tissue.

The tenor of new knowledge changed. Unexpectedly, he sensed that Vananda Hadley missed him. He would accomplish nothing unless he maintained precautions for his own safety.

Yes, Mother. Jahn smiled. She must have taken advantage of her Salbari connections and contributed to the transmission.

That seemed to be all. He opened his eyes. His reply would include the odd sensation he'd felt in Osun Zavijavah's presence. Nothing like it had been mentioned in training, and empaths were always ordered to report new phenomena. Athis Pallaton had issued that directive.

But he must prioritize. First: who stood to inherit authority here?

Later that afternoon, he put Alun to work on a printout and donned his view-glasses. He found the Casimir home records without difficulty and scrolled through the roster. Old Donson, whom he had met rambling the halls, had been Head Regent for forty-eight years. Donson no longer remembered current events—Jahn had synched deeply with the old man and come up with a wealth of outdated information. Here, he found a list of early accomplishments. Donson had materially supported the drive to colonize the other Concord worlds, but at the same time, he had maintained a predominantly independent Tdegan economy. In several of Donson's inventive economic institutions, such as Central Credit of Tdega, Jahn spotted details that now fed the discord between Tdega and other Concord worlds. Central Credit offered incentives for independent production and local investment. Apparently Donson hadn't known his reforms would punish those who wished to purchase out-system.

Or had he?

Donson had passed authority—although not his title—to his only son Aeternum when Aeternum turned forty-five. Evidently Aeternum had considered secession for years. Jahn spotted hints in the way Aeternum had molded Bkellan University's historical records into an oddly skewed account that implied Tdega had always dominated the Concord.

It made a fascinating story, written in vague language that required information-flow training to interpret, but Jahn had that training.

This shed light on the Tdegan mind-set. Keeping an eye on Alun, who sat engrossed in his work at another table, Jahn reached toward the floor. He had slipped off his shoes in his bedroom, dropped his smallest mneme unit into a shoe, and carried it out. Now he loaded it with this data.

He tucked the mneme back into his shoe and kept reading for potential heirs.

Aeternum had three offspring. Eldest son: Hutton Casimir, destined for despotism. Beginning his first year at Bkellan University, Hutton had taken the presidency of every organization he joined. Jahn shook his head. He'd known people who excelled at intimidation and manipulation. Hutton fathered two sons, Bellik and Alun. Hutton had been assassinated at forty-two. Gamal's doing? Maybe in self-defense. Perhaps trying to survive Hutton's paranoid suspicions made Gamal ruthless.

Jahn skipped Gamal's long entry for the moment, intending to return and read all its hypertext. He scrolled down to see what the record showed about Aeternum's third child.

He'd had a daughter, Evadne Casimir Tambor. She'd produced four children and left Bkellan. Her husband owned rich backcountry holdings. Jahn guessed she had left to raise her children somewhere safe. She seemed wiser than either of her brothers.

The Tdegan attitude toward women perplexed him. Maybe his vision was skewed, since he'd been raised by one of the most talented women on Antar, but he had no trouble respecting talented women *or* men. Vananda Hadley—Mother—had taught him to respect his heritage and its responsibilities. She had admitted only once how deeply it hurt when Jerone Emlin abandoned her because she was "too heavy a load to handle."

Vananda Hadley … a load to be handled? That label insulted not only Vananda but her Creator.

Evadne Casimir Tambor's three male children were potential heirs if Bellik and Gamal vanished, according to the Concord's inheritance system. Their names would go onto the mneme.

He scrolled back to Gamal's entry. Gamal's Bkellan University record showed a long struggle for barely moderate evaluations. He had joined few organizations and worked single-mindedly. Married young to an heiress, who gave him five children. Danza and Gonsalve, the eldest pair, had been convicted of poisoning their uncle, Hutton Casimir, and they were executed.

The children had done it?

Maybe. Jahn scratched his chin. Hutton's death had boosted Gamal into position to inherit power, Bellik and Alun being too young at the time. Jahn couldn't help wondering whether Gamal encouraged the assassination. Hutton probably had made life miserable for Gamal. For all of them.

But that was only speculation. He read on.

Gamal Casimir's middle son Siah, recently gone into exile, had studied political science, pleased his instructors, and appeared devoted to religious activities. Another potential heir, and one who appeared somewhat normal.

Gamal's last two children, both daughters, had no University record.

Evidently, both died young. The youngest, Ora, had even died on the same date as their mother Joyan. It actually looked like a childbirth fatality.

Jahn whistled between his teeth. Was that possible in this century? He pointed at the screen and requested hypertext.

It was genuine death in childbirth. Gamal had taken his family to a country resort, where Joyan's time had come unexpectedly—and quickly.

Shaking his head, Jahn scrolled backward again. Gamal's second-youngest daughter had been named Luene. This child's early school evaluations had been recorded for posterity, because they were superlative. The child had achieved fluency in three languages by the age of eleven. There, her record ended.

That was too tantalizing to ignore. He ran media and in-flo checks and found nothing for seven years back.

Frustrated, he shut down the terminal and slid off Alun's view-glasses. Outside the suite's window, the sky lightened. Soon it would be second dawn, time for the evening meal.

"How is that coming, Alun?"

"Oh, it's coming. I'm just slow."

Jahn sat down on the arm of an oversized chair. "Do you want to take a break?"

"No. I want to finish."

He had to admire Alun's dogged persistence. "Alun, do you remember somebody named Luene?"

Alun screwed up his face "Luene? I think I used to have a cousin named Luene."

"What do you remember about her? What happened to her?"

Alun bowed his head, squeezed his eyes shut, and struggled visibly. "I think she died."

Yes. Too many Casimirs had died. But why? Who could have perceived such a young girl as a threat? Hutton? "What happened?"

"I don't remember."

Naturally. Jahn shrugged. "It may not be important. I'm going out for a minute, though." He glanced aside. "Stay away from that window."

Alun laughed. "Don't worry about that!"

Jahn hid the mneme and put his shoes on. He strolled out into the hallway. Rich carpet lay underfoot, and the wall coverings' color changes still fascinated him. Around the corner stood a bored-looking Security guard.

Several minutes of small talk later, when he sensed he had the guard's confidence—and the guard's inner frequency—he slipped into synchrony and said, "Seems like it's been forever since we heard anything on young Luene."

The guard glanced at him sharply, slightly alerted. "We don't need to hear anything on Luene now. Anyway, that excuse died years ago."

Baffled, Jahn quickly probed through the guard's schema of Luene.

He came up wealthy. A group of Antaran educators—fresh from Nuris University—had arrived at Bkellan, claiming to offer advanced schooling to a small number of exceptionally gifted children. Making a grand gesture of cooperation, Gamal Casimir enrolled the brilliant Luene. Eight months later, the researchers disappeared with all ten children. This guard recalled scathing excoriations that Casimir sent to the Concord, but the Concord was unable to find any of the children.

Jahn was stumped. "Strange, how Antar never even acknowledged the matter," he said. Antarans had never heard of it.

"I think we received one message here at the Residence. A quiet formal apology from Nuris University."

Jahn reached deeper, knowing now that he was in danger of detection. The guard hadn't quite believed that the apology originated on Antar. Jahn didn't either. He doubted that Nuris University had even heard of this incident. It had surely never sanctioned kidnapping. More questions came to mind, but he couldn't ask them. The Tdegan guard had to think he'd been here all his life. He should *know* this.

But he also discovered that for several years the Casimirs had used Luene's name in local news releases, subtly reminding the Tdegan people that Concord politicians were untrustworthy.

In light of that memory, the guard's comment made sense. Casimir didn't need the "excuse" of Luene anymore. Antar's attempt to nationalize Tdegan resources had finally sparked the Tdegans' desire to secede from the Concord, and it ignited the Casimir clan's interplanetary ambitions.

If Jahn searched enough files, he'd probably find some record of a command erasing all references to Luene's alleged abduction. Now that

146 | KATHY TYERS

Casimir no longer needed to scandalize the Tdegan public, he probably preferred to forget her.

So what really happened to her? Had Gamal considered her a threat at eleven years old? Or had Hutton? When had Hutton died?

Jahn carefully terminated the conversation, got a cup of tea from the guard station dispenser, and strolled back into the suite. "Almost ready for supper, Alun?"

"Almost."

"Take your time."

This time he used the i-net leech he'd been issued for accessing data streams undetected. It had come from the Antaran embassy, and it resembled a Tdegan personal reader.

Careful not to issue any commands that would leave a record of leech use, he found the erasure command buried in a series of household requests. Someone wanted the alleged abduction forgotten, all right.

He pulled off Alun's view-glasses and retrieved the mneme he'd loaded. He must send his fifth transmission pod tonight.

Working quickly, he transferred data off the mneme into his transceiver. Then he VTT-recorded the new data on Luene Casimir. Gamal Casimir's plot to reorient the Concord might lose public support if Antar could prove that Luene Casimir was living somewhere, unharmed and happy to have escaped her family's machinations. She would be eighteen now, and brilliant.

If she survived.

And the Concord would need to be able to conclusively prove her identity. Jahn searched the net until he found Luene's personal locator frequency. He recorded that in his transceiver program, too. As he did, he reminded himself that PLs could be removed or altered.

A gene scan would have been the best ID he could send, but this family record did not include genetic data.

He rubbed his face. A visit to the private Residence clinic was in order.

He stashed his leech and transceiver, then packed his smallest mneme in a shoulder bag. From his emergency supplies, he dug out a palm-sized needler. He loaded three tiny darts into its firing chamber. Each would deliver a five-minute stun charge for a seventy-kilo person, longer if he or she were smaller. He ordered downstairs for dinner and spent the long daylit evening with Alun. By second sunset, he was running on caffeine and tomorrow's energy.

He rode an elevator down to the office floor, where he peered up the hall for several seconds before hurrying toward the small clinic.

The door was open. A woman well under seventy kilos sat at a multi-net terminal. She seemed absorbed in the murmuring hand-dance of data switching. Before she could look up, Jahn flicked the needler.

Her hands relaxed down to the surface, but she remained sitting erect, staring at space over the projector. This stun charge maintained muscle tension, and she would regain consciousness sitting in more or less the same position, with her eyes still open. Needler loads were time-limited to prevent ocular damage.

Cautiously he slipped her view-glasses off her nose and slid them onto his own. He reached around her shoulders, blanked her terminal, and traced data flow upstream to genetic records.

Luene Casimir's had not been deleted. Jahn switched on the mneme. As chromosomal sequences paraded up the screen, he concentrated briefly on each one. Taking the complete scan required four and a half minutes while the woman sat blank-eyed. Hastily Jahn slid the woman's view-glasses back over her ears and shut down the terminal. He'd experienced occasional power outages when he worked in the west wing. A power-down would be easy for the woman to dismiss, easier than it would be for him to try to retrace her path back to her previous screen.

He also raided a drug cabinet for the medicine Filip Salbari had recommended he give Alun. He slipped back out the door with seconds to spare.

Now he had information worth spending another pod on.

He returned from his countryside transmission trip to find Alun sitting up at the table in his bedroom. "What are you doing there?" Jahn exclaimed, casually dropping his shoulder bag in his own bedroom's doorway. His bed looked wonderfully inviting.

"Just thinking. Where have you been?"

"Out in the country."

"But it's midnight," Alun exclaimed. His stubby new queue stuck out at the nape of his neck. He tapped absently on the side of his multinet. "There's nothing to see."

"There are stars. And cool air."

"I remember—" Alun said. He stopped.

"What?" Jahn stepped closer.

"Going outside," Alun said in an awestruck tone. "Being very young, and going out one afternoon to play. It had just rained. The stars were very bright. It's so vivid, Jahn."

Jahn folded his hands and smiled encouragement. "Good, Alun. Let those memories come whenever you can. They'll help you remember other things. What else comes back from that afternoon?"

Alun sat down on the nearest chair, a deep leathery one. He shut his eyes and drew several deep breaths. "Nothing, I guess. I wish there were more."

"That's all right. How about bed now?"

Alun rolled his eyes. "I'm not sleepy. Don't you want to play a game or something?"

"Not tonight. Please, Alun. Go to bed."

"I don't *want* to go to bed. Not until you go to sleep too."

Suddenly Jahn understood exactly why Alun had waited up. There was mischief afoot. He faked a yawn. "I am very tired." He turned down his bed. Nothing slithered out at him. "Just a minute, Alun."

Jahn undressed in the personal and hurried to bed. "Good night," he called loudly. Then he swung his legs up onto the bed and climbed in.

His feet caught, trapped in folded fabric.

Evidently some pranks were universal. "Alun!" he shouted in mock anger.

Giggles erupted behind his bedroom door. "Oh, no," Alun exclaimed. "The maid must have done that!" His head appeared around the door's edge.

Jahn flung a pillow. Alun retreated, laughing loudly.

By the time Jahn remade his bed, Alun had bedded down. Jahn hesitated before climbing back in. While Alun lay drifting off—but before he fell asleep—would be an ideal time to try pushing a synch deep enough to detect the remains of Alun's previous personality. If he could find more childhood memories, hitch a subliminal nexus to them, and draw them up into Alun's consciousness, he might encourage regrowth. Medical psi-ologists sometimes used that technique.

And—he rubbed his rough chin—if empaths had possessed the full circle of telepathy, with the ability to project as well as listen, then helping Alun could have been simple. But they were not full telepaths. And he doubted he could draw up Alun's buried memories. That would've taken his grandfather's skill.

The thrill of this afternoon's discoveries had worn off. He had prob-ably squandered a pod. Why would the public care if Gamal Casimir's daughter lived in the Concord? Tdegan women did not inherit.

In the morning, he would empty the capsules he'd stolen from the clinic into a vial, refill them with … with sugar, probably … and return them to that bottle. Any inventory that turned up this medication miss-ing could implicate him and Alun.

One dose would go into Alun's coffee tomorrow.

His eyes burned, he was so tired. He buried his head under the covers.

13

Seats at the Conclave table had been randomly assigned half a century ago, grouped system by system along three arches of a roughly Y-shaped table. Filip Salbari sat at the northern arch's center.

The table occupied the middle of the estate's smaller atrium. A sunken pool surrounded the platform, providing privacy even on less solemn occasions. A concealed mechanism pumped water from a fountain at one corner toward a rivulet surrounded by ferns at the opposite corner. Beyond the pool, five steps led up to an outer square of lawn cornered in broad-leafed evergreen trees.

Filip frowned. Alcotte's wife Gladwyn, plainly past the shocked state of grieving and well into anger, was finishing an impassioned plea that the Concord wreak retribution at Bkellan University on Tdega. She sat as far as possible inside the Antaran arch of the table, away from Tdega's three empty chairs at the southeast arch's center. Regents from Crux and deputized delegates representing Kocab sat closer to each other than usual along that arch.

Ilzar's also-vacant chairs, left of Filip, had been pushed to the east end of the table. That enabled another Antaran to sit with the Salbaris: Asa Sheliak, looking haggard and wearing several cold bandages, had spent twenty-one hours buried under rubble. Filip had just nominated him to one of the vacant Vice Regencies out of respect for his family, but he hadn't spoken all day.

"There must be justice," Gladwyn finished. Sonic ridges at mid-table amplified her pained voice. "We cannot allow Tdegans—nor anyone!—to believe that violence against living planets will be tolerated. We all suffered too much from the Devastators." She spread her hands dramatically. "They are still out there. We must stand together or crumble separately."

She sat down. Instantly, a thick layer of tears drowned the fire in her eyes.

Filip opened his hand on the table, asking for the right to speak next. When no one else laid out a hand, he said, "I cannot countenance retaliation, but all of you needed to hear that such feelings run strong on Antar."

Delegates nodded to each other.

"I could favor a blockade," Filip continued. "Tdega means to take Ilzar and Sunsis, and we have no evidence that either system desires secession. Interfering with Tdegan domination of either world is an option."

"So is liberating them." His uncle, Boaden Salbari, spoke without opening a hand. "I suggest a direct assault on Tdegan forces at Sunsis or Ilzar."

Filip nodded. Boaden had readily agreed to suggest this.

"Blockade?" Dio Liion, University Regent of Unukalhai, spoke up. Her braided topknot was a brilliant copper-auburn. "Do you realize how many ships it would take to blockade a planetary system?"

Far to Filip's right, Admiral Gehretz Lalande pushed to his feet. As a youngster, he had coordinated war game tournaments on board his generation ship. He had added fifty years and fifty kilos and lost all but a fringe of white hair, but he claimed that he'd lost none of his talent. He had told Filip privately that he refused to let younger men take over now that the Concord was at war. "One shipload of gravel," Lalande said, "unloaded in orbit around Tdega, would suspend space travel into and out of planetary spaceports for at least fifty years. Minimum expenditure, maximum result."

Still standing, Filip shook his head. "But then how would we feed our people? We have a two-year store of Tdegan grain to supplement our produce. When that's gone, we begin to starve."

"Then I suppose destroying Tdega Gate is out of the question?" Lalande asked.

Sober silence filled the atrium. Straining his ears, Filip could barely hear the false stream trickling behind him.

Destroy a Gate, and strand a system back in the sub-lightspeed universe? It was unthinkable. Anyway, he doubted that even Lalande had any idea how to do it.

Vatsya Habitat kept a Regent in residence on Antar. He asked for the floor. "We must negotiate with Tdega," he said heavily. "Vatsya will run out of food sooner than Antar will."

Sal Megred of Crux sprang to his feet. "Never," he shouted, his round face almost purple. "That is exactly what they want. Do we reward violence?"

Kocab's newly deputized delegate, a white-haired woman, spread her palm on the table and stood slowly. She glanced left to where two empaths on duty sat between Crux's station and the empty Sunsisan chairs. Then she looked over at Filip. "How many listeners do we have on Tdega?"

He rose to answer. "Our official Ambassador is not empathic. We have one undercover agent, and he is transmitting regular reports while he can. He was only given a tenpod ship for communicating with us. Five pods remain. We must assume that transmitting out-system has become extremely dangerous."

The Kocaban woman clasped her hands. "He'd best lie low."

Boaden sprang up. "No." When he shook his head, his jowls kept shaking. "We need information now!" Uncle Boaden had never believed in coddling empaths simply because the Concord had so few. Off the record, he had called Filip a mutant to his face.

Filip imagined Jahn Emlin's predicament on Tdega: he must protect his life and yet draw as close as possible to some of the most dangerous people in the Concord.

Formerly in the Concord.

"What can you tell us?" Dio Liion asked.

"Keep your security clearances in mind, please. A man will die if Tdega learns what I am about to tell you." Filip paused. "Our agent has taken a job that requires him to live in the Casimir Residence. It is an information-flow position in service to a disabled family member."

Even Boaden seemed impressed. He nodded slowly.

Asa Sheliak finally spoke, looking shrunken under his bandages. "We can be thankful for every bit of information he gets to the Gate relay."

"True," Admiral Lalande said. "Would it be possible, would it be ethical to have him kill Gamal Casimir?"

"From what he has communicated regarding prevailing attitudes," Filip said with some reluctance, "someone else would step into Gamal's shoes. There are too many Tdegans in the power caste who want to secede from the Concord. If he's going to shake their attitude, he must do it in an unexpected way."

Gladwyn exhaled heavily and laid a hand across the top of her belly. "It's late. I suggest we adjourn for the night."

Startled, Filip checked the time. In less than an hour, it would be midnight. He stood. "Does anyone wish to continue?"

Dio Liion's head shake set her topknot dancing. "Perhaps the morning will bring new developments." She looked across at Gladwyn and arched an eyebrow in sympathy.

"If we all sleep on it," Boaden said, "I think we will see the logical path more clearly. We must not hesitate to follow it."

Filip had no doubt what Boaden meant. "Tomorrow, then."

A thin-haired man from Miatrix sprang up and walked over to join Sal Megred of Crux. They spoke earnestly in low voices.

Favia joined Filip as soon as Boaden left the chair between them. She looked him up and down with intelligent eyes and laid a hand on his shoulder. "This is hard for you," she murmured.

Favia was the most empathetic non-empath he'd ever met. She slid her hand down his arm and clasped his hand, and she walked silently beside him down the steps to the atrium's sunken level. Her sister Vananda had returned to Nuris to help supervise salvage and rescue efforts.

Filip paused beside the water channel. An orange fish lazed upstream, beating the water with transparent fins. Flagstones lay underfoot between green pillows of moss and sweet chamomile. The Salbari estate was teeming with people, both University and military. He and Favia had housed six in each suite—crowded conditions for the estate, but roomier than Vatsya Hab and other high-quality living spaces. No one had complained. Probably no one had slept much, either.

"If you don't head for the bedroom," Favia said gently, "I'll drug your wine."

Filip squeezed her hand and led her across the watercourse on the nearest stepping stones. "Don't bother."

He caught three and a half hours of sleep before a voice in his left ear awakened him. "Message," it said softly. "Message."

There would be a ten-second delay before the infernal implant restated itself. He slid off the bed, careful not to wake Favia. He pulled on a robe and got out the door before it repeated. "Message. Message."

The outer room was as dark as his bedroom, but a motion sensor turned a on dim overhead light before he reached his desk. Efficient instead of ornate, the private office's only touch of luxury was a set of bookshelves: real wood, from Tdega.

He sat down and said, "Screen on."

He recognized the junior staffer who appeared. "Sir, a relay message has come in. Cover code indicates that the source is Jahn Emlin, origin Tdega. Shall I feed?"

"Absolutely."

The message, already decoded from mneme format, appeared in letter type. The first page's contents shocked him. He had never heard of Luene Casimir nor any kidnapping charge. Gamal Casimir had managed to wreak public-opinion havoc on Tdega without leaking word to Antar. It was an accomplishment Filip grudgingly admired.

Of course, he would cooperate in the attempt to locate her. This might be the unexpected lead he had hoped for. He pointed at another panel to print the gene readout. As letters appeared on the top sheet in his printer box, a thought struck him.

Llyn.

Quickly he reviewed the dates Jahn had sent. They jibed within weeks of Llyn's estimated age. And Karine Torfinn had reported that when she first saw Llyn, the girl looked as if she'd been recently moved, although—what had been the wording?—her mental involvement suggested years in the AR.

Jahn's other news detailed military preparations and Casimir family background. Filip keyed the military information to Admiral Lalande's quarters and put a message alert on his private line. It would serve the old war gamer right, waking him after so little sleep.

Next he checked Rift Station's medical records. There'd been no gene profiles done on the residents. "Inmates," internment staff labeled them. He must have Llyn tested immediately.

If his suspicion was correct—and he quickly came up with several more reasons why it might be true, including Llyn's obvious intelligence—then he must explain this to her himself. Sending a messenger would not show enough respect.

Llyn Torfinn, a Casimir? He couldn't send her home to a family that murdered each other.

But he could encourage her to broadcast a message to the Tdegan people via Gate relay. The Conclave might also make other suggestions.

He keyed an order for his ground crew to fuel and check the family's small jet for takeoff, and he requested a single bodyguard. He barely had time to shower and deputize Alcotte to convey this news to the Conclave. *Tell them I'll be back by noon,* he murmured into the VTT recorder. *With or without her.*

Half an hour later, he was airborne. Surface winds required an easterly takeoff, which took him toward Nuris. He didn't want to see it, but passing this close without surveying seemed counterproductive. He leaned forward and touched the pilot's shoulder. "Flyover, please."

There wasn't much to see. It was still hours before dawn, and the main dome's big arches lay mangled and twisted. Steam jets lit by construction lamps showed that the magma plume continued to move upward.

What had the Tdegans done to Antar's fragile crust?

"Enough," he told the pilot. "South, please."

14

Llyn tried to shake off the hand gripping her shoulder. "No," she insisted. "'S too early. It's still dark."

Actually, the room light shone overhead. Karine squeezed tighter. "Get up and get dressed. We're wanted at the infirmary."

Llyn sat up and shook her head, feeling stupid. "What is it? An epidemic?"

"Get dressed. Don't argue."

"What is it?"

Karine backed away. "Do you want the first shower? Keep it short."

Llyn straightened her back and tugged her cover. "Karine," she said. "What. Is. It?"

The empath raised her chin. "They want a full genetic ID on you."

Llyn eyed the clock. "At three-thirty?"

"Fine." Plainly disgusted, Karine clipped her words. "Don't shower. I'll be out in two minutes."

By the time Karine emerged, Llyn had dressed in a pair of old, comfortable culottes with a dangling fringed belt. She had also roused enough to realize that genetic testing meant they must have found a suspected match. That didn't justify awakening her before dawn, but she was too sleepy to think that through, and definitely too sleepy to care whether she showered. It'd be easier to doze off again if she didn't.

She shuffled to the medical center with Karine at her elbow. The night-shift medtech muttered as she pushed a stool toward one of her mysterious black boxes. "We could've drawn blood samples on day one and done complete workups on everyone, but oh, no. The civil defenders would've screamed." She pointed at the stool. "Sit."

Llyn sank down.

"One finger in that little hole, and hold it there."

Llyn steadied her arm on the countertop and stuck in the ring finger of her left hand. She felt a little pressure on her fingertip, a slight chill, and then pressure again.

A tone sounded. The medtech waved her away. "All done, missy. Wait in the cafeteria."

Karine tugged her out of the laboratory.

"I know the way." Llyn shook her arm free.

Karine tossed her head. "Snappish this morning, aren't you?"

Llyn walked a little quicker.

Karine steered her into the kitchens, where they found a baker overseeing a row of automated kneading vats. They thumped out ten different rhythms. "Any coffee?" Karine asked the baker. "We're waiting for a medical test."

"Then get out of the kitchen."

"Nothing contagious." Karine filled two cups from a pot and said over her shoulder, "This way."

Llyn had to follow. She obviously wasn't going to get any more sleep. Karine set the mugs at one end of a table, one across from the other. Then she sat facing Llyn, watching hawk-eyed.

"Sleep well?" Llyn asked conversationally, trying to soften Karine's stare.

"As long as I did."

"What's going on?"

"They wanted a gene scan, and they wanted it now."

"Who's 'they'?"

Karine tapped the table with her index fingernail. "I don't know what the problem is."

"Couldn't we go back to bed?"

"I want to wait up and find out the results."

She'd sipped only a little coffee. "Maybe I could go back to bed." On the other hand, voices buzzed in her brain: *They've found me, they know who I am, it's all over, it's all beginning, it's all going to be different.*

"Stay here," Karine said.

As Llyn lifted her mug, she thought she felt its warmth in her hand. She sipped again cautiously. The bitter brew must be last night's batch. If only it tasted as good as it smelled.

And if only she had a mouse hole to hide in. Karine obviously knew how excited she was. Her frown looked jealous. Maybe something was afoot. Karine wouldn't answer, so why ask questions—or even make conversation? Llyn concentrated on her coffee, sniffed herself, decided she should've taken that shower, crossed her ankles, uncrossed them, and stretched out on the bench, shutting her eyes.

Footsteps pounded toward them. Llyn opened an eye and saw Director Graybill hurry closer. Surprised, she sat upright. What was he doing up at this hour?

"Llyn," he said, "come with me. Regent Salbari wants to speak with you."

Llyn blinked, awake in an instant. She hadn't felt this delighted since the day she accidentally scored a Z-ball goal.

Director Graybill looked from Llyn to Karine and added, "He just arrived. Did you know he was coming here?"

Karine nodded as she stood.

"Why didn't you tell me?" Llyn cried. She would've showered if she'd known.

"Let's go." Karine tugged down her shirt hem.

"Ah," Director Graybill said, "no. Llyn only, please."

Karine's neck stretched. She twitched her mouth twice. "I'm Llyn's guardian."

"Karine," the Director said, "I have orders. Llyn is to come with me. Only Llyn."

Llyn followed up the hall, wishing she'd been able to record the open-mouthed expression on Karine's face. Then she wished more than ever that she'd showered and put on presentable clothing. She liked Head Regent Salbari as well as she'd ever liked anyone. She didn't want to impress him, exactly. She just didn't think she ought to meet him wearing last night's clothes and yesterday's sweat. Had he come all this way to see her?

And what did this have to do with her three o'clock awakening?

Director Graybill opened a small door that Llyn had never been allowed through. She walked in.

Regent Salbari sat on a metal-and-cloth institutional chair beside a small window. The bloodstones glittered on his white collar, and a man stood behind him wearing a long, open jacket over his tunic and culottes. Bodyguard, Llyn guessed. Rift Station Internment Facility might not be the safest place for Regent Salbari.

He stood immediately. "Thank you, Graybill. Good morning, Llyn. Sit down. Would you like coffee?"

She remembered that voice. She'd thought of it last week when a language arts instructor asked her to define "serene."

Director Graybill backed out. Llyn was about to tell Regent Salbari that she'd had all the coffee she could stomach when she caught a whiff from the urn on his table. This was fresh. Not only that, she decided once she'd sipped from the cup that his bodyguard poured, but these beans were not related to those ground for institutional use. "Thank you," she said sincerely. "I'm sorry I'm rumpled, Regent Salbari. I—"

"Don't even think about it. I threw on the first clothes I could find this morning."

She couldn't see any wear on his red-belted culottes or tunic, but he probably dressed grandly most of the time. "Karine wouldn't tell me what's happening," she said. This warm sensation in her middle—was it hope? "Will you?"

"Yes." He set down his cup. "Fully. But would you humor me for a few moments and tell me how you've been treated?"

She saw no reason to hold back. He was an empath. He would know if she hedged. "The schedule's no worse than Karine's clinic. Staff—they're wonderful. No offense, sir, but it's nice to deal with people who can't tell everything that I'm feeling. I spent five years with an empath. Here, there's—there was, anyway—a chance to escape."

"I think I can empathize," he said softly. His eyes sparkled between age lines she didn't think she remembered. At first, she didn't get the joke.

Then she laughed. He joined her. "Be careful with that cup," he said. "It's very hot."

"Oh?" She set it down and went on. "I've even got a couple of friends. I think I could've made more progress, except that for the last week, Karine has confined us both to one room."

"One room? That was never our intent. Around the clock?"

She explained about Jink Band and soft-tonal.

"You had no difficulty at the concert in Nuris." He frowned. "Only afterward, and that might not have been directly related."

"Exactly, sir. And after we got home, I experimented. Harmony doesn't put me into a trance. Only single melodies or duets, and only if the pitches coincide with intervals from a seventeen-tone scale."

His eyes widened slightly. "What's that?"

"You …" How to explain? "You divide the octave into smaller steps, and there are more of them. It was the music in my AR. The chords are incredible."

He rubbed his smooth chin. He apparently had taken time with his appearance. "It does seem from your records that environmental tones disrupt your brain activity more often than full musical scores. In fact, full scores in our tonality would probably cover up birds or clanking dishes."

And now even those didn't seem as potent. Llyn had never dreamed that he had followed her case so closely. "Why didn't I think of that? Would you tell Karine? She respects you."

He actually winced. "Llyn, there has been a remarkable development in your case."

She folded her hands and wedged them between her knees.

Regent Salbari's eyebrows rose in an expression she didn't understand. "Not only are you Tdegan by birth, but this morning's gene test proved that you are a member of one of Tdega's University families."

Now she recognized the expression: compassion. Llyn sat stunned. She was related to … to the murderers who had set one Concord world against all the others?

Five years with Karine had trained her to converse circumspectly with empaths. Regent Salbari's silence didn't demand a quick answer. He would watch her deal with her feelings.

She'd searched for a family. She'd fantasized an ideal set of parents somewhere in the Concord. She had even tried looking for them. Now that she had parents, she wasn't sure she wanted them. She wished she hadn't found out.

She stopped twisting her fingers around each other and looked up at him. "Okay," she said. "I'm dealing with that. Which family?" She knew of four.

He smiled sadly. "For a girl who lost so many years of seeing, you're blessed with excellent perception. I must assure you that neither I nor anyone else on Antar will hold your parentage against you. Do you understand?"

What he was saying, yes. She understood. But she didn't believe him. "Yes …"

"Evidently," he said, "you are the youngest surviving daughter of Vice Regent Gamal Casimir."

Her throat went dry. The very man who claimed responsibility for Tdega's secession—and everything that followed? No. A thousand times no. She would rather be Karine's.

Regent Salbari laced his fingers and dipped his chin. "Take a few moments. Think through the idea."

He showed a different kind of empathy from the kind she had experienced for five years. She had to be grateful. She tried to imagine herself sired by the butcher Gamal Casimir, murderer of Nuris University. After a few more moments, she realized that her Tdegan friends probably thought of Regent Salbari in similar terms. But he hadn't killed anyone! Caught in a steel mousetrap, she writhed and struggled and resisted the notion as long as she could.

Once her emotions lay down panting to rest, she asked, "How do they think I got to Antar?"

"Our details are sketchy, and there are long gaps. On Tdega, Regent Casimir claimed you were kidnapped by Antarans pretending to be educators. As far as I know, that is false." He spread his hands. "Evidently, Regent Casimir has used your disappearance in the past—from time to time—to incite public feelings against Antar."

She felt numb. At least that was an improvement over her previous

162 | KATHY TYERS

panic. And her path forward seemed obvious. "I should go back there, then."

Regent Salbari shook his head. "Llyn, the Casimir family has a reputation for violence. You would be in danger there."

But he couldn't leave her here. "I must go back anyway, mustn't I? That is my family. Regent Salbari, you can't keep me from going home to my real family. Maybe I could help to placate him—Vice Regent Casimir, my—is he really my father?"

Regent Salbari nodded silently.

Perhaps she'd feel more unified on Tdega, less pulled in all directions. Perhaps some of the automatic responses that Karine had tried so hard to train out of her actually resulted from a normal Tdegan upbringing, and not sensory deprivation at all.

Tdega had a different culture. Would she adjust—one more time?

Maybe she had a real mother. "I might feel less abnormal there," she muttered. Already, her mind had changed about one thing. "Sir, please don't leave me here at Rift Station with Karine. Not one more day."

"I will not. But you do not need to go directly to Tdega."

"I am a Tdegan alien," she pointed out. "The Antaran government has declared that we ought to be confined."

"Then it shall confine you to the Salbari estate for the present. I would like you to record a transmission to the Tdegan people, if you are willing. They only need to know that Antar had nothing to do with your abduction, and—"

A thought struck her. "Who put me into the AR unit?"

He didn't glare at her for interrupting, but he answered soberly. "No one knows. Our only clue is the report about those alleged educators. Tdega claimed they were Antaran. Maybe that story was invented to cover some other circumstance."

"Where did you hear it?"

He glanced away for barely a moment. "We have sources in Bkellan."

She shrugged. "That's history anyway. And you're right, I can decide later whether I should go to Tdega. But for now, just get me out of Karine's bedroom. Please."

The compassion lines deepened on his forehead. "Tyranny," he said, "is no less tyrannical when it is well meant. In fact, it becomes inescapable."

He laced his fingers around one knee and leaned back. "Would you let me observe the way Karine has been treating you?"

"You mean empathically, don't you?"

He nodded.

She shrugged. "I suppose so. After all, Karine has been doing it for years."

He stared up at her for several seconds. At last he said, "Bring some memories up to the surface. Don't be selective. Let them come."

Once Llyn started reflecting on the way Karine had treated her, images tumbled one after another like crates from an overstuffed closet. She shut her eyes and ignored Regent Salbari. Restrictions followed evaluations. Discussions, discipline, demands, and more restrictions.

When the flow trickled off, she stared at the floor. "I'm being unfair," she muttered. "You're only seeing one side of the story. Karine has told me that fantasy and false interpretations feel exactly like reality."

"Yes, but I will see the other side. I promise. And I won't be the only one."

"What do you mean?"

"There'll be a board of inquiry."

Llyn stared. "Good," she whispered. Instantly, guilt jabbed her. "I just want to be free."

"Every freedom," he said, "carries as a correlation its own set of restrictions. And every restriction carries implied liberties. Does that make sense?"

"I think so," she said. "Niklo learned to drive. That made him free to go where he wanted. But it also made him subject to laws he hadn't needed to know before."

When Regent Salbari smiled, the scrambled universe seemed friendlier. "People of my faith call these freedom-restriction groups 'spheres.' Some spheres are more complex than others. Our Creator demands that we choose the sphere of our own moving. I believe that the heart of your rebellion against Karine is that she requires you to move in her sphere, and you are not suited for it."

"Should I be ashamed? She seems to think so."

"Absolutely not. You must order your own life. If you don't, you become guilty of impersonating another sapient being. There are complications, of course. Some liberties are meaningless, even destructive."

"Gamal Casimir was free to destroy Nuris University," she said bitterly. That beast was her father?

"That is an extreme but excellent example. The Creator's sphere encompasses all others. Once you have been freed, you cannot remain free if you go on serving yourself. The self is a cruel master."

Filip studied her with his inner sense. He had seen terrible things in her memory, done in the name of "parental care." Although her view was naturally slanted, he had been trained to take that into account.

He probably could persuade her not to return to Tdega, but he could not leave her at Rift Station for one more day. At the Salbari estate, he would introduce her to the Conclave.

In fairness to Karine, he must explain one more concept. "The paradox of freedom," he said, "is that its goal is to become a better servant."

She eyed him with keen curiosity.

"Only an individual who has taken full responsibility for her own intellect, conscience, and actions can find the sphere she was created to occupy. Then she can offer fully human service—in the sphere to which she is suited."

"Fully myself," she said. "If only you knew how badly I want that."

He drew a deep breath. "Would you like to be present when Karine is told who is your father?"

She had wished, a little while ago, that she could capture a certain stunned look on Karine's face. Now she knew that had been nothing compared to what was coming. She hesitated. She would have to face Karine as Llyn Casimir for the first time.

Another thought struck her. "Is my name really Llyn?"

He pressed his palms together. "Luene."

"Luene." She tried it on her tongue. It sounded right in a way she didn't understand. "Luene Casimir. Huh. I wonder how I made it 'Llyn' in my mind."

He stood and walked to the intercom. "Would you like to stay?"

"I would." She crossed her ankles firmly. Regent Salbari offered a ticket out of the hawk's reach. So did she have the courage to use it?

Karine appeared within seconds. Llyn wondered if she had been waiting outside the door. Karine looked from Regent Salbari to Llyn to the bodyguard and back again several times, obviously synching with each, trying to lessen the information advantage that Llyn had temporarily gained.

Empaths needed few words to communicate. The moment Regent Salbari spoke, Karine's cheeks flushed. They grew darker as he explained. She clenched her hands in the lap of her culottes, and then she gripped both sides of her chair and moved it closer to Llyn. "No wonder the University was threatened with violence," she said.

Llyn's hackles rose. *Don't blame me for that!* she wanted to scream. Just thinking it was enough, with these two. Both glanced at her, Karine sharply and Regent Salbari with … well, with empathy.

"And no wonder people were looking for her," Karine added. "Is this a safe place for her, Filip? Should we take her someplace even more isolated?"

"The matter has been discussed." Regent Salbari's gaze remained steady. "And we are not convinced that the Nuris University attack had anything to do with Llyn."

"You didn't answer my question," Karine said. "Where should we take her?"

Regent Salbari shook his head. "Llyn's safety is not the issue we face at this moment. She has offered to return to Tdega."

"What?" Karine seized Llyn's hand. Her fingernails dug into Llyn's palm. "How could we trust Gamal Casimir to care for Llyn? He has the war that he wanted."

"Surely he also has a father's love for his daughter." Regent Salbari glanced aside at Llyn. "It would be easy to announce to Tdega—publicly, the same way Bellik Casimir spoke to Antar after their attack—that we had found Gamal's missing child. If the Tdegan public knew she was coming, she would be watched by more people. She would be safer."

Karine's fingernails dug in. "That puts us in a bad light. It hints that we had her all along, and that we're sending her home because they attacked."

"You are right. We must attempt to trace her history first, of course. We lost whatever information Rakaya Shasruud could have given us, but we—"

"Trace information? The i-net is destroyed!"

The gripping hand loosened for an instant. Llyn tugged her hand free and sat on it.

Karine was now fully distracted, arguing with Regent Salbari. "Even if Gamal Casimir didn't lock her away in a grimmer institution than this is, moving worlds would put Llyn under stress. She might find another artificial reality. Or if they don't care for her properly, she could have a fatal accident. Look how easily she has these episodes."

"Karine." Regent Salbari spoke so softly that Llyn scarcely heard him. He and Karine must have communicated subliminally, because Karine cut off her litany of doom. "I am afraid," he said, "that you are more concerned for your own happiness than for Llyn's. Please try to see the situation from her perspective."

Karine sat perfectly upright. "Llyn is my daughter."

My daughter. Two very different words echoed in Llyn's memory: *unique subject.*

With another side glance at Llyn, Regent Salbari answered. "I have interviewed your daughter. As I have said, she is mature enough to make many decisions for herself. We demand that of our youngsters, you know."

"They make mistakes," Karine whispered.

"And learn from them."

Karine shook her head. "And sometimes they are destroyed."

"They must take that risk. Our parents had to release us. They had to accept our humanity. The ability to choose one's destiny is evidence of possessing a soul."

He had followed her case closely, including Karine's speculations!

Karine glowered.

"I see no evidence that you have trained Llyn to make decisions. Each small choice, during these past five years, should have prepared her to make larger ones now."

"Exactly. She's not ready."

"Despite you, she gravitated directly toward a course of diplomacy."

Llyn blushed. She wondered how harshly Regent Salbari would have spoken in her absence, if he was this harsh with Llyn listening.

"She always gravitates toward danger. She's drawn to it." Karine looked pale. "She can't get to Tdega on her own, no matter what she wants. The Concord can protect her from the Casimirs by denying her transportation."

"Llyn needed to be separated from you months ago," he said, and a wave of delight washed through Llyn. He continued, "If I hadn't been busy with other concerns, I would have foreseen this confrontation and made it easier for all three of us."

Llyn felt as if any movement she made would set Antar spinning backward.

Regent Salbari turned toward her again. "Your ... adoptive mother is correct on several counts. Returning to Tdega would not end the war. You could remain safe and comfortable here. You spoke of new friends. Perhaps, once you slept on the idea, you would prefer to stay with them."

"If I slept on the idea here," Llyn murmured, "Karine would change my mind for me."

Karine's whole face flushed. "You can't accuse me—"

"Control yourself." Regent Salbari's quiet interruption thundered.

"How dare you shame me in front of my child!"

"Control yourself," he repeated. "Llyn, go back to your room. Pack your belongings. You may spend ten days at my family's estate—more, if you need it. After that, I will send you wherever you choose to go."

Llyn sprang up. Karine leaned forward as if she meant to leave, too.

"Stay with me, Karine," Regent Salbari said firmly. "We must talk."

Llyn squeezed out the door and away. She swung her arms as she strode up the long, straight hall, almost giggling.

Freedom ... freedom ...

Karine's insides seethed at a roiling boil. She would not synch with Filip Salbari, not after this, not even to make communication easier. How dare the man?

"She would be in danger on Tdega," Salbari admitted, "but she would not be alone. Jahn Emlin has penetrated the Casimir Residence. He will—"

She glanced at the bodyguard. Who did Filip think he was, traveling with an escort? "That boy has ridden his mother's coattails all his life. You can't expect him to perform without her."

"He is doing an excellent job. He has matured under pressure, exactly as I expected. I only wish I'd had time to check on you more frequently. I spent several minutes in synchrony with Llyn. You have almost subjoined her. You have tried to make her an extension of yourself."

Ridiculous! "For five years I struggled to translate the chaos of that girl's mind. I taught her human culture from scratch, from nothing. Wall rheostats. When to say 'please.' How to use eating utensils." She knew her voice was rising. She didn't care. "Physical rehab alone was full-time work. I have returned Llyn to the real world. Never belittle me in front of my daughter. Never." She'd never felt so uncontrollably angry. This was a man she had trusted. Respected. Even loved, in an appropriate way.

"You *have* been this angry," he said. "Your rehabilitation work with Llyn has been excellent, but an intellectually and emotionally abusive situation has arisen, and I deeply regret that I was too busy to become aware of it."

"That's nonsense. And just because Llyn wants something, that doesn't mean she ought to get it. 'All things are lawful,'" she quoted, "'but not all things are profitable.'"

"And 'Why is my freedom judged by another's conscience?'" He shook his head. "You gave Llyn the wrong kind of freedom. You made her free of a vital responsibility, that of maintaining her own personhood." He steepled his fingers in front of his frown. "Once affairs calm down with Tdega, I must step out of one of my offices. Obviously, I am not competent to hold both."

"Obviously," she exclaimed. "You are also wrong in your suspicions, and especially in accusing me of abusing my child. How dare you?"

"I have the right to discipline any member of the Order. Must I resort to that?"

"For what?" she cried. "I have done nothing wrong."

"You could be accused of criminally abusing a fellow human. Llyn is competent to press charges."

"No inquiry board would convict me."

"Don't be so certain."

In that moment she hated him.

"Get hold of yourself." He stood and glanced at the bodyguard. "I am taking Llyn north. I will arrange her transport to and from the estate."

"I will pack quickly," she said.

He stared as if he didn't believe that she meant it. Softly, exaggerating each word, he answered. "You will remain here. You are to consider yourself confined, awaiting the evaluation of your peers."

Her stomach churned worse than ever. "That is ludicrous!"

"Unfortunately, the inquiry must be postponed until we settle the Tdegan conflict. For now, Karine, stay here at Rift Station. That is your own choice. Stay in this room until Llyn has left the facility. You may keep her in your prayers, but that is all."

How dare he? Her anger coiled up and rendered her mute. Salbari's blank expression did not change. Either he did not feel her fury, or he too had drawn back out of synch. He wasn't a strong empath. He'd been elected for other reasons.

Reasons that obviously had no basis.

"I'll stay in this room until I calm down," she said.

He turned and walked out. His bodyguard followed.

15

Gamal Casimir snuffed a cigarillo in a small crystal bowl and tossed it behind the fire grate. "Sit here," he said.

Across the fire room, Osun Zavijavah settled into a deep chair. With his classic nose, chin, and cheekbones—and that drooping black mustache—he looked elegant, even handsome, as long as he kept his glasses on. "I don't honestly think it will work."

"I have doubts, too. But it's worth trying." Gamal reached into a cargo crate. From its depths, he drew out a transparent helmet. It didn't look bulletproof, but his Chief of Engineering Development had assured him that the clear material could deflect large-caliber projectiles. Why, asked the engineer, should Regent Casimir restrict his vision in any direction?

Gamal, who had retained his monocular blindness to stop the Chaethe from choosing him as a carrier, had nodded sagely.

Anchored inside the helmet's broad padded collar, small, clear tubes ran up the interior every four or five centimeters. They would provide ventilation without introducing weak spots. Pumping units were concealed inside the collar.

Gamal had asked the engineer for two additional features. First, there was a lock-down neck clamp to make it irremovable, except by coding a touch sequence onto the clamp lock. That should keep infested humans from removing non-infested individuals' protection.

Second, there was a high-band transceiver built into the collar tab. Certainly the Chaethe spoke among themselves. Once Gamal tapped their network, Rider would no longer be able to claim extra levels of intelligence. He hoped that the Chaethe used ultrahigh frequencies to communicate.

As Gamal donned the prototype, Zavijavah removed his dark glasses. He rubbed his eyes and temples, blinked and squinted. It made him look irritated. There'd been a long period after Zavijavah's infestation when he'd rarely complained about discomfort.

The helmet rested heavily on Gamal's shoulders. His engineers had placed controls on a tab that extended from the helmet's collar on his left. He could see and reach them easily. "Ready?" he asked Zavijavah.

Zavijavah straightened in the deep chair. "I'm listening," he muttered.

Gamal switched on the transmitter. "Hello, hello," he repeated. "Hello, testing." Slowly, he turned up the gain. "Hello, testing. Hello, Rider. Hello, Chaethe. Can you hear me?"

Zavijavah squinted and winced. He flung both hands over his ears. "Stop!" he exclaimed.

Gamal ignored him. It was Rider he must contact. "Are you listening?" Gamal asked again. "Rider, I wish to make a mutual defense treaty with your people. I am Gamal Casimir, Vice Regent of Bkellan University. I speak for the Tdega system. I have brought new people to Sunsis, helping to accommodate your folk. If you can hear me, have Zavijavah say so."

"Stop!" Zavijavah sprang to his feet. "Stop," he shrieked.

"You wanted proof that our people could fight, that we could protect you from the Devastators—"

Zavijavah screamed.

Disappointed, Gamal turned down the gain. "Was that too loud?" he asked through the transmitter. "Is this better? Do you hear me? Have Zavijavah say so—"

"Please," Zavijavah said. "Stop. It's wailing at me."

Gamal exhaled in disgust, briefly fogging his helmet. He flicked the main switch and pulled off the headgear. "What do you mean, wailing at you?"

Zavijavah slumped against one side of the chair and blinked up at Gamal. His pale brown irises filled the ocular orbits, surrounding enormous pupils. "I've told you. It shrieks. Right between my ears—"

"Did it speak to you?"

"No."

"Nothing?"

Zavijavah glowered. "I said so."

"Is it hurting you?"

"No worse than normal." Zavijavah squeezed his huge eyes shut. Water trickled out of one of them.

Gamal replaced the transparent sphere in its crate. "I'll ask the engineers to install fine frequency tuning and we'll try it again."

Zavijavah shot him a baleful look.

Gamal opened a cabinet. "Let me pour you a drink." Of all Residence employees, he wanted his Security Chief's support, especially now that he spoke for Rider, the alien ambassador. Gamal also didn't want Bellik supplanting him by buying off Osun Zavijavah.

"I'll—hm." The last bottle of his favorite liquor, red ruin, had only a dribble left. "I'll send for more."

Zavijavah slid on his dark glasses and sprang out of the chair. "I'll go down and get some."

Was Zavijavah preparing to bolt? Gamal stalked to the room terminal and called up a trace of Residence employees by personal locators. One employee who might logically walk Zavijavah to the kitchens without offending him was right down the hall. "Wait a minute," he said. "I'll have Arne Vayilis go with you."

Maybe it would be better to concentrate on trying to develop a vaccine to keep the creatures from infesting the wrong people.

Jahn sat at a vacant desk in Personnel, researching the Lahoma shipbuilding plant for Alun Casimir—and for Filip Salbari. He had sent his sixth pod, carrying a week's worth of military intelligence. Now, he must gather data for his next report. Upstairs, Alun was engrossed in a projected three-dimensional puzzle. As Jahn sorted information, he practiced maintaining the listening stance that had earned his worst evaluations from Grandfather Pallaton. It was difficult to maintain vigilance with his mind occupied. He must practice more.

To his surprise, he caught the odd, vacillating frequency again. The one that was not typically human. He suspended his hands over the control board.

Voices approached his open door. His former supervisor, big Arne Vayilis, strode past. Security Chief Zavijavah walked with him, easily recognizable in his dark-red uniform coat, drooping mustache, and wraparounds.

Jahn slid off his view-glasses. "Hello Arne," he called. It would be better to announce his presence than surprise that pair.

Arne looked through Jahn's door. "What is the upstairs tutor doing down here with common employees?" He laughed. "Don't you like it up there?"

Jahn grinned back at the big man. "It's a good position, but the hours leave something to be desired."

Arne's belly shook when he chuckled.

Zavijavah peered around Arne, eyes invisible, expression unreadable.

"Good afternoon, Gen Zavijavah." Abruptly Jahn realized that he had slipped off his listening stance. Frustrated, he reopened it.

The eerie sensation rose and fell, pulsing behind Zavijavah's inner frequency.

Instantly, Zavijavah raised a hand to rub his temple. The gesture looked as if the custom-fitted glasses bothered him—but could he have felt Jahn's synch? When empaths listened, people didn't notice.

Jahn squelched his synch. Vayilis turned to leave. Zavijavah followed, still rubbing.

This confirmed Jahn's earlier observation. But what was it he'd heard?

He'd had no trouble finding Zavijavah around the Residence, but every prior opportunity to listen had fizzled. He'd stationed himself outside Zavijavah's office and been interrupted by Security staff. He'd strolled past Zavijavah's rooms at midnight, but heard nothing—and on both occasions, the hallway guards had been too alert to catch with needler charges.

Obviously, though, Zavijavah was the key to something.

Jahn slipped his glasses back on. The Lahoma plant was heavily committed to components that could be destined for warships. Alun would be interested in many of these figures. As Alun slowly recovered, numbers and parts and ways of assembling them had begun to fascinate him.

Jahn enjoyed watching Alun regain his senses. Alun had no warmon-gering intentions. Jahn had cautiously but consciously slanted lesson data, increasingly aware of the enormous power educators held over their students.

This data proved that Casimir's commitment to military action went back much farther than last month. Lahoma had gone into full produc-tion almost as soon as it opened. The line robots necessary for producing these ship components must have been designed and built over a year ago.

By the time he pulled off his glasses with the file fully sorted, the regular shift had long since passed, and then all his free hours between quitting time and nightfall. Fog slunk down into Bkellan from the mountains, shrouding the grounds in weird stillness. It was time for bed. Almost midnight, according to his body.

But he needed to hunt Osun Zavijavah. He would explore the east wing's third floor first, then walk past Zavijavah's room. Maybe by then, Zavijavah would have retired but would not be asleep. In case one of the ubiquitous hall guards appeared, Jahn also needed to be ready to fake a delivery. Such as a vital new printout.

He copied the data he'd condensed for Alun, mounted it in a display folder, and tucked it into his document case. That data could be bound for Casimir himself, if anyone challenged him. He closed up the terminal and left.

Standing in the silent hallway, he breathed a prayer for success and protection. That made him wonder how all this skulking was molding his soul. The Hadleys had a tradition of serving society, but surveillance work was teaching him to be devious.

The responsibility of spying out the enemy also gave him odd free-doms, such as carrying a weapon. The doctrine of freedom-responsibility spheres had proven uncannily applicable to his people. Accepting respon-sibility to the Creator's own sphere had given the empaths—as a new creation—a much-needed sense of place.

Clanking noises and heavy food smells drifted from the kitchen far down the left hall. Many kitchen staff came on duty at second sunset and worked all night. He turned toward the elevator nearest the kitchens. Sweeping his authorization badge in front of the reader, he asked for the third floor.

The elevator disgorged him there. He heard voices from the left, so he turned right and slipped through a door, listening hard for other mental presences.

A light switched on overhead. He'd stepped into a storage area piled with art objects and elegant furniture. There could be interesting material here. Pressing his hip pocket to make sure the slender needler was there, he walked past a stack of old portraits. Ornate frames of various sizes leaned against each other at all angles.

"Who's there?" a voice asked behind him.

Jahn spun around. He'd slipped off synch! A Security guard stood in the doorway, one hand on his sidearm. Jahn kept his hand away from the needler. It was too late for that. "Korsakov," Jahn answered. "Personal staff, Alun Casimir's tutor. I'm looking for something to put on Alun's wall." He didn't bother to synch now. The guard was obviously suspicious, and Jahn needed to concentrate on his alibi. "According to the household net, this room has several good pieces."

"Did you get authorization?" the bulky guard asked.

"At this hour?" Perhaps the guard had a sense of humor.

The guard beckoned. "If Regent Casimir's still awake, I think he might want to ask you some questions."

"Sure." Jahn strode back toward the main door, clutching his document case one-handed. He was as ready for this as he ever would be.

The guard took him down a level to the second-floor hallway. "Wait." The man recited a code to the guard station. When a light came on, the guard grunted. "This way."

Jahn followed up the hall and past several doors. His escort opened one. Jahn took a deep breath and walked inside.

At the far end of the room, a line of flame devoured several massive wooden logs. The fire threw so much heat that Jahn felt it four meters away. Gamal Casimir sat beside it, wearing a thick black nightrobe. The deep V on its front showed a carpet of black hair on his chest. He set a drinking glass on a wooden table.

Osun Zavijavah also cradled a drinking glass. Even in this dim room, he wore the glasses. Jahn glanced at him and then quickly away. For the first time in weeks, he felt sticky. If Osun Zavijavah ordered him frisked, he had three shots in the needler. He could take Casimir, Zavijavah, and the guard.

If he was fast enough. And the guard must fall first.

The guard saluted Casimir and then Zavijavah. "Gen Korsakov was upstairs, sir. Family storeroom."

"Oh?" Casimir beckoned.

As Jahn stepped closer, he caught a whiff of liquor. Casimir's eyes looked red. Obviously, he was deep into his cups. A drinking man could become far too friendly and voluble, or he could fly into a rage. This would be a wire-walk.

Keeping an eye on the guard, Jahn made the customary bow. "Good evening, Regent Casimir. The Residence net said there might be paintings suitable for Alun's suite upstairs. I apologize for neglecting to secure clearance. I should have realized it would cause a problem. May I go back tomorrow?"

"I don't think 'snecessary." Casimir folded his hands on his robed lap. "Alun doesn't know good art from bad."

"No, sir." Jahn glanced aside. The guard had returned to attention beside the door. "But I hope to surround him with quality. His taste will improve if I whet it." He shifted his document case to his right hand. "I had also hoped to give you these figures from the Lahoma plant. This will be Alun's lesson tomorrow." He passed the document to Casimir.

"How's th'boy doing?"

Jahn didn't want these two to know how much Alun had improved. "He is learning. Slowly." Jahn loosely clasped his hands and tried to look relaxed. He imagined he could feel Osun Zavijavah study him through hidden eyes. "At the moment he is fascinated by numbers. He loves the way they can be manipulated." He pointed at the printout. "This will give him a chance to compare many kinds of figures and refresh his memory of a vital operation."

"Sounds good." Casimir glanced aside at Zavijavah. "D'you want him detained?"

Zavijavah barely shook his head.

Relieved, Jahn spotted the half-empty crystal carafe on Casimir's side of the hearth. "I am sorry to have disturbed you."

Something in the fire exploded. Jahn almost jumped out of his skin, but neither Zavijavah nor Casimir reacted. They must be accustomed to the noises wood made when it burned. To Jahn Emlin, destroying wood seemed criminal. To Jahn Korsakov, it must seem a normal privilege of the wealthy.

"'Sreally not a good time to go nosing around upstairs."

"Very good, sir. Once again, I apologize for disturbing you."

Casimir waved a hand in front of his face.

Jahn risked listening deeply for a moment. There was nothing inhuman about Zavijavah's surface sense this time. Surprised, he groped across for Casimir's inner frequency. The man was more alert than he acted.

In that case, it was time to leave. Jahn backed toward the door and into the hallway, then turned on his heel and headed for Alun's suite, thoroughly puzzled.

As the door closed behind Jahn Korsakov, Osun Zavijavah sat up straighter in his chair. He took a quick sip from his glass. Drunk straight, red ruin tasted like poison.

But to his surprise, it seemed to be keeping Rider quiet.

Casimir shook his head. He'd lost his sleepy-eyed languor the moment Korsakov hurried out.

"That was interesting," Zavijavah said. He'd seen Casimir fake drunkenness before. "Why did you and Bellik hire Alun a tutor, anyway?"

"When Rider takes Alun, if he seems to recover suddenly, that will explain it," Casimir drawled. "But where was I?"

Truly, human intelligence was extraneous for Rider's needs. "Hunting catamount on the Huuterii Pass."

Casimir studied his drink, appeared to decide it was full enough for the moment, and continued a long, tedious narrative that freed Zavijavah to ponder a question that had been occupying him for an hour.

He hadn't heard Rider since the second drink vanished. The parasite drove him to take fanatical care of his body, but tonight—after the shrieking caused by Casimir's experiment—it had let him relax and tipple.

The second-spore migraine had faded away with that second glass, too. Painkillers no longer relieved it. This last hour had been blissful. He studied the hand that held his glass. He thought he spotted a freckle appearing on the back of it. He would have Medic Jackson remove it tomorrow. He was not vain, but freckles ruined the contrast between his fair skin and his black queue, mustache, and glasses.

Casimir finished his tale with a dramatic imitation of firing his antique slugthrower. Zavijavah made appreciative noises on cue. Casimir smiled and drank deeply. They both stared into the fire's living heart.

Finally Casimir spoke. "How are you feeling these days?"

"Terrible, of course." Zavijavah took another long, careful drink, more of a dose than a pleasure. His last sips were making him agreeably sleepy. "I have decided I will be glad to pass on these spores. Even if another human or two gets a headache ..." He grinned at his own joke. "It's time to get rid of mine." As before, Rider would stay with him, but he now was willing to help it reproduce.

"That's a switch. Are you finished being altruistic?"

That kind of thought had always made him feel like a traitor to humanity, but not at the moment. He must, he must regain this blissful, pain-free state for the sake of his sanity. "Right," he said. "If it wants Alun, can we do it now—tonight—before I lose my nerve?" For the moment, that hideous memory didn't distress him. "Choose someone else for the second spore. Anyone. Korsakov would be fine. Or Vayilis."

Casimir shook his head in a languid arc. "You have to wait eight ... yes, eight more weeks until the second spore matures. Then you've got a window of, oh, about two weeks to transmit them before a third starts to form. But ..." He tipped his glass toward Zavijavah. "We shall toast the occasion aforehand, and I'll let you drink liberally before, before, before the big event. Just to make things go easier. What do you say? What does it say?"

Rider said nothing.

Maybe Rider was susceptible to alcohol and didn't know it. That might give Zavijavah a bit of power over the creature!

On the other hand, it was adept at reading his intentions. If he reached for a drink, consciously hoping to silence it, it would wail at him. He might not be able to drink fast enough to thwart that.

Then what was the harm of staying slightly tipsy?

He might be reprimanded for drinking on the job, if they smelled it on his breath. But there were ways of hiding that.

Casimir was staring at him, smiling, looking as if he were waiting for him to speak. "It's much easier to cooperate," Zavijavah said, hoping that would answer whatever Casimir had said last.

Casimir poured another half glassful for himself and offered Zavijavah the carafe. Although his glass was still nearly full, Zavijavah took the carafe to keep Casimir from spilling it. He poured a token splash into his glass. "Nine years," he mused.

"What?" Casimir asked. "Oh. That you've lived with our friend Rider. It liberated two spores, too." He rested his chin on one hand and fingered his lower lip. "Spores can stay dormant for ten years, but they usually don't. They still have one sense when they're loose."

"What's that?" And how did Casimir know so much?

"They seek heat. Somewhere out there," Casimir said, gesturing with his glass, "there is at least one other Tdegan whose Chaethe is about to reproduce. They are loose on our world already. So I must communicate with Rider. We will try the helmet again. And we'll try whatever else it takes."

"Perfectly sensible," Zavijavah said through gritted teeth. He recognized the threat in Casimir's voice. "When you learn to communicate with it, tell it that it's welcome to leave at any time."

Casimir frowned. "Don't think you want that."

"I want it," Zavijavah whispered, "more than anything."

"It would probably kill you if it left."

Zavijavah almost dropped his drink. "You never said."

"You never asked." Casimir smiled magnanimously and waved his glass. "I am, after all, the Concord's foremost expert on the Chaethe life cycle."

"From watching Rider." Zavijavah gritted his teeth. He'd discovered that Casimir did own a medical scanner, the only one in the Residence. "Would you care to share what you've learned?"

"Moment of penetration," Casimir said. "Spore sheath breaks. Several hundred cells escape inside your skull. The sheath doesn't dissolve—I think that must be how Rider leaves, if it decides to. That's what I think would kill you."

"Why?" Zavijavah demanded. "How do you know?"

"It left its previous host to take you. It wanted seer eyes. So it got them."

So the man Zavijavah barely remembered had died. He shuddered. "Go ahead."

As Casimir rambled, Zavijavah picked out new bits of data. Once Rider had made a body for itself, it had lain down a copy of its chromosomes. Creating a sheath for that spore took years. When that phase ended, its reproductive system went temporarily dormant. Fissures opened along the spore's inner end, and its moisture content rose. If the parent Chaethe signaled, the spore literally rocketed toward the skull opening its parent had used to penetrate.

"So you saw that happen?" Zavijavah asked.

Casimir waved a hand. "Yes. Apparently if it doesn't decide to liberate the first spore, the process starts over. It can't send one off and hold one back, so the ripe one has to stay put if a second starts forming."

Zavijavah grunted. "So I've got three aliens alive in my head? I only hear one."

"No, just one. They come to life—they're born, in a sense—when they get their first gray matter."

Fascinated against his will, Zavijavah leaned forward. "Why Sunsis? Why not just do it here?" He would love to avoid making that trip.

"More private." Casimir raised his glass. "How did we get so deep into that subject?"

How like Casimir to change the subject. "You were telling me," Zavijavah said, "not to encourage Rider to leave."

"Ah." Casimir gulped his drink. "Don't. I need you, anyway. We have to perfect the helmet transmitter."

"Not the helmet itself?"

"It's been rifle-tested. The little tigers penetrate like bullets. No offense, but I'd rather keep my friends outside my skull. I'll deal with them from a distance."

Be thankful you have a choice, Casimir. "Why not just send me alone? Or send somebody else to help me, if you're worried about—"

Casimir waved both hands in front of his belly, belched, and smiled again. "I can't send an agent to Sunsis to represent me," he said with a grandiose sweep of both arms, "because I am the only uninfested Tdegan who knows what's afoot."

A door chime brought Casimir's head up. "What was that?"

"Someone at the door." Zavijavah stood.

"Tell them t'go away."

No. Anyone calling on Casimir this late must represent an emergency. Zavijavah stalked to the door and thumbed the entry switch twice. His cheeks burned. He almost wished Casimir hadn't told him anything.

The door opened. One of his staff guards stood outside. "Is the Regent here?"

"He's busy," Zavijavah said.

The guard wrinkled his nose, probably at Zavijavah's fruity breath. Zavijavah didn't care. He was off duty.

"Head Regent Donson just had a massive stroke," the guard said. "He might not live through the night. If you can get Regent Gamal upright, he'd better come down the hall if he wants to see his grandfather alive."

"I'll tell him." Zavijavah pushed away from the door. The staff guard didn't close it but stood outside at attention. "Your grandfather's had a stroke." Zavijavah cleared his throat. "This might be it."

Gamal rubbed his face with both hands and swore as he tottered upright. "Get me a cup of coffee. Double strong. Then call Jackson. This is an emergency."

As soon as Casimir staggered up the hall, fortified though not sobered, Zavijavah emptied the liquor carafe into his glass. Carrying it cautiously, he returned to his room by way of the kitchens, where he claimed two more large bottles "for entertainment purposes." Back at his apartment, he set them inside a pair of high boots. He drained his glass before falling into bed.

When he woke the next morning, old Donson was feeble but responding, expected to recover most of his faculties—and Rider remained silent. Zavijavah toasted Donson's recovery at breakfast, morning coffee break, and at lunchtime. He felt human again.

16

Filip asked his bodyguard-pilot to pop above the cloud cover on the way north from Rift Station. As soon as the glare eased outside his window, he peered up and out. "Llyn. Look."

Five members of the nearby star cluster hung in the heavens this time of year. Although dawn was approaching, Crux, Kocab, Miatrix, and Unukalhai were easy to identify by their distinctive colors, and brilliant Vatsya shone overhead like a blue-white jewel. Llyn gasped.

"I haven't forgotten my first trip above the clouds," he said.

"Tdega has stars every night, doesn't it?"

"Almost. Look, there's a seeder plane." He pointed out the window. "Look quickly ... I'm sorry, you missed it. We are clearing the clouds that the Devastators left us. I have seen a difference in my lifetime. In yours, there might be gaps of blue sky daily instead of monthly."

"I'll probably be on Tdega, sir. I won't see them."

He respected her silence as they dipped back into low atmosphere. Gradually, the world grew light. She sat nose-pressed to the window, plainly fascinated by a mountain range that the pilot kept on his left wing. For the moment, he felt like he was seeing it through new eyes, like a set of stone wrinkles on the world's crust.

But he had work to do. He opened the terminal on his lap and punched up the Conclave frequency. Antar had received word from Ilzar a few hours ago, an independent radio operator calling for help. Ilzar Gate relay had transmitted it automatically to Antar Gate. As Filip suspected, there were many frightened Ilzarans who did not want to secede with Tdega.

He composed a private message to the Conclave: Rift Station had matched Llyn Torfinn's DNA with Luene Casimir's, and she was with him.

He wished he could sleep for an hour. Or two.

"Regent Salbari?" Llyn pointed out her window. "Is that where the garnets are dug?"

Wondering why she asked, he leaned across her to look down. An open-pit mine scarred a mountainside. "No. That's a conductive metals site. The garnets are south of here." Favia's father had told him how the first gem strike on Antar was of blood-red garnets, and how he'd had one trilliant-cut like an abstract droplet. He'd made it the empaths' emblem, and he'd pinned Filip's first stone to his collar. Filip was only the fourth head of the Order.

The small jet swung around the mountains' eastern flank and then headed out over rocky flats and deep-green algae paddies. He asked Llyn, "Would you like to stop at Lengle? There might be things at the clinic you'd like to have with you."

She shook her head. "No. I really don't own much. You can send to Lengle for anything I need, can't you?"

"It will be difficult."

"Then I'll do without."

He thought he understood her determination. He closed down his leech. They would pass over Lengle anyway. "See if you can spot the clinic from the air."

She pushed her face closer to the window, filling it. He couldn't see out, so he eyed her. She had thrived at Rift Station. A disinterested observer might still call her thin, but no longer bony. Pulled severely back from her face, her black hair hung in a bunch at the nape of her neck. He saw the resemblance to Gamal Casimir in the curve of her nose, her full lips, and a pensive expression that often concealed Casimir's next move from careless politicians.

He had also seen tiny signs that her tactile sense had not fully recovered, such as the way she'd comfortably cradled that hot coffee cup.

He closed his eyes, synched deeply with her, and listened. Llyn carried

184 | KATHY TYERS

the scars of her isolation in a hesitancy to commit herself—she wasn't certain of the right things to say—but she was flattered by his attention.

She seemed to bear Antar no grudge, although her eagerness to escape Karine had felt like a caged creature's desperation. Llyn was beginning to realize she could function outside her prison, if someone bent the bars.

As Filip anticipated, the little jet touched down lightly at the middle of the estate landing field. It was just a smoothed strip of volcanic ground, but Llyn exclaimed, "You're free to come and go whenever you please, wherever you please."

"Almost." Filip was almost sorry to have arrived already. The pilot taxied straight toward the estate house, as ordered. "The only trips we're making under emergency restrictions are those that are necessary. Today," he added, "you were a legitimate political crisis."

She grinned. "I'm honored."

He felt stiff and old leading up the east ramp to the family wing. Blue ceiling panels gave off light at balanced wavelengths like a cloudless sky, illuminating a line of monochrome family portraits. "Most of our guest rooms are occupied, I'm afraid. I'll give you one of the children's suites. I hope you won't mind."

"Will the children?"

"Not these two. They camp with each other half the time anyway."

Llyn walked alongside him, up a long hallway with white fabric-covered walls. She paused at a doorway to run a hand up and down its textured surface. He wondered whether she could feel it. "Lovely," she murmured.

He could easily imagine what was going on in her mind. Had she had a home like this, unremembered, on Tdega?

A thin, matronly staff woman strode up the hallway. "Gen'n Favia said you'd want me."

Filip stood away from Llyn. "Cilla, this is Llyn Torfinn. She'll be staying with us for several days. Please move Uri into Locke's room for a week and make Llyn comfortable. I'm giving her family access." He turned to Llyn. "That means the run of the estate, kitchens and all, twenty-four hours. I'd only ask that you not disturb the Conclave meeting in the atrium."

She raised a hand. "I wouldn't dream of it."

Two small girls dashed up the corridor and swung into a bedroom. Filip didn't recognize either of them. "The house is full," he said. "This wing will be noisy."

Her eyes widened. "Wonderful."

Sweet girl.

The two children exploded back out into the hall and sped on in the opposite direction.

Filip needed to get back to the Conclave. "Please don't leave the grounds. It's a long way to civilization in any direction."

She fidgeted with her fringed belt. "Yes. I saw how isolated this place is when we flew in. Why did your family build so far from any city dome?"

He shrugged. "We were traditionally a frontier family. We lost some of our isolationism shipboard, but the moment my grandfather could separate himself, he did."

"It saved your lives this time."

"Yes." He looked around soberly. Always before, the isolation had seemed unnecessary to him. "It did. And he saw to it that we'd be able to offer hospitality. Ask Cilla for anything you need. Clothing, food …"

"I'll be fine. Thank you, sir."

In the atrium, Filip hurried toward the Conclave table. Alcotte tilted his head in greeting and turned away, stroking his beard. Dio Liion of Unukalhai stood with a hand spread on the table. She wore her long, red hair clasped at the nape of her neck this morning, not in her usual ornate knot. Unukalhai, closer to its Gate than any other remaining Concord world, planned to respond with full military support. "… so if Kocab can feed them, we will supply enough recruits to staff a full-sized cruiser and two pocket battleships. I see food as the limiting factor." She bowed toward him. "Welcome back, Filip. How is the Casimir girl?"

Filip folded his hands on the table. "For the moment, she is as happy as she remembers being."

They responded with murmurs and nods.

"Has anything more been heard," he asked, "from either of our sources on Ilzar?"

Sal Megred of Crux raised an eyebrow over an almond-shaped eye. "The emergency message repeated at seven-minute intervals for just over an hour and then went silent."

Filip frowned. "Nothing from Jay Li at Zjadel?"

"Nothing."

A message appeared down on the tabletop, on his eyes-only screen. "Essentially waiting for you to get back so we can make the vote unanimous. A."

He touched his T key, signaling thanks to Alcotte.

Alcotte stood. "I wish to make a formal motion," he said. "That this Conclave send an expeditionary force to the Ilzar system consisting of Antar's remaining Outwatch ships and three from Unukalhai. Then each of the five remaining Concord systems possessing Gate ships shall arm five more of them. They shall rendezvous here to defend Antar from further attack, or stand ready to do battle elsewhere."

The vote was unanimous, the strongest symbolic gesture they could make for history's sake. But Filip had to wonder, once they settled in to haggle troops, weapons, and provisions, how history would remember this meeting: as a step toward reunification, or as a second stumble toward dissolution and human extinction?

Llyn stood in front of an enormous window and stared out over the northern plain. She couldn't imagine why anyone would settle up here, except to be alone. Or had the elder Salbaris hoped to turn volcanic waste into cropland, once the clouds cleared away and there was more daylight at plants' favorite wavelengths? That would make more sense.

"Llyn? Hello?"

She turned. Beyond cabinets packed with brightly colored toys, two young women stood by the door. One—tall with a small-featured, feminine face—had cropped her brilliant red hair so short that her head looked almost cubical. The other had pulled back her brown curls with a stiff hairband, but behind the band they expanded as wildly as if she carried a static electricity generator. She wore a long, flowered dress in shades of pink and rose.

"Yes," she answered. "I'm Llyn. Hello."

"We came to see if you'd like some company." The tall, red-haired girl's plain brown tunic and culottes looked as if she'd just come off some kind of duty shift. "I'm Rena Tourelle. This is my cousin, Stasia Hadley."

"I'm—" Llyn cut off her own introduction. She spread her hands and shrugged. Regent Salbari had suggested that she keep her other identity quiet, at least until she decided whether she meant to return to Tdega. But she didn't want to be dishonest. "Everybody calls me Llyn."

"We're sworn to secrecy," Rena said. "Don't worry about us."

Stasia sat down on one of the room's quilted beds and shook her wild hair back behind her shoulders. "I wanted to meet you." The eagerness in her voice intrigued Llyn, because it also carried an edgy undercurrent of unfocused hostility. Two emotions at once! "Father says we're supposed to talk you out of going back to Tdega."

"Father?" Down at Nuris, she had met two Hadley women: Regent Salbari's wife Favia, and her sister Vananda.

Stasia smoothed her flowery dress over her knees. "Regent Salbari. He's trying to give up on me." Now the hostility came through more clearly. "He's trying to pretend that he doesn't care that his eldest doesn't approve of him."

"What is it you don't approve?" Llyn asked, startled.

Rena sat down on the other bed without offering any clue. Was this a test? Llyn remembered the social games of Rift Station. The stakes seemed higher here.

Stasia leaned back on both arms. "The list's too long. Mostly, he expects me to live up to the family ideals. I might've had a life of my own by now, if it hadn't been for this idiotic war."

Llyn frowned. "But I didn't—"

"I'm not blaming you. Not even the Tdegans, really. I wanted to go to Bkellan University. Mother and Father wouldn't let me."

Oh.

"You can imagine what life would've been like for you there," Rena put in.

"Look at her." Stasia pointed at Llyn. "She doesn't seem to be suffering here—"

"Llyn," Rena said firmly. "We'd be happy to show you around the estate, provided you don't mind putting up with a certain ongoing discussion. Maybe you could even shed some new light."

This promised to be fascinating. "Take me anywhere," Llyn said. "No, wait. First, I really would like to clean up."

Filip called Llyn into his private office one week after she arrived. He felt eroded by those passing days. He had probably spent more time in desperate prayer than asleep. Every Regency family had sent word to his or her system, and military recruits would arrive within three weeks to be trained for warfare—using learning programs created long ago to defend the Concord in case the Devastators attacked again, and then mothballed as decades passed and no enemy reappeared. How ironic that when an enemy came, it showed a human face.

Llyn sat down in his office, wearing a flowered housedress that looked to be one of Stasia's. It gave Llyn the look of a tiny wood nymph.

"Are you well?" he asked.

"Very well." Her face had a new luster, and she clasped her hands steadily in her lap. His chief of staff, Cilla, had reported that Llyn had carefully explained her "medical condition" and what to do if she appeared to black out. According to reports, she hadn't.

"I've had my taste of freedom and luxury." She smoothed the dress over her knees. "Thank you for both, Regent Salbari. But as much as I enjoy your family's hospitality, I don't think the delay is accomplishing anything."

He frowned. "I don't want to send you into danger."

"But you promised to send me if I asked to go. And I think that Tdega is the sphere where I am meant to serve."

He shook his head. "But is this your choice or Stasia's? I hear you've been together most of the week."

She smiled. "Stasia pushed. She wants me to test you."

"Did she say so?"

"No. But it's obvious. Still, this is my decision. Stasia …" She hesitated. "Stasia is—"

"Go ahead. I know her well." It hurt to see Gamal Casimir's daughter showing more maturity than his own. "Don't be shy. Be honest. People will admire your candor."

"All right, then. Stasia thinks she is competing with you. She doesn't realize how good a life you have given her. The sad thing is that she will only find out when she leaves you."

He rubbed his face. "I think you should stay, Llyn." He wished she would. She and Stasia were undoubtedly good for each other.

"I can't."

He glanced at his terminal. "My staff tried to trace your history on Antar this week. They came up with an opening date for the Rakaya Shasruud Laboratory, but no additional information on Shasruud herself. If she was Tdegan, your father could have sent you here to Antar to dispose of you."

"I've thought of that."

"Then why do you want to go back?" Why in all of the worlds?

"Because I want to find out who I am and what I am. I'd go publicly, wouldn't I?"

He nodded.

"Finding my family has been the only idea that was mine—not Karine's—for as long as I can remember. Here, I'm a well-treated prisoner. I expect to be a well-treated prisoner on Tdega, too. And you have said you could take steps to help ensure my safety."

"I would. But you would be far from safe." If only he could do more.

She clasped her hands in her lap. "I think my father—Regent Casimir—is likely to make me a symbol of how terrible Antar is. And, you see, once I'm there, I can speak out—carefully—and say that Antar is not terrible. That I was treated well. I know I won't end the war, sir, but I could make a difference."

He knew how deeply she wanted to feel valuable. To her, this had to look like the first real opportunity of a lifetime.

He had called her old enough to make adult decisions. He had told Karine that she must be allowed to take risks. He must believe the words he had spoken.

She spoke earnestly. "I want something to show for my life."

He hesitated. He wished he could tell her that his nephew lived with the Casimirs. Jahn could help protect her. Still, she would be questioned when she arrived. She could unwittingly betray him. Better to have Jahn seek her out. He would alert Jahn through the embassy. "I have a fast private ship available. If I send it to Tdega, that also gives me the chance to recall our Ambassador. I will not inform your father of your return until you pass Antar Gate."

"That would be excellent. Then, the ship won't be able to disappear unnoticed or have an accident, like the *Aliki.*"

He had to admire her. "You're afraid, aren't you?"

"Of course," she murmured.

"Good. You will be welcome to change your mind at any point until you pass Tdega Gate."

Karine had stayed inactive for a week, hoping to hear that Llyn hadn't made up her mind, hoping to be consulted regarding the decision. She had thought of several compelling arguments.

But not even Niklo called in.

Now that Salbari had taken Llyn away, Karine had to spend time with her fellow inmates if she wanted conversation. She detested them. During one attack drill, a woman had sneered, "Nice of them to bother protecting us," and another had answered, "Who says they'd alert us if there *was* an attack? This is just to make us complacent."

On the eighth morning, Salbari finally contacted her via text. Stripped of arrogant double-talk, it contained one vital fact.

Llyn had departed Antar.

"No!" she cried. She glared into the north. *Coward!* she thought at Filip Salbari. *You didn't dare tell me in person. You sacrificed my daughter to suit your philosophy.*

Then she lay down on her bed and sobbed. Llyn was gone, and Karine could not follow.

Not yet. The moment hostilities ceased, she would find a way to get to Tdega.

If Llyn were still alive.

For the rest of that day, she grieved. But she despised inactivity, in herself and in others. The next morning, she petitioned Facility Director Graybill for an i-net linkage.

"It's not worth much." Graybill spread his hands over his desk. "But you're welcome to it."

"It's time someone did something about that," Karine retorted.

It took two hours online to find someone who was already working on it: Professor Ochus Ysander, formerly of Nuris University. *We've sorted less than one percent of the EMP gibberish* appeared on her screen. *There's plenty of material for anyone willing to spend hours decoding.*

I have hours to spare. She jabbed each key, typing rather than dictating because it made her feel marginally better. She recognized the symptoms of deep frustration. She'd seen them dozens of times in her patients. She'd underestimated the depth of anger that accompanied this. When she returned to Lengle, she'd push her patients deeper and harder to work them through it. For the present, she would treat herself.

The mess EMP had made of Nuris University's data bank gave her a new "patient," so to speak. Professor Ysander assigned her a clump of data that looked like rubbish from several collapsed buildings. She sorted and labeled the rubbish one fragment at a time, and she transferred each labeled segment to a file someone else would attempt to reassemble. She was also assigned a "building" file into which others dumped decoded data. The work was unspeakably tedious. So much time, so little reward.

Perfect.

Filip worked around the clock for three days. The warships finally arrived through Antar Gate from Unukalhai. Goaded by Boaden, Filip processed data on strike points, provisions, armament, and a dozen other factors.

And then, with a burst of speed, the strike group—Antaran and Unukalhaian—left Antaran space for Ilzar Gate.

He stumbled into his private quarters. Favia pushed him onto their bed and shut the curtains. An overhead fan rustled floral bed hangings that Favia had designed herself. They surrounded him with brilliant pink shooting-star blossoms. "Antar's defenses are stripped," he murmured, staring at the ceiling. "What if—"

192 | KATHY TYERS

"More reinforcements are due in three days from Unukalhai," she said softly. "You have done all that you could."

"It will take seventeen days for our strike force to reach Ilzar—"

"Filip. Go to sleep."

His mind would not shut down. "I could have sent Jahn another tenpod. It might have gotten through to him while Casimir monitored the ship that's delivering Llyn. He only has four pods left. Did we do the right thing, letting her—"

"Filip," she said ominously, "enough." She slipped into bed beside him. "Creator, still his thoughts."

Clasping her hands, he shut his eyes. "Amen," he whispered.

On Karine's fifth day online, she sat down, pushed on her view-glasses, and scowled at her terminal. Why was she doing this to the exclusion of all else? She was helping Antar and the Concord, but she had gained nothing for herself. She pointed to the switch that set her display to record without transmitting, and she dictated text.

> *Regent Salbari:*
> *I am now involved in the NU Reconstruction Project. I feel that this goal would be better served if I could work from my personal terminal at Lengle. Request permission to return there.*

She studied it. Concise and to the point. Nothing would tug at Salbari's notorious sensitivity. He relied on emotion more than an administrator should. That came from his counseling experience.

She frowned at her window. She was sick of this room. Sick of it. Why not take advantage of that sensitivity, knowing it existed?

She sent the request.

Her reply arrived the next morning.

> *The choice of internment was yours. Sorting programs are available to all NURP workers at the following address. Director Graybill informs me that he would find your*

assistance invaluable. Two of his inmates show signs of impending emotional crisis. Please report to him at your first opportunity.

Karine scowled at the virtual keyboard. She had less respect daily for Director Graybill, who didn't know an emotional crisis from a temper tantrum. Now she was stuck more than ever.

Ignoring Salbari's request, she keyed up her first hour's workload. She hit a roadblock almost instantly. One data fragment keyed clean—it originated within a single transmission—yet yielded to no local sorting program. She saved it, downloaded the NURP sorting battery, and fired one program at a time at the fragment. It was only half a page long, but it refused to crack. Tempted to upload it for expert decoding, she hesitated. This could be something valuable. It might give her leverage over Filip Salbari.

She sent out a call for lingual programs. Several had survived intact at outlying terminals, where on-site and satellite schools kept printed copies. Teachers were reloading them into the world's master program.

She returned to her terminal that evening and found sixteen lingual programs listed in her menu. Normally, she would begin with the likeliest prospect. This time, smarting from conversations with the Tdegan inmates and feeling perverse, she keyed up the shortest, most fragmentary recognition program. It wasn't even an attempt to translate.

When the recognition program ran positive, she almost jumped into her display. This half page of data, still totally untranslatable, was—according to the recognition program's hypertext—a mysterious subliminal language long credited to the Devastators, or else their mysterious enemies, the Chaethe.

Karine let herself exult. Then she tackled the fragment's underlying electronic signature. Each decoding program sorted for origin by characteristic "thumbprints" left on the data by its transmission over miles or light-years. Threads of information, pulled together, pointed to its origin at ...

Sunsis? Not Tdega?

She rubbed the bridge of her nose. No Devastator artifact orbited Sunsis's primary. The system had two marginally habitable planets. Sunsis

B was too cold for open-air habitation and was colonized under a necklace of domes around its equator. Sunsis A was closer to its sun and habitable within climate control zones at both poles. All of the colonies were small, but both worlds had rich mineral resources.

Sunsis, she repeated. Probably Sunsis A, with its larger population. The significance of her discovery slowly ripened in her mind. Tdega meant to take Sunsis out of the Concord, allegedly because of its citizens' dissatisfaction, although the Concord's Regents believed the true reason was access to minerals.

But if this data fragment was recent and not archeological, there could be Devastators—or Chaethe—active in the Sunsis system.

Her exultation faded. She keyed the new i-net for more data. Nothing came up.

But plainly, the Concord's enemies were back.

And the Concord was Gate-linked so closely that it functioned like a single star system.

And Llyn had gone to Tdega.

She spent the next hour online, researching every myth, each rumor concerning Chaethe aliens. At the end of that hour, her insides roiled.

She requested a line to the Salbari estate. "Personal interview, please," she told the virtual microphone. "Filip Salbari. Double-star the request." That was the most urgent symbol of Order business, with appropriate penalties for misuse.

Filip took most of an hour getting back to her. By then, she sat cracking her knuckles.

"Karine," he said all too politely, "is something wrong? I had a second request from Director Graybill—"

"This has nothing to do with Tdegan internment, Regent Salbari. I'm coding a sublevel transmission to your printer." She'd loaded the lingual fragment. She pointed at the SEND key. "Is that something you can read?"

He reached into a printer bin she couldn't see, lifted a sheet, and scanned quickly. "No. What is it? Where did you find it?"

Smiling grimly, she told him. When she'd finished, he stroked his chin and whispered, "Creator."

It felt good to see those knitted brows. "It might explain Gamal

Casimir's erratic behavior," she said. "And you may have sent my daughter into terrible danger, if Sunsis and Tdega are influencing each other."

His projected face looked up into hers. "We have no evidence of alien activity on Tdega yet. Please don't panic."

"I am not panicking."

"Don't quibble words. Thank you for the information. We will move on it immediately."

"Speaking of moving—"

He raised an eyebrow. "Obviously, you're accomplishing more for the Concord there at Rift Station than you could contribute back at the clinic, with so many distractions. Since we remain on wartime footing, I must consider that first."

"I don't like sitting in a cage."

For some reason, he smiled for an instant. "No one does. I'm feeling caged myself. But we're both doing our jobs. I'll be in touch. Thank you." His image vanished.

She had experienced hot anger ten days ago. This time, her fury felt cold and decisive. It was time to take a step she had long avoided: lobbying other empaths to recall Filip Salbari from headship. So far as Karine Torfinn was concerned, that man had lost his manifest to lead the Empath Order.

And while she was at it, Antar needed to know about the Chaethe aliens.

17

Llyn had a hard time believing that space travel could be accomplished with a crew of four, but the transport Regent Salbari had provided—so small it had no name, simply a hull number—seemed to be leaving Antar at a good clip. The four crew members said the ship was programmed for absolute autopilot, including life support, from the time it left Antaran local space until Tdegan tugships would nose it toward an orbital station—except for a few hours on approach to Antar Gate.

Temporarily weightless, Llyn wormed upship behind the only crew woman, Lieutenant Elna Metyline. The transport's central corridor opened beside exposed pipes and conduits (mostly life support, Lieutenant Metyline explained) toward the command cabin. Engines thrummed a deep rhythm around her, and tiny gurgles ran up and down inside the conduits. Lieutenant Metyline's head, shoulders, and then her body and legs vanished through a hatch. Shutting her eyes, Llyn pushed toward it. Once certain her head had passed through, she opened her eyes again.

Two crew members sat belted into seats in front of an instrument array. Hoping to see out, Llyn craned her neck and looked for a viewscreen or porthole. The only bulkhead space that wasn't covered with instruments was flat gray metal. She didn't bother to suppress her disappointment. Hiding her feelings was no longer necessary. Karine was eight days behind her.

And she shouldn't feel so happy about that, she told the corner of her mind that was still leaping up and down, singing joyously. She owed

Karine—her accurate diagnoses, healing techniques, and perseverance—a huge debt. She could function as a human again.

But it felt fabulous to be free.

Lieutenant Metyline clung to a handhold just above Llyn's. "We'll open the visor in a minute," she said. "Just get comfortable."

Llyn groped for another handhold and slipped her wrist through it up to her elbow.

"Two minutes to Antar Gate. Mark," an officer said. His voice sounded mechanical, like a poorly coached news reader.

Llyn whispered to Lieutenant Metyline, "What does he mean?"

Lieutenant Metyline's brown hair floated around her face. She whispered back, "One minute and we'll open the visor. It's so remarkable that crews rebelled when ship designers didn't include retractable visors on early models of this antique."

Llyn returned the other woman's smile. Regent Salbari had sent her off in one of the oldest small transports in the Antaran inventory. As he told her, Tdega would tear it apart looking for new technologies. Everything on board could potentially be used against Antar.

Including its crew? They were frighteningly religious, all four of them, ultra-prepared for their own deaths—in case Gamal Casimir tried to question them or executed them outright. Llyn hated to think of her father in that light. She would've preferred to think of him as Regent Salbari with a long, thin black pigtail. But the crew obviously feared interrogation, and Lieutenant Metyline had shown her a suicide implant inside her upper jaw.

"Ten seconds," announced the same crew member. "Five. Four. Three."

He touched a control. A slit appeared in front of him. It widened as the visor slid back to reveal an unbelievable chromatic display. Llyn had seen holographic auroras over online projectors. This vista was one long curtain of red, streaked with pale rose, pink, and white. Antar Gate.

At the edge of the window, she saw part of the Gate itself. It was unreflective black, pocked and scratched but otherwise featureless, almost as dark as the space alongside it. Its workings were internal, so she had heard, protected from meteoric impacts by a surface so impenetrable that no probe had given any clue to its workings. It had been jokingly suggested that the unknown Gate builders mined an alternate universe for energy to run and maintain them. Humans had used them for three centuries with hardly a mishap, and the Devastators had left them strictly alone.

Llyn couldn't get her perspective. "Is it a meter thick or a kilometer?"

"Eight point six three kilometers," Lieutenant Metyline answered in an awed voice.

Llyn gaped. If the Gate was eight kilometers thick, then it was hundreds of kilometers across. She'd heard that approach angles varied, depending on what system a crew meant to target. Transfer would not be instantaneous. Not even information traveled from Gate to Gate simultaneously. Llyn had also read that time did not seem to pass between Gates for passengers, although ship travel took objective days. She was about to find out firsthand.

Would this little transport go *poof* like the *Aliki?*

"Secure grips." The crew member's voice sounded stressed.

"Just hold on," Lieutenant Metyline said. "You won't feel much. But watch."

Llyn clenched the metal handle and tucked both feet behind a silent conduit.

The crew member counted down. "Three, two, one, mark."

Without any hint of a purple middle state, the pale pink aurora became pale blue, still streaked with white. Llyn gulped, almost too overwhelmed to appreciate what she was seeing. This was real space, its appearance distorted by light waves and particles playing tricks at inter-Gate speed. Slowly, the streaks resolved into coldly gleaming stars. Llyn stared, crouching close to the bulkhead, as visors once again swallowed the view. Plain bulkheads enclosed the crew once more, and a wave of claustrophobia washed over her. The transport had never seemed so small.

"We're in Tdegan space now," the crew member said. "Lieutenant, take her below. We can assume we'll be challenged momentarily."

"Are you all right?" Lieutenant Metyline spoke softly.

"I will be." Llyn shut her eyes, She needed to imagine herself someplace huge. The Rift Station cafeteria popped into her mind, so she reconstructed its visual details until her head felt less light. How could it be less light when it was weightless? It wasn't, but eventually she felt more or less normal.

She opened her eyes. "Thank you," she said. "Thank you all."

The front-seater who hadn't spoken turned around and squinted at her. Huge eyes, almost all pupil and iris, bulged from his face. Seers saw too well in darkness to function comfortably planetside, but they excelled at starship navigation. "It would be a crime," he said, "to bring someone out so far and not let them experience this."

Llyn wondered what miracles of color and darkness he'd seen. Was Gate passage his equivalent of her inner-world paradise?

The crew would broadcast Regent Salbari's message momentarily. If no Tdegan challenged them, the ship would remain in free fall for a few more hours and begin deceleration. There would be gravity again. Unfortunately. Weightlessness wasn't wafting, but she liked it.

"I'm right behind you," came Lieutenant Metyline's voice. The woman had been friendly, although her religious lecturing had sounded as if she were trying to prepare Llyn to die, too—just in case.

At the bottom of this section, the crawl hole opened almost into a "room." Faint hissing noises, so soft that Llyn had to strain to hear them, distinguished the compartment from her silent cabin. She took a hand-hold and waited for Lieutenant Metyline to catch up. She considered groping for a drink bulb from the cabinet, but she decided not to bother. She wasn't that thirsty. She had tried a sip of juice an hour ago. It was too much work to drink now. She would wait until deceleration imitated gravity.

Lieutenant Metyline groped into the wide space and anchored her feet, then straightened toward Llyn at an impossible-looking angle. She looked like a hydra in Director Graybill's aquarium, glued to the glassy side with its tendrils waving out into the water. She groped at her ship suit's collar and pulled out a delicate chain. "I wanted to show you something," she said. She fumbled at the back of her neck for a moment and flung something into the cabin.

Llyn plucked it out of midair and untangled it with both hands. A triangular garnet floated on the chain. It looked all too familiar. "Oh," she said. "I've seen these."

Lieutenant Metyline's eyebrows rose. "Has anyone explained them? At the center of our sphere is a Creator who—"

"Yes. I've heard that story. Many times."

Lieutenant Metyline pulled her feet loose and pushed off so that she drifted toward Llyn. "You won't live forever. None of us do. What will you experience after you die?"

"Nothing, I assume." Despite Karine's lectures. She handed back the garnet.

"Suppose that isn't true? Suppose you are accountable—"

Oh, enough. Llyn let go of her handhold and pushed toward her cabin in the lower passage.

Lieutenant Metyline caught her by a pant leg. "Has it occurred to you that Tdega might not send out a tugship? The easiest thing in all the worlds would be to just let gravity catch us and burn us."

Llyn bumped the bulkhead beside the passageway. She turned around and shook her leg free. "It doesn't take much imagination," Llyn said, "to realize that Gate travel is dangerous. Always."

"Or they could shift us off into space. That's a major reason for sending any crew at all in a preprogrammed transport. We're supposed to be able to steer to safe haven. But there's no haven we could reach with the fuel we're carrying, not inside three systems that have seceded."

Llyn had hoped that these crew people wouldn't infect her with their pessimism. Now, worry grabbed her other pant leg and shook shivers up her spine.

She tried to shake it off as easily as she'd shaken off Lieutenant Metyline. "Karine says your faith is a matter of free choice, though she presented it as factual. But once she started giving me choices, I had to get free of her. Had to. You can't know what it was like for me."

"You're right." Lieutenant Metyline reached the next bulkhead and anchored herself by an arm. "I can't know. Nearly all empaths hold to the sphere, though."

Karine had used the same lingo. "You're an empath?" That was disquieting.

"No. I had an empath grandmother, but I didn't get the mutated gene." She sounded as if she felt cheated.

Llyn, on the other hand, felt relieved. "Thanks for your concern," she said, mentally adding, *If that's what it really is, and you're not simply recruiting.* Before the other woman could speak again, Llyn dove downship.

She was bolting the hatch of her silent cabin when she remembered that Regent Salbari wore two of the garnets. This was his view of the universe, too. Which of them lived by it, Regent Salbari or Karine?

Until she found her own sphere, she decided, she would serve Regent Salbari. *If anyone's listening,* she formed words silently, *is it all right to ask for a safe landing? I'm scared.* She pictured Regent Salbari when she imagined a higher authority. He had known she was frightened. Did everyone who finally escaped a terrible situation reach this point—when they also realized they'd left everything familiar?

She curled up and reoriented her hammock. Incredibly, this narrow space had bulkhead bolts for four of them. The crew had given her the cabin to herself, squeezing Lieutenant Metyline in with the men. Llyn hadn't paused to wonder about the arrangement. How did they find privacy?

Maybe they were so convinced they were about to die that they didn't worry about civilized details.

At the end of her module, inside a bulkhead cabinet, she'd found an AR helmet with one-eighty-degree projection capacity. Lieutenant Metyline said spacefaring crews often carried AR units to let crew members refresh themselves with a sense of open spaces. Llyn had bolted that compartment shut. She was determined not to fall back into that addiction. She'd been delivered.

Delivered, she repeated as she wrapped her hammock around her, keeping both arms free. Antar had been a womb of rebirth for human settlement, and for Llyn Torfinn. She'd never seen an infant being born, but it was reportedly both sudden and slow, joyful and anguished. Like her long, slow, and painful-at-the-end deliverance from Karine Torfinn. In that sense, she could finally think of Karine as her mother.

The cabin's other compartments held a beautiful new Tdegan wardrobe, created for her at the Salbari estate—including one of Stasia's flowered dresses, a parting gift. Maybe Stasia had felt that the next best thing to going to Tdega would be knowing her dress was worn there.

Llyn also missed Ilke and Tana. She wished she had asked if they wanted to send messages. She intended to tell Tdegan authorities about them once they started "debriefing" her, as Regent Salbari delicately described it.

Abruptly, she noticed a taut string of the hammock pinching her arm. She *felt* it. Karine's surgeon had said this might happen eventually. Artificial nerves he'd implanted at the biochip site might one day kick in and start functioning.

Delighted, she anchored herself against the other strings of her cocoon and rubbed her arm back and forth.

A voice from her bulkhead startled her. "We are being hailed and told to prepare for boarding," the crewman said. "Secure for full deceleration."

Llyn had drilled for this maneuver with the crew. She double-checked her orientation relative to shipboard g-forces, secured her hammock straps, and made sure everything was well tucked into bulkhead compartments.

So much for Lieutenant Metyline's imaginative worries.

Welcome me home, Father!

18

Filip Salbari sank into the chair in his private office. He picked up a hand-painted miniature of Favia, fingered its filigreed frame, and set it back down over his terminal.

He had asked even Favia to leave him alone this afternoon. A looter had been caught today, robbing demolished apartments in Nuris City: an empath, using his listening ability to avoid detection. Filip had synched with the looter to see if he'd made other excursions. The man had tried not to think about them, but in the end Filip discovered that this had been his fifth thievery trip in three weeks. He'd planned to make more of them. He had only been caught because he'd been momentarily distracted.

Declared and undeclared empaths who misused their abilities always vanished. The Order's laws regarding criminal actions were merciless. Filip Salbari, head of the Order, had just authorized a man's execution for a crime that would earn anyone else just a few months' imprisonment. Not even the looter's family would be notified as to what had happened to him.

Every war in history had been, in essence, suffering individuals. At least this man would not suffer pain or long anticipation. He would be given exactly enough time to make his peace with the eternal before joining it.

Filip knelt in a corner of the floor and leaned his head against both walls. He spent half an hour praying before he felt ready to pick up his burdens again. Several members of his Order had told him, over the past few years, that they'd voted to elect him because they knew he would never end another life unless the offender were unequivocally guilty. They felt safe with him as their head. He was known as compassionate.

That did not comfort him today. He remembered Athis Pallaton saying, "When your strength is finally gone, you will learn for certain that something exists beyond yourself."

He asked for strength to go on. The secrecy of his headship, besides keeping others from coveting the position, also protected him from public accusations of injustice. But why hadn't he already stepped down from one post? Exhausted, he had not searched out a candidate for either position, although Alcotte assured him that his sense of inadequacy was one sign that he knew his limitations.

Today he wanted to shed both offices.

He pushed up into the seat beside his multinet terminal, pinched the nerve that lowered his viewing implants, and pointed to his terminal's activation switch. No matter how inadequate he felt, he must stay current.

Sitting at his command station in Bkellan Defense Base's battle center, Gamal Casimir also watched a virtual board. When he moved his head, he momentarily perceived its three-dimensional imagery.

An antique Antaran ship had cleared Tdega Gate two days ago. Immediately it had sent a widebeam transmission over Tdega's general communications net: allegedly, it carried his daughter, Luene. Antar had its revenge for Bellik's public-channel announcement. Now, he couldn't even sequester the girl until he found out what she had become.

… If this was Luene. The reader balanced on his left knee would tell him momentarily. Twenty minutes ago, the fast transport that was bringing the woman—and four Antaran crew members—had broadcast a gene sequence. Casimir had relayed that sequence to the Residence. Logan Jackson would cross-match it with Luene's sequence of record.

If this was Luene, how had the Antarans discovered her identity? He had left no trail linking the name with her. All of the other children in his experiment died, despite his confidence that it would succeed.

He'd sent Luene—what was left of her—to Nuris, in case he needed to "discover" her there and accuse the Concord of kidnapping, corroborating the story he released on Tdega. He'd been led to believe she, too, had died. Hadn't his agent on site reported "experiment terminated" five years ago?

She could have been hospitalized for those five years. Whatever killed the other children had surely affected her. Over on Antar, mentally disturbed patients were often given to the mutant empathic healers.

He rubbed his chin. Empaths. There were also empath intelligence agents. Antar obviously had operatives here. One of those could have recently ferreted out information linking Luene with the woman who would arrive at Bkellan Base tomorrow. That would imply a deep-cover agent with access to privileged data. Casimir must alert Zavijavah's staff—

Unless the operative was on Zavijavah's staff?

Disquieted, he touched the VTT button on his reader and held it to his mouth. "Zavijavah only. Rerun full background checks on all Security employees. Report any connection with Antar or the Empath Order."

As he set down the reader, its corner light blinked. He touched another panel. A message appeared: "100% positive cross-matching."

Then this was his lost daughter, young Luene. Really, retesting her—with samples that Casimir would watch from draw to screen test to display—would be only another formality. Antar would not have sent her unless they were confident of her identity.

Somehow.

Was she crippled? Functional? Cogent? Could she even walk?

He set his reader on the virtual board and paced out into the battle center. Occupying the top floor of a hexagonal tower, it had a magnificent view of Bkellan's rooftops and streets. It had been the first room on the former Outwatch Base that Gamal modernized, including a central non-polarized view display. Over its projector hovered another multidimensional image of Tdega Gate and the ships that surrounded it. As he walked past, images shifted in its depth.

A sharp whistle announced the arrival of another command-level officer. Gamal eyed the main door.

Bellik marched through, uniformed as usual. He pumped a fist as he walked. Gamal imagined the boy holding a swagger stick. It would be precisely the prop for him.

Bellik glanced around and strode over. Gamal had asked him to report in person. He'd ordered another takeover but left Bellik free to organize that operation.

Bellik snapped off a salute.

Oh, pipe down, Bellik. "How did it go?" Gamal asked softly.

"The Antaran embassy is now occupied by our people." Bellik remained at attention. "There was no difficulty. We have the Ambassador in custody—"

"Where?"

"This base. Secure quarters. Only my people saw him arrive."

"Good. If anyone attempts to contact him at the embassy, notify me immediately."

"That goes without saying. We also found the embassy coding room."

"Ah," Gamal said. "The home link."

"Exactly." Bellik pursed his lips. "There have been spies among us."

Obviously. "I assume you put our top people to work on the coding circuits."

"Naturally." Bellik pointed around the battle center. "Any news—?"

"This woman's gene sequences match your cousin's."

Bellik was uncharacteristically silent.

"Why does that bother you?"

Bellik frowned. "I remember having my grades compared with hers, even when she was ten years behind me."

And of course, that nettled Bellik. Bellik's father had been a comparable menace to Gamal. "We don't know what effect the immersion will have had on her."

"What are you talking about?"

Gamal turned away to keep Bellik from seeing his embarrassment. Bellik knew nothing about that experiment—or the Chaethe. So far. "She has been immersed in Antaran culture for many years," he answered with a shrug. Bellik was too self-absorbed, too incurious to catch a lie. "They might have harmed her."

For an instant, Bellik stared as if he wanted to ask another question. He must have decided that would've been beneath his dignity. "I will be in my office, entering my final report regarding the embassy." He pivoted on a heel and headed for the door.

Another alert whistle sounded. Osun Zavijavah strode in, sporting a new bandage on his left hand. He must have had another freckle removed. Bellik dodged him on his way out.

Gamal walked to the middle of the room and met Zavijavah beside a projectech's terminal. "How do you feel?" Gamal asked.

Zavijavah smoothed his mustache. "Good enough." He touched his right ear. "Four weeks."

"I haven't forgotten. I can get you to Sunsis in fourteen subjective days. We'll leave at the earliest opportunity." He would not give Alun to the Chaethe without accompanying him to Sunsis, but he did not want to leave Bellik behind, in charge of the military. Bellik might get ideas.

"Is that your daughter?" Zavijavah asked.

He'd lost her twice. Now she was back in his grasp. "It looks that way."

"Will you make her a Regent?"

Gamal folded his hands. "Possibly. We have no idea if she will be mentally capable." He had loved her, in his way. He would enjoy having her home again, if she was still the same sweet child. He would take good care of her.

Was there a chance of recovering his talented, doting daughter?

Admiral Gehretz Lalande relaxed in the command chair of his Concord destroyer *Fire Dance,* glad it had taken eighteen days to reach Ilzar. He'd needed most of that time to convince his crew of mostly nonmilitary volunteers that they really must follow orders.

In the crunch, they had done as he'd told them. His electronic warfare ship had remained in front of Ilzar Gate relay, jamming all signals. The rest of his battle group had swooped down on Ilzar itself, five days from the Gate. Tdegan forces in residence hadn't even scrambled. They must have thought the cowed Concord would not strike back. Only two small Tdegan cruisers had been in orbit, guarding a freighter loaded with strategic denzite ore.

Lalande commanded twelve ships, nine from Antar and three from Unukalhai. All were older and slower than the Tdegan cruisers, but the commanders opposing him had proved they couldn't think in three-dimensional space or rotate their sense of "up" and "down." Maybe they hadn't played enough immersive AR games. Lalande had always contended that the Outwatch needed to train ten-year-olds, not twenty-year-olds.

The Tdegan cruisers had managed one significant counter-stroke, dispatching a scout ship to disable the EW jamming ship that remained in Gate position. Now the damaged Tdegan cruisers drifted, broadcasting on too many frequencies for the *Fire Dance* to disrupt. Still, by the time those signals reached Tdega, Lalande's flotilla should be reinforced by Ilzaran resistance or else headed back toward Ilzar gate.

When Lalande surveyed planetside damage from Tdega's missile attack through cloud-penetrating scanners, his mission lost all resemblance to a game. No one would be able to hold the Concord together if Gamal Casimir slammed another world with the missiles that had blasted those craters into Ilzar's western seacoast.

One of his commtechs called, "We're getting a message from below."

"Receive," said the deck officer.

A projector dangled from an overhead metal support. Three holograms appeared below it, two men and a woman who stood facing him. All three looked young and athletic.

"Thank you," the smaller man exclaimed. "We cannot thank you enough. How can we support your efforts?"

More youngsters. Lalande glared at his transmission pickup. "Tell me. Did the Syyke City Council really vote to secede from the Concord along with Tdega?"

"Never," the woman growled. "That is a lie. Tdegan troops in Syyke are holding most of the Council hostage, but we will not surrender."

Then it had been as Lalande suspected. Ilzar would prefer to remain in the Concord. "I assume you will need help dealing with Tdegan troops groundside."

She nodded vigorously. "We will. I escaped the city, but many didn't. Tdega has demanded overtime production. The ore concentrators are running around the clock, and until today we were launching five or six shuttle loads to orbit daily. If I were Gamal Casimir, I'd send my shining new fleet straight to Ilzar and try to catch the Concord flotilla getting resupplied."

The tall man raised a hand. "Casimir has held his fleet close to Tdega Gate for some time."

This wasn't really news. Lalande had dispatched a scout drone through Tdega Gate. He would barely have time to prepare an ambush. If he was lucky. If these elementary children on his crew kept following orders. If Casimir stayed busy at home for two or three days. "You have one ore ship already loaded, is that correct? May we buy it in the name of the Concord and pay you when the war ends?"

"I suppose so." The woman looked puzzled.

So did Lalande's deck officer when Lalande cut the connection and turned aside. "What are you going to do with a load of denzite ore?"

Lalande evicted a commtech from the nearest terminal and confiscated his view-glasses. He slid them on, pointed his way into the file that he wanted, and studied the image of Ilzar Gate that appeared. "We brought along seven ship-killing mine charges and four detection fields. Using ore to fill the gaps with gravel clouds, we can block traffic into and out of Ilzar system."

"Doesn't that waste ore?"

"No, it's perfect. With the Ilzarans' extraction technology, they will be able to clean up the cloud within five or ten years. And it's already up in orbit."

"What about peaceful ships, though?" The DO's wide blue eyes made him look alarmed. "They'll come through the Gate and—"

"We'll lay our barriers far enough from the Gate that a ship traveling at conventional speed will have enough time to see them, slow down, and stop for inspection. But a warship will destroy itself. We will hang off to one side, wait, and challenge any survivors."

He signaled a Kocaban woman who sat at her comm station. "I need a message relayed to Antar. We can't wait for advice, but we can warn home what happened here and what we're going to do. Tell them to stand ready in case Tdega retaliates there."

19

Tdegans in formal dress clustered near a platform along the magnificent, wood-floored reception hall's east wall. Several rows of heads separated Jahn and Alun from the platform. Most of the men sported thin, dignified black queues, and the women showed as much variety of hairstyle as Jahn would have expected at a formal Antaran affair.

A gold curtain on the back of the platform hid a door. Whispers echoed a silent excitement that Jahn heard full volume when he touched people around him with a shallow synch. Was she genuine? Had she been a prisoner? What would she be like?

Filip Salbari must have located Luene shortly after Jahn's report arrived. Tonight's festivities resulted from his own agency, which gave him a sense of professional satisfaction. Still, he worried. Gamal Casimir's daughter would have been safer on Antar.

She'd arrived at Bkellan Base three days ago. Jahn and Alun had stood with a crowd as a shuttle settled to the ground behind a metal barricade. A slight young woman had appeared on the shuttle ramp, wearing Tdegan clothing, standing beside a woman in Outwatch blue-gray. She waved hesitantly.

The four Outwatch personnel vanished immediately as Luene was whisked to the Residence clinic. Jahn and Alun followed in a Residence maglev, speeding and jumping drive grooves like University students between terms. Then they waited in the grand hall with other staff. Medic

Jackson emerged a few minutes later to announce that gene testing had proved the girl was unquestionably Luene Casimir.

Then she had vanished again, probably closeted with her father and his aides for a grueling debrief. Now guards stood outside Siah Casimir's former suite, down the hall from Alun's, but neither Jahn nor Alun had glimpsed her again.

Perhaps Gamal Casimir had secluded her—or worse—and was presenting someone else tonight, a substitute.

Bellik Casimir mounted the platform and strutted toward the gold curtain's center, dressed in full formal blacks. They made him look like an unlit shadow beneath the tiers of light rods.

Next, Gamal stepped out from between two guards at the center of the long gold curtain, resplendent in his own gold-trimmed blacks. Gamal had declared himself Commander of Tdegan Forces several weeks ago, but tonight he appeared in the dazzling new uniform for the first time.

"Can we get closer?" Alun asked. For three days, he'd seemed almost desperate to see his cousin.

"I think so." Jahn edged forward. Alun followed like a puppy. He looked gawky, all arms and legs, in his cutaway jacket. Even after all these weeks, Jahn felt equally conspicuous wearing clothing that fit so snugly.

Alun's attention span and vocabulary had improved so much that they would be hard-pressed to conceal his progress much longer. Alun took enormous pleasure in surprising people, so Jahn had explained the need to "dumb up" as a long, complex prank to be sprung on Uncle Gamal. Tonight's socialization would test Alun's resolve and maturity to their limits.

Jahn looked for Antar's gray-haired Ambassador. Several days ago, online news interpretations coming out of the embassy had been cut off. Jahn suspected a Tdegan takeover. That made any attempt to contact the Ambassador perilous, and the man would have attended this presentation if possible. He must be a prisoner, or in hiding, or dead, so Jahn must find another way to get news from Antar.

He'd also better urge Kai Oldion to find them both a way offworld.

Gamal Casimir stepped to the edge of the platform. Bellik swaggered up behind him and posed at attention.

"This is a joyous day." Casimir's voice seemed to come from all four walls. He plainly wore a vocal amplifier somewhere amid the gold hard-ware on his uniform.

The crowd quieted. Ignoring Alun for a moment, Jahn tried to synch with Casimir, but too many excited people stood between them, creating too much emotional noise.

Alun glanced up at his uncle, then around him. He bent to whisper, "This is embarrassing. People are staring at me. They think I'm an idiot."

"You're getting better every day," Jahn whispered back. "Never forget that he still wants to make you a Regent. When the time comes, they'll see what you really are."

"I'll be all right," Alun muttered. "I will be all right." He squared his shoulders.

Casimir kept both hands at his sides and called, "My daughter Luene has returned. You remember the charlatans who kidnapped her, pretend-ing to offer the best education in Concord space. You have heard that she has been sent home.

"This is an obvious ploy on the part of Antar and the Concord. It sickens us to think that they imprisoned her for so long. We also had word early today of an Antaran strike at our Hegemony ally world of Ilzar."

Voices grumbled. Jahn had heard this last night, over the Residence i-net, and he'd kept abreast of the counter-preparations Bellik and Gamal were making. The first counterstroke would occur at Ilzar, but Antar would also be targeted. He'd sent Salbari his eighth pod this afternoon while Alun napped. In his report, he'd requested a second tenpod. Soon.

Gamal raised a hand. "We will keep you informed. But now, please welcome the prisoner who has been freed. She will be presented by my grandfather, Head Regent of Bkellan University, Donson Casimir." Gamal stepped backward, applauding.

Alun beat his hands together, wildly enthusiastic. Around Jahn, people clapped and whispered. Head Regent Donson hadn't made a public appearance in three years. Jahn had heard the commotion five weeks ago, when the old man nearly died. Donson's stroke that night probably had spared Jahn from a full investigation.

Donson tottered up the platform steps, assisted by two guards in dark red, one on either arm. The applause seemed to batter the old man. Donson had been a peacemaker, though proud and independent. Jahn wondered whether he remembered that his grandson Gamal had attacked the Concord.

Donson freed his arms from his helpers and lifted both hands, grinning toothily. "My great-granddaughter," he said in a thin amplified voice, "is lovelier than I remembered. Please welcome her back. Come forward, Luene."

Red-coated Security men drew the gold curtains apart. The slight woman Jahn had spotted on the shuttle ramp, or else an excellent double, stepped through. Almost a head shorter than either Security guard, she looked slim, awed—childlike, in a long white formal gown. Her hair hung loose over her shoulders, barely waved at the ends. She seemed to be dragging her feet along the platform. Jahn sympathized, remembering his early days in Tdegan gravity.

Luene walked to the old Head Regent and kissed his cheek. She curtsied to her father, holding both of her hands low along the gathers of her long dress. Finally, she waved a white-gloved arm out into the room.

"She's pretty," Alun murmured, "for a skinny woman."

A thought struck Jahn like sunlight and woke him up. Alun wanted to court his cousin! That was a perfectly normal development. "Let's get you closer." Jahn tried to push forward, but the press had thickened. Stepping back, he nudged Alun. "You know, we'll see her at the Residence. These others won't have that chance."

Alun grinned. "You're right."

"You could leave flowers beside her door," Jahn whispered. "Make her wonder who they came from."

Alun blinked and frowned. "No," he murmured, "I don't think so."

"She might think someone else left them?"

"Yes." Alun glared up at the platform.

Bellik, Donson, Gamal, Luene, and two other dignitaries from Bkellan University's Board of Regents had formed a reception line. That seemed like heavy pressure to subject Luene to so soon after a long voyage. "Maybe they'd let us cut the line," Alun suggested. "I'm family."

"Then you should uphold family dignity." Jahn grasped Alun's arm. Alun blinked at Luene, stared, and blinked again.

"Are you remembering something?" Jahn asked.

"I'm not sure." Alun looked away.

Torn between Alun's desire to get closer and his own dislike of lines, which rarely formed in a terminal-based society, Jahn hesitated. The line was almost fifty persons long before he let Alun drag him in.

A fiftyish woman wearing a formal blue gown stepped up behind them. Jahn greeted her somberly and offered his arm. That was the proper gesture to make when joining an unaccompanied woman on Tdega.

She waved him off. "I was fending for myself before you were born. Who are you?"

Her independent attitude surprised him. She acted almost Antaran. "Jahn Korsakov. Residence aide to Vice Regent Casimir and Alun Casimir." Jahn touched Alun's shoulder. "And you, madam?"

"Rhetta Baranak, professor emeritus. They retired me last year, but I stay active in University recruiting. That bought me a ticket tonight. What do you think of the girl?"

Jahn shuffled forward a few steps. He could barely see Luene's white gown between the heads and shoulders of other curious greeters. He shrugged. "There's not much to think yet. I wish she'd said something."

"Ah," said Professor Baranak. "Be careful. Remember, Gamal Casimir doesn't like his women to speak in public. Bad memories."

That eldest daughter must have been trouble. Step by step, Jahn, Alun, and the professor approached the platform. At the stairs along its south edge, Residence guards swept weapon scanners up and down Alun and Jahn. They waved Professor Baranak toward them. "Silly," she said, scolding. "Where would I hide a gun—and what for? Ideas are more powerful than armament."

Jahn pivoted on the steps and faced forward. A Residence staffer introduced him to a University Fellow, who in turn presented another Fellow. Jahn synched briefly with each. Both were bored, but Casimir required this charade. A few more hours and it would end—and then, the second one believed, no one would hear from Luene Casimir again.

Jahn frowned. He'd heard nothing about Luene from Filip Salbari, but with the embassy link cut, he must wait for word from other sources and use his best judgment. His instinct was to protect Luene from the other Casimirs.

Gamal clasped Jahn's hand disinterestedly and reached with his eyes for Professor Rhetta Baranak. Jahn wondered whether they knew each other, or if Gamal Casimir merely found her attractive.

Head Regent Donson Casimir stood beyond Gamal. He took Jahn's hand with a surprisingly powerful grip for a man who had almost died five weeks ago. "What was your name?"

"Jahn Korsakov. I'm young Alun's tutor." Jahn smiled warmly at the old man, a relic in the flesh.

Then Luene Casimir's stance caught his eye. She stood like an Antaran woman. They grew up wearing culottes, coached by their mothers to tilt their hips away from anyone watching. She posed into the line of well-wishers, looking up at Alun with her head slightly cocked, as if she found hearing Alun more important than seeing him.

Jahn worked into synchrony. Beneath her rehearsed poise, Luene bounced between conflicting feelings, evidently unable to experience two simultaneously. One moment she felt terrified of making a mistake. The next moment she rejoiced, ecstatic about having gained her freedom.

Had she truly been a prisoner? Had she so hated Antar?

On second thought, her relief focused on a shadowy individual. Someone had made her life miserable—

Abruptly he realized he was sinking deeper into her emotions than surface synch ought to allow. He pulled back and concentrated on looking alert. That kind of mistake in this kind of public situation could destroy his cover.

Her face delicately mirrored Gamal Casimir's, particularly her lively, intelligent eyes. He dismissed the worry that Casimir might have secluded the real Luene.

She clasped his hand silently.

Professor Baranak bumped his right side. "My turn," she said. "Hello, Luene. Welcome to—"

Jahn hadn't even spoken. Quickly, he said, "Luene, I'm Jahn Korsakov of Residence Staff. I hope to see you again soon."

He stepped along the platform and followed Alun off the other side. He'd heard of empaths occasionally being pulled into deep synch. If her mind used the same inner frequencies as his, he would be able to listen in on her thoughts almost effortlessly.

The thought made him uneasy.

He and Alun passed a group involved in lively debate. Jahn caught the word "parasite" and understood. Two days ago, word had arrived via Gate relay that Antar had been stirred like a roaches' nest. Rumors were flying, though no source had been identified. Those rumors sent Tdegans to their superior i-net for information, and a name surfaced: Chaethe, the aliens the Devastators allegedly feared. Data was sketchy but sensationally gruesome, including the notion of parasitism.

Jahn spotted Osun Zavijavah standing near a refreshment station. Jahn had wondered, hearing that rumor, whether Zavijavah's odd extra frequency meant he carried an alien parasite. But he'd synched several times with the Security Chief since the fire-room encounter, and he'd heard nothing unusual.

So that might be a dead end.

"Alun!" A stout young man in a yellow shirt clutched Alun's arm. "Remember me? I'm Jojo. Jojo Sarkish."

Alun punched the newcomer's shoulder. "No, I don't remember you, but I'll bet you were my friend."

Jahn stayed long enough to make sure that Jojo Sarkish was genuinely friendly and that Alun didn't seem likely to forget himself and speak too intelligently. It could put him in serious danger. Jahn relinquished his student to old friends and walked around the room's perimeter, trying to look as if the crowd fascinated him. He was searching for the Antaran Ambassador.

He didn't spot the man, but he did find Luene. She stood next to her other cousin, Bellik, who kept her within touching distance. She was trying to converse with five other men and women, including Professor Rhetta Baranak. Each time Luene struggled for words, Bellik suggested several.

Alun was right. He had competition.

Jahn eased into that circle next to Professor Baranak, who passed him a plate of hors d'oeuvres. He chose a tiny sandwich with a dozen thin layers and sent the tray along.

The man on the other side of Professor Baranak was asking a question. Jahn caught only the last few words, "...in your Nuris University studies?"

"I had not applied to University." Luene's voice had a faint melody that wasn't an Antaran accent. "Anyway, Nuris University was destroyed. I thought you knew."

The man who had asked the question spluttered. Bellik laughed.

Jahn bit his flaky sandwich and took a deep mental breath of Luene's feelings. They'd settled on one sensation. She felt like an insect pinned to a card, and she was particularly uncomfortable standing close to Bellik Casimir.

Jahn listened next to Rhetta Baranak, ascertained her inner frequency, and tugged her toward nexus. She glanced at him. He tilted his head toward the long glass doors along the north wall and raised an eyebrow toward Luene.

The professor marched forward. Jahn kept close to her side as she slipped an arm through one of Luene's. "This is too much for the girl," Professor Baranak said. "Luene, you look drained. Would you like to slip out for a breath of air?"

Luene's eyes went wide. She looked as if she'd been dying of thirst and someone offered her a liter of cold water. "Please."

Jahn hurried to pass the tall older woman and the thin young one, opened one of the glass doors, and followed the women out onto the porch. "I won't ask questions, child," Professor Baranak said. "You've probably had enough to last all night."

"Thank you." Luene sighed. She glanced back and up at Jahn.

He spoke quickly but softly. "Jahn Korsakov. Residence staff. I tutor your cousin Alun."

"Oh, yes." Her almost-smile vanished. "Bellik's brother."

"Yes, but Alun isn't pushy. I hope to introduce you soon. Another day. We live in Residence."

She finally smiled. Jahn would have loved to synch and find out whether her happiness was eagerness or relief, but he held back.

"Is Bellik always like this?" she asked. Jahn noted she was careful not to define "this."

"Be careful of him." Professor Baranak spoke quietly. "He wants two things. Control, and information so he can control people better."

"Oh." Concern lines appeared between her eyes. Her nose wrinkled. "I've known people like that."

"I don't see Bellik often," Jahn said. "But I guarantee you'll see him as often as you allow it."

The wrinkles spread to her forehead.

"Just don't allow what you don't enjoy." Professor Baranak glanced back into the room. "Haven't you had boys chasing you for the last few years?"

She looked down at the stone porch. "I've been isolated."

Chilled, Jahn asked the dreaded question. "Were you really a prisoner?"

"In a way." She shrugged. "Father has asked me not to say more."

Only vaguely reassured, Jahn stared at her eyes. Large, brown, and alert, they were edged by delicate lashes. She looked back steadily. Again he listened for her inner mind, drawn into a deep and pleasant synch. "I'm sorry," he said. "We didn't mean to bother you with questions. You need a rest." Her stress and fear were not quieting, even after she'd escaped the crowd. "You're under pressure right now."

She took a deep, slow breath. "I know. Thank you for the warning, Gen Korsakov. And thank you both for helping me escape for a minute."

She stepped away. Jahn glanced down, off the narrow porch, and caught a whiff of something blooming. He wanted to pick her a blossom to complement her delicacy. Tdegan greenery had deeply impressed him when he first came from Antar.

But not tonight. He touched Professor Baranak's shoulder, excused himself, and walked back inside. He'd better check on Alun and get away from this lovely young temptation. He'd gleaned some of Luene's history by synching with Residence Medic Jackson earlier today. He knew of three empaths who operated emotional disturbance clinics. He would have been glad to escape one of those, too.

Whether at a clinic or locked into the AR before that, she'd missed learning to interact with other human beings. He thought he could understand her fearfulness tonight, her desire to escape the reception, and her bewilderment with Bellik Casimir's overpowering ways.

Maybe in a day or two Jahn could talk with her about Antar. She obviously felt homesick. He could say that he'd visited—

No. His cover story did not include any trips to Antar. He had separated himself from Antar as much as was humanly possible.

And he must keep it that way.

Stars. Thousands of them!

Llyn breathed deeply. The garden smelled like exotic perfume, and it sounded as if thousands—millions—of night insects were calling each other. Truly, Tdega was a garden world.

Still, she felt heavy and weary. She'd napped at first sunset today, but reading about Tdega's double day cycle was a far cry from living through it.

This was not home yet.

Sensitized to manipulation, she had immediately recognized it in her father. She'd only been here two days, so she must give him a longer chance ... yet she'd been warned again and again about the dangerous Casimir family. As soon as she knew enough about Tdega to get by on her own, she would like to move out of the Residence and settle in a safer place. Then, she could debunk Tdegan propaganda about her having been kidnapped by Antar.

She hadn't been allowed to visit Lieutenant Metyline, which worried her when she remembered to think about it.

Her father had put on a kindly face as he asked about her encounters with Regent Salbari. He'd asked dozens of questions about Rift Station, which she could interpret as concern for his citizens interned there. Her "debriefing," as Regent Salbari had predicted it, hadn't been as much of an ordeal as she'd anticipated.

Is this what I was born to do? she asked the stars. *Does it have to be this lonely?* She ran a hand along the porch's concrete rail. She had to push down to feel it, but she did manage an impression of roughness. Then she looked up again. The sky sparkled like jeweled velvet.

Seeing the stars reminded her of Regent Salbari and their flight together. He had also shown them to her. She wished he had come here, but she understood now that he didn't dare.

She lifted her hand. Rubbing the rail had turned it red, but it wasn't scraped. Her tactile sense had become stronger.

Well. She drew a deep breath of the fragrant night. That Tdegan man had been right. She needed to calm down. Her inner self longed to escape all this stress, and she knew where it would try to hide. She couldn't let it. She had requested that no music be played at the reception. With the cacophony of voices in there, no one would've heard music, anyway. The tumult echoed off every reflective surface. The hall's only acoustically deadening features had been human bodies and high tiers of light rods, and she hadn't missed the fact that the higher rods became smaller. She rarely missed geometric details.

Men wearing pigtails had looked odd at Nuris University. Surrounded by them tonight, she felt vaguely threatened. Again she wished that Karine had given her more of a social education.

Yet in one way, she had. Llyn had instantly recognized Karine's need to control people, made darker and stronger, in her father and her cousin. Professor Baranak hadn't intimidated her, though. Neither had the Tdegan man who'd been with her. His voice had soothed.

She stared out at the garden. Lights glimmered, creating green patches surrounded by darkness. She wondered how many of the fragrant plants and chirruping insects were native to Tdega, how many were imported from Earth, and how many were genetically engineered. Also, how Tdega's human settlers had imposed a stable ecology on such a wild, fertile world.

She turned around. Professor Baranak still leaned against the Residence's outer wall, looking up at the stars, but the man had gone inside.

She probably should, too. She strolled back along the porch. Professor Baranak pushed away from the wall. "Feeling better, Gen'n Luene?"

She must get used to that name. "This is difficult for me. I haven't spent much time in public situations."

"You'll probably learn to cope quickly. You were a brilliant child."

"Was I?" Llyn clasped her hands. "I don't remember."

"You had one of the brightest young minds on Tdega. I think it's still there." Professor Baranak straightened the waist of her long gown. "There's no rush to go back inside, if you're not ready. They've all had a look at you. Now they just want to talk to each other."

Was she ready? Did she feel human enough to face that mob again?

To her surprise, she did.

"I feel much better, actually. I'd like to rejoin the party."

Gamal Casimir touched Jahn's shoulder as Jahn walked Alun past him. "A word with you, please."

Disquieted, Jahn excused himself to Alun and followed Casimir toward a corner. Regent Gamal might have been told about his excursion outdoors with Luene. Jahn wasn't about to offer any details unless asked.

"You'll be speaking with my daughter regularly," Casimir said once they were alone. "She needs tutoring as much as Alun does if she's going to function in Tdegan society."

"That makes sense," Jahn murmured, masking his delight. Did this mean—?

"I will send you to evaluate her education soon. She will challenge you, Korsakov." He turned away.

Jahn spotted Alun standing near the platform, watching Luene from a distance. Jahn sneaked up behind him and whispered loudly, "Alun."

His student spun around, spotted him, and smiled. "What?" he asked in a deep, mocking voice.

"Your Uncle Gamal has decided that Luene should join our lessons."

"Lessons?" Alun beamed, openmouthed. "Jahn, that's—that's perfect."

Luene stood near the bottom of the platform steps, talking with two elegantly dressed young women. Donson Casimir beckoned her up onto the platform. Mounting the steps, abruptly she froze in a straight-ahead stare. The rigidity lasted only a few seconds.

Then she tumbled backward into Bellik Casimir's arms.

"Luene?" Alun whimpered.

The crowd pushed forward, taking Jahn with it. Donson Casimir cried out for help. A Security employee shoved through, shouting, "Get back. Give her air. She's not used to this much attention."

Nor this much gravity, Jahn guessed. He planted both feet to slow his forward momentum, shouldered into the front circle, and slid toward synchrony. Was she conscious?

As before, she drew him deep. She was not seeing this room, but she was mentally active, deep in an uncannily vivid, weird dream.

Bellik lifted her in his arms and carried her around the platform's side toward a service door.

"What happened?" Alun bit his lower lip and watched Bellik take his cousin away.

Jahn shook his head. "You saw what I saw. She fell down. Bellik caught her. That's all I know for certain. I think she wasn't over her long trip yet." And what else?

"I hope the Antarans didn't do something terrible to her." Alun frowned.

Jahn wanted to follow Luene into the clinic, but he'd already drawn the attention of Residence Security, and Luene's return surely suggested a leak in Gamal Casimir's information-flow pipeline.

So he stood with Alun and worried.

Llyn roused through a grid-lined fog, mortified to have lost control after all. Obviously she hadn't relaxed enough, and she must have heard some tinkle of glassware, someone whistling to signal a friend. Or something.

Subdued masculine voices came to her first: her father's, and the Residence medic's. Next, she focused her eyes. She lay in a small room with medical-electronic walls, one of which wasn't quite ninety degrees from the others. She'd endured an examination and a battery of immunizations here two days ago. Immigrants from thin-air worlds might carry all kinds of mutant infections, and so they worried Tdegan medics.

Evidently the medical staff had pulled off her constricting formal clothing, because now she wore a loose hospital gown. The gown and her soft sheets made an eerie but pleasant sensation against her skin.

Two days ago, she had told Medic Jackson how to bring her around, "just in case." It had been embarrassing, but now she was glad she had done it.

Her father stood talking softly with Medic Jackson.

Her father. His long cheekbones fascinated her. So did his thin, dignified queue and the keenly intelligent look to his eyes. Laughing, those eyes were beautiful. Narrowed now, they looked hostile, if she read him right.

"Father?" she croaked.

He turned toward her, frowning. "Are you all right, Luene?" At least he sounded concerned. He didn't seem to blame her for having a flashback, the way Karine always did.

She pulled a deep breath. "I'm all right. I'm sorry. I've had these odd episodes ever since the AR."

He sat down on a stool close to her head and leaned toward her. His heavy eyebrows lowered so far that he almost squinted. "What do you remember about the AR? What is your oldest memory?"

Through three days of questioning, he'd touched on her inner world but kept a cautious distance. Now—now that she'd humiliated him in front of his friends, staff, and officers—he must have stopped worrying about losing dignity in front of her. She'd lost all her own.

She wondered how Karine would interpret his behavior, as well as hers. Then she chased the question out of her mind like a dedo from the kitchen. She must manage this situation. Karine Torfinn lived a twenty-day journey away.

"I remember colors," she sighed. "And music. Musical notes have triggered several of my flashbacks. Particularly if they're spaced in a seventeen-tone scale."

"What's a seventeen-tone scale?"

Llyn tried to explain. "Most of our music divides each octave into twelve half-steps—"

"How does that make you faint on the stairs?"

Again, she had the sense that his concern was not for her well-being. She clasped her hands over the thin sheet. "If I heard something clink or someone's speech inflection that was at an interval from the seventeen-tone scale, it could have triggered the flashback. I was stressed, Father, and stress seems to make me vulnerable. I'm truly sorry."

"That was why you asked not to have music played?"

She nodded.

"What else do you remember about the AR?"

She explained it in loving detail: the grid lines, the playful geometrics, the sense of wafting. He listened with obvious interest. His beneficence went to her head like a flight through the grid. Maybe she'd misjudged him.

Maybe if Karine had tried to make her happy in the outer world, there would have been fewer relapses.

Abruptly glancing up, Llyn spotted her father's Security Chief. Gen Zavijavah stood at the doorway. He'd dropped in occasionally during the past two days. She'd never seen a man wear dark glasses indoors, and she wondered what he was hiding. What she could see of his face looked distinguished, like an e-net actor's. When he'd bent close at the receiving line, though, he had smelled like strange medicine. And he acted erratically.

"Father?" She pointed over his shoulder. "Gen Zavijavah is here. I think he wants to talk to you—"

"No." Zavijavah stepped into the room. "I was fascinated. Please go on." His voice seemed oddly slurred.

Her father eyed him, momentarily looking like Karine conducting a synch examination. Zavijavah drew back, looking guilty, or frightened, or ... Actually, she couldn't interpret his expression.

Her father turned back to her, and now he smiled again. "Go on," he urged. "Gen Zavijavah is interested in your inner world, too."

She distrusted his abrupt change of voice. "That's about all," she said. "It was a land of pure pleasure for me. I never accomplished anything there, but there was no need to accomplish anything. Karine said it made me lazy."

"I don't like what you've told me about this 'Karine.' I also dislike the fact that Antar forced you to live with an empath."

Feeling guilty for having maligned Karine again, Llyn shrugged. "She wasn't as kind as she might have been. She tried to control me instead of letting me learn things. But still, she is a gifted clinician. She taught me—"

"You could have learned from someone compassionate."

If only! "True. Still, I didn't realize how much she'd taught me until she wasn't around."

"Ah," he said. "But if she succeeded, she did so because you are a brilliant young woman. You were always brilliant."

Professor Baranak had said the same thing. Had that been her reputation? What would she have been by now if she'd been allowed to live normally? Maybe she could have helped keep the Concord from going to war.

Or she might have disappeared, like her brother Siah—or been executed like the others.

She should try and find Siah. He might take her in.

Arching her eyebrows, she whispered, "Thank you. I don't remember anything before the AR unit. Are there records from my childhood? Pictures? Could I see them?"

He glanced away, pursing his lips, then looked back down at her. "I may be too busy over the next few weeks. Antar is being as difficult with me as it was with you. But I'll check on you, and Gen Zavijavah will keep you safe from outsiders." He pointed at his small, handsome aide.

Gen Zavijavah tipped his head toward her. Even from that angle, she couldn't see his eyes.

"All right," she said softly. She would not let Gen Zavijavah intimidate her. She had her own set of rooms now, and a full-time servant. She could order even Gen Zavijavah away if he bothered her.

Incredible.

Gamal walked back out into the hallway. Zavijavah followed.

He must direct more energy toward finding the security leak that brought Luene home, glad as he was to see her. Every Residence employee had already been rescreened for errors in retinal scan or DNA typing. Each background check had been repeated. Whoever it was, he or she had the means to circumvent normal security checks.

He'd find them.

Bellik waited outside the clinic, standing at stiff attention. Gamal was tired of that self-important pose, tired of all Bellik's posturing. "Will she be all right?" Bellik asked.

Gamal nodded. "An odd episode. Probably related to her experiences on Antar."

"Luene is a lovely young woman." Bellik fell into step with Gamal. "I am interested in applying for permission to court her, if she recovers."

Gamal frowned. Marrying Luene would strengthen Bellik's position as a potential heir, and Bellik would make her a good spouse, but Gamal hesitated to decisively disinherit his son. Siah had surrounded himself with guards at his mountain retreat. Not enough muscle to menace Gamal down in the city, but enough of a presence to protect himself. Maybe Siah was a Casimir after all—though for the moment, he was decisively out of the picture.

At least he was no Antaran agent.

Gamal turned to see if Zavijavah had reacted to Bellik's romantic request. He kept walking. Zavijavah seemed absent lately, probably because of the headaches, though more than once Gamal had smelled red ruin on his breath.

Gamal touched Bellik's arm and stopped, letting Zavijavah walk ahead. Zavijavah seemed to shrink, framed by the floor, ceiling, and walls. Gamal blinked. Someday, after he'd won the Chaethe as allies, he would like to get that eye fixed. "You may court her," he said, "but don't count on my naming her to my Board of Regents."

"Why not?"

"Someday this Board will control nine planetary systems. Until tonight's episode is investigated, Luene must remain under observation. She will begin reacculturization immediately, though. I have a tutor on the grounds."

"Alun's?"

"He seems nonthreatening."

Bellik grimaced. "He's also young and male, even if he's as homely as a newborn pup."

"I'll make sure he knows how to keep to his place."

Bellik glanced up the hall. "What's wrong with Zavijavah? He's getting even stranger."

"Zavijavah," Gamal said, "is a mutant. He carries the seer gene. Sometimes it gives him headaches. No mutant is ever totally comfortable."

Bellik squinted, perhaps in sympathy. Or, knowing Bellik, distaste. "So," he said, "it's time to answer the challenge at Ilzar."

"We've dawdled too long." Gamal agreed with his nephew on this subject. It felt good to have taken a strong lead in the war, which gave him time to step back and greet Luene. Now, though— "Teach them a lesson at Ilzar. Don't waste time or ships. Do something for the Concord to see and remember."

Bellik saluted. "I'll meet you at the base tomorrow morning."

20

Outside the Salbari estate, a hot, damp wind swept the plains. Based in hastily constructed Quonsets along the airstrip's runway, Antar's remaining Outwatch troops guarded the strip and estate.

At the Y-shaped table indoors, Filip perspired despite his loosely woven white tunic. Other Concord leaders looked weighted down by fifty days of crisis. After another four-day break to allow communication to return, there was much to catch up on.

Filip had opened the morning session with a review of recent events. A report from Admiral Gehretz Lalande at Ilzar had arrived by Gate relay shortly after the previous Conclave session. Concord forces had established a beachhead and closed Ilzar Gate.

On the other hand, in all six settled systems, new e-net dramas were feeding a horror of Chaethe infestation—from whatever source, perhaps a rumored Tdegan agent on Antar. Karine Torfinn also continued to badger him regarding her translated fragment from Nuris University's archive. It pointed unequivocally to Sunsis.

He'd done what he could to preserve peace and calm. A travel ban might keep any localized infestation from spreading. Still, no one could stop information, nor its hangers-on: misinformation and panic.

A representative of Teemay Engineering's research department appeared in hologram over the Y table's center. Electronically facing all directions, he explained Chaethe parasitism in as much detail as Antaran research could support, as well as what could be done to prevent or at

228 | KATHY TYERS

least detect it. "An adaptation of available technology could produce a scanner capable of detecting infested individuals," he claimed, "based on the spore sheath's metal content. As soon as you authorize funding, we will develop the project."

"Discussion?" Filip asked.

His colleagues merely sat looking stiff.

Very well. "Is there a motion?"

Sal Megred of Crux, leader of the military reactionists, stood and glared with black-almond eyes. "I move we fund production. I also wish to requisition fifty such scanners for Crux."

Filip seconded the motion, heading off wholesale requests. It passed unanimously. The Teemay rep's image vanished.

Filip sat down and exhaled heavily. "Do any of you want to break at this point?"

Sal Megred spoke without formalities. "We've had plenty of time to stretch and wait and talk things over. As Salbari said, Sunsis could harbor a Chaethe infestation in advanced stages. If it spreads, this could end human civilization in the Concord region. Again. What are we going to do about it?"

"We must discuss that now," Filip said. "We will not follow point of order unless the discussion becomes unruly." He glanced at Megred.

Dio Liion of Unukalhai opened the discussion. A velvety green gown set off her ornate hair this morning. "Can we send reinforcements to Ilzar?"

"Not quickly enough to help Admiral Lalande," Boaden Salbari answered, stroking his jowls, "so he didn't ask for any, as you'll note. He knows we have to defend Antar."

"Have we sent any ships to Sunsis?"

"No." Boaden glared at Filip.

Sal Megred nodded. "The obvious solution is one I don't like, but it must be suggested. Thanks to our old enemies, we know how to sterilize a planet."

That idea must be quashed. Filip spoke quickly. "Sunsis A has no ocean anymore."

Sal Megred pushed away from the table. He folded his arms. "I meant Tdega, of course."

Filip straightened involuntarily.

"Not Tdega," Favia murmured. "It's the closest thing in the Concord to a truly habitable world. That would be a terrible crime."

She was correct. This Conclave was at war with a few Tdegan individuals, not with their whole world's web of life. "Sending a force to Sunsis with scanners and impounding only the infested individuals would make more sense. Surely the non-infested Sunsisans would be glad for help."

"True," Favia said. "Surely they don't want to be consumed."

"Unless they all are." Boaden pushed back from the table. "Already. Also, if that mission failed, the aliens would find out what we're doing. They could declare war on the Concord. Could we fight two enemies at once?"

"Maybe we already are," said Sal Megred.

Several other options were proposed and discussed. Finally Filip spoke into a gloomy silence. "We might try communicating with the Chaethe."

Boaden snorted. "You empaths would suggest that."

He tried not to sound irked. "Yes, we would. Maybe the Chaethe don't know how their actions appear. They could think in truly alien ways. Is it right to try wiping out any intelligent species? That would be an act worthy of the Devastators." Even the Chaethe were children of the Creator, although they might not know it.

But this was no time to point that out.

"Do we have time to talk with them?" Megred cried. "It would take three weeks simply to get there. And why? We know what they want. They want to eat us alive. Understanding the enemy doesn't mean sitting down to tea with him! If we have to wage war, we should strike quickly." He pounded one hand with the other. "Decisively."

Boaden waved Megred back down into his seat. "This situation will require all our intelligence and courage," Boaden said. "We must make quick decisions and demand immediate obedience. And may I add, no popular assembly can wisely direct a war."

Filip eyed his uncle. Boaden stood halfway between Filip's caution and Megred's vengefulness. Too much caution could slow down the Concord enough to defeat it.

A path seemed to open before him. A way forward.

Gladwyn looked uncomfortable in the heat, with her child three days overdue. "You could send an attack force one week behind the diplomatic delegation," she said. "Surely we could wait one week to open another front of this war."

Boaden rubbed his chin. "Filip's suggestion bears consideration," he grumbled. "I move that this Conclave conscript a team of empaths and send it to Sunsis A to try negotiating with these aliens, if that's what we're really facing. Then we should send a strike force five days behind it. Better to lose a week and sacrifice a few ... individuals," he said, charitably—perhaps—avoiding his usual term *mutants,* "than to incinerate a habitable world. Even a marginally habitable one. We must try to communicate first—with Tdega, at least." He rested his hand on the table. "If that fails, we blast Sunsis."

"Why conscript the empaths?" called a Kocaban delegate. "Conscripting an unwilling human is too much like destroying a habitable world. Especially since this appears to be a suicide mission. Put out a call for volunteers."

Suicide mission. The words made Filip hesitate. Was there really no hope of success? He pondered as other voices took sides. Asking for volunteers would bring in a dedicated group, many of them with small children. He would not orphan those youngsters if any other choice existed. Volunteers would also offer an unrealistically homogeneous idealism. They would not fairly represent humankind if talks were established. Finally, if humanity must communicate with an alien race, the effort must be made by the most skilled communicators, not the most unselfish.

He could create teams of three empaths. In each team, one member must be strong in the nexus skill that allowed linkage and influence. Another member must have the strongest synch gift he could find, to hear any frequencies used by the Chaethe. The third should know as much as possible about organisms such as Chaethe parasites, particularly any known linguistic patterns, in order to translate. Three empaths had done such research: Bord Marlon, himself, and Karine Torfinn.

Abruptly, he realized he was ignoring Concord issues to concentrate on Order business. He must stop procrastinating. It was time to walk that way forward, to trust others and the Creator. Finally, he knew which post to resign. At the next lull, he spoke. "On this issue, I side with Boaden."

Alcotte shot him a sharp look.

"A conscripted group, balanced to offer all of our skills and resources, would serve the Concord better than a mismatched band of well-meaning volunteers."

Boaden grimaced. "Easy for you to say. It's a fair guess you won't be chosen."

Something else occurred to him, a thought that confirmed his decision: a different Head Regent should be in place, ready to take charge, if he did not return from Sunsis.

Dio Liion sprang up.

Filip silenced her by standing too. "I would not ask anyone to undertake a mission I was not willing to undertake myself. I will volunteer."

Sal Megred rocked his chair. "You just said you wouldn't allow volunteers. Are you so certain you would be one of the best?"

"You're resigning as Head Regent?" Alcotte asked. Sarcasm hazed his voice.

Alcotte should know him better. Filip cleared his throat and said, simply, "Yes."

The mid-table sonic ridges picked up and amplified the softly spoken word. All heads turned toward him.

"Respectfully and with apologies," Filip said, "I do resign the Head Regency of Nuris University. I nominate Boaden Salbari to serve in my place. He will be exactly the leader we need in this crisis."

Boaden tilted his head, looking as stunned as Alcotte. He flattened both hands on the table. "I move that this Conclave discuss whether to allow Filip to resign in order to go to Sunsis. As for you—" He pointed up the table at Filip. "You are excused for the moment, of course. Submit this plan to the head of your Order."

"All right," Filip said, silently laughing. He wondered whether Boaden would figure that out before Filip told him. As Head Regent, Boaden would need to know. It amazed Filip that seventy-plus trained empaths had been able to keep his double leadership secret. "I will spend the next hour on the c-net."

Favia fidgeted. He knew she was afraid for his sake. Still, she had always said she respected his judgment.

He walked down the steps, away from the table, one part of him deeply relieved and another part wrenched with regret.

But still wholly certain.

Isolated in his office, he murmured a prayer of thanks for the assurance that he'd made the right choice. This mission would call for his strengths. Defending the Concord against invaders, if Filip failed, would require Boaden's different talents.

He stared at his terminal, set to c-net but sorting information instead of sending it. Each triad must defend itself against psychological takeover by alien-influenced human carriers. There must also be physical defenses. The sparse old reports had it that Chaethe parasites could penetrate a human skull. That suggested the notion of helmets.

"Helmets," he said aloud. "Consult Teemay Engineering." The voice-to-text circuit recorded a note on his reader.

There were only a few other things that empaths could do for defense. Their mission would demand candor and vulnerability.

He asked his computer to rank all trained empaths by synch skills, nexus ratings, and counsel or persuasion grades. Those were re-measured every five years. It produced four lists, ranking all seventy-eight trained empaths in order of all four abilities.

From those lists, he had it eliminate all younger than thirty and any who had children under eighteen. Bord Marlon, unmarried, and Karine, whose son was attending University, fortunately qualified—as did Filip, whose scores were median across the board.

He'd found his three translators. But the synch list had shrunk to one name—fortunately the best, Vananda Hadley. The nexus "list" was only seventy-two-year-old Joao Pallaton, the late Athis's younger brother.

Filip frowned. He asked the terminal to add empaths whose children were no younger than fifteen or who were older than twenty-five and unmarried.

That added one name to each list. Still not enough. He secured full teams only when he allowed parents of children over twelve. He hated to conscript a twelve-year-old girl's mother. Still, Lyova Waverly had excellent synch gifts, and with the fate of human-settled space potentially at stake, he must fill the position.

He asked the computer to formulate the three most compatible triads if he added the six skilled individuals to his Chaethe-knowledgeable core of three. He also keyed for strong counsel and persuasion scores, distributed evenly among the triads.

A list appeared. He stared at it. He must ask eight other people to sacrifice their freedom and probably their lives. This looked like one of Nuris city's casualty lists.

What happened to a soul if a Chaethe entered its body?

"File," he said, and the list vanished. In less than a month, the Concord looked likely to tear itself apart. If the Chaethe aliens had sparked Tdega's secession, then in the hope of averting wholesale warfare, he would gladly spend his own life. Surely the others would, too.

He fingered one of his collar garnets.

Karine blinked. Hadn't she turned off the light when she bedded down?

Two men and a woman stood at the foot of her bed. All wore Outwatch blue-gray. "We're sorry to wake you, Medic Torfinn," said the man in the middle. "The head of your Order has issued a formal summons. Please pack quickly and come with us."

A formal come-along? Had Filip decided to call her before a board of evaluation now? She shouldn't have been rude to Herva Metyline.

On second thought, he would not send the Outwatch for a counseling offense. Rubbing her face, she swung her legs over the side of the bed. This must have something to do with the war. That, or—

Had something happened to Llyn? Maybe Filip had decided to mount a rescue effort. "How many days should I pack for?"

"Only your personal essentials," the woman said. "The Order will take care of anything you need."

Then this was a genuine conscription, and nothing to do with the call block she'd installed last week. Herva Metyline had repeatedly suggested that Karine was stuck in an inappropriate stage of grieving—had been stuck, in fact, since Namron's death eight years ago. There was no answering that. Herva would label any answer "denial." Karine had blocked the connection, preventing Herva Metyline from trying to counsel her any further.

Actually, this probably concerned Llyn.

Karine stuffed a duffel with the barest necessities. If the Concord meant to send her to Tdega, it would clothe her there. She held her head high as the group passed Director Graybill, who stood at the entrance offering a handclasp. "Good luck, Karine. Whatever it is."

She brushed Graybill's fingertips with her own and strode out the door.

At Rift's small airfield less than a kilometer outside the city dome, a twenty-seat jet waited. Karine climbed on board. To her surprise, three people already sat aboard, all empaths. Dropping her duffel in a locker, Karine sat down beside Vananda Hadley. "What's up?" she asked, buckling in.

"Nobody's telling. I tried listening," Vananda added, "and either the crew hasn't been told or they've been warned not to think of it."

If Vananda Hadley, Filip's sister-in-law, didn't know why they were being conscripted, nobody did. Across the aisle, a dark-skinned man with intelligent eyes—wasn't that Bord Marlon?—leaned forward. "We're assuming something to do with the war, but I wrote my thesis on theories of alien civilization years ago. That could be a factor."

Karine preferred to avoid that topic. "Could they be sending us to Tdega?"

Vananda pressed her palms together as the jet taxied forward. "I don't know whether to hope so or not," she said. She, too, must have been awakened unexpectedly, since her brown curls pointed every which way. "If I went to Tdega, I would want to check on Jahn, and I mustn't."

Of all the young empaths Filip Salbari could have sent to Tdega, he'd chosen the coattail rider. Karine should have known months ago that Salbari's judgment did not match his reputation.

The craft accelerated for takeoff.

Vananda kept staring. She was going to ask. She wouldn't be able to resist. Here it came: "Didn't I hear that it turned out Llyn was—"

"Gamal Casimir's daughter." No use pretending otherwise.

"Perhaps she learned not to be a Casimir while she lived with you." Vananda positively oozed sympathy, with slumped shoulders and wide eyes.

"Llyn was rebellious." Karine answered firmly, keeping her tone businesslike. "Very strong-willed. But not untrainable. I miss her."

"Has anyone explained why she was found on an artificial-reality machine?"

"No." Karine had long stopped wondering. Perhaps that was a mistake.

"Or if that had anything to do with Tdega declaring war?" Bord Marlon asked from across the aisle.

"People will always conjecture." And conjecture was cheap. Karine clutched her armrests. "No one knows."

"Then maybe," Vananda said, "something has finally come up. Maybe we're going to check on Llyn."

"I hope so." The words were out before Karine could stop them.

They flew in darkness under the clouds. The plane landed next at the manufacturing city of Elhem, on the North River between Nuris and the Salbari estate. The Outwatchers debarked again, leaving Karine and the others to hypothesize connections between Chaethe and Tdega.

The Outwatchers had been gone less than an hour when a blast of pain struck Karine. Vananda doubled up, pressing her chest to her knees. Bord Marlon's seatmate Joao Pallaton unbuckled and stood up, light on his feet for a man past seventy. "What was that?" he cried.

Bord palmed sweat off his high, dark forehead. "The last time I felt something like that was the day Tdega hit Nuris."

"This was closer." Vananda straightened, passing a hand over her eyes.

Karine cocked an eyebrow. She hadn't gotten that much meaning out of the blast, only pain.

Abruptly a voice spoke. "Prepare for takeoff." The jet taxied forward in darkness.

Karine exchanged startled looks with Vananda. Joao sat down. The Outwatchers who obviously debarked to pick up another empath hadn't returned.

The atmosphere on board became subtly fearful. With four empaths in a small space, they reinforced each others' feelings, just as—earlier—they had reinforced each other's excitement without knowing it.

Interesting.

"We're all short on sleep," Vananda said quietly. "We'll find out what's happening when we arrive. I'd like to nap."

If they were headed for the Salbari estate, there wouldn't be much napping time left. Elhem was close to that northerly enclave. Karine didn't care if she never saw Filip Salbari again, but it looked unavoidable.

Perhaps Llyn had been locked away. Perhaps she had vanished and Salbari was sending empaths to retrieve her.

Yet Salbari had warned that after Llyn left Antar, he could not answer for her safety. Karine could have struck him for saying that.

Vananda opened one eye.

"Sorry." Karine mustn't think about Salbari—or Llyn—just now. She slumped in her seat, shut her eyes, and tried to rest. The jet engine lulled her into a fitful doze.

Karine had been to the estate several times, assisting with Order business. This time, the complex was almost silent. It was several hours past midnight. Filip Salbari met them in the private office adjoining his family suite.

She took the seat farthest from Salbari's narrow desk. Eight people fit comfortably into this carpeted sanctum, with room for several more. Its single small window looked out over the inner lawn, orchard, and flower gardens, all artificially lit.

How nice for Salbari that he never had lived in a prison compound.

The fruit trees, which looked dull by lamplight, reminded Karine of teaching Llyn to pick apples without destroying fruit spurs. She wondered if she had finally won and they were going to retrieve Llyn after all. Llyn would have become extremely undisciplined after living without supervision all these weeks.

Salbari solemnly swiveled his chair away from the wall-mounted desk and made it part of the group's circle. He laced his fingers in his lap. He cleared his throat. His hair had gone gray at the roots in less than two months.

"This isn't easy," he said.

He was not a strong leader. He never had been. Karine glanced left. Vananda sat staring into Salbari as if she could see his synapses firing.

"We have received another transmission from Jahn Emlin, warning of counterstrokes planned against Ilzar and Antar. The situation is worse than we had thought. Yesterday afternoon, the Conclave asked the

Empath Order to do a dangerous job. If it fails, there is a chance of death or worse."

Worse? Karine mocked him in her mind.

"You are being conscripted, rather than being asked to volunteer—partly to keep you from deliberating with fears that might not let you volunteer, and partly because you are the most talented individuals in areas where we need strength."

He paused and returned Vananda's stare. His wife's sister dipped her head in a slight, solemn nod. She would have looked much more dignified if her curls hadn't stuck out in all directions.

Next, he glanced at Bord Marlon and the aging Joao Pallaton, holding each man's eyes for only a moment. He skipped Karine, which surprised her, moving instead to Qu Yung, one of Antar's rare citizens of almost unmixed ethnic heritage and a descendant of Antar's pre-Devastator Regents. Lyova Waverly, bone-china fair without even a freckle, had studied under Karine several years ago. Karine remembered her as easily distracted by the boys. Kenji Emlin, a blond young man with a broad, perpetual smile, was a recent trainee.

Finally, he looked at Karine.

She cocked an eyebrow and let her feelings spill over her strong inner boundaries. He meant to send her on a potentially fatal mission? She did not like the idea. She would rather volunteer, and she still did not believe that the "mission" existed. How did this relate to Llyn?

Salbari faced the middle of the circle. "There is suspicion," he said, "that Sunsis A harbors a Chaethe infestation in advanced stages. Karine, you have known that for some time."

She crossed her arms. "It's a theory."

"This team, plus representatives from the other remaining Concord systems, will travel there. We will attempt to talk with the aliens if they are there, and if they can be persuaded to communicate. If they occupy human hosts, surely they can speak our language."

Karine's throat constricted. Communicate … with alien parasites?

"Talk?" Bord Marlon spoke before she could object. "What should we tell them? Get out of our space—that's simple. Why send us?"

"Even if they can communicate with us, they could be so culturally different that they can't comprehend human values. They might not understand how heinous their actions appear to us."

"Or maybe they don't care," Qu Yung said. Karine remembered him from Nuris University. She'd studied one year behind him. He'd seemed sensible, with good grades and no social life.

"Or they don't call us intelligent beings as they define intelligent," Vananda suggested.

Irked, Karine leaned forward. "This entire idea is not intelligent. Who proposed this trip? Why are we cooperating?"

Vananda pulled her chair away from Karine and turned back to Salbari. "Personally, we stand to lose everything. But I am honored to be chosen. Thank you."

Salbari rubbed one of his cheekbones, temporarily smoothing the dark circle under that eye. "Thank you, Vananda. The Conclave will speak with all of us in two hours."

"You say, 'us'?" Qu Yung stared at Salbari. "Are you coming?"

"I don't want to either. But I will."

Karine crossed her arms. It was only appropriate that Filip risk his life if the rest of them must do so. That did not make her like him any better.

"What about the Concord?" Lyova Waverly asked. Abruptly, Karine remembered that Lyova had a twelve-year-old daughter. Surely Salbari didn't mean to send her on a hazardous mission.

It was easy to believe he would draft Karine, though. He obviously despised her.

He folded his hands. "This has not been publicly announced," he said, "but I resigned the Head Regency yesterday afternoon."

Karine glared. The man had cracked. She wondered what actually happened yesterday afternoon. Was he forced out of office?

"This means that the Conclave's balance has slipped," he said. "The war party is stronger now. We, here, will represent the last hope of peace. We can hope to succeed and return, though. We will form three triads …" Salbari talked for several minutes about listeners, linkers, translators, and the balance of counsel and persuasion that he hoped to achieve.

Now she understood why she had been chosen. She knew more about Chaethe speech than any other empath, except possibly Bord Marlon, and she had taken a double major from Athis Pallaton himself in counsel and persuasion.

Resigned? Salbari? She doubted it.

"What happened while we waited at Elhem?" Joao asked, shaking his head.

"We aren't sure." Salbari shifted in his seat. "The Outwatch agents went to pick up Tam Vandam, an excellent nexus specialist. One of them activated his distress beacon inside the Vandam home. A local police officer answered the beacon. She found all three agents and Gen Vandam dead without a mark."

"A wild talent," Karine muttered. The empath mutation was comparatively new, and no one fully understood its capabilities. Unexplained phenomena did crop up. The Order needed stronger leadership if it hoped to control them. Salbari was doing the right thing, volunteering for a suicide mission.

Who would succeed him, with the Concord and with the Order?

"We felt terrible fear," Vananda murmured.

"It's been thought that empaths could die if they felt others' final terror," Salbari said slowly, stroking his chin. "And the Outwatch agents did know why they were calling on all of you. But that does not explain what killed them."

"Perhaps he panicked," Karine suggested. "The nets are full of Chaethe rumors." She had seen to that. The public needed to know what was at stake.

Vananda raised an eyebrow. "Projected emotional anguish? If Tam did discover what the conscription was about, could he unwittingly have drawn the Outwatch people into nexus and disrupted all their inner frequencies to the point of ... stopping them?"

"It's a terrible theory. I don't think we would care to have others hear it." Salbari looked suitably somber. "At any rate, our plan to balance three perfect teams has already gone awry. We won't have Tam Vandam at one nexus."

"Are we canceling, then?" Lyova sounded hopeful. A wisp of light brown hair curled toward her thin eyebrows.

"No."

Karine listened hard. An undercurrent of panic was rising in the room.

Evidently, Salbari finally picked it up. "We will find another nexus. As conscripts," he added, "you are entitled to every consideration. But meanwhile, can each of you give me a pledge of cooperation?"

If they wouldn't, Karine imagined him locking them up.

She nodded reluctantly.

He lowered his voice. "Karine, I had thought that this mission might be a blessing for you. Only something this urgent would take your mind off losing Llyn."

I would not have lost her if you hadn't interfered, Salbari.

Vananda winced.

Salbari dismissed the others to sleeping rooms but asked Karine to stay. He claimed he wanted to talk with her privately. She sat stiffly with her hands in her lap.

Once the door slid shut, he tipped his desk chair and looked sad. "Obviously, you still blame me for allowing Llyn to leave you."

Obviously. "It was a mistake."

He seemed to be waiting for her to speak again. She could outwait him. She was glad to see him ousted from the Head Regency. As soon as he dismissed her from this room, she would speak with the other empaths about replacing him in the Order, too.

"There was additional information in Jahn Emlin's report," he said after almost a minute. "Llyn had passed Tdega Gate, and a Tdegan medic had repeated the gene test that identified her. A suite in Casimir family quarters had been set aside for her, but when he sent that transmission, he hadn't yet seen her."

Karine hated depending on Vananda's son for news of Llyn. She refused to soften.

"I kept you here to make an offer," he said. "Eventually, you must appear before an inquiry board. Assuming we will go to Sunsis, I thought you might wish to face that board before we leave. You seem confident that your record will be cleared—"

"You think I'd rather die on Sunsis with a clean record than under suspicion?" She laughed. "Why should I care? The whole inquiry board idea is ridiculous."

"If you feel that confident, we should—"

"It can wait."

He stared at her for several seconds, resting an elbow on his desk. "Karine, you need help. There are half a dozen people at this estate who can—"

"You've lost your balance." No clinician could help someone who didn't want help. Somehow Filip still thought he was fine.

"We need your help on this mission."

He'd been synching. She refused to open up in return. "I will do what I can for the good of humanity. But I'll do it for my own reasons, not yours."

His eyes narrowed. "Very well. Tonight. Here. A board of inquiry will decide whether you should be charged with any offense regarding your treatment of Llyn. I will nominate two empaths. You may nominate two others. You'll have to choose from those who are here, but that gives you several options."

Two of the others had seemed reluctant to accept this mission. "Bord," she said without hesitating. "And Qu."

"Very well," he said. "I will call them—and you—to come back here this evening at seven."

Filip closed up his office and headed for the Conclave. Karine's attitude could poison others. Did he dare to take her to Sunsis? Was her knowledge worth the risk, or should he choose another?

Who? Had any non-empaths studied Chaethe language or culture? There was too little knowledge to draw from, and he had no authority to conscript someone outside the Order.

Maybe a board inquiry would shock her out of complacency. Now that he felt free to concentrate on the Order, he realized he should have done this weeks ago.

He caught up with Boaden halfway across the atrium's outer lawn. "We need to talk for a moment." There'd been no chance yesterday evening.

"We certainly do." Boaden stepped off the direct path and walked several steps toward the atrium wall, farther from the delegates arriving for an early morning session. "I would appreciate a little more warning next time you plan to drop a bomb."

Filip shrugged. "Waging war calls for quick decisions and immediate obedience," he quoted. "When I realized that the Concord needs you and not me, I acted."

Boaden backed against the stone wall. "I hope you decide that history justifies your actions."

"One other thing," Filip said.

Boaden raised an eyebrow. "Is this your next bomb?"

"I did not have to contact the head of our Order yesterday. I am the head."

The skin around Boaden's eyes crinkled. "I'm not entirely surprised."

"I didn't think you would be. As Head Regent, you need to know for certain."

"Are you still sure you should go to Sunsis?"

"More certain than ever."

"I think so, too. Whoever heads that mission will have to be extremely sensitive and a creative communicator."

That was high praise, coming from Boaden. "Thank you."

Boaden eyed the table. "Were they all willing?"

"Some more, some less. One is marginal."

"That's why you conscripted." Boaden stepped out. "It's time."

Filip took his place as Boaden opened the early session. *Early? It already feels like afternoon.* Listening around the table, Filip detected urgent undercurrents that had been missing before. Everyone seemed to have focused.

"Report, Filip." Boaden clasped his hands on the table.

Filip stood. "We found only eight empaths. The ninth nominee has died. We must enlist one more who is extremely strong in nexus linkage if we are to put together one more triad." He glanced beyond Gladwyn toward the end of the Y table. Karine and the other conscripts had joined the session.

"Thank you all," Boaden said. "On behalf of the Concord—of millions of other people—I wish you success and offer our full support."

Alcotte and Gladwyn had been communicating via keyboard. Alcotte cleared his throat. Boaden tapped the tabletop and raised an eyebrow at Filip.

"No," Filip said firmly, eyeing Alcotte. "Gladwyn is about to deliver, and she just lost most of her birth family. You may not go."

Gladwyn stared at the tabletop. "If it means sending the strongest team possible, Alcotte and I have agreed that he would volunteer. You need another nexus, don't you?"

"Would the Conclave accept my offer?" Alcotte asked.

"Just a minute," a young voice called. Between Gladwyn and the other empaths, Gladwyn and Alcotte's twenty-year-old daughter Rena had sprung up. Her cropped red hair shimmered eerily, but she wore a conservative white tunic and culottes. "My nexus scores are almost as high as Father's," she said. "I have no children. I know you wanted older and wiser people, but I'm qualified. Send me."

Gladwyn's cheeks lost their high color. "Sit down," Alcotte said gently. "You're too young."

Rena shook her head. "I'll fight and die here, if the war comes to Antar. You're sending representatives of all Concord systems. Let me represent its young people."

"You're honestly willing?" Sal Megred stroked his chin, studying Rena. "I am."

Filip eyed Rena, too. It was tragic when young people died, but they did not cling to life like their elders. Young people understood themselves as immortal. By middle age, many lost that faith.

Rena might be right. If the mission failed, Alcotte and Gladwyn would not be left childless. Gladwyn's fourth child—a daughter, who also carried the empath mutation—could arrive momentarily. Every solution to this problem demanded risking someone's life.

"I suggest a secret vote," Boaden said. "Shall we send Alcotte or Rena?"

"I second," called Alcotte. He and Gladwyn reached for their keyboards. Other Conclave members took longer about deciding.

Filip prayed that he might remain sensitive to wisdom's leaning. Then he voted for Rena.

After another minute, Boaden stood. "The vote is for Rena. Three votes to two."

"Good," Rena said boldly. "Thank you."

Gladwyn lurched forward, burying her head in her hands. Alcotte pulled her close to his chest. Vananda sprang up from her place at the table's end and threw her arms around them both.

Boaden offered Rena his hand.

Close to eleven o'clock that evening, Filip withdrew from Joao Pallaton's nexus. Qu and Vananda, the best synch listeners in residence at the estate, had probed Karine's memories, intentions, and desires for nearly four hours. He took a few seconds to study his fellow empaths' faces. Bord was dark and straight-nosed, and Qu retained the epicanthic eye-fold of his ancestors, while Vananda's genetic heritage couldn't be guessed—but all of their faces reflected the concern that showed on Joao's forehead as four dark, parallel lines.

Karine pivoted and sat up, facing sideways out of the deeply reclined chair where she had endured her ordeal. She shot Filip a look hot enough to boil water. He understood her pain. Board inquiry was a devastating invasion of privacy.

Joao Pallaton rubbed his lined face. Normally proud and straight-backed, he looked ashen. "Are you all right?" Filip asked him.

"Yes," Joao said. "It's been a while."

Bord Marlon crossed one leg over his knee and clasped his hands around it. "Thank you, Karine."

She stalked out of the room.

Filip sat in his desk chair, facing the circle. He looked around at the other empaths. "Discussion?"

Qu reached out a hand. "This was plainly an attempted enmeshment. She had begun to subjoin the girl. But Llyn has been removed. What would be the point of disciplining Karine?"

Vananda shook her head. "Before we consider any consequences, we must evaluate the situation."

"Karine may also need treatment," Filip said. "If she does, we must try to help her."

"There is little else to say." Bord uncrossed his legs. "Karine has become unable to function without controlling other individuals. She cannot trust them or herself to interact in a healthy manner. This is a tragic loss of a fine clinician."

Filip folded his hands. "Evaluation, then. Attempted enmeshment?"
They all nodded.

"Attempt to subjoin, with intention?" If this board agreed unanimously, Karine would be charged and tried. Her clinic might be taken away, as well as her place in the Order.

"Absolutely," Vananda whispered.

"Yes," said Joao.

Qu folded his hands and leaned forward. "With some justification."

"Justified or not, the subjoining was attempted," Bord said.

Filip nodded. "I agree. Can we take her with us to Sunsis once she has been formally charged?"

"What better place for her?" Vananda spread her hands. "We may be the only people who can help her see what she has become, and why, and the danger she poses to everyone she cares about."

Filip nodded. If Karine submitted to treatment before going to trial, any judge might be more lenient.

Karine strode through the door wearing a confident smile, but once past the threshold, she hesitated. Her eyes widened. "No," she whispered. "You can't think—"

Joao stood. Coming from Athis Pallaton's brother, the words might sting less. "Karine, you were closely controlled as a young woman. You gained mastery of your own situation, but Namron's death wounded you more deeply than you realized. You tried to counsel yourself instead of seeking the help you needed, and somehow that heightened your terrible fear of being abandoned again.

"You tried to subjoin Llyn instead of gradually relinquishing control over her. That is the unanimous charge of this board. But you may begin treatment immediately. Come with us to Sunsis. We are not clinicians, but we can help you."

"Do I have a choice?" Her hands trembled.

Joao glanced at Filip.

This had been another difficult decision. He nodded.

Joao eyed Karine again. "You may choose," he said. "When an individual is free, she will take damages—but so will slaves, and they have no choice in the matter. You may remain here, confined at the estate. If we do not return, you will be tried by the Order's new head. If we come back, Filip will judge your case."

Filip felt her anger seethe and then slowly crumble. She must have felt certain Bord and Qu would not recommend charging her. She clenched her hands. "You feel I acted wrongly?"

Joao stepped forward. "You did try to do what was right. But you must develop a sense of grace, a trust in the Creator and in other people. There is a time to relinquish control. Filip set a fine example yesterday."

She scowled.

"We would like to see you offer recompense to Llyn, if the opportunity ever comes. But first, you must relearn the source of your own significance. Your freedom and Llyn's are both of utmost importance." Joao spread his hands. "That is one of the great mysteries."

Karine covered her face. She stood still for several seconds. Synching, Filip felt if-then pairs tumble through her mind. They slowed and settled.

"I'll come with you," she muttered, but he sensed that she barely accepted the idea of treatment.

It would take twenty-two days to reach Sunsis A. By then, she might change her mind.

In any direction.

21

Llyn lounged on the foot of her enormous, internally heated bed and stared out a tall window into the garden's rectangular maze. From this angle, it was easy to spot the convoluted escape route. Someday soon, she hoped to try it from the inside.

After last night's crisis, she'd slept in the larger of her two spacious bedrooms. Her personal servant, a wrinkled little woman named Peatra, had drawn and scented a warm bath this morning and laid out a snug but attractive outfit, then shown her how to order breakfast.

Llyn's private multinet was in the office-sized room adjacent to her personal, with unlimited c-net, i-net, and e-net time. All at the flick of a finger, with no Karine monitoring—although, now that she thought of it, someone else probably would watch her selections.

And she was lonely. She wished she could have brought Tana and Ilke. They could've had wonderful times with such a palace to explore. She had freedom and space, but no one to share them with. With all the new freedoms she could claim, she hadn't enjoyed them yet.

She yawned and rubbed her eyes. This was a depressing development. She didn't feel any more "normal" among her Tdegan kin than she'd felt on Antar with Karine. Regent Salbari had hinted that she'd have to find a major part of the answer inside herself, which would take time.

So far, she hadn't asked about the nearest artificial-reality ARcade, but she guessed the urge would grow stronger before it went away. Already she wished she could plug in and vanish. She felt as if the day had gotten away from her, too, because she had just eaten breakfast, but the outdoor shadows indicated afternoon.

A bell rang somewhere. She hurried out into the office area and checked her multinet terminal. Nothing blinked. The sound repeated. It seemed to come from the other side of her bedroom, or else the narrow entry hall. She spotted a small light gleaming on a panel near the front door. She hurried over and touched it.

A voice said, "This is Jahn Korsakov."

Now what did she do? Experimenting, she touched the light again.

The door slid open. Two men stood just outside. Both wore snug shirts and pants that did not camouflage their lean young bodies. "Gen'n Luene," the one in front greeted her. "May we come in?" His voice sounded familiar. She must have met him at the reception. There had been so many people there.

"Who are you?" she asked, trying to sound curious instead of challenging.

"I'm your tutor. I live in Residence with your cousin, Alun. I don't suppose you remember us?"

Now she did. This was the man with the soothing voice. The taller, lankier, younger man hung back, grinning. The smaller man wore a more penetrating expression on a face that was shorter and more square than most Tdegans'. "You're the man who was kind at the reception," she said.

He smiled. "You heard too many names last night. Are you feeling better?"

She nodded. "Sleepy, but fine. Come in, both of you."

Her tall cousin strolled around her suite and peered into every corner. "It's empty in here," he said. "Siah had lots of pictures on the walls."

His voice had an odd singsong inflection, like one of Karine's severely depressed patients. "Siah," she repeated. "That's my brother in exile?"

Gen Korsakov nodded.

Siah's departure must have opened this suite for her. "Well, welcome. Sit down." She led them into the room with the terminal, the extra chairs, and the conversational table.

Her tutor sat down in a huge, luxurious black chair without even looking at it, as if he were accustomed to this lifestyle. "Are you lonesome yet?"

"Yes," she admitted. "How did you know?"

"Anyone would be lonely, having moved back to a world where they didn't remember anyone." He sounded hesitant. Wary, maybe, after her inexplicable public behavior.

"I suppose I'd better tell you why I blacked out at the party." She couldn't believe this. She was warning someone from the first moment, just as Karine would have done.

"Don't say any more than you want to, Gen'n Luene." His voice, like Regent Salbari's, accepted without criticizing.

"Would you do something for me?" she asked. "On Antar, I was called Llyn. *Luene* sounds right, but … I guess when you're feeling lonely, you like something to be familiar."

"I will call you Llyn. But don't call me Gen Korsakov. It's Jahn."

"And I'm Alun," put in the younger man. "I'm your cousin. I fell on my head several weeks ago. Jahn has been teaching me the things I forgot."

Jahn flickered an eyelid in a gesture Karine sometimes used. It meant, "Do you understand?" She returned the half wink.

"Tell us what happened at the reception and afterward, if you care to."

Gingerly, Llyn sat down on a quilted chair with fancy rolled armrests. It looked like it was worth everything she had owned before. "It was a flashback. They're apparently caused by the time I spent living in artificial reality, and they're triggered by environmental sounds—and certain emotional states. My brain became programmed to respond in certain ways to seventeen-tone music." She eyed his face. Usually at this point, people looked confused. His expression did not change. "Do you want me to explain that?"

"Later."

Relieved—the concept took some explanation—she went on. "Music controlled the AR environment, and me while I was in it. So when I hear music in that tonality, especially if I'm vulnerable and stressed, I go down. Boom."

"How do you come back?"

She flicked one thumb with the other, enjoying the sensation. "I usually need help. They shine a light in one eye. Or pinch my arm, but they have to do that very hard. My tactile sense was blocked when I lived in the AR. I think," she added, "it's starting to come back."

"The episodes must be awkward for you," Jahn said.

She didn't need to answer that.

Alun leaned forward. "What are your flashbacks like?"

Jahn shook his head slightly. She felt assured that she didn't have to say more than she wanted. Still, she described a composite flashback: the grid, the wafting, the shapes, and the beautiful music. While she talked, she studied Jahn. Something about his posture, his face, or his mannerisms reminded her of Karine, although not in a bad way. He simply seemed vaguely familiar. She decided not to tell him, since she'd said so many negative things about Karine.

He couldn't know what she was going through, actually missing Karine Torfinn. She had molded to Karine after five years. She didn't enjoy knowing that.

He stared down at the rich carpet after she finished. "Your private world sounds lovely," he murmured.

"It's tempting to try and go back."

"Do you have some compelling reason not to?"

That was a new question. Karine had always implied that the time she spent in flashbacks was wasted. "I want to live," she said. "To accomplish something."

"Then you will." He unfolded his hands and laid them in his lap. "Your father has asked me to tutor you and Alun because he wants both of you to be considered for his Board of Regents one day."

Fortunately, the notion had occurred to her shipboard, so she didn't choke or do anything else idiotic—but it wasn't much of a compliment if Alun would also be eligible. "I think it would be wise to see if I can still learn, first," she said dryly.

"That is wisdom. Your father wants me to inspire you to aspire."

"When will we start lessons?"

He laced his fingers around a knee. "Let me ask you some questions right now."

As Alun sat listening and occasionally moving his lips with a knowing smile, Jahn grilled her for most of an extended Tdegan hour. He covered

Tdegan history and geography—and the Casimir family—in some depth. She felt grateful to Regent Salbari for the data he'd fed into her ship-board terminal. She was able to answer more than half of his questions. Probably a failing grade, but not total ignorance.

Jahn looked impressed when she finished. "How do you know so much? I had thought the average Antaran was less knowledgeable."

"I had help. And Tdega is much on the minds of Antarans these days."

"People here assume that your mind was destroyed by the Antarans who linked you to that AR unit. I think you're going to surprise them very pleasantly." He stood. "That'll do for this morning. I scan information coming into the Residence and decide what is critical for you and Alun to learn. Now that I know where you are beginning, I'll call you in tomorrow morning for a lesson."

"You should probably start with the basics. I don't want to miss things just because you think I already know them."

He nodded. "Come on, Alun."

Alun rocked out of his chair. "You're pretty, Luene." He kept smiling at her.

Flustered, she backed away. She looked down at the indigo carpet.

Jahn took Alun by the arm. "Honesty is wonderful, Alun. You're recovering quickly, and I hope you never unlearn your directness. But don't be overwhelming."

He sounded as if he were agreeing with Alun. Her cheeks warmed. She didn't feel pretty. She felt tired. And heavy. "Thank you," she said. "Both of you."

They left her in the big suite alone, but considerably less lonely. As Regent Salbari would have said, she'd brought someone inside her boundaries. She hoped Jahn wasn't the kind to take advantage of her vulnerability.

But she could send him away, too.

Did she want to?

She rummaged in wall compartments until she found a warm scarf. She ran it up and down her forearm and along her fingertips. Soft. Other sensations came through, too. Her muscles ached faintly, and the Residence felt cold.

She wrapped the soft scarf around her shoulders.

After checking with Zavijavah to make sure Luene had awakened and seemed healthy again, Gamal Casimir headed for Bkellan Base. An arterial lay southeast along the edge of the city, which looked as lively as ever under the brilliant sun of first afternoon. A supply district—mostly raw-goods distributors for home manufacturing—lined the arterial for most of the way. Heavier industry separated residential Bkellan from the base-spaceport zone, and here, wartime dampened no spirits. Steamy smoke poured lustily out of a tall new stack at the Lahoma shipbuilding complex.

Gamal thought ahead to the base. He had housed the Outwatch crew of Luene's transport in the new barracks, promising to send them back to Antar by the next peaceful ship. He had not told them that that ship would stop first at Sunsis A to pick up other passengers. Alien ones.

Was it wise to offer the Chaethe Alun's voice on his Board of Regents? That would divide his family's loyalty. Still, now that he'd hit on the idea of winning the Chaethe as allies, he couldn't give it up. If the Devastators returned, he couldn't defend the star cluster without knowledge that his Chaethe allies would have gathered over centuries of fighting them. And he couldn't cut Tdega loose from the Concord so long as those Gates existed.

Destroying Gates was out of the question. He envisioned the future Tdegan Hegemony as Gate-linked to Bkellan University, with Bkellan Base benevolently ruling eight satellite worlds.

As for the security leak …

He had exhausted his conventional lines of investigation. If he wished to continue, he'd have to drug and question his employees. Not even Zavijavah would be able to keep that a secret once he started. The spy would bolt. So instead, the next employee disciplined for any reason would be in for a rough hour. And then the next employee, and so on.

He dismissed his driver outside the hexagonal tower and rode to the top floor. A whistle announced his arrival. Low-ranking personnel stood and saluted.

Bellik passed him a reader. "I've dispatched three of our new war wagons through the Gate to Ilzar. We'll have them through Ilzar Gate in two days."

Gamal calculated aloud. "So they'll reach Ilzar itself in eight." He considered sending another ship to menace Vatsya Habitat. Vatsya, the least-populated Concord system, was a logical fish to net for the Hegemony.

But that would take time. He needed Ilzar and its minerals first. "Good," he said. "I don't think it will take much to dislodge them." He pointed at a column of figures on one side of the screen. "Deploy another ship to Antar, too. Arm it with two of the new missiles."

Bellik raised an eyebrow. "I was about to suggest that."

"Can you make it a Gate launch?" If that were possible, they could strike in just seven days.

"No. The next pair of missile clusters only passed inspection two days ago."

Gamal shrugged, disappointed but not discouraged. "Ten extra days won't matter in the long run."

Bellik raised a booted foot onto a chair and rested an arm on his thigh, another of his conqueror poses. "Any luck breaking those embassy codes?"

"Not yet." Several more messages had arrived at the Antaran embassy since it fell into Tdegan hands. He was anxious to read them. "We're working on it."

Osun Zavijavah stumbled into the Residence clinic. He had left work without checking out. Even after a tumbler of red ruin, his head pounded. Medic Jackson stood beside his aide's terminal. "What is it, another freckle?" He glanced over and straightened. "Zavijavah, what's wrong?"

Zavijavah had just swallowed a zinger mint. That ought to cover his breath for the ten minutes it would take to get some relief. "Headache," he blurted. "It's awful."

"Sit down. Shirt off."

He took a chair near Jackson's black-box array and partially undressed.

Casimir had banned scanning units, even portable ones, from the Residence clinic. No imaging facilities here would betray Rider's presence.

Jackson pointed to a box. Zavijavah stuck his left ring finger into its opening and waited as Jackson stood behind him and pushed things against his back. A series of numbers appeared on a wall.

"Mm," Jackson said. When he lowered his head, his chin quadrupled. "Your symptoms are indicative of swelling of the brain. It must be terribly painful."

Zavijavah grunted assent.

"I'd like to send you across town for a scan."

"It wouldn't show anything." He tapped his glasses. "Seer skulls are different. Boss wants me here at beck and call anyway."

"Boss might lose you if this swelling doesn't go down. And you've got a second problem that could be causing it. Aggravating it, at least."

"Oh?"

"Don't 'oh' me, Gen Zavijavah." Jackson reached up and rapped one of the numbers. "Your blood alcohol is off the register."

He hadn't known that would show up. "How could that have happened?"

"How much have you been drinking, and for how long?"

"Just today, just for the headache." He stood and backed toward the door, grabbing his shirt. "Give me some pills. Then I'll leave you alone."

"I don't think so. With a count that high, you ought to be flat on your back. You're up, you're moving, and you're reasonably coherent. That means you're addicted. Blood work says your liver's all right, though, so we've caught it in time."

Liver damage. Wouldn't Rider love that? "Give me my pills."

Jackson whistled. A big aide walked into the doorway and blocked it. "You need bed rest, and you need an ethanol purge. You can do both simultaneously."

Zavijavah bolted under the aide's arm, but he stumbled. A hand grabbed his shoulder. His glasses clattered to the floor. The other two men wrestled him toward an examining table under lights that were far, far too bright.

Jackson clicked three broad belts across his midsection, securing his arms along his side. "This isn't necessary," Zavijavah cried, watery-eyed and helpless. "Don't—"

Something chilled his arm. "This will break down the ethanol into water and soluble carbon dioxide," the aide said.

Zavijavah squinted an eye. Jackson stood close, watching the aide. "Your lungs and your bladder will finish the job."

He glanced down. The hypodermic was a huge, shining blur. He yanked his arm underneath his body, leaving the aide holding the hypo in midair.

Jackson frowned. "Do we have to knock you out first?" He reached into a drawer, ripped open a pouch, and drew out an oval cloth. "All right, then." He dropped it over Zavijavah's mouth and nose. "Breathe deeply."

Slammed by the memory of what he'd done to Alun Casimir, Zavijavah tried not to inhale. Gradually, the room faded to black.

When he woke up, he was panting and Rider was shrieking. He tried not to think about his alcohol cure, but of course, that had exactly the opposite effect. Spinning out of control, his stream of consciousness rewound to that night in the fire room, then rapidly reviewed all he had learned since then.

Take me to Casimir. Take me now, Rider's thin voice screamed. With his very skull vibrating, Zavijavah writhed against the restraining belts. Somebody shouted—Jackson's aide, maybe. He couldn't even gather enough presence of mind to tell Rider how much attention it was attracting.

A huge voice, bigger than planets, bigger than suns, roared through Zavijavah's universe. *He was right. I can leave you. That would kill you. You are not what you were.*

Gasping, Zavijavah opened his eyes. Someone had replaced his glasses. The clinic door hung askew.

Do you understand? the voice boomed.

"Yes," he squeaked. He'd half hoped that Rider wouldn't notice what he had done when it finally resurfaced. The alien needed his senses to survive but spent little time communicating with him. The physical world obviously wasn't its home.

His disobedience hadn't even gained him a memorable respite, because looking back over the last two weeks, he had walked in a fog.

Take me to Casimir.

"He isn't here," Zavijavah muttered. "He left from the base for dinner and a live show. He'll be back in a while."

Take me to Casimir.

"I can't." Zavijavah raised his voice and pleaded. "Jackson won't—"

"I won't what?" Jackson scurried through the doorway, followed by his aide.

"It's all right." His voice warbled like a sick bird's. "I'm okay now. I was ... hearing things."

"DTs?" Jackson peered into Zavijavah's left eye. "You'll be shaky for a day or two. You probably deserve it, but I can give you something that'll help."

"Please." Zavijavah gulped. "I'll need to apologize to the boss as soon as he gets back."

Jahn had been walking Alun out to the gardens for a second-dawn dinner picnic, taking a route that brought them past the clinic door, when he faintly heard a scream. It sounded like Osun Zavijavah. He'd told Alun that he felt a chill coming on and didn't want to eat outside after all, and he lured Alun back up to his second-floor suite.

Several paintings now decorated its walls. He'd followed through—immediately—after claiming in Gamal Casimir's fire room that he was looking for artwork.

Alun sat out on the balcony now, eating a stuffed game hen while Jahn manipulated Alun's terminal. He'd claimed to be working up tomorrow's lessons. Actually, he hoped Residence security was down with Security Chief Zavijavah temporarily out of commission. And why was he screaming in the clinic?

Jahn asked to see his own confidential dossier. Employment information appeared over his screen. He'd been right! No one was keeping Residence terminals secure for the moment, and he could leech other people's hardware at will. Virtually no one ever shut down a terminal when they stepped away.

Before checking on Logan Jackson's clinic, he tried the normally locked military files. The newest data looked sinister. Two days ago, Gamal Casimir had shuttled two Advanced Cluster Missiles up to a Gate ship in orbit. Those missiles might pound Antar in seventeen days. He hoped the Concord had sent Regent Salbari adequate reinforcements, because it would be too late to call for help now. On the other hand, if Jahn sent his ninth pod ship tonight, population centers—and the Salbari estate—could evacuate.

He switched over to Jackson's clinic to see why Osun Zavijavah was inside, screaming.

An audio pickup was live, and he listened, appalled. Addicted? He didn't mind learning that Zavijavah was a seer. But more and more often lately, the man had reeked of hard liquor. Jahn had never dreamed that a man could slip so quickly.

The line fell quiet for a few minutes. He wondered if anywhere on a Residence line he might find his final orders from Antar, sent before the Concord realized Tdega had seized the embassy. Hopefully not. They might contain hints of his identity.

He had listened to Llyn-Luene's surface thoughts while he interviewed her, pleased to discover that he'd made a good impression and impressed by her quick deductions—but alarmed to find that she found his face and mannerisms familiar. He must invent some explanation before she drew the obvious conclusion.

It spoke well for her character that she liked Filip Salbari. She had not mentioned the Head Regent, but his name had passed through her thoughts several times. He wished that he didn't need to keep a strict silence on Antaran issues. They could have talked about Filip Salbari. That would have eased his loneliness, too.

Abruptly, Logan Jackson called Gamal Casimir's suite. Jahn's line leech followed the burst. Suddenly, Jahn had access to Casimir's terminal too, and through it, to the reader he often carried. Casimir had just returned from his evening out. He was leaving his suite, headed for the clinic.

Jahn prayed that Alun would eat slowly. He leaned close to listen.

This time, the gray shape looming over Osun Zavijavah resolved into Gamal Casimir. "What is this?" he demanded. "Jackson says he's got you in detoxification, of all things. How long has this been going on?"

Zavijavah spoke honestly, in fear for his life. "Since that night up in your study. I discovered that I couldn't hear … Rider … when I was drinking with you. Ethanol must put it to sleep."

Casimir waited for Rider to add a comment, but Rider gave no orders. "I see," Casimir said. "Then you need to stay totally away from alcohol."

Yes, Rider hissed. "Yes," Zavijavah relayed. Rider added, *There are medicines.* Zavijavah echoed that too.

"Medicines? Oh, to make you sick if you tipple. I've heard of that. I'll have Jackson give you a good, big dose." Casimir laid a hand on Zavijavah's shoulder. "Daily. That way you won't be tempted."

"I won't." He hated making the promise. Hated abasing himself to Rider. And to Casimir. Hated himself thoroughly. But there was no other way.

"Eleven days." Casimir pointed at his chest. "You have eleven days until we take Alun to Sunsis. I expect impeccable behavior."

Rider seized his voice. "Your daughter has come back?" it asked.

Casimir flinched. "Yes. But—"

"I want her. I will have two offspring."

Casimir spread his hands, and for once in his life, Zavijavah pitied the man. "She has been mentally damaged," Casimir said. "She—"

"That is no concern. Bring them both to Sunsis."

Then Rider let go. Zavijavah shrank into the table. "I didn't tell it—"

Casimir raised a hand, his expression blank. "Be quiet. My treaty with the Chaethe depends on you. Do you understand?"

"Yes—"

Rider sent up one last thought bubble. *I'm ready to get up.*

"It wants me to get up." Zavijavah wriggled his elbows against the restraining band, agreeing with Rider for the moment.

"That's right. You haven't exercised for a couple of weeks. You were religious about it for a while."

"That was Rider's choice."

"It's yours now."

Zavijavah squeezed his eyes shut. If for one instant the universe granted him omnipotence, he would have dissolved it. All of it.

"I'm finished, Jahn," Alun called, interrupting the distant voices. "Are you feeling better? Can we go down to the hedge maze? There's plenty of time before bed."

Stunned, Jahn slapped off Alun's terminal. His throat had constricted. He cleared it. "Just a minute," he called back. "I've got a few bites left." His game hen lay almost untouched on his plate. He'd heard enough to kill his appetite. Chaethe—the parasites that allegedly sent spores out of one victim's skull into another's—were here. Zavijavah carried one. Casimir obviously knew it. What did Casimir plan for the Concord if he wanted a treaty with such creatures?

That enormous issue shrank, though, as a closer horror seized Jahn's attention. Now he knew why Alun had not been killed.

And that Llyn faced the same fate.

He must warn Filip Salbari tonight, sending that pod ship.

And he must not let Casimir destroy Llyn or Alun. Within the next eleven days, he must invent some way to keep them from being taken to Sunsis. Should he warn them as well?

Did he dare?

After tonight, he could dare. With his embassy link cut, his usefulness to the Concord had almost ended. If Filip Salbari had been able to send another tenpod, it would have arrived before now. After Jahn sent his ninth pod tonight, he could justify sacrificing his cover to help two human beings escape Gamal Casimir's scheming.

Maybe he could spirit them away, with Kai Oldion's help, and spend the tenth pod telling Antar where to find them.

He waited until Alun was snoring in the other room to load his mnemes. As fond as he'd grown of Alun, he doubted Alun could keep such a terrifying secret. Llyn, though—if he read her right, she had lived for years with a guardian she distrusted. She would have developed defenses.

260 | KATHY TYERS

Tomorrow he would take the two of them someplace where surveillance was minimal. He would distract Alun and tell Llyn all he dared.

"What are you doing?"

Startled, he spun his chair.

Alun stood in the doorway, blue pajama legs dragging the floor.

"Alun," Jahn said solemnly, "I'm thinking about Luene."

"Me too. Could we just go down and see her?" Alun grinned. "She's very pretty."

"I'm afraid, Alun." How much did he dare to say? "I'm afraid someone might try to hurt her."

Alun glowered. "Someone named Bellik." He narrowed his eyes, probably trying to look shrewd.

"He might."

"We have to help her."

"We will, Alun. Good night. Thank you."

"Not tonight?" Alun's eyebrows rose as his shoulders slumped.

"No. But soon."

Alun sighed. "Good night, then."

Jahn waited another long Tdegan hour before packing his mnemes into a small Residence convertible-drive car. This time, when he switched off his PL, he thought about activating the chip in his ring and leaving it under his pillow.

Not yet, he decided. Not even this was a last-resort situation.

He laid his leech on the front seat and set it to audibly monitor a local law-enforcement band, and he steered onto a deserted Bkellan street. There he parked. Within a few minutes, he found and switched off the Residence car's transponder.

Now he was untraceable. He headed out into the countryside. Kilometers away from any public landmark, he sent off his burst.

The law-enforcement voice from his leech instantly started reciting numbers.

He'd been monitored. *Creator, help!* Leaving his transmitter and long wire lying in the weeds, he gunned the car and accelerated up the long country lane. He roared through the next several corners, charged with an urgency that he hadn't felt since the first time he'd transmitted.

A new voice came on the enforcement channel. It read off a fresh string of numbers. Triangulation coordinates, no doubt. Lights appeared in the sky, swooping close to ground level. Hovercraft approached his transmission site from three directions.

Heart hammering, he slowed to a country crawl and watched them. One landed at the transmitting site while two kept hovering. Three kilometers farther west, his road intersected a thoroughfare. He accelerated into traffic, momentarily relieved. Within minutes, he started worrying about roadblocks.

Unfortunately, the car was checked out on his Residence card. Zavijavah's staff would know he'd gone out tonight. That transmitting site would be watched. He didn't dare go back for his equipment—nor to transmit there again, even if he could replace it.

He pulled over and activated his leech again. He keyed up the Residence and accessed the garage line, hoping to remove any record that he'd taken out a car.

No data appeared.

They had tamper-locked the garage line. This meant they already suspected a Residence employee of making unauthorized transmissions. He had researched the c-net yesterday, using the leech to leave no record of his search. If he could have found one unsecured access to Gate relays, it had seemed an obvious way to communicate with Antar.

Unfortunately, the c-net was locked in local mode.

Then he must leave Tdega immediately. The tools and weapons he'd been issued to stow away on an outbound ship might have gotten him aboard—if he could have found one—but they would not be enough for three stowaways, and he was not leaving without Alun and Llyn. He must contact Kai Oldion. Tonight.

At least he had sent one more information burst through the Gate relay. That had to be victory enough, a fit end to his mission.

He stopped at a public self-wash and steamed the car clean, and he drove back to the Residence from another direction.

All the halls were quiet.

22

Alun was snoring in the next room. Jahn leeched the i-line again, routed a call out through a circuit he normally used to order clothing, and tried Kai Oldion's access number. He'd called Oldion several times but gotten no answer. He worried that Oldion might try to regain his position by reporting Jahn to Casimir. But Oldion also might be out of town hunting an escape ship.

This time, the engineer answered. "You're still here," Jahn exclaimed. "Have you found anything?"

"Yes. I made a contact out of town. I was getting ready to leave you a message, but it's intimidating to call the Rez."

Jahn heard no deception in Oldion's voice. He had to speak frankly now. "I'm glad you didn't. We need to leave immediately. Did you find a way?"

"Yes."

"When? My two students need help getting out of the Rez."

"Is this serious trouble?"

"Serious enough."

Oldion cleared his throat. "We're going to Unukalhai. That suit you?"

"Perfectly."

"We've got to mute a surveillance satellite. That will take about two days. We plan to meet at—" He gave detailed directions into the mountainous countryside north of Bkellan. Jahn committed them to memory.

"Small private craft, ground launch. Can you and your passengers arrive before 0900, two days from now?"

"We'll be on foot," Jahn said. "It'll probably take most of a day to get that far."

"Then start walking tomorrow night."

"We'll start as soon as I can get away. Don't try to contact me at the Residence. I won't be there. If we don't make it, leave without us."

"We will."

"If you think you're being watched, don't wait for me."

Since Alun was still snoring, Jahn took the time to assemble a small emergency pack. He'd already obtained two data suits. The larger one looked too small for Alun, and the smaller one looked too big for Llyn, but gelskin—normally associated with AR synthesizers—also blocked personal locator frequencies when activated. He'd connected power cells.

He couldn't leave his mneme units behind, even if he had no further use for them. They, too, went into the pack, as well as the variable-frequency transponder he'd used all along to deactivate locks and alarm systems.

He'd also concocted four thermal outsoles, copying the pair in his emergency pack. He would have Llyn and Alun wear them over their shoes to avoid leaving warm footprints for IR scanners to pick up.

Good, basic precautions.

With less than an hour and a half until dawn, it was too late to get a good start during this darkness. They would have to wait until first sunset this afternoon.

After eight days of Gate watch, Admiral Gehretz Lalande's forces had begun to let surveillance details slip past them. Making unannounced rounds, he found two scantechs chatting with each other on watch and a gunner on duty with his turret set for target simulation. He ran the battle group up to full readiness. He held them at red-alert status for two hours.

Then he kept them watching Ilzar Gate.

After three more hours, an enormous shape blurred through. "Full scan," Lalande ordered. "Whatever that is, it's not going to get far—"

A row of scanners flashed and darkened to prevent overload. The emergency siren howled. By the time *Fire Dance's* instruments came back online, the scanners showed an expanding cloud of debris sending shock waves through the ore cloud.

"All slips, full particle shielding," Lalande ordered. As the first shock wave crashed past the *Fire Dance*, another ship emerged from Ilzar Gate. The scanners flashed again.

"I hope we haven't destroyed two civilian ships," his deck officer murmured.

Lalande turned to a scantech. "Any preliminary indication of what they were?"

She straightened her chair and shook her head. "They were big, fast, and on their way to hit Ilzar hard. Definitely looking for us, sir."

Lalande led his deck officer away from the scanning station. "If I have Tdegan strategy anticipated, the next ship through will be their counter-invasion force, and it will be slower. Fast enough to sustain damages, but it won't be destroyed."

The deck officer crossed his fingers.

These children. They'd never learned to detach themselves from life and death and think of war as a game.

Lalande's watch took two hours, but his patience was rewarded when a massive personnel carrier sped out of the huge oblong Gate and abruptly hit full deceleration. It swerved away from the trip-line area and plowed into a cloud of denzite ore that had been tugboated into a corridor near the emergence vector from Tdega. "Watch that," he directed the scanning officer. "Was she breached?"

After a few minutes, the woman answered. "Leaking air, sir."

The carrier drifted from boulder to boulder so slowly that their relative velocities would not damage it further.

"Also leaking transmissions," the scantech announced. "In two days, Tdega will know it's got personnel stranded on this side."

"Well done." Lalande straightened his back. It felt good to give honest praise. "They'll know we're here, waiting to fire. Any rescue squad they mean to put through, they'll have to send crawling. We've likely got about five days. The forces outside Tdega Gate will send word to headquarters and await orders."

"Are we going off full watch status, then?" his deck officer stood straight and proud.

Lalande eyed the young man. "Off full watch, but we're not going anywhere. Let's see what else comes through."

An unwelcome visitor interrupted Llyn's breakfast. Bellik Casimir arrived in his dark-gray uniform, carrying a bundle of gorgeous red flowers spotted with black. She pressed her face to them and breathed deeply. They had no fragrance.

"Thank you." She tried to sound gracious. Maybe she misread the man. "This is a wonderful world. Everything's either green or blooming."

"I think you're blooming." He rested a hand on the back of a chair and leaned on it, transparently trying to catch and reflect light on his gold half-moon collar pins. "Every time I see you, you look more assured. You'll be a full Regent in no time."

And Commander Bellik plainly was interested in snatching a Regent. "I think it will be quite awhile," she said, ringing for Peatra. When the wizened little servant woman arrived, Llyn asked her to put Bellik's flowers in water.

"Would you like to ride out to the defense base with me later today?" Bellik asked. Even his voice seemed to swagger. "We've got a force on its way to Antar."

"To Antar?" That was terrible news. Why was he telling her?

"Don't look so unhappy. They attacked our defense group at Ilzar. We don't want this war to drag on forever. This time, we'll end it. If you'd like to drive out to the base … ?" He dipped his chin and raised his shoulders. Maybe the gesture was supposed to look like a playful shrug.

"I'd like that," she said carefully, "another time. I don't feel well today. Nothing serious, just … well, women are like that." The handy universal excuse.

He sighed. "Oh. Another time, then. Enjoy your breakfast." He strutted out.

Peatra returned with her flowers in a tall vase and set them on the conversational table next to Llyn's congealed breakfast.

She picked at the food. She barely had time to feel relieved by Bellik's departure before Peatra poked her wrinkled face around the corner into the study again. "Excuse me, Gen'n Luene," she said, "but it's time you joined your tutor. You're to meet him in Alun's rooms."

Llyn sprang up. She didn't need a big breakfast, anyway.

It was pleasant to join Jahn and Alun this morning. She no longer wanted to be fully independent. She simply wanted interdependence, real community instead of being dominated.

Jahn surprised her by announcing that they were going to do this morning's lesson at the Residence kennels. Alun jumped out of his chair. "Great," he exclaimed. "Thank you, Jahn!"

"Do they keep dedoes?" Llyn needed to hear a loud purr. She wanted comfort. If Antar was attacked again, who would survive?

"No," Alun exclaimed. "We have purebred Labrador retrievers. Real dogs, originally bred on Earth." He held his head proudly.

"I'd love to see them." Maybe they wouldn't comfort her as Squeak would have, but she'd never seen a purebred dog. Jahn escorted them down the lift and out a back door. Alun strode ahead. "I can't keep up with him," Llyn exclaimed. Her knees and hips already ached.

"Don't try," Jahn said quietly. He glanced aside, then said, "I need to talk with you alone, anyway. I know you haven't been here long, but your father's Security man isn't to be trusted."

She'd almost forgotten that concern in the flood of other ones, especially wanting to warn Filip Salbari that another attack was coming. "Gen Zavijavah? In what way?" she asked cautiously.

Jahn studied the path and walked slowly. Smooth pebbles crunched under both their feet. "I learned something alarming yesterday. Your father has plans for you and Alun in addition to seating you on the Board."

His tone of voice confirmed her concerns. He was preparing her for a shock. "I'm used to unspoken agendas."

He raised an eyebrow.

"I was, well, supervised too closely by the woman who adopted me. I learned to keep my defenses up. It wouldn't surprise me if Father had invented some plan."

"It's a terrible one, Llyn."

She shortened her stride. Wasn't Jahn Korsakov another one of her father's trusted employees? Why believe him, why trust him? But she plainly couldn't trust her father or Bellik. They were attacking Antar again. Tdega might be her planet of birth, but Antar was home, and she'd lived through the horrors of the previous attack.

Jahn hadn't yet spoken with the manipulative overtones that Karine, Bellik, and her father used. He talked to her as an equal, even though his position as a teacher set him above her.

Well, she liked him, but she didn't trust him yet. Maybe later. He might help her try hunting for Siah.

"You're wondering why you should trust me," he said.

"What are you, an empath?" She meant it as a joke.

But it fell flat. Oddly, he flushed pink. "If you don't trust me, that's only natural."

"True," she said, startled. "Tell me what you think they're planning. Then I'll decide whether to trust you. And," she added, "I won't repeat anything to Gen Zavijavah. I knew you were thinking that, and obviously, I'm no empath."

"You certainly must have learned to distrust them." That was an odd tone of voice, simultaneously hopeful and strained. "What's wrong?" he asked into her hesitation.

"It wasn't what you said. It was the way you said it." Come to think of it, he had given her extra time to react when he said something provocative. Could there be Tdegan empaths?

Or was he Antaran?

"Did I offend you?" he asked. "I'm sorry."

She shrugged and looked down the path. Geometric flowerbeds dotted and striped the lawn on both sides. They were still several meters from the kennels. "There was one empath I liked and respected," she said. "I have met Head Regent Filip Salbari. He is not the megalomaniac that you Tdegans make him out to be."

Jahn smiled for an instant. "I don't believe the i-net accounts of him either." His smile faded. "You've heard the rumors about intelligent alien parasites?"

She felt a chill. "Yes. Who hasn't?"

"It appears—and I hope I am wrong—that your father knows that Osun Zavijavah carries one."

A little gasp escaped her.

"It will need to reproduce soon. Your father has apparently selected you and Alun to become carriers. I think this alien race wants two seats on the Board of Regents."

She froze in midstride. Several meters away, a flock of birds landed on the sloping lawn.

It had been hard to imagine such a horrible creature. She wanted to scoff at the rumors. But Jahn's voice—sincere, convinced, and deeply concerned for her well-being—was nothing like Bellik's. He might be mistaken, but he was not trying to deceive or manipulate her.

"So far as I know, I'm the only one who has found out. I was …spying on him," he admitted. "Just to see if I could do it," he added, and this time, his voice cued her plainly. He was not telling the whole truth.

Her heart jumped. Was this man an Antaran? Maybe he could warn Filip Salbari!

"I'm going to get you two off the grounds." He raised his head and eyed the distant garden wall. "Today. They're looking for me."

Her emotions tumbled as she processed all that. Looking? They? Then he *was* under suspicion. Did standing with him implicate her, too? But he wanted to get her away, and she wanted exactly that. "If you're … being looked for, why are you still here?"

"To help you. Things are happening quickly up there." He glanced back at the Residence's long façade. "Your father's situation has gotten too deep to handle, and I can't let you be dragged in."

They reached the kennels, a low building of weathered wood. Llyn hadn't had a chance to tell him about the attack force. Maybe she didn't dare. Maybe he wasn't that kind of a spy.

But as he glanced up at an electronic gate that surrounded the dog runs, she looked across a distinctly squared chin.

Oh, my. This could change everything. If he was an Antaran spy, why hadn't he had that chin surgically altered? On the other hand, most people weren't this keenly aware of shapes and angles, or so she'd been told.

And she wanted to trust him. He wanted to take her out of the Residence, and she wanted to get out of the city. So far, their goals—even the timing—agreed perfectly.

She eyed the electronic gate. A small, round glass lens peered back down. Within the gated area, dog runs lay separated by rows of short flags. She guessed that they indicated electronic fence lines.

Security. Gen Zavijavah might be watching and listening anywhere, at any time.

Zavijavah had acted oddly, hadn't he? Even more suggestively, she'd already noticed that he spoke not with one man's tone-of-voice repertory, but with two. She wished she had studied more science. She felt dangerously ignorant on the subject of parasites, and she didn't need Jahn to warn her not to check the net on that topic ever again.

Inside an electronic aisle marked by yellow-gold flags, Alun was already crouching beside a large black animal. Its collar was also yellow-gold, and it lay on its side, surrounded by pushing, shoving smaller versions of itself. "Is it safe?" Llyn asked Jahn.

Did she believe him? Could she trust him?

She would rather trust Jahn than Bellik. That had been her first impression, but after this morning's visit from Bellik, it was even stronger.

"It's safe for Alun," Jahn said. "He raised Bear from a puppy. But I wouldn't recommend our crossing that fence line. She's got pups of her own now."

"So I see." Llyn had experienced enough maternal protectiveness to last a lifetime. She sat down cross-legged several centimeters outside the line of yellow-gold markers and called to Alun, "So, that's your dog, isn't it?"

He looked up over his shoulder. "She's such a good mother," he exclaimed. "The puppies are already twice as big as last week. Llyn, when they're big enough to take away from her, would you like to have one?"

"I don't think Bear would like that." Llyn glanced at Jahn, expecting disapproval.

Jahn murmured near her ear, "That's the most generous offer I've ever heard Alun make."

She nodded and called back to Alun, "But they're beautiful. Thank you, Alun. I'd love one."

Alun beamed. She'd never seen a man look so totally happy—and the pups did look exquisitely soft. She wondered what it would feel like to stroke one.

Alun seemed occupied for the moment, and Jahn didn't act eager to

270 | KATHY TYERS

start a lesson, so she pressed back up to her feet. She walked out over the fence line and a few steps downhill. As she'd hoped, Jahn followed. She stared at the rooflines of the main kennel, wondering if any observation cameras were mounted on top of them.

She turned to stare back at the Residence. "What did you see or hear that made you suspect that about Gen Zavijavah?" she asked.

After hesitating almost a minute, he asked, "You're familiar with the Sunsis colonies?"

"I know where they are."

"They appear to be the source of infestation. According to your father, he intends to take you and Alun there next week."

"Do you have any idea where my brother Siah is?"

"I wish I did. I'll get you off the grounds. I'll hide you. I promise."

"I'd like to find Siah."

"That's not far enough. Your father probably knows where he is."

Should she tell him to warn Antar? Maybe Gamal Casimir's daughter had the right to demand cooperation from her tutor. "I want to find Siah." She mimicked the firm, confident tone Karine always used.

———

Startled, Jahn kept his eyes on Alun. He'd been almost ready to confess his identity, but Llyn's lunge for control of the situation caught him off guard. He had thought she felt helpless here. He was the helpless one, with his transmitter seized and a desperate plan to run away exactly as the whisperers had predicted. Run, in fact, with a female student. This would look unforgivable.

He was already maintaining a shallow synch touch. Momentarily, he probed more deeply.

Llyn felt as totally curious as she had been frightened earlier. *Who was this man? Could she warn Filip Salbari through him?* She pulled him deeper—

He bailed out. She was testing him, and that was appropriate. He would not leave her behind, as Jerone Emlin had abandoned Vananda and Jahn. "Siah has a direct line to Bkellan University," he said, tugging her toward nexus. "Even I found that. Your father can find him, too."

Then Siah wouldn't be able to help hide her. Maybe she should—

She strangled the thought. After living with Karine, she rarely let herself finish surreptitious thoughts until she was alone.

But Jahn was no empath.

She glanced at him again. He tilted his head and looked up into the trees, as if she'd surprised him synching. As if he were … signaling her? Telling her he *was* an empath?

Why put herself under an empath's control again, if he was?

But if he was, maybe he could warn Antar.

Memories of Karine threatened to panic her. Memories of Filip Salbari kept her calm.

"I'm going to walk around the back of the kennels," Jahn said softly. "Please talk to Alun for a while."

"All right." Llyn strolled back over to the kennel, sat back down on grassy ground, and got Alun chatting about his dogs. That gave her time to think.

Jahn could be an empath, an Antaran spy. In fact, she would almost bet on it. Why else would he be staying on to help her? If that was the case, his talents might help her escape.

But she did not trust him. Not yet.

And that felt like a shame.

After only a few minutes, he ambled back around the building. "Alun," he said, "Let's go inside. There's a morning i-net to check."

Alun sighed and said, "Okay."

Jahn glanced sharply at Llyn. Again, she found herself trying to interpret his expression. Was he synching? Did he realize what she was thinking?

To her shock, he nodded.

A chill raced down her back. She stood up, looked directly at him, and formed words in her mind: *I haven't been here long enough to trust you, Jahn Korsakov. Don't betray me.*

"No," he murmured.

"What?" Alun turned around with one hand on the kennel latch. "Did I do something wrong?"

"No, Alun." Jahn kept staring at Llyn. "You're fine."

The eye contact was electric. Llyn made herself look away before he did.

They walked back to the Residence. Alun chattered about dogs while Llyn tried to control her thoughts, keeping them private—but they sped out of control. If he was an empath, he was a spy. If he was a spy, he had ways to communicate with Regent Salbari. He must already know about the attack they were sending to Antar—

And if he didn't know before, he knew now.

23

Jahn abbreviated Alun's morning lessons and kept listening. Security guards passed in the hall, but none acted suspicious. Over and over, he wondered: Luene Casimir had a reputation for intelligence, but she had taken only two days to realize what he was. Who else might have seen through his cover?

Only someone equally familiar with empaths and who would recognize empath mannerisms—he hoped. He should be safe for a few hours. He'd left her in her room, reading the i-net, but as soon as he returned to Alun's suite, he had leeched her line, ready to rush back outdoors if she transmitted any kind of report.

She didn't. She plainly did not trust him, but he found himself almost trusting her.

At midmorning break, her terminal went into hibernation. She had probably finished her reading assignment. Jahn sent Alun out for a jog around Residence grounds and walked back down to her rooms. A Security guard stood three doors up the hall, ignoring him. Jahn synched for a moment. The guard was not consciously watching him.

But something was afoot. There wasn't normally this much security in the hall.

Llyn's servant Peatra admitted him. Llyn sat cross-legged on the edge of her bed, cradling a Tdegan lyre against her body. A breeze that smelled like three kinds of flowers ruffled the room's gauzy curtain. He synched shallowly. She seemed tense.

"Aren't you supposed to leave music alone?" he asked, praying she would say nothing incriminating in front of Peatra. "I thought it brought on your flashbacks."

"Sometimes." She stroked the strings. "Peatra just brought this in for me to see. And look. Nothing happens."

"It's pentatonic," he observed.

She looked up with sharp eagerness in her eyes. "Are you a musician?"

"I was, a long time ago. But you're taking a risk."

"No." She shook her head. "I've discovered something wonderful. This lyre has no half tones."

"Not if it's pentatonic. The notes of that scale are farther apart than—"

"Exactly! The music in my artificial world was set in a very tight scale. The octave was divided into seventeen tiny steps, with hundreds of shades of meaning. This music is peaceful. It has no tension. It doesn't drive me in any direction."

She was anything but calm, though. "Many people find pentatonic music boring," he said, "because it doesn't go anywhere."

"Exactly." When she smiled, her face radiated peace. "You said you'd been a musician. Was it vocal or instrumental?"

"I sing. Sang, anyway. With a performing group."

Her eyes widened. "Really? Do you have any recordings?"

Oddly, he did. He'd wondered what sentiment had driven him to include those files in his limited confidential storage when he left Antar's i-net and came to Tdega. Now it seemed miraculous, a possible key to her confidence. "Yes, on a personal reader."

"I'd like to hear what you sang. Can you go get it?"

"Well—all right." Once again, he walked out into the hall. He ignored the slow pace of another Security guard strolling toward the elevator, but he synched to make sure he was still safe. Again he sensed no particular vigilance.

He found his personal reader in the pocket of an old pair of work pants, suitable only for crawling around in storage areas. He had rarely needed it here. When he walked back out into Alun's entry hall, Alun stood there panting. Perspiration bedraggled the sparse hair on his chest. "That was great," he exclaimed.

Jahn slapped his shoulder. "Go shower. Then order yourself an early lunch." It would be dark by 0600, lunchtime. Time to leave.

He walked to Llyn's room again. She laid down her lyre when he pulled the reader out of his pocket. "Thank you," she exclaimed.

Not seeing Peatra, he gestured toward the door of Llyn's extra room and raised an eyebrow. "She's watching i-net," Llyn said softly.

Jahn thumbed the reader's control sequence to start the music.

It was an old popular song. Immediately after his University grad, he'd spent an evening with friends making this recording. He would have liked to listen to it. Instead, he adjusted his mental stance and synched with Llyn. She sat on a chair and stared at the floor with her head cocked sideways, as if she were listening to something that threatened to sneak up behind her.

Her emotions, always enthusiastically single, focused on the music. They stretched into it, becoming alarmingly galvanized. Sensitized.

Hastily, he shut off the recording. He needed her trust, but he hadn't meant to seduce her!

She stirred. "What did you do that for?" she exclaimed. "I was enjoying that. Your voice blends well with the others."

"You picked me out?" he asked lightly.

"I hear voices very well. Why did you shut it off?"

"You looked upset." Not quite true, but it would suffice.

"No," she said, avoiding his eyes. "I wasn't. I hadn't felt so ... good ... since my last really deep flashback." She laughed lightly. "Turn it back on. Please."

"I don't think I should. Music pulls you too deep." He knew that for certain now.

To his surprise, her voice rose in anger. "If you surround me with restrictions too, I'll—I'll send you away."

"But you'll—" he began, and he stopped. She hadn't blacked out. Hedging her with restrictions would never heal her, and her anger was healthier than blind cooperation. She might make terrible mistakes with her freedom, but she must be free to make them.

Besides, if she had deduced his empathy, she would soon realize he'd felt her reaction to the music.

He cleared his throat. "I spoke out of turn. I'm sorry. That would be a wrong thing to do." He made himself say the words, knowing they were the right words to say, even though his inner man longed to protect her. From himself, if necessary.

"Turn it back on." She stared at his face as if daring him to refuse.

"Are you sure? You're making a dangerous choice."

"Give me the credit for knowing that."

"Please do me one favor, then," he said gently. "Don't listen to music unless I'm here to help you … ah … cope."

She actually laughed. He'd never heard her laugh before. It sounded like the upbeat of a song he ought to remember. "Would you turn that on, Jahn?"

He pressed the repeat button. The song started over.

He didn't synch with her this time but listened. He winced at every cracked note and amateurish harmony.

The song ended. She handed back the reader. "I'm healing. I can listen and resist now, even this soon after a flashback."

"Be careful," he begged. "We feel strong at the beginning of every learning curve, when we're acquiring new skills—but at that point, we have very little actual power."

"I do feel strong." She stretched her arms over her head.

"When you have fully learned a skill, it's different. You feel how small you really are, how little you really know. Haven't you experienced that?"

She whispered in a teasing voice, "Yes, teacher."

He flickered an eyelid at her.

"I've been addicted to a memory." She pushed back into the chair. "But I do prefer this world—your music—my life—being a free moral agent—over the inner world. So I will participate in my own healing."

"You've barely begun."

"And I'll keep on until I die." Her hand clenched. "But if you try to fence me in, or fence the music out, you'll kill me. Don't you understand?"

"I think so," he murmured. "You've taken responsibility for your own actions, right or wrong."

"Fully human. At last." She closed her eyes and squeezed out a tear. "But it used to be very sweet in there."

In where? *Oh. In the AR.* "You need something sweeter. Something you can choose for, not against." He synched momentarily and found that her distrust had vanished. His inner man, which had almost kept him from playing that recording, exulted now. "I understand that your … Antaran mother … kept you on a rigid regimen."

"Karine Torfinn." She practically snorted the words, glaring at him.

He formed the word *Oh* with his lips. Karine Torfinn had spoken at one of his training sessions. His classmates decided the woman had an authority fixation.

"She did shape me from a pleasure-seeker into personhood." Llyn seemed to be staring into a far distance. "And in hindsight, I respect her. But she couldn't let go. You—right now—could walk out of this room and go where you pleased. Even now, I can't do that."

"Freedom without purpose accomplishes little," he insisted. "If you serve no one, you serve yourself. And the forces of chaos. Those masters will charge a hefty price for what you thought was pure freedom."

"Are you a religious person?" Her eyes narrowed.

"I've chosen what seems the highest sphere."

"That sounds like Regent Salbari."

Alarmed, he touched his lips. If anyone were watching or listening—anyone—a statement of agreement could hang him. But he was glad she was talking again, and thinking. He despised the thought of seducing her, although willingness still softened her large brown eyes. He wished she would go on looking at him that way.

"I'm going to take Alun down to the kennels again in an hour," he said. "Right about sunset. Come with us."

"All right." She glanced at the door. "I'll dress warmly."

Llyn watched him walk out. She must have embarrassed him, getting so deeply involved in his music. She wished she hadn't. But when he'd played that song the second time, despite her first reaction and the danger of a flashback—simply because she'd insisted—she had decided to accept him. He probably knew that, too.

Because he was an empath.

She was plagued by them!

The door shut.

Yet it had felt good to hear him sing. To imagine touching him was a warm new experience. She let herself imagine it just a little bit longer: strong arms, a gentle embrace—

Stop that! She recalled his warning and shuddered. It had been bad enough living with someone who could listen to her thoughts. It terrified her to imagine an alien creature living inside them.

In a way, Jahn had been right. If she flashed back to the inner world again here at the Residence, she would be helpless.

She must escape.

So why not go alone? Every service-shop area in the Concord had an ARcade.

The idea shot through her mind like a flash through the grid lines, followed by another: it would be harder for Gen Zavijavah's Security force to track one runaway alone than three together.

But an AR would be no escape. Sooner or later, they would find her. And she did not want to be alone.

She laid aside the lyre and rested her head on one arm. From this angle, she could see the old Casimir family scrapbook Peatra had brought her. Not one image, not one class trophy had stirred her memory.

She must stay calm for an hour. Until first sunset.

24

Osun Zavijavah's private office was spartan, without windows or wall decorations. He had shuffled in for work half an hour late today, dragging his feet so not to jar his head. At least Rider was quiet.

Last night, word had come in that Ilzar's reinforcements were stranded, Ilzar Gate blockaded—but that was Bellik's business. The first work on Zavijavah's screen was an urgent report from garage staff. During last night's crisis, when that burst transmission was triangulated, three Residence cars had been checked out. All three employees were now at work, one pretending innocence plus two probably noninvolved: a kitchen employee, the kennel master, and the young Casimirs' tutor.

Zavijavah rubbed his head. Jahn Korsakov had been caught once in a secure area. That'd been the night he'd discovered red ruin, for all the good it had done him.

Res-net was no longer considered secure, so Zavijavah hunted down a pad of paper and jotted a note to his employer. He sent it off with an aide. When the aide returned, he brandished several printed sheets. "Sir," he said, "Gen Orrican arrived with your printouts."

"Ah!" Decryption expert Orrican had been decoding those final broadcasts to the Antaran embassy. Zavijavah reached for the papers as his aide shut the door behind him.

First, Casimir's reply: he wanted all three employees interrogated this afternoon. Zavijavah should select an effective drug and schedule one-hour blocks at the clinic.

He set that aside and eyed Gen Orrican's translation of the embassy papers. As he scanned the top page, something seemed to crawl up his neck. Empath lingo. Unmistakable. He and Casimir had suspected, but this looked like confirmation.

He eyed the three names again. Obviously, the tutor was in the most vital position. Therefore, Korsakov was the likeliest spy. If he was an empath, no one else must know he was under suspicion until the last possible moment. Also, he must be questioned first.

Zavijavah made a final note on his paper pad: *armed escort.*

He read on.

Antar ordered the security leak to eliminate the "infested individual."

Zavijavah frowned. He'd been targeted for death. Still, Korsakov—if Zavijavah guessed his identity right—had not received this order.

Zavijavah's mouth twisted upward. He could arrest the tutor immediately.

Still, Korsakov had done nothing hastily. It was obviously not his style. He only needed to be watched by guards who did not know he was their specific subject—

Zavijavah's screen flashed twice, signaling priority news. He swiveled his chair to face the monitor.

The burst was brief. Filip Salbari had resigned the Head Regency of Antar, effective immediately. Boaden Salbari was the new officeholder.

Zavijavah pressed his aching temples again, pushing the pain in deeper. Boaden Salbari would pursue a more aggressive defense. Bellik was probably rubbing his hands, eager to battle a real militant.

As for Korsakov, he'd been here for weeks. The embassy link was down, the transmitter seized. He was almost netted.

At the next coffee break, Zavijavah called Casimir and requested permission to report personally. If Casimir refused, he would know he was still out of favor over the red ruin episode.

Word flashed back: *Report to the fire room.*

Relieved, he adjusted his dark glasses and hurried out of his office.

Casimir stood by the unlit hearth. "Are you feeling all right?"

"Moderately. Did you hear about Filip Salbari?"

"Yes." Casimir set a mug on the hearth and stepped toward one of the room's inner doors. "I'm sure Bellik will have plenty to say about it."

"There's something interesting afoot at the Rez, too. I believe we've found the leak."

"Really." Casimir paused in the side doorway. "Sit down. I've got something I need to finish up. Keep talking, though." He pointed to a deep chair and walked through the doorway. His voice filtered through. "Who is it?"

Zavijavah couldn't believe Casimir wasn't hanging on every word, but he sat down. "Korsakov," he said softly. "The tutor. And he's also—"

His world exploded.

Gamal peered around the door. Zavijavah had slumped onto the floor.

Definitely effective! Particularly when the subject was caught by surprise. Gamal glanced back into his inner room. Enormous coils topped a massive wheeled machine he'd requisitioned out of defense base supplies. It was a huge electromagnet, one of several ways he'd thought of protecting himself on this upcoming Sunsis trip. A powerful magnetic field should affect an iron spore sheath. He was glad he'd thrown the switch for only an instant.

Had he hurt either Rider or Zavijavah?

He shut the side door and slipped into the fire room. He knelt beside Zavijavah, probed at the side of his throat, and found a pulse. Zavijavah was breathing, too. Gamal had pocketed a stimulant patch down at the clinic. He peeled off its backing and stuck it on Zavijavah's neck.

Then he stood up to watch Zavijavah. He'd tried to move quickly, so neither Rider nor Zavijavah would know what he'd done. This would be his last-ditch defense against allies who might turn on him.

He lit a cigarillo and waited. He did hope he hadn't injured Zavijavah. He didn't want another brain-damaged dependent.

Luene, like Alun, was not what she'd been. He had thought she was dead years ago. And she still could be an assassin. But she was not what he remembered.

He'd intended to offer her years ago. Now he hesitated. His helmet experiment still might succeed.

But so might using her as a cultural bridge. It was always wise to have alternate plans, and if Luene recovered, she would make a splendid ambassador to the Chaethe. If she was an assassin, seeing her infested would end that threat.

At any rate, he didn't want her told anything certain about the Chaethe. He could not control net rumors, but until the last moment, she should know as little as possible to spare her the terror of anticipation. She would adjust after the fact, as Zavijavah had done.

Groaning, Zavijavah pushed up on stiff arms.

"What happened?" Gamal demanded.

"Don't know," Zavijavah grunted. He pulled off his glasses and squinted. "But you probably do."

Interesting. An immediate, intelligent guess. Evidently he hadn't taken any serious damage. "No. I took my message and when I came back in, you were lying there—"

"What happened?" Zavijavah interrupted, using the atonal Rider voice.

So it'd also stirred up Rider. "I don't know." Gamal shook his head. "I'm deeply concerned."

"Something endangered my symbiont's life. I need to know what it was." The tone still sounded like Rider.

"So do I," Gamal exclaimed. "I will put Zavijavah to work immediately. He will try and find out what happened."

Zavijavah slumped and sighed. He wobbled to his feet and pushed his dark glasses back on. "What was that all about?"

"I don't know." Gamal flicked ash off his cigarillo into the fireplace. "But you were telling me you'd found our spy. Maybe he just sent off a signal that affected Rider."

Zavijavah sat back down in the chair. "No. We've got his transmitter."

"Maybe he has another. We'll take him today, one way or another."

"Be careful and quiet," Zavijavah said. "According to those final embassy transmissions, he's an empath."

"Oh, ho. Another one." Mutants were everywhere. "Whether he deliberately attacked Rider or it was an accidental side effect, it can't happen again." He jerked his head toward the door. "Call up your off-duty people and meet me in the Oak Room. I'm going to call Bellik over."

"As soon as I get another headache dose from Jackson." Zavijavah shuffled out.

Gamal smoked thoughtfully and stared at the fire. Korsakov was high in the information-flow hierarchy and in direct contact with Luene. Gamal had paired them himself. Korsakov's records had looked clean, but with in-flo training, he would have known how to circumvent security. If he was an empath, that would explain how he had operated.

But it would not help him beat interrogation. With the leak stopped at last and a way to defend himself against Chaethe, Gamal could go safely to Sunsis.

He snuffed his cigarillo. So all it took was a simple electromagnet. Why hadn't he thought of this before?

Because he'd been trying to communicate. The key was control.

Alun and Luene could be two Chaethe voices on his Board of Regents. And now he could control them all.

Llyn sat bolt upright, sweating. Her room lights had come on. Food smells drifted up from the Residence kitchen. Her shoulders ached, probably since she'd fallen asleep in an odd position. She flung herself off the bed and walked to the window, needing to wake up, hoping she hadn't missed Jahn and Alun.

The sun had just set. A few stars pricked tiny holes in the sky.

She'd been having the strangest dream, almost a flashback. But she'd emerged on her own!

She dug in her closet and found a dark shirt and a pair of snug pants. She wished she could take more things with her, but she didn't want Peatra to think she meant to do anything more than walk down to the kennels.

She was running a brush through her hair when the door chime sounded. She opened it, and Jahn and Alun hurried in. Jahn held out a rolled bundle, gave his head a slight sideways jerk toward her personal, and said, "Here, Alun. Sit down at Llyn's terminal."

Now that it was about to happen, she wanted to hustle. Clutching the bundle against her chest, she slipped into the personal. As she unrolled it, a slip of paper fell out of a black gelskin data suit. She picked it up and read: *PL chips won't transmit through gelskin. Put this on under your clothes.*

Shaking out the garment, she found a small battery hooked to it, just enough to create a weak field. Something else dropped on the floor. It separated into two limp objects, like thin, baggy socks attached to sole-shaped cards.

She stripped and slid on the data suit. It was too big. When she put her clothes back on, they held it in uncomfortable bunches against her skin.

Having her tactile sense back wasn't going to be all feathers and soft blankets. The most important self-defense sensation was pain. Hadn't Karine taught her so?

There she went, thinking about Karine again.

Guessing the booties should go outside her shoes, she slipped them on, too, then walked back out of the personal. Jahn, she saw, had also changed into dark clothing, and she spotted black gelskin at Alun's neckline. They both wore the flimsy booties outside their shoes. She had guessed correctly.

"Hi, Luene," Alun whispered. "You have to be very quiet. We're going down to see what the puppies act like when they sleep. Jahn says they wiggle and kick."

"Okay," she whispered back. She eyed Jahn more closely. He wasn't wearing a data suit.

He said nothing about it then, but as they walked out the back door, he murmured, "I can turn my PL off."

He'd known what she was thinking, naturally. A chip he could turn off? Wonderful—and illegal. "You found a gate?" she asked. "How will you unlock it?"

As they strode away from the building, down the pebbled path, he pulled a small, black object out of a pocket. It fit on his palm and looked like a miniature i-net leech.

"What is it?" she asked.

"Forgive me if I don't tell you. What you don't know, you can't tell anyone else."

"I wouldn't—"

"They could make you."

"Oh." The idea made her want to shrink down to insect size.

The data suit bunched between her legs as she walked, and she grew uncomfortably warm. As they walked under a tree, she glanced up. A flock of birds had settled to roost away the dark hours.

She eyed Jahn's pack. It was the same dark gray as his jacket, and it didn't look very thick. "What about food and water?" she whispered.

"There's habitable country around Bkellan. We'll do all right. Alun is much better than he was," he added. "I don't think you've been here long enough to notice."

Thinking about Alun kept her from flinching at every noise. "His voice already is less singsong, more spontaneous than when I met him."

Jahn nodded slightly and kept walking. "If someone follows us," he said softly, "we'll have to separate. Quickly."

"Shall we meet somewhere?" She shivered.

"Don't try to find me. I'll find you. I can do that."

"True." She remembered Karine at the library. It seemed like a lifetime ago.

What was she doing, running away with an empath?

Evidently, she'd learned to believe in their abilities.

When they reached the kennel, Bear and the pups were nowhere to be seen. "Aw," Alun said. "She's inside her little building."

Jahn pulled Alun close and talked against his ear. Alun mouthed the word "Bellik" and nodded seriously. His expression became shrewd.

"Okay," he whispered to Jahn. He glanced over at Llyn. "Let's go."

Bellik marched pompously into the Oak Room. "I hope this is important," he declared. "I can contact the base from here, but I belong with my forces. There are six hours left in my workday. I don't want to waste them."

Gamal sat at the oak table's head and let him spout. Zavijavah stood by the door. The display wall showed only the Residence's façade, gleaming by first sunset's sidelight. Zavijavah had assured him that his people had cleared out of the halls and were tracking all employees by PL chip this afternoon. Korsakov was in Alun's rooms. "Sit down," Gamal ordered.

Bellik frowned. "What's so important?"

Gamal took his chair at the table's head and leaned his elbows on both armrests. "I have been thinking. Someone else should know about you, Zavijavah."

Zavijavah stroked his mustache, frowning. "I don't know about that."

"I do," Gamal said firmly. As the secession conflict heated up, Gamal found himself spread thinly. Before they all went to Sunsis, Bellik needed to know some things. "Bellik," Gamal opened, "I want to give you information that only Gen Zavijavah and I possess."

Bellik took a seat halfway down the inlaid table, trying to look modest.

"No," Gamal said. "Closer. Zavijavah, you sit, too." He pointed across the table. Bellik sat down next to Gamal. Zavijavah took an opposite chair, but he glanced at the door, and his nose twitched.

Gamal swiveled to face Bellik. He pulled a tiny folding knife from his pocket and opened its blade. Razor sharp, it was less than half a centimeter wide. "I need a blood oath of secrecy."

Bellik raised an eyebrow, obviously startled, but he offered a finger. Gamal reached forward and nicked it, or so he thought. He'd missed. He must get that eye fixed. He flicked again. This time a red streak appeared. Bellik wiped his finger on a pocket tissue.

Gamal waved at a wall rheostat, dimming the lights. "Zavijavah, take off the glasses."

The Security Chief complied. Bellik stared as Zavijavah squeezed his eyes shut and slowly opened them, then opened them farther, then opened them all the way. Gamal had forgotten how enormous the brown irises looked.

"He's a seer," Bellik exclaimed.

"That's a start. Thank you, Zavijavah."

Zavijavah maneuvered his glasses back into position. Gamal raised the lights again. "We are dealing with an alien race, Bellik."

Bellik rolled his eyes. "Seers aren't alien. They're mutant humans."

"Don't interrupt. Nine years ago, an associate of mine returned from the Sunsis system, where he had gone on a business trip. He informed me at that time that the race known to us as Chaethe had returned to Concord space. They wished to establish an alliance with Tdega."

"Wait. What? Chaethe?" Bellik could be a little dense. "The aliens in all the rumors?"

"The same."

Bellik examined his finger and wiped it again. "They wanted a treaty with Tdega, not the Concord?"

"Our world is fertile. The others are not."

Bellik narrowed his eyes. "Is that why we left the Concord?"

Gamal glanced at the display wall. Soon the Residence that it showed would be the star cluster's center of power. "No. It's not." He didn't want to discuss his goals in Zavijavah's presence. Rider could be listening, even though Zavijavah insisted it usually wasn't. He'd stirred it up badly today. "The difficulty has been establishing two-way communication. They hear us, and they can control a host and speak through him or her, but they see us as creatures to be trained. Correct, Zavijavah?"

Still stroking his mustache, Zavijavah nodded.

"Gods." Bellik gulped. "Is he—does he—"

"He does. Looking at you through Osun Zavijavah's genetically enhanced eyes is the Chaethe individual who first contacted me. I might add that it has released two offspring on Tdega. One apparently made it to Antar. That's probably our rumor source." He shook his head. "I'm afraid we lost the other."

Bellik leaned away from Zavijavah.

"With Gen Zavijavah's assistance, I devised an experiment seven years ago. The first host had also brought back from Sunsis a highly advanced artificial-reality unit, developed by the Chaethe themselves. It seemed possible that if …" How should he phrase this? "If a group of young, impressionable humans would be completely wiped of conscious memory and conditioned into Chaethe deep thought, they might learn to negotiate on humankind's behalf. We need these aliens as allies."

Bellik eyed his finger, which had stopped bleeding. He tossed his tissue into a recycle bin. "Go on."

"Unfortunately," Gamal said, "nine of the ten children died within months. I did not—"

Bellik straightened. He pushed forward and laid both elbows on the table. "Was Luene the tenth?"

"Let me finish," Gamal growled.

Bellik folded his hands.

Gamal continued. "I did not ask a medic to determine cause of death, but I suspected the intellectual equivalent of failure-to-thrive. It kills babies who aren't touched and stroked."

Bellik clenched his hands. "Go on," he said, "but I know where this is heading."

"I had intended, after three or four years of AR conditioning, to present the children for infestation. If they proved able to communicate with their own—"

"You what?" Bellik exclaimed.

This was becoming tiresome. Gamal fingered an inlaid square on the table. "It was a wrench, sacrificing Luene. But if you recall, she was the brightest eleven-year-old on Tdega. Holding her back might have doomed the experiment."

"As I recall, she already spoke a couple of ancient languages when she vanished."

"Yes. I felt she had the best chance for success. The highest resilience scores. She did survive when the others died."

Bellik nodded. Zavijavah picked at the tabletop, too. His cheek twitched.

"I always meant to see that she was treated well," Gamal said, "carrying only one offspring spore at a time to minimize her discomfort."

Zavijavah winced.

"As I said," Gamal repeated, "I hoped that once infested, she and the others would be able to negotiate with the aliens, since the Chaethe have already settled inside Concord space. We can have them as predatory enemies or permanent, powerful allies. But we have them. Here."

Bellik glanced at Zavijavah and tapped the table. "Luene survived. Why?"

"I don't know. And she never regained consciousness. When the other children died, I canceled the experiment. I sent Luene to Antar some time later, when she lingered in what looked like a vegetative state. I hoped to cut my losses. It was a hasty idea, not as well thought out as some others. For a few weeks, I hoped to implicate the Antaran government in her kidnapping. By that time, of course, I had lost any hope of her regaining independence."

"But she recovered." Bellik stared at his folded hands. "Rather well, considering."

"Considering that her intellect was stripped and then immersed in an alien environment, yes."

"What is your next step, then?" Bellik asked.

Good. Bellik was back on track, working toward their common goal.

Maybe there was hope for the boy. "Zavijavah's partner, his—Rider—will need to liberate two spores in a few days. I am giving the Chaethe Alun and Luene."

Bellik blinked. He hesitated. Finally, he said, "Will that harm Zavijavah?"

"Not if he cooperates. And he will."

Bellik looked up from his hands. "You will forgive my speaking frankly, Uncle. Some will accuse you of a lack of paternal empathy."

Gamal shrugged. "I gave Luene up for dead years ago. It is good to see her physically alive, but the woman in our Residence is not my daughter." This had been the decision that steadied his resolve. "She has been rebuilt by an Antaran empath."

"But perhaps she still could communicate with a … parasite?"

"It's a dubious hope," Gamal admitted. "I'm not certain what motivates Zavijavah's Rider, but since its needs dovetail with my own, I shall continue to cooperate. I hope to show the Chaethe that I will make them a desirable ally. They fear the Devastators even more than we do." He addressed these last few words to—and through—Zavijavah. Zavijavah kept staring straight ahead.

"Why him?" Bellik pointed. "Because he's Security?"

"That particular Chaethe wanted seer eyes. They use our senses. It's only natural they would want enhanced specimens."

Bellik nodded, obviously thinking things through. He slid back his chair. "Is that all, sir? I have business to—"

"No. Zavijavah, you had more news on last night's burst transmission. Tell Bellik."

"We found the transmitter," Zavijavah said. "We screened it for biological debris, but it came up clean, so we can't identify the sender that way. But we can pinpoint its planet of origin. An amateur comet watcher recorded an energy burst from an object in geosynchronous orbit that night."

"I meant to mention that," Bellik exclaimed. "We sent up a shuttle to check it out. It was an Antaran tenpod. Nine berths were empty."

"Fired?" Gamal asked.

"Yes."

Zavijavah folded his hands and addressed Bellik. "Other evidence implicates Jahn Korsakov."

Bellik raised both eyebrows and looked to Gamal for confirmation.

Nodding, Gamal tapped the tabletop. "You hired him to tutor Alun," he reminded Bellik.

"He was already top-clearance staff."

"And," Zavijavah said, "new evidence says that our security leak is empathic."

"Then he'll know if we're coming for him." Bellik frowned. "That could be dangerous."

"That's probably why he hasn't made any sudden moves. He knew we didn't suspect him. But now we do. Where is he now?"

Zavijavah touched his reader. "Still in Alun's rooms."

"We will question him immediately." Gamal eyed Bellik.

Bellik folded his hands. "Am I required to attend? I would like to, but I have pressing business this afternoon."

Gamal shrugged. "We'll give you a transcript."

"Thank you."

"Zavijavah?" Gamal turned to his Security Chief. "I wish to speak with Bellik alone before he leaves."

Zavijavah pushed back his chair and hurried out.

Bellik stared after him. "He does act oddly."

"He's in pain. Imagine carrying a foreign object inside your brain."

Bellik shuddered. "Why have you told me?"

"I have legally disowned Siah."

Bellik raised his left eyebrow again. It seemed to be his gesture of the day.

"I have not made the action public yet, but I will." Gamal did not add aloud that he would be watching Bellik just as closely. If he balked now, he must be silenced. "When I leave for Sunsis," he added, "I want you in charge of the Security squadron I will be bringing. Zavijavah will be otherwise occupied."

"I am honored. Sunsis?"

"There is a Chaethe liberation site there. I want Luene's experience to go well."

Bellik straightened his shoulders.

"Are you still interested in courting her?" Gamal asked, amused.

Bellik shuddered. "I think not."

25

Filip Salbari stepped off a Cruxan shuttle onto the consular ship *Woodman*, which would be his home for the next month or more. Several Outwatch people and the Miatrixan delegate followed him. The Crux system had supplied the *Woodman* in exchange for economic considerations, if the Concord survived.

Maybe they were chasing shadows. Maybe there were no Chaethe on Sunsis, Filip reflected, peering into his small cabin. He would love to be mistaken.

Before boarding the shuttle, he had walked up a hillside north of the estate dome and made peace with his Uncle Boaden. They'd hiked silently, panting in Antar's delicate atmosphere and sweating like wrestlers. The plains stretched in all directions.

Filip raised his pony bottle of oxygen and breathed deeply through its mask attachment. He stirred a gravel pile with one foot. "I should have passed the office to you weeks ago," he said. "I wish you all success."

"Each system will send a delegate to Sunsis in case you can get the aliens to talk." Boaden stared toward the horizon. "If you do get that far, present yourself as Head Regent. They don't need to know you resigned. You did earn the title."

Now that Boaden had taken the job, that could be construed as an order. "I will," Filip said.

Boaden raised his own breath mask. He stared for several more seconds and asked, "Have you designated an heir for your share of the estate?"

Filip shrugged. "Stasia is immature, but she's my oldest. She'll grow into stability."

"Does Favia approve?"

"Wholeheartedly."

"You two are so trusting." Boaden flattened his free hand on his thigh and leaned forward. "I hope you're not trusting yourself to death with this mission of yours."

So did Filip. "Eventually, we must trust. There will always be people who'll take advantage, but trust is the basis of civilization."

"I understand that philosophy."

Even if he didn't agree.

Filip had also designated his brother Alcotte as pro tem head for the Order. He had ordered his files and handed estate business to Favia. They'd been more passionate lately than they'd been since their first years together. There was nothing like knowing a person could lose something to make him value it. If only he could always live that way—

No. That was impossible. How could anyone maintain that much tension and remain sane?

The Cruxan Captain, Burgin Hardette, saluted him in the *Woodman's* narrow passageway and handed him a reader. Filip eyed it. There'd been another pod message from Jahn. It confirmed that Gamal Casimir's Security Chief carried a Chaethe parasite, and that Casimir sought a treaty with the aliens. It also confirmed a major Chaethe presence at Sunsis A.

So much for that hope.

Also, Jahn intended to spirit his young charges away from the Residence because they had been selected for infestation. Filip scanned that sentence twice to make sure he'd read it right. How could Casimir subject Llyn to that fate? He prayed with all his heart that Jahn would succeed.

"Thank you." He handed back the reader. Captain Hardette's gold-seamed gillie prosthesis rode on shoulders that were broad and muscular from years of carrying it. Hardette intended to stand for the Crux system if talks occurred. He had promised Filip a fanatically loyal crew, determined to make a quick end to the conflict. Also on board were Dio Liion of Unukalhai, the only other University Regent coming along; a young military man from Vatsya Hab; the middle-aged career diplomat from Miatrix; and the group's elder statesman, Senator Urban Igrim of Kocab.

"We received another Gate relay, too," Hardette said. "Admiral Lalande repeats that Ilzar is liberated, loyal, and eager to remain in the Concord. Lalande is laying in defenses and getting ready for a counterattack."

"I trust his judgment. As does Boaden." It had been a week since Lalande arrived. Every day of that week, he'd expected word of a counterstrike there. Gate relays, which had always seemed amazingly swift, now struck him as slow.

"He's on his own now." Hardette's posture never softened. "Tdega could get ships off its Gate to hit him before we could send word back to Lalande, let alone ships."

They walked up the narrow passageway. The Miatrixan delegate vanished into a cabin she would share with Karine Torfinn. Karine had seemed subdued and embarrassed when they boarded, and she had offered to remain accountable to Vananda for the trip. Filip hoped nothing changed her mind. Obviously, she ought not to be told about Jahn's transmission and the specific threat to Llyn.

Rena Tourelle peered out of a hatch, her vivid hair the brightest sight shipboard. "Uncle Filip," she exclaimed, "I've got two Outwatch women and the Unukalhaian representative in my cabin."

"Everyone has been mixed. The triads will train long hours. You'll be glad not to sleep with another empath." Twenty Outwatch troops would bunk in the same cabins as the empaths and delegates. Filip hoped by small strategies to mold them into an effective team in the twenty-two subjective days they would spend between planets.

Rena grinned and ducked back inside the hatchway.

"How old is she?" Hardette asked softly after they passed that hatchway.

"Twenty."

The Captain cleared his throat. It gurgled.

"I didn't want to risk her, but she was the best choice available," Filip said.

"I hope you know what you're doing."

"So do I."

Hardette tapped another hatch. "We're out of the housing corridor now, and into cargo. This one contains headgear. Bulletproof, or so I'm told. Hot and uncomfortable, though. I can vouch for that."

Llyn followed Jahn around the kennel into its shadow, brushing a metal security flag with her leg as she passed. Alun came last. As her eyes adjusted, a long, black wall seemed to appear across the back of the grounds. They stayed close together and sprinted toward it. She hadn't been this far north on the Casimir property. "Access for emergency vehicles," Jahn explained. "I found it one day, exploring." He held up the small box and twisted a dial. The gate swung open.

"You're right," she said. "I don't want to know what that is."

Behind the grounds, a hillside sloped up into dark forest. "Can you run for a while?" Jahn asked.

She drew a deep breath of cool air. Its smell—evergreen woods and freedom, however brief—exhilarated her. "I'll do my best."

He led uphill at a slow, steady jog. Alun stayed beside him, and she followed. Her booties slipped and slid, keeping her slightly off balance.

The third time Jahn stopped them to rest, Alun grabbed her pant leg. "You're hurt!"

By dim starlight, she spotted a shiny area on her dark clothing. She felt it with one hand. It was damp, and her hand came away smudged.

"I must have cut it when I walked past that security flag," she said, feeling stupid. "But I didn't feel any pain, and my sense of touch is much stronger—"

"Clean cuts are sometimes painless." Jahn frowned. "But it's possible that we left a blood trail." He slid up her pant leg and exposed a short, straight cut.

"Oh, no," Alun exclaimed. "Does it hurt, Luene?"

"No," she said. Unfortunately, it was the truth. If it had hurt, she would have noticed sooner.

Jahn dug something out of his pack and wiped the wound clean. "It's already stopped bleeding." He rested a hand on her shoulder. "Worrying won't solve anything."

She wondered if he was using some empathic skill to comfort her. She'd heard that they could, although Karine never had. Not that she

296 | KATHY TYERS

could recall. "All right," she mumbled. From this clearing, she could look down into Bkellan. Its lights twinkled across a wide arc of horizon, more beautiful than any domed city could be. "How far are we going this afternoon?"

"Until we can't carry you one step farther," he said soberly, "or we find a secure place to hide."

"I'm almost ready," she said.

He pulled several objects out of his pack and laid them in the weedy dirt. Then he led uphill at an angle from their previous path, probably trying to put searchers off a straight trail. She wondered what evidence he'd wanted to abandon outside the Residence. She didn't mind zigzagging, or even covering the same ground twice, so long as it got them away. She pictured Karine soaring overhead, hunting. Karine-hawk had a new companion today, an eagle with Gamal Casimir's face.

She plodded on in darkness.

As Gamal beckoned to the hall guard, Zavijavah drew his needler and stalked toward Alun's door. Two more Security men followed them. Gamal touched the security override on Alun's entry panel, and the door slid aside. Gamal stepped out of the Security men's way. They rushed in.

The suite was empty.

Gamal touched his comm unit. "Locate Jahn Korsakov," he directed the main Residence terminal. One of his aides walked to the window and stared out.

"Gen Korsakov is in Alun Casimir's suite," res-net answered.

But he wasn't. Frowning, Gamal cleared his throat. "Locate Alun Casimir."

After several more seconds, the voice circuit spoke again. "Gen Casimir is not on Residence grounds."

That, at least, appeared to be accurate. "Locate Luene Casimir."

"Gen'n Casimir is not on Residence grounds."

"Find that PL," Gamal growled. "It's somewhere in this suite."

Zavijavah drew his reader, touched several buttons, and swung it in front of him. Brandishing and sweeping it, he walked into the tutor's bedroom. There, he set it down on the bedside table. He flung back the bedclothes and dumped the pillow onto the floor.

A man's ring lay where the pillow had covered it. Zavijavah scrutinized it and handed it over. Gamal hefted it, a square agate mounted in silver. "I guarantee," Zavijavah said, "that if we take that apart, we'll find a personal locator chip."

Gamal headed out the door. Seconds later, he stood beside Zavijavah in his daughter's empty room. The servant Peatra had admitted that she hadn't seen Luene for an hour. A Security aide stood rifling through drawers.

"We'll find them." Zavijavah turned toward the door. "It won't be hard. I'll check the surveillance satellite." He punched his display again. His pale cheeks lost what little color they had. "No signal. Evidently he's shielded them all somehow. But we'll find them," he repeated. "It'll just take a little longer."

"Maybe," Gamal said. "But think about this, Zavijavah. Before, she might have gone willingly to Sunsis. Now, we'll have to take her against her will."

"At least she isn't Luene anymore. Remember that."

Gamal squared his shoulders. "Yes," he said. "I remember."

26

His furious Rider—and ten or twelve cups of strong coffee—kept Osun Zavijavah awake through the night and into the next workday. Rider, who seemingly spent most of its time in another world, had stayed at the surface, alternately goading and stroking him.

By evening light, Zavijavah had personally tracked Luene, Alun, and Korsakov to the emergency gate at the back of the grounds, following a trail of bruised grass blades since infrared scanners picked up no trace. Then he'd lost their trail on the scrubby hillside.

At least they were afoot and couldn't get far, though plainly they were using anti-surveillance technology. Since dark had been falling again, he'd called off his team until morning, when other people could see. Rider howled over that idea.

Zavijavah had reminded it that this break would give him time to search Korsakov's bedroom and the other escapees' suites for more evidence, enlist some of Bellik's troops, and strip the net for information: tools that empaths might use, tricks that they might try, ways that they might be caught.

Examining Korsakov's closet, he moved a stack of clothing. "What's this?" He leaned forward. Blood rushing to his head made it throb.

His partner, a weighty woman who usually worked outdoor security, poked her head into the closet. "What's what?"

"Get back," he said. "Get me a light."

A faint set of circular depressions in the carpet showed that something had been stored and removed. Ordinary eyes would not have spotted these, including Korsakov's. Zavijavah had proved twice, now, that seers' talents should be respected. He shoved the clothing farther out into the room and looked closer.

When the big female shone a light over his shoulder, the depressions almost vanished. "They show better in shadow," Zavijavah muttered.

What are they? Rider asked.

The i-net had projected images of empaths' mneme units. "I think," he said, "this is evidence. Get a lab kit. Calculate size and weight of the objects that would've left these impressions."

A flush of pleasure started in his midsection. It spread in both directions, Rider rewarding him using his own nervous system.

Behind his shoulder, Casimir's voice asked, "What did you find?"

Zavijavah straightened. He waited for his aide to leave the room, then answered. "Gold, I think."

"Good," Casimir said. "The other team found blood near the back gate. Jackson says it's Luene's."

The pleasant flush turned to prickly heat. "Did Korsakov hurt her?"

Casimir didn't answer directly. "I have worse news. That surveillance satellite just went down. They must be headed for a ship of some kind. If we don't find them before it's launched, you're cooked."

Zavijavah's collar seemed to draw tight. "Rider can sense empathic listening." So it had said, while he conducted his research. "I'll go out now. Personally." *Hurry,* Rider howled. "Wait," Zavijavah exclaimed. "I have a wonderfully primitive idea. Perfect for tracking an Antaran."

"What?" Casimir's frown looked fierce.

Zavijavah lifted his reader. "Connection," he ordered into its small square pickup. "I want the kennel master."

"Llyn? Llyn!"

Jahn's low voice sounded urgent. Llyn groaned and rolled over. A tree root, or maybe a rock, poked the side of her head. Scrapes and scratches covered her hands.

They'd jogged through the sunny evening and far into nocturnal darkness up a hillside covered with conical trees and leafy bushes. She'd asked

Alun the name of one bush. Plainly delighted by her interest, he kept pointing them out. He even knew which were wild and which descended from terraforming stock.

By starlight, Alun had found this hollow. The root ball of a long-fallen tree sheltered it. Using a trowel from his pack, Jahn had helped dig it deep enough for Alun to fit inside. She and Jahn had stretched out close to the root ball and fallen asleep. Now shadows were lengthening again, and soon, first sunset would dim the woods. She didn't want to move. Jahn's back had felt warm and comforting against hers. Alun had looked like a young mountain curled up in the root hollow.

"Llyn!" Jahn's voice sounded more urgent.

She sat up and rubbed her eyes. The gelskin felt amazingly heavy. "We'd better get going," she mumbled. "I suppose."

"Listen." Black stubble covered his chin. One side of his face had odd red dents where he'd slept on it.

She strained her ears. Then she too heard distant barking.

Alun scrambled out of his den, blinking and rumpled. "That sounds like Bear! Somebody took her away from her puppies."

Jahn sprang to his feet. "They're using her. Tracking us."

"We can't shoot Bear to get away," Alun exclaimed.

Llyn nodded. She'd been ready to blurt the same thing.

"We won't," Jahn said. "We'll separate. Remember? Alun, Bear will try to come to you. Get over that ridge." He pointed at the forested hump eastward. "There should be a stream. Get your feet into it. Keep them wet. Head upstream, but stay in the water. Dogs can't track you in water. Understand?"

"Yes."

"Then go. Hurry. I'll come for you."

"Wait," Alun cried. "Jahn, if anything happens to me, please take care of Luene."

"I will," Jahn promised. The warmth in his voice quickened Llyn's pulse.

Alun sprinted into the darkening woods.

"I'll head west and down a little." Llyn peered into the forest. "I can get farther away from you two that way."

"All right. Hurry." Jahn stroked her face with his scratched hand. "If they catch you, I'll come back."

"But how will you know if—"

"I'll know. But I can't let them catch me now." He ducked his head and ran straight uphill.

"Right," she muttered. She darted away from their lair, slipping frequently on the slick booties. Should she shed them? No, she didn't dare. Soon, her cut throbbed and her leg muscles ached. She wanted this, she reminded herself. She wanted her tactile sense back. She gritted her teeth and tried not to limp. The barking gradually faded.

Her limp got worse. Every step wrenched thigh and calf muscles that she'd never worked so hard. Each bush seemed to grab her, trying to dig another painful scratch.

A soft hum swept over her head. She shut her eyes and dove into another thick bush, wishing she couldn't feel it scratch those long, red streaks into her skin. The humming grew louder. It stopped overhead.

Jahn had known Security might locate them by their body heat. Maybe they'd found her. Still, she had enough energy left to draw them off Jahn's track. She, at least, could hope for her father's mercy. She disentangled herself and sprinted another twenty meters west across the long hill.

Out of a thicket of trees downhill on her left, two big men in red appeared as suddenly as if projected by a terminal. Llyn froze, panting, almost glad that they'd finally chased her down. Pretending innocence, she exclaimed, "I'm here. I'm all right. Is anything wrong?"

One security man raised a weapon.

"Wait," she cried.

He fired. Her arm stung momentarily. Shocked, she opened her mouth to protest—and crumpled onto prickly ground.

Months ago, when Jahn had made his way from his pod ship across country into Bkellan, the folded mountains had only been barriers. Now they offered cover. Tdega was as huge and beautiful as Filip Salbari had promised. The only ugly things here were humans.

He reached the ridge as the sun sank toward the horizon again. From here, he watched a Residence hovercraft swoop low over an area Llyn might have reached. He glanced down into the creek drainage north. Behind it glowered another jagged ridge.

Before plunging into that next drainage, he looked back. A long, thin shadow running far below must be Alun. Faintly, he heard the dog barking. He prayed Alun would reach the stream.

Alun scrambled up a long rocky outcrop several meters short of the streambed, then turned around and peered into the trees. Obviously closer to Bear, he must be listening to her.

Jahn stretched his synch sense to the limit. *Hurry, Alun! Run!* He barely heard Alun's inner frequency from this distance, but when he'd arrived on Antar, he wouldn't have been able to do that. Alun wanted … to catch Bear and bring her along.

He mustn't! Jahn tried to push Alun toward nexus. From this distance, he could barely synch.

Alun dashed down the rock outcrop, parallel to the stream.

Abruptly, Bellik's amplified voice echoed off stone: "Alun. We see you. Stay where you are. Don't move, or we'll shoot."

Jahn didn't expect Alun to obey Bellik, and he didn't. He spun and dashed uphill.

There was a sharp *crack*. Alun stumbled and fell hard against rock, bounced, and fell a second time.

Jahn clung to the ridge, aching with fury. Wind whistled over his head. The cloudless sky darkened.

A big black retriever dashed up to Alun, wagging her tail. She bent to sniff. She raised her head and howled.

Alun didn't move, but Jahn had no sense of his death. He was only unconscious.

Five men appeared out of the trees. Jahn rolled across the ridge toward the open slope on the other side, pressed to his feet, and ran down a long, loose stretch of scree. It slid with him, accelerating his run.

Anger goaded him on. Whispering voices darted out of the darkness. Casimir's forces had recaptured at least one of Jahn's students, and here he was, still running.

He had to stay free, he reasoned—flailing to keep his balance on loose rock—to sneak back and free them both. But that also meant he couldn't go far. He could not take off with Kai Oldion without Alun and Llyn.

Help! Please!

Below another snowfield that had lingered into summer, he jumped into a small creek. He ran downstream, following his own advice. Other searchers might also have dogs. Icy water seeped into his shoes.

Many kilometers downstream, running by starlight, he slipped for a third time as a hovercraft slowly approached out of the south. He hoped being this cold and wet would make his body less visible on scanners.

The stream had widened. He stumbled around another bend and saw a large shadow that hunkered midstream, looking like a clump of bushes growing on an island.

He would be a boulder, slightly warm from the short day's sunshine. After a brief roll in frigid water, he curled up as close to the bushes as he could push in. The hovercraft probably was flying a standard search pattern. Once it passed, he would be safe here for several hours.

He held his warm, bare face and hands close to the ground.

The humming engine hovered briefly. It moved on. He stayed in his crouch and breathed shallowly. His nose brushed a patch of some wild herb. Slowly, he reached into his pocket. First he came up with the needler. That wouldn't do—not this time. He slid out a dart gun he'd loaded with lethal charges.

After he had listened for several minutes, he dared to hope they'd passed over him. He could afford a few seconds to listen for inner frequencies. He turned the mental corner—

Someone yelped. A circle of noisy minds surrounded him. One had an eerie double presence.

He refocused in time to hear an amplified voice. "Come out, Korsakov."

He crooked his elbow and steadied the dart gun.

Something prodded him.

He rolled, firing blindly. A hand seized his. Another grabbed his arm. There must be three of them. He shouldn't have gone off synch—

He lunged forward. They gripped and held. Hard metal circled one of his wrists. He flung himself toward the water.

"I don't think so." He knew that voice. Zavijavah. "If we wanted you drowned, we'd do it ourselves." Something caught and secured his other wrist. "Get up."

Jahn levered his thighs under his weight, struggling while outside forces stretched his arms in both directions.

"Light," Zavijavah shouted. Beams appeared from several directions. Jahn staggered upright.

Osun Zavijavah held his dark glasses down at his side, sheltering his eyes with one hand. The man's eyes were huge—

Of course. Zavijavah was a seer. He wished he had known that. "You must be quite a tracker," Jahn said softly.

Zavijavah's cheek twitched. "We can make this as hard or as easy as you like, Korsakov." He leveled a needler at Jahn's midsection.

Llyn blinked herself awake. She lay in Medic Jackson's clinic again. Her blood-soaked pants and bunchy data suit had been stripped off. A bandage constricted her throbbing leg where she'd cut it. Through the open door, she saw her father standing in the outer room. He spoke with Jackson, both of them using low voices.

Had they caught Jahn? If he had stayed free, she still might escape. Should she try to convince people she'd gone for a walk alone? As soon as her father came in to talk with her, she would tell him—

He walked out of her line of sight. A door whooshed open somewhere she could not see. It whooshed again, obviously closing.

Medic Jackson appeared in the inner doorway. He lowered his head, creating several extra chins. "Welcome back," he said dryly. "Does the leg hurt?"

"It's throbbing."

"Want something for that?"

"Sure." If he intended to drug her helpless, he would do it without asking.

"Any other pain? I found only scratches."

She examined her hands. A network of red lines crisscrossed them both. She shook her head. "I ache all over, but I'm fine. Honestly. I'm sorry I got everyone stirred up. I just wanted to go for a walk."

Jackson raised an eyebrow. "I'm afraid you're going to wish you hadn't."

"Oh?"

"Your father doesn't want to speak with you. He left as soon as my remote indicated you'd awakened. His only orders are that you are not to be left alone."

"Do you ... have any other patients?"

"Not at the moment." His mouth twitched. "Perhaps soon."

"What do you mean?"

"What do *you* mean?"

She refused to ask whether they'd caught Jahn or Alun. "Nothing," she said.

"Good." He strolled away from her bedside. "I would prefer to know as little about this as possible."

"This is not pleasant to watch," Gamal Casimir said. "In case you wondered."

"You've made your point." Jahn spared Casimir one glance. Then the other man, the stranger in this concrete room, moved again. A whip-like string dangled from each of two devices he held in heavily gloved hands. Jahn's left ankle was anchored by a heavy metal strap to a ring on the concrete floor.

Osun Zavijavah stood behind Casimir's chair, wearing his glasses again. So far, they had only demanded Jahn's name. He'd regained consciousness shivering on the floor here, still wearing his wet black clothing. He didn't know whether he was in the Residence, at Bkellan Base, or elsewhere. He couldn't imagine how he would escape, but he must.

The other man circled.

"I may have made one point," Casimir said smoothly, "but we have barely begun. I want you to understand how you will be treated if you refuse to cooperate. If my people have to resort to expensive drugs, it will cost you."

"As I said, you've made your point."

Casimir nodded at the other man.

The big man swung his right hand. A whip-like tendril wrapped around Jahn's fettered ankle. The big man swept in with his left hand. Jahn raised his hand to shield his face.

The other tendril caught his wrist. Pain blasted from his ankle up his body and out his palm.

The big man stepped back. Jahn folded forward, catching his breath. He straightened.

Casimir leaned back in the chair, arms crossed. "Next time, the power will be higher."

"Be careful." Osun Zavijavah leaned down. "There mustn't be permanent harm."

Casimir waved a hand. "Tell your friend not to worry. He's taking no damage."

Jahn stared at Zavijavah, momentarily distracted from watching the other man circle. Why would Zavijavah's "friend" care if he were harmed?

Unless … unless they meant to take him to Sunsis, too.

"Korsakov," Casimir snapped. "Pay attention."

Jahn stared at him.

"Your name."

"Jahn Korsakov."

"That's a lie."

"No."

Casimir flicked a finger at the circling man. Jahn braced himself. There'd be no permanent harm. He'd heard Casimir say so.

The jolt knocked him to his knees.

"Your name," Casimir asked again.

Jahn didn't bother standing back up. "Jahn Korsakov," he repeated.

"Jahn Korsakov," Casimir said, "do you have any idea what the penalty is on Tdega for kidnapping?"

On Antar, it was lifetime commitment to therapy and public service. Jahn stared but did not answer.

"Can you guess how you should pay for kidnapping the Vice Regent's daughter and nephew? Give him another taste, please."

"Wait," Jahn cried. "Is Alun all right? I saw him fall when Bellik … challenged him."

The big man kept coming. Jahn tried not to flinch, but now his body knew what to expect. It ducked forward. It writhed as tendrils caught and bit again.

Jahn tucked into a fetal position and concentrated on breathing. On staying warm. A chill breeze was blowing in this room.

"Get up," Casimir called.

Jahn managed it.

"Alun is comatose." Casimir folded his hands in his lap. "Jackson says he will die shortly. You'll be charged with his death."

Jahn gulped. "If he's alive, please try to save him. Don't … finish him off." Alun deserved better than that.

"You will be charged with his death," Casimir said again.

"I was nowhere near him. Bellik's people fired something at him just before he fell."

"Can you produce witnesses? I can."

Jahn's throat constricted. He tried to swallow, but his mouth was dry. Alun deserved to live!

Osun Zavijavah stepped forward, swaggering almost as convincingly as Bellik. He carried a reader. "If you'd care to hear them," he said, "I have your final orders from Antar. They were received by the embassy before it closed down."

Surely they hadn't decoded that transmission.

On the other hand, Tdegan technology surpassed most Antaran equivalents.

"Want to hear them?"

"I don't know what you're talking about."

"Mm." Zavijavah stepped closer. "Your gentle, peace-loving, *former* Head Regent Filip Salbari has ordered you to kill somebody, Korsakov. Lest an infestation or its influence spread."

Former Head Regent? Jahn stood and shivered, straight-faced. Again he resisted the temptation to speak.

Another Security man handed something to Zavijavah. Zavijavah traded him the reader for two other objects and stepped closer, brandishing a thermal oversole and an agate ring. "Tell us about these, Korsakov. Where did you get them?"

"The ring was my father's."

"I don't think so." Zavijavah glanced at the man with the whips.

"Oh, that's enough." Casimir made a fist and struck the arm of his chair. "Use the drugs. Send me the information. Particularly," he said, lowering an eyebrow at Jahn, "how this man insinuated himself into the data system. And I want a full body search. I want him bleeding when you're done."

The whip man set down his weapons and pulled off his gloves.

Casimir rocked forward and stood. "You're a lucky man, Korsakov," he said in a bland voice. "In three days, you'll be taking an all-paid vacation. Transport time will give you a chance to heal."

The other man applied a thin tool to the ring near Jahn's ankle. His foot came free.

Jahn had so little strength left that he didn't try to kick. Instead, he synched with Casimir as he and Zavijavah walked out, leaving Jahn in the big stranger's tender custody.

Casimir was thinking about his allies at Sunsis A, the center of their activity in Concord space. About hundreds of infested humans, and the steady stream of victims the Chaethe needed now. The Antaran who claimed to be "Jahn Korsakov" had a strong young body—

Casimir's thoughts faded out.

Jahn's tormentor pulled out a pencil-like object. "Might as well lie down," he said. "You're going to be transported unconscious again."

Jahn had awakened the last time with a throbbing right elbow. He must've hit something on his way down.

Lesson learned. He lowered himself to the floor. "May I have some dry clothes?"

The stranger bent over him. "Isn't Tdega warm enough for you, empath?"

Llyn lay on her own bed, back in her own room. Still disoriented, she wasn't sure if it was supposed to be day shift or night, but the sun was setting.

Jahn might be dead. Or a prisoner. Or he might still be free. He might be trying to get back to her. What about Alun? If Gen Casimir caught him, would he hold him responsible for trying to escape? Did Gen Casimir even know that Alun was improving daily?

She must get away. Jahn would find her if she left the Residence. He had said so, and she believed him.

Her door chimed.

She sprang off the bed and called, "Come—"

It was already sliding aside. Her father stepped through, glowering like Karine on a bad day. Osun Zavijavah followed him. Zavijavah's black hair, glasses, mustache, and his dark-red Security tunic made his face look almost white in the dim light. A second man wearing Security red slipped through behind him and stood next to the door.

The door of her room. In her family home. She'd come here hoping to be part of a real family and to help bring peace to the Concord. How could she have been so naïve? "Father," she said solemnly, "I want to apologize for—"

"Don't call me 'father.' Sit down." He grasped the backrest of a chair at her conversational table.

She took the seat. Her heart thumped. She thought she saw pain in Gen Zavijavah's face. What must it feel like, to carry an alien parasite? At one corner of her mind, a tiny, frightened presence crouched screaming. The man was sick. Unclean. Infested.

Gen Casimir sat down facing her. "How long have you known that Jahn Emlin is an Antaran empath?" His tone of voice pinned her to the wall and dared her to squirm.

"Jahn who?"

He crossed his legs. "Your tutor. Born on Antar. He is a fully trained, registered empath. How long have you known that?"

"An empath?" Panic curled through her. Had they caught Jahn, or were they looking for him? Had they interrogated him, or were they guessing? "Father … Sir, haven't I made it plain how I feel about empaths? How did your staff let one of them get close to me?" Her pulse thudded in her ears.

"You're not convincing me." He moved only his mouth. "You're not a good actress. Not only is Jahn Emlin an empath, he is the nephew of Filip Salbari, who just resigned the Head Regency of Antar."

Gen Zavijavah stood behind Gen Casimir's chair with his arms crossed.

Llyn glanced up at the Security man. "He did?" She gulped. "Why?"

Her father spoke again. "How long have you known Jahn Emlin is an empath?"

"I don't … don't know what you're talking about."

He stabbed the table with a fingertip. "You ran away with Jahn Emlin and your cousin Alun. Is—"

"Where is Alun?" she pleaded. "Is he all right?"

"He fell. He hit his head on a rock."

"Again?" she whispered.

He scowled. "He's in a coma. If he dies, we will charge Jahn Emlin with murder."

She swallowed on a dry throat. Had they caught him, or was this another "if we catch him" statement? And what had happened to Regent Salbari?

"Is Jahn Emlin your lover?"

"What? No!" she exclaimed, but the accusation stung. She'd tried to hide that hope, even from herself. But she had hoped. He was kindly, and smart, and gentle. All a man should be. There simply hadn't been time.

"You accept the fact that his name is Jahn Emlin?"

"How would I know that?" she begged.

"Is he your friend?"

She pressed her hands to her face. "If he is from Antar," she said, dropping her hands and folding them on the tabletop, "something about him must have seemed familiar. You know I don't remember my Tdegan upbringing."

"You never will remember it. It was electrically wiped from your neocortex."

Her chin quivered. "How do you know?"

"You were part of an experiment." His tone remained dry and clinical. She'd heard Karine speak this way. "You and nine other children were stripped of memories to impress you more deeply in an artificial reality. We—"

We? "You did it?" she breathed. Her own father?

His eyes narrowed. "Stop interrupting."

He had! Her own father had used her as an experimental animal— had locked her into an AR and swallowed the key—had killed the young girl she once had been! Why? She wanted to scream it. *Why?*

"Is Jahn Emlin your friend?"

"Yes." Angry now, she slumped and rested both elbows on the table-top. "A good teacher tries to be friendly. He seemed vaguely familiar, too. Of course he—"

"Is he your confidant?"

"I have no confidant." She tried to snarl the words. She wanted him to hurt the way she hurt. She belonged nowhere. To no one.

Her father shook his head. "You're not even remotely convincing." He stood. "I have wasted enough time on you. You are not Luene Casimir, my devoted daughter. She died long ago in a great cause. You are Llyn Torfinn, one empath's reconstruction and another empath's lover. You will see him in two days."

Then, was Jahn alive—but was all hope of rescue gone? "What do you mean?" she asked, trying to sound bold, tempted to retort, *If Luene Casimir died, you killed her.*

He stalked toward the door. "I have had bad luck in my descendants," he said. "You will redeem the line." He left the room.

Gen Zavijavah stepped around the chair toward her. She backed away.

His left cheek twitched. "Evidently you've been made privy to some personal information regarding me." His voice gloated. She felt like a morsel being inspected before consumption.

"Gen Zavijavah," she blurted. "I'll … do what you want, if you'll … do me a favor in return."

"What I want?" He raised a black eyebrow.

She cleared her throat. "Yes." Her voice quavered. She cleared her throat again. "I want to ask—to beg, if I have to. Don't … involve Jahn Korsakov. Can you use your influence with Father to get him released?"

A serene smile spread over his face. In other circumstances, he might have looked handsome. "No," he said. "Rider wants Jahn Emlin now. Rider doesn't explain. It demands. You'll understand how it is. Soon."

Then they had caught Jahn, her only remaining ally. She felt as if something huge were squeezing her chest, making it hard to breathe. She had to ask—she couldn't resist: "Is it as terrible as it sounds?"

He tilted his head forward. "Of course it is." He strode to her multi-net. He touched three panels and said, "Security clearance, Zavijavah. Deactivate. Full exclusion."

Exclusion? "What are you doing?" she cried.

"Confirm." He looked back over at her. "I think it really would be best if you remained incommunicado, Luene. The ship will leave soon."

Then he also left.

She hurried to her desk. The terminal had gone dark. Alarmed, she pointed at the switch.

No image appeared. No sound came.

Gen Zavijavah had shut off her access.

She sat down and crumpled onto her forearms, so angry and frightened she barely could think.

Wait. Angry and frightened? Was she actually feeling two emotions at once?

Yes. She was. She had been mentally and socially crippled, declared worthless by her own father. Now he would throw her away a second time.

If Alun was dying, would they punish Jahn by offering him in Alun's place? Jahn had talked as if there were only a few days left.

Where was he?

She pushed back her chair. Feeling like an automaton, she stood and walked to her window. She tried opening it. It would not budge. Leaning against the wall, she stared outside.

When the sky darkened, she lay down and tried to sleep, but for hours, she couldn't. Voices outside her door confirmed that she was guarded in the hallway.

She could have stayed at Filip Salbari's estate. Safe. Cared for. With his daughter as a friend.

We never know all the dangers that come with our choices, she heard in memory. Regent Salbari had honored her decision. She had certainly learned because of this mistake, hadn't she? She could never be blithe about consequences again. But they could not have guessed at this danger.

And what had happened to Regent Salbari? Had the Antaran populace turned against him? Was he ill?

Karine never would have let her come home to Tdega, of course. Maybe Karine was not a normal empath, as Llyn had once thought. Karine was nothing like Regent Salbari or Jahn Korsakov. Had Karine been born with a twisted personality, or had she acquired it over years of dealing empathically with sick and twisted minds? Or—was something even worse wrong with that woman?

Llyn clenched her hands under the pillow and forgave Karine everything. That hawk, at least, had tried to turn her from an eaglet into a hatchling hawk and keep her forever in its nest. Her father, the eagle, intended to feed her to his friends.

She had barely dozed when a meal tray slid out of the chute over her conversational table. It had a bowl of steaming—what was that, cereal or pudding?—at the center. She ate mechanically, wondering if her appetite had vanished or if this tasted like metal.

She must do something. Maybe she could at least warn Residence staff that a Chaethe was among them. She would be ready as soon as someone arrived to pick up her tray.

No one did. Another tray slid down on top of it five hours later.

Jahn? she thought out into the unknown distance. *Where are you?*

27

Five days out from Antar and two days short of Gate passage, Filip sensed trouble on board the *Woodman*. Karine, Joao, and Vananda—his third triad—seemed unanimously unhappy. It didn't surprise him to find Karine roaming the passages wreathed in depression, but Joao Pallaton had conquered too many crises to let minor trouble bother him. If he seemed unsettled, something was gravely wrong.

Filip called Vananda into the galley. He had already told her that he'd heard from Jahn, but not about Casimir's plan for Llyn. Knowing about that would not help any of his coworkers, and only Jahn could thwart it.

The galley had satin-finished metal walls, metal chairs, and a metal-topped table anchored to the deck. Voices took on a slight echo in here.

Vananda crossed her legs and studied her fingers.

"What is it?" he asked. He did not synch with her. After a full day practicing with his own triad, he craved privacy.

"With training?"

"Start there."

She shrugged. "Uncle Joao is excellent at nexus. He links me solidly with Karine. But the nexus wobbles. We can only hold it for a few minutes."

"Why?"

Vananda sighed and looked up. "Karine tries to accept my supervision, but linking daily with her, I find myself less certain that we have any chance to establish contact with the enemy."

"Enemy?" Filip asked, alarmed.

She spread her hands. "You see? I'm picking up her attitude. I know better."

He inhaled deeply. Shipboard air smelled clean but processed. "You said that the nexus wobbles?"

She rested an elbow on the metal galley table. "When nexus is that uncomfortable, it becomes difficult to sustain."

No nexus was completely comfortable. He, Rena, and Qu had spent two all-day sessions establishing a warp-woof balance that didn't make one or another of them too queasy to continue. They'd moved on to experiment with back-feeding. The boldly talented Qu listened to an Outwatch volunteer as Rena amplified the volunteer's inner-frequency thoughts while holding nexus. Filip amplified Rena, then Qu strengthened his perception. With another week of practice, they should be able to feedback without conscious thought. Rena, although relatively untrained, had stunning strength and almost boundless enthusiasm. Perhaps that enthusiasm, sensed by them all, was part of what kept them persevering.

"I was afraid of that." Filip leaned on the table, too. "I might rotate Karine to another triad."

Vananda shook her head. "You can't spread her negativism. We should have taken Llyn out of that clinic months earlier. She must have been miserable."

He rested his chin on one hand. "Is Karine cooperating with treatment?"

"She seems to be going through the motions, but I don't think she believes in them."

"She'll have to pass a full evaluation before we renew her clinician's license."

Vananda finger-combed the curls on one side of her head. "Surely it was at the back of your mind that one or another triad might not function. Wasn't that one reason for drafting nine of us?"

"I'd hoped not to lose a triad before we left Antar Gate."

"I want to believe in the mission," she said. "I don't like what's happening to me."

"I will switch you to Lyova's triad, then, with Bord and Kenji. And I will dissolve the third triad."

She looked up, startled. "What will Uncle Joao and Lyova do?"

"Lyova could help the system delegates listen when we open negotiations. Joao could nexus-link the other two triads. I think he's the only one of us who could do that."

"And Karine?"

"Record events, maybe."

"I worry." Vananda stared aside. "I've seen her talking with the two Outwatch lieutenants."

Filip rubbed his chin. "Perhaps I should speak with the lieutenants again. Fearful voices can be all too persuasive." He shook his head. "System reps are meeting daily, too. I could address them as well, or talk with each one privately."

"Will you speak to Karine?"

Confront her? "I will tell her I am dissolving your triad," he answered heavily. If Karine meant to sabotage the mission, she had begun well.

His frustration suggested another thought. "I haven't taken the chance to compliment you for the way you raised Jahn," he said. "He has exceeded all of our hopes. I only wish we had some way to get him off Tdega, along with Llyn. Her safety depends on him now."

She lifted her chin. "He was ordered to find his own way home. I believe he would sacrifice himself for Llyn, if that did not conflict with the work he is doing for you."

"He may not have received my last transmission. There is at least one Chaethe carrier at the Casimir Residence." He could tell her that much. He avoided thinking about the other news.

"He has probably discovered that Chaethe. He has talent. Despite," she added with a wry smile, "some people's opinions."

He glanced away, at a bulkhead lined with storage compartments. It hurt to hear Vananda talk about her son sacrificing herself. It seemed somehow wrong.

"Isn't that what I'm doing, Filip?" Her smile lost its sarcastic twist and became wistful. "Sacrificing myself? I'm not just his mother. I'm his fellow worker."

Antar's strongest living listener had been scanning his thoughts, and this time, he didn't object. He laid his hand on hers. "Jahn is truly your son."

Before confronting Karine, Filip sounded out several other people. Each interview gave him the impression that the delegation was dividing, slowly and nonviolently like a splitting amoeba, into two camps. The representative from Miatrix—Karine's cabinmate—and the one from Vatsya Hab were manifestly losing faith in the mission. The Outwatch lieutenant he questioned answered with proverbs about eternal security and life after death.

Even Dio Liion harbored doubts. She stood in front of her tiny cabin mirror, twisting her hair into the ornate topknot that marked her as Unukalhaian, frowning at his image. "I disagree completely with Gen'n Torfinn," she said, "but we have been arguing about what conditions to lay on the Chaethe. You've only been to half of our systems council sessions, so you haven't seen the worst fights. We all want them gone, but I feel that the humans they already inhabit should be free to remain in the Concord. Captain Hardette refuses to consider furnishing the Chaethe with ships to leave in. We circle and never arrive."

"We're less than halfway to Sunsis." Filip wanted to soothe her, but the poison had obviously spread farther than he anticipated.

Karine denied nothing. She sat with her hands folded on the other side of the mess table. Maintaining a shallow synch, Filip observed her stiff poise. "I have been thinking." Her voice rang against metal bulkheads. "If you mean to go through with this mission, since I know more about the Chaethe language than anyone else on board—and since my triad has been dissolved—then I should take charge of the encounter. Between your triad work and performing as an official delegate, you'll have your hands full, while I have both hands free now.

"And I hear the delegates have been arguing," she finished.

He stuck to the subject. "That was not the plan, Karine. I have taken responsibility for this mission."

"We adjust. Do you have one good reason to hold me back, other than the fact that you've decided you don't like me?"

He would have laughed at her preposterous reversal of the personal dynamics if she hadn't looked so serious. Her inner frequency never wavered. Obviously, she had convinced herself.

Apparently, he needed to remind her how she honestly felt. How bizarre! "We must work together," he said, "regardless of dislikings. Your work at Sunsis might prevent further trouble on Tdega. This is an opportunity for you to contribute to Llyn's safety—"

Finally, an honest emotion: her anger flickered. "Don't talk to me about Llyn. If she is in danger, you are to blame."

"Be careful. Remember, you have been charged with an inappropriate attempt at control."

"This is different."

"Of course it is. Are you being faithful with your treatment readings and meditations?"

She glared.

"You will not be given command of this mission, Karine."

"I never said I wanted it."

But she had. Just moments ago. She'd learned to play both sides of an argument and remain convinced of her own single-mindedness. "You asked to take charge of the encounter."

"That is also different."

"No. That is the heart of our mission. Please go back to your cabin." He lowered his voice, speaking as persuasively as possible. "Look inside yourself for anger. Let it rise, and then face it down. Confess it. Try to purge it. If we arrive on Sunsis bickering, we have little chance of succeeding."

"We have no chance, Salbari."

He inhaled sharply and flattened his palms on the galley table. "Do not speak like that to me. Nor to any other person. I am giving you an order. I will enforce it if you choose to disobey."

She sprang to her feet.

"Just a minute," he said sternly.

She stood glaring at him.

"Your life—and the life of everyone on board this vessel—depends on our full cooperation. If you hope to survive, you will do the best work you are capable of doing."

She stared several seconds longer. "Anything else?" she asked.

"No."

She stalked out of the galley, footsteps ringing.

Gamal Casimir had packed his travel kit late the previous night. As part of final preparations, he examined the modified helmet his Chief of Engineering Development brought to the grand hall.

It still looked like a fishbowl. "You've given it a broader transmission range?"

The engineer stood near a curtained door at one end of the hall. At this early hour, with the sun rising for the first time, the hall was empty of staff. "Three times broader." His voice echoed in the huge glass-and-wood hall. "We have added frequency modulation and single sideband, and it transmits simultaneously at narrow intervals across all three bands."

"Good idea." Gamal fingered one of the small, clear ventilation tubes. Sunsis A was hot and arid. When the Devastators boiled its oceans away, most of its water vapor had escaped into space. "Will it fog?"

"We tested it to ninety percent humidity, Regent Casimir."

"That should suffice."

Bellik stood near the middle of the floor, adjusting his black uniform belt. His fresh haircut made his head look unevenly stubbled. Gamal turned back to the engineer. "You have one for Bellik?"

The engineer handed Bellik a carton.

"Excellent. What about the electromagnet?"

"Already on board, sir."

He had ordered nonmetal projectile rifles for his troops, and two kinds of cartridges: explosives and dummy loads. He dismissed the engineer and spotted movement. Osun Zavijavah walked through the hall door. He had dressed in civilian clothing, a simple white shirt and brown trousers. Gamal had never realized how well Security reds suited him. Without them, he looked small and pale.

"Did you want me?" Gamal asked in a respectful voice, as between equals. Zavijavah carried the Chaethe Ambassador to Tdega, and this was Rider's trip.

Zavijavah's cheek twitched constantly. "Luene is here. She is asking to speak with you."

"Perfect timing." Gamal glanced aside, at Bellik. His nephew nodded, face bland. "No second thoughts?" Gamal asked. He couldn't resist. "If you still want to court her, once she's infested—"

"No!"

Gamal shrugged to conceal his amusement. He had other plans for Llyn Torfinn, anyway. "Then bring her here."

Bellik hurried out. He returned with Llyn, the woman Gamal had briefly called Luene Casimir—and would call Luene Casimir again publicly, once she sat on his Board of Regents. She wore a simple, belted summer-weight shift. He wondered why she had asked to speak with him this morning, after two days in confinement.

Seeing Zavijavah, she stopped walking and stared. "Sir," she said softly, "I don't … want to go to Sunsis. But I will go without complaining, if you leave Gen Korsakov here on Tdega."

He hadn't actually told her that he'd caught Emlin, and she hadn't asked. Interesting that she assumed it now. "Will you confess to having a relationship with him?"

She dipped her chin, held her hands down at her side, and nodded.

"Good," he said. "That clears the air."

She raised her head. "Then will you leave him here?"

"No. But I will let your relationship continue." And his experiment, as well.

He still hoped—as he had hoped long ago—that Llyn might be able to communicate with the Chaethe. Therefore, he needed total control of her. Once she and Emlin both carried Ambassadors, it would be easy to dominate her. He would simply threaten Emlin. The scheme would work in reverse, too.

"I don't understand." She glanced over her shoulder at Zavijavah.

Bellik tapped her elbow. "Worried?" It was a useless question, asked to torment.

She eyed Bellik. Her jaw twitched.

Bellik stared back with a bland expression. She might have been a logical spouse candidate, but now she was valuable to Tdega in her own right.

The guard who'd escorted her down from her room remained at the doorway. Gamal beckoned him forward. "Take her to the base. We will follow shortly."

Llyn's eyes widened. Her hand trembled as she flicked hair away from her face. "Now? I thought we had at least one more day."

He'd meant her to think that. "We shuttle up in an hour. Would you like a tranquilizer?"

She shook her head, pressing her lips together.

Gamal nodded at the guard. The man grasped Llyn's elbow and turned her toward the door. She shuffled away.

Zavijavah sighed as their backs receded.

"Soon, friend." Gamal gripped his shoulder. "Your reprieve has almost arrived. Go with her if you want to. Oh, and tell her about Alun."

"Ah." Zavijavah walked off at a smart clip.

"Wait," Gen Zavijavah's voice called.

Llyn turned to see the Security Chief following her and the guard. "I will ride to the base with you," he announced. "And I'm authorized to tell you that Alun died of his injuries two hours ago."

She groaned. Alun's near recovery made his death even more tragic.

"It's all right," Zavijavah said blandly. "His place has been reassigned."

Llyn shuddered. "It's not all right. He was my friend." But at least Alun would never carry an alien parasite. "Shouldn't I go upstairs and pack?" Maybe she could stall Gen Zavijavah. Maybe she could jump out a window and be safe—as Alun was safe now. "We'll be gone several weeks," she added.

"Everything you need is on board." He gripped her shoulder. She felt it clearly. "This way."

He took her out a back door. Crossing from the Residence to the garages, she looked up and back at the huge building with its stone cornices. If she ever saw it again, she would not be alone in her own body.

She shuddered.

A nonmaglev car sat idling when they reached the garage. The driver held open a back door. Zavijavah motioned for her to get in. The broad garage door swung open, and Llyn glanced in that direction. Could she escape that way?

Gen Zavijavah cleared his throat. She glanced at him. He'd drawn a hand weapon. "Get in," he said.

She slid into the car. As he walked around the back, she tried the rear door handle. It was already locked.

He joined her.

"Why is he doing this to me?" she asked.

Zavijavah seemed to be looking through her. He said nothing.

Llyn watched every detail of Bkellan—every housing tower, each tree, even the smoking factories—as the chauffeur took the vehicle across town. Gen Zavijavah sat against the other rear door, and although she could not see his eyes, she felt as if he were staring at her.

Maybe he wasn't, though. Maybe it was his Chaethe, studying her.

They passed through an open gate in the former Outwatch base's new fence and out to a large, glassy crater, the chauffeur steering without slowing until suddenly he braked. As Llyn climbed out of the back, another group arrived in a van. It settled to the ground, and two Security men emerged. Since Zavijavah didn't push her forward, she stood and watched. The first passenger out was the Antaran woman she had met on board her transport ship, Lieutenant Metyline, the religious one who'd taken comfort in her suicide implant. Now Llyn understood the temptation. Why hadn't Lieutenant Metyline used it?

Maybe she didn't know where they were headed. Nor why.

The huge-eyed navigator climbed out next. Gen Zavijavah stepped toward him. The navigator squinted, obviously suffering under the bright morning sun.

"Watch her," Zavijavah ordered their driver as he strode forward. Llyn recognized the next two people off as the rest of her Outwatch crew. They wouldn't be here if she'd stayed on Antar, and she felt worse than guilty. A dignified older man followed them. Then several others. Llyn wondered whether any of them had any idea what was going to happen.

When Gen Zavijavah reached the Antaran navigator, he drew a spare pair of dark glasses out of a pocket pouch on his belt. He handed them to the teary-eyed seer. "Here," he said.

The Antaran hesitated.

Gen Zavijavah pulled off his own glasses, and then Llyn understood. She recognized his huge round eyes, almost all pale brown iris and inky pupil.

The navigator took the glasses and slipped them on. "Thank you."

"You're welcome, brother."

Maybe Zavijavah had not totally died to human sympathy. He returned his own glasses to the bridge of his nose and strode toward Llyn. A squadron of Tdegan troops herded the second group toward a wedge-shaped shuttle that stood in the crater.

As Zavijavah led her closer, he said, "To answer your question 'why,' they wanted me for my abilities. They want you for your parentage. You're to provide a Chaethe voice on the Board of Regents. The only one, now that Alun's dead. Walk."

She followed the other group slowly, realizing how bitterly Zavijavah resented what had been done to him. She could not ask him for sympathy.

But there must be some way she could redeem this hideous situation.

She hurried to catch up with Lieutenant Metyline. There were things she needed to ask about.

Hours later, she stepped off the suborbital shuttle onto a huge transport ship, holding Lieutenant Elna Metyline's hand and thoroughly briefed regarding the Sphere sect. Elna's reverence for creation's Creator reminded her of a choral hymn she'd heard ages ago, seemingly in a different life-time. The sect's founder had submitted to be sacrificed on humanity's behalf—and (Elna stressed this) he even forgave his executioners, assuring his adherents of life after death. Elna had spoken fearlessly. Llyn had nothing so lovely to explain in return. Only the aliens awaiting them at Sunsis.

Saving her new knowledge to consider later, Llyn stared up the transport's boarding ramp. The dignified-looking man in the group had apparently been Antar's Ambassador to Bkellan. Allegedly, he'd been recalled by Regent Salbari and taken back to Antar by Lieutenant Metyline's crew. They had all vanished at the same time, anyway. Now she knew they'd all been imprisoned.

She honestly wasn't surprised.

But none of them had seen Jahn.

Perhaps he was dead after all.

Another escort peeled Llyn's hand out of Elna's and hustled her up a long corridor to one of several identical hatchways. He touched a control, opening the oblong hatch. "Inside." He shoved her through.

She spun halfway around, trying to grab the hatch's edge. Someone inside seized and held her. The hatch shut with a loud, ominous click as she struggled against strong arms that pinned her own arms to her sides.

"Llyn," someone said behind her ear. "It's me."

She went limp. The strong stranger had Jahn's voice.

28

Llyn pulled out of his arms, looked down, and studied them. Tiny scabs and dark purple bruises covered them—and his face, and his hands. His queue had been cut off. His hair was black at the ends, but the roots were reddish-brown. Red stubble covered his chin, too. She knew the square jaw and his broad forehead, but she'd never seen them without edge shadings of dark pigment.

He did look Antaran.

"Jahn?" she whispered.

He rested his hands on her shoulders. "I'm sorry I frightened you."

She reached up and touched a scab on his chin. "Is your name really Jahn?"

"Yes. It's Jahn Emlin. Vananda Hadley is my mother. Filip Salbari—your friend—is my uncle."

It was a relief to hear it from his lips. "Regent Casimir knows."

"He knows everything," Jahn murmured.

"You look different."

"I had an implant that darkened my skin and hair. They found it."

But his soothing voice was the same, and hearing still was her dominant sense. This was her friend. She fingered his cheek, shuddering to think about the kind of search that would turn up a cosmetic implant and leave such scabs and bruises. "They hurt you."

"I'll heal."

She stared at his eyes, understanding too well. They wanted him in prime physical condition. At least his eyes were still warm, brown, empathetic. She leaned toward him again, and this time, his arms closed around her. He held her and stroked her hair. She couldn't think of anything else to say. She didn't want him to let go. Here were comfort and strength enough for the moment.

Eventually, he loosened his grasp. She looked around the tiny cabin. It reminded her of her quarters aboard the Antaran transport, with its metal decks and bulkheads, but instead of hammock rings it had a pair of bunks. Several cases of crates were piled on the top bunk. "I don't know why they put us together," he said, "but I'm grateful."

"Father means to pair us off. And it's not that I don't like you. But we've got to … to be careful."

He looked as if he meant to answer, but the deck tilted. She grabbed his shoulders as one bulkhead suddenly became "downhill."

"Engine burn," he said. "We're underway."

She looked all around. "Can't we hide—can't we get out of here—" She knelt beside the hatch.

"Don't touch it!" He seized her arm.

She turned around. "Why not?"

"Voltage lock. It threw me onto the bunk. That's why I pulled you away when it first closed you in."

"Oh." Defeated, she wrapped her arms around herself. The cabin was warm, but she felt cold. "Our only real chance to escape would be to overpower the whole crew," she said without much hope. "Can you people do anything like that?"

"No. Only listen."

That made sense. "We might outnumber them." She glanced from one metal bulkhead to another. "I came on board with twelve other people."

"I've heard them through the bulkheads. The crew says Sunsis is seventeen days away." He climbed onto the top bunk, perched on its end, and started tapping. Three quick raps, three slow, three quick. An easy pattern.

She knelt again and imitated his rhythm. When nothing happened, she crawled ten centimeters farther along and tried again. If all the prisoners could signal each other, they might coordinate something—but what?

Eventually, too tired to continue, she straightened. "Have they left us anything to eat?"

He slapped a crate on the top bunk. "It's all labeled 'rations.'" Even his palms were dotted with scabs. He looked strange, queueless with two-toned hair and a new beard. She wondered what invisible scars Gen Casimir had inflicted on him. If he'd suffered, it was partly her fault. Yes, he was a spy. So yes, he'd taken that risk. Still, he'd been caught trying to help her and Alun escape.

On the other hand, she and Alun had provided Jahn with information he wouldn't have gotten otherwise. She must let Jahn take responsibility—and the consequences—for his own actions. Wasn't that a concept Regent Salbari had taught her?

What courage it must have taken, though, to leave Antar for Tdega.

Alun. Poor Alun. "Did you hear?" she asked softly. "Alun died."

He looked up with furrowed brows and narrow eyes. "I thought so. He took a terrible fall."

"Fath—" No, she would not call him that. "Regent Casimir told me he lingered. He had said that if Alun died, he would charge you with murder—"

"They told me that, too."

"Well, I don't think he will now. He's more likely to hold charges over you as a threat." She sat down beside him on the lower bunk. "I'm sorry Alun's gone. I liked him."

"So did I." Jahn stared at his feet. "And I assume you heard Regent Salbari resigned."

"Yes. Why?"

"No one's saying." Jahn reached up into a crate and pulled out a soft metallic pouch. "No label." He tore into it. Thick brown pudding oozed out. He cleared his throat.

"I've been eating that for two days already," she said, "if it's what I think." She dipped in a finger and licked it. At first, it tasted oddly sweet. Then oily undertones came through. "That's the stuff, all right."

Jahn spoke in a flat, detached voice. "We're being prepared as hosts for a parasite with massive iron requirements. It encases its spores in metal."

She shuddered. "At least we won't starve."

"They won't let us. I tried refusing a meal."

She didn't ask for details.

"Here." He handed her the pouch. "I'll finish what you can't choke down."

She squeezed pudding out of the pouch's ripped corner into her mouth. She swallowed as much as she could, horrible though it tasted. She needed her strength.

"We've got to get out of here," she muttered. She glanced up at the top bunk, piled with food crates. Their captors had left only one bunk vacant. She would sleep on the deck rather than tempt fate the way her father seemed to intend.

Was he watching? She didn't see any surveillance eyes on the bulkhead, but if he'd set someone on watch, she wouldn't give them the satisfaction of watching her search the cabin.

Jahn climbed into the top bunk's vacant corner. "I'll hand these down to you," he said. "We'll pile them on the floor."

Thank you, she thought at him, wondering whether he'd synched with her previous thoughts, too.

"You're welcome," he said.

———

She took the bottom bunk and undressed under the covers. Several minutes after Jahn stopped rustling above her, she hadn't gone to sleep. The lights hadn't dimmed, either. She whispered, "Are you awake?"

"Yes." His clear voice suggested strength and courage.

She hoped she wouldn't let him down. "Did they hurt you, Jahn?"

"Why are you asking me again?"

She'd been thinking about some of the things Lieutenant Metyline said on the shuttle. And hadn't she been told that most empaths followed Sphere teachings? "If you have to forgive them, how do you do it?"

She listened to a long silence before he answered. "It isn't easy." He didn't sound condescending or scornful, and plainly, he knew what she referred to. "You start by acknowledging that they owe you a debt—of comfort, or dignity, or whatever they stole." He was silent for a moment. "You're thinking about Karine? Or Gamal Casimir?"

"Karine." She still carried so much anger, even after trying to forgive the woman. And that was to say nothing of her father and what he was doing—

"Well, she owes you plenty. You have to realize that you can never collect. Nor from your father."

How much of her thoughts could he follow? Or was that simply a logical guess? "I'll deal with him later," she said. She thought through that idea of debt, as it applied to Karine. Truly, she felt robbed. Really and truly robbed of her freedom, dignity, and hope of independence. She dredged up a vague, bitter memory. It made her feel hot inside. Clenched. "All right," she said. "Next?"

"Since you can't undo what's been done, your pain harms you more than it hurts Karine. It stresses you, now that you're letting yourself feel it."

"Oh, yes."

"You will need," he said softly, "to let Karine take the consequences for her own specific actions. Give them back to her. To the Creator, too."

That sounded familiar. It wouldn't solve anything—not magically, as she might have wished that it could—but it was something she might work on. And maybe, if the Sphere people were right and an eternal Creator existed, she could ask for his help.

Especially if this was the requirement for life after death. Because she would almost rather die than cooperate.

"I'll try," she said. "Thank you. I hope you can sleep."

"You too."

"You should probably stop synching now."

He laughed softly.

She lay still and tried to think of every insult, every restriction, every anguish Karine had heaped on her. Each memory was a debt. Not one could be repaired or repaid.

Nor, come to think of it, could she repay Karine for the good things she'd been given, such as her education and training.

So. If she hoped to find any lasting happiness, it had to come from inside her—or else by way of that Creator.

All right, then, she announced silently into the void. *Elna says that you're out there. Regent Salbari says so, too. And Jahn seems to believe. I don't know enough to buy in, but if your sphere is real, I'd like to join it. I want to stop feeling afraid. I'll—I'll forgive them all. Is that really all it takes?*

She waited for the dread curling around her heart to loosen its claw-like grip.

It didn't. Apparently, she'd missed something.

Well, thanks anyway. She turned toward the wall. Jahn's breathing had become heavy and regular. Evidently, he had respected her thoughts' privacy.

But would it be too much to ask for some sign that you heard me? Elna had said honest doubt was expected. *Whenever you're ready. Hopefully soon.*

She still heard only Jahn.

Eventually, his breathing lulled her into a dream. Karine dangled by her feet from a glimmering grid line, hanging head-down over the crater-ous yellow surface of a planet that was supposed to be Sunsis A. Hawk-wings folded over her back, she waited there for Llyn, wearing Osun Zavijavah's wraparound glasses.

Jahn woke before Llyn did. He hadn't slept well since Casimir's people worked him over. His bones still felt as if they were buzzing with pain, and imaginary needles still probed and sparked under his skin.

He had no idea how long he'd slept. If they were under surveillance, the cabin lights might not dim. Ever.

He slipped off the top bunk, careful not to jostle Llyn on the bunk below. Her relaxed face looked utterly peaceful, and he envied her. Curled around her pillow, she looked almost like a child with a stuffed animal, her hair thrown behind her head.

Smiling, he stepped across the cabin and eyed the hatch. He lay down next to it. Then he closed his eyes and listened.

Llyn's dreaming came through clearly. He synched his inner frequency to hers, wondering if he would be able to make sense of any imagery. She seemed to be operating an exercise machine. Exercise ...

He opened his eyes. She'd almost pulled him down into sleep. They were uncannily matched, almost as if they naturally thought in a kind of nexus. Again he studied her sleeping face, remembering the determination she had shown during their dash up the long hillside. To have come back so strongly from the mental crippling Casimir inflicted on her, she had to be as brilliant as that Tdegan Security guard had remembered. Llyn had returned from a deeper fall than Alun's. She would fly higher, once she learned to catch air in her wings.

She had also stirred instincts that he could not indulge here. He shut his eyes, determined not to spring Casimir's trap. Casimir stood to benefit if they relaxed their guard and loved each other. They also would need all their wits about them if they hoped to escape the Chaethe at Sunsis.

He dismissed regret, exhaled, and centered himself in a mental posture of listening. Then he tried eavesdropping again, tuning out Llyn's dreaming mind. He heard faint inner frequencies in all directions, like fuzzy stars on a hazy Tdegan night. He focused on one at random and synched.

The frequency fluctuated, anticipating something and relaxing, in a long slow rhythm. Someone was apparently playing a gambling game on watch.

He lay still for most of an hour, sampling presences, until someone awoke in a cabin close by. The instant he achieved synch, he recognized Gamal Casimir. Gamal had been awakened by a communiqué reporting an attack ship's approach to Tdega Gate. In three days, it would emerge at the Antar system.

Jahn tried to tug Casimir into nexus and urge him to turn that attack ship around. He managed to keep Casimir awake for half an hour, but Casimir did not respond with any decision. Eventually, the other frequency faded as Casimir dozed off.

Jahn glared up at the bulkheads and wiped sweat off his forehead. If he'd been Athis Pallaton, he might have succeeded.

Well, he wasn't. He climbed back up the boxes onto his bunk, turned over twice to wrap the blanket around him, and tried to sleep. His buzzing bones and thousands of tiny itching scabs made it impossible.

Two days and six nauseating meals later, Llyn had rapped every bulkhead a thousand times. She sat down on the lower bunk next to Jahn. Her knuckles ached as she closed her hand carefully around his forearm. His bruises were fading, and he never complained, but she didn't want to hurt him. "You've done all you could," she said. "So have I."

"You're upset." He probably was synching. He looked more and more tired, napping often but never for long.

"Well," she said, "yes. But …"

He bumped her with his shoulder. "But what?"

"I want to be brave for your sake. I'm sure you've felt my fear for two days."

"I don't listen all the time. And touching your feelings always comforts me."

"How's that?"

"It's so easy to synch with you."

She smiled.

His voice softened. "I'd like to try to hear all that you are. Would you let me?"

How many times had he already synched with her? It had never harmed her. Not that she could tell, anyway. "It would be good—while I'm still myself—to know that someone had known me completely. Do you think you would still like me?"

"I know I would," he murmured. "You honor me by showing that much confidence."

"Would I feel anything?"

"Tell me if you do. So far, you haven't."

"Try it, then."

She closed her eyes and waited. Nothing happened for a long time. She counted tiny ridges on the pad of her thumb.

Jahn sighed softly. She felt cheated.

"I like you very much," he whispered. "Do something for me, would you? Think of that melody."

"From your recording?"

"Yes."

She recalled it to mind, wishing only that they might escape together.

The featureless bulkhead shifted, although no grid lines appeared. She sensed someone beside her—but not in human shape. The amorphous presence glimmered blue-gold. She sang herself toward it. It grew to surround her. She burst its wall and plunged through. It laughed, shrank through her, and doubled back.

She had played games like this with the gentle geometries of her inner world. She saw no reason to try and escape now. She dove into the blue-gold presence again and clung, singing a wall into existence. It surrounded them both.

When her control song's echo returned, she cringed. The seventeen-tone scale had turned bitter. She still responded automatically, controlled by it exactly as she used it to control other shapes. She had grown accustomed to living as a free agent instead of wafting along, steered by external music as often as not.

Years ago, she had invented a silencing sequence of tones that rose through three octaves. She sang it now.

The echoes silenced. Triumph and joy flooded out of her spirit's center. She hadn't even known she had joy inside her. She'd thought she was full of pain. Jahn's presence seemed to amplify her joy.

Wanting to tease him the way she had teased programmed presences, she tried dashing away. He clung. She couldn't break free. She struggled, singing discord into the gridless vacuum. That seemed not to affect the other unmistakably human presence. "No," Jahn murmured. His echo filled her mind. "Please don't fight me. Don't drop me."

She relaxed into the blue-gold embrace and listened. She listened keenly and closely. She seemed to hear herself singing out of his heart.

His voice sounded again. "That's love, Llyn. That's what truly caring sounds like. That's how I feel about what I saw in you."

Flushed, she hung in place and listened. Abruptly she sensed something both deeper and vaster than Jahn's presence, and she realized it was both inside and vastly outside of her. Turning herself inside out—the gesture made her feel a little like a Klein bottle, with no inside or outside—she sang herself toward it.

It spun, a pure, blinding light. The closer she drew, the less frightened she felt. Simply approaching it seemed to muzzle her ability to fear. She couldn't tell its true shape. Rotating at a speed approaching infinite, it looked spherical. It spun off garnet-red droplets in all directions.

One droplet whizzed toward her. She plunged into its path, and in an instant of pain, it pierced her through. Either this liquid was more solid than she was, or it was no droplet but the brilliant shard of a jewel. A gift. The pain that its passing left morphed into a shivery new joy.

"What are you?" she sang at the spinning sphere.

"I am." It expanded explosively, as things sometimes did in the inner world. But it also remained outside her, so completely beyond that it seemed to enclose the universe.

Awed but puzzled, she made the inside-out gesture again and found herself next to the blue-gold presence, the one that soothed like Jahn's voice. "Did you see that?" she sang. "The ... the bright center?" And what made her so sure it was the center?

"What are you talking about?"

"What's happening?" Llyn asked, confused but entirely at peace. She'd begged for a sign. Was this it? "Why are you here?"

"I'm still synched with you," Jahn's presence answered, "and I think you pulled me into one of your flashbacks—"

"No, no! This isn't a flashback. Nothing like this ever happened before. And I won't apologize."

"I'm not sorry, either. This is something empaths can't do. I don't want it to end. We might never do it again."

"Maybe we have no choice. Maybe we can't stop. Maybe it's ... permanent?" She cracked her eyes open.

She sat beside Jahn, not the blue-gold presence but a man with a short red beard, holding him so tightly that her shoulder hurt. His eyes opened, too. She let him go and leaned away.

The sense of communion flowed on. He loved her. On the inside, where he could not deceive.

"Something's different," he whispered. "Something just happened."

Llyn blinked. Then she, too, noticed that only her visual imagery had changed. The inner-yet-outer world sense of melody, space, and time flowed on. So did the electric awareness of Jahn Korsakov. Jahn Emlin. Jahn.

Relaxing against him, she shut her eyes. "Whistle something," she whispered.

"What?" he asked, and she felt his confusion. Had he changed her into an empath?

He laughed at the thought. His merriment infected her, and she laughed back. It felt wonderful to laugh. It meant cherishing the unexpected. Comprehending it. Delighting in it.

"Whistle something," she repeated. "Random notes. Try to hit one of the seventeen-tone intervals. I have a hunch."

He puckered and blew an unlikely series of tones. Llyn envisioned inner-world responses to the intervals, but the bulkhead remained solid in front of her.

"I don't know what has happened," she said solemnly, "but I'm free. I'm in control."

"This time, I think you truly are."

Should she be afraid? They had done something to and with each other that she could not understand—but the sensation enchanted her. She relaxed into it again. "What color am I?" She wondered if he would understand.

He answered without hesitating. "Blue. You shimmer."

Somehow, that didn't surprise her. "You're the same. You're one of us. Whatever *we* are."

"You're beautiful."

"No. You are."

She was losing track of which identity was speaking.

"I think," Jahn said softly, "this must be something the trainers called interactive enmeshment. It was supposed to be terrible."

"I think it would be, with the wrong person."

He nodded. "Not just terrible. Unbearable."

If this killed her, she would die happy—and uninfested. She pulled closer to Jahn and deeper, farther from the world of bunks and bulkheads.

Something amazing had begun.

Jahn felt helpless in Llyn's universe, but her sense of belonging made him hope he could adjust.

This state truly would be intolerable with a person who used other inner frequencies. It would drive one or both mad within minutes. He

336 | KATHY TYERS

couldn't believe he and Llyn had stumbled into it together. They must have been led to it.

Yes, echoed Llyn-inside-him. *It feels that way. Led.*

If Gamal Casimir enslaved their bodies to aliens, might they escape together into this other plane of existence? Alone, he would have refused to return to it. This weird, extra-dimensional existence had to be part of creation—but surely they were not meant to linger here. It would never be his home.

Still, Llyn might be happier here than living controlled by an uncaring "Rider."

Her alarm accelerated the nexus frequency. *Don't deny yourself everything just to make me happy. That's what Karine tried to do, only in reverse. It's just as wrong. And I don't think the outside world is unimportant. It's created, too, isn't it?*

He tried to think himself smaller, as a gesture of apology. Nothing happened. In this strange inner world, he could only cling to her. "Actually," he said, "if Osun Zavijavah is any indicator, I might be happier here, too."

Still, it felt like temptation.

Favia Hadley eyed the estate nerve center's overhead monitor. A standby message had been repeating for twenty hours. Delegates, planetary representatives, and family members, remaining at the Salbari estate for word from Ilzar or Sunsis, had squeezed close together on the floor under this monitor.

She stood beside Boaden Salbari, knowing he wouldn't stay much longer. He had taken to pacing the nerve center's circle of multinet terminals. His frown deepened the jowls beneath his chin. As Head Regent, Boaden had deployed the few reinforcements that had arrived from Miatrix. One Miatrixan gunship remained close to Antar Gate, where it could respond if an invader emerged. The other two stood in high orbit, ready to defend this continent. But what good could two midsize gunships do against the war wagon her nephew Jahn had described in his transmission?

Boaden had also made evacuation arrangements. Fifty kilometers from Nuris, Rift, and two other industrial cities, and upwind from the estate, crews were digging deep bunkers. As soon as Boaden ordered general evacuation, Antarans would flee the obvious targets.

Favia did not expect to hear from Filip until he announced the mission's success, and that might not happen for weeks. She could only pray for him. Maintaining her hugely expanded household, including the other systems' delegates, kept her scurrying. Alcotte had stayed close to Boaden, assisting when Boaden let him, particularly with Antaran domestic affairs.

But Boaden itched to assemble a strike force and send it to Sunsis behind the empath delegation. So far, although Vatsya and Kocab had promised five warships each toward the effort, none had arrived.

Yesterday, they all had been shaken loose from their routines by the standby messages appearing over c-net terminals. The Tdegan star-and-ring emblem had flashed, as before, but no further communication appeared. As Jahn predicted, a Tdegan warship had emerged through the Gate and launched a dozen defense fighters. One destroyed the Miatrixan defender.

Now only two gunships stood between the world of Antar and a new round of Tdegan missiles. They could arrive in six days. Digging crews had gone on triple overtime.

This morning, her daughter Stasia lingered next to one of the six multinet transceivers. Favia stared, loving the girl. Stasia had inherited Favia's thick, curly hair and Filip's passionate eyes. Some people had claimed her parents gave her too much freedom, because she refused to do anything that didn't hold her interest. In the past, Stasia had kept to her rooms during a crisis.

But Filip had spent several hours with her before leaving for Sunsis, and the next morning, Stasia had volunteered to help wherever needed.

A tremor rattled the floor. Two techs who'd been standing under the main projector backed away. Favia guessed the tremor had been strong enough to unsettle even the people who hadn't been nervous.

She missed Vananda. Vananda had always been as close as the c-net during a crisis. Gladwyn was also absent from the nerve center. Two nights ago, she finally brought one more Tourelle into the world. Gladwyn and little Feith were resting together.

Boaden bowed his head and muttered, "I wish they'd get on with it."

"You're ready?"

"With two warships." He sounded disgusted. "Where are the reinforcements the other systems promised? Only Miatrix—"

The ringed star vanished. A man's head and shoulders appeared. Favia recognized Bellik Casimir. "Antar and the Concord," he said brusquely, "we find it difficult to believe that you could not take our promise at face value. By striking the Ilzar system, you have opened war against the Tdegan Hegemony. That is a war you will not win, and we are about to end it."

A flurry alongside one of the multinet terminals momentarily distracted Favia. Boaden strode toward it. She turned back to the pigtailed image near the ceiling.

"We warned you that the weapons we used against Ilzar would be brought against you if you challenged any world of the Hegemony. We will arrive in Antaran orbit within six days of your receiving this transmission. At that time, we will launch missiles. You probably expect us to strike your cities." He paused, smirking.

Favia glanced at Boaden. He lowered his eyebrows. Where else might they strike?

The smirk faded. "We will target your sea, Mare Novus. That will send up enough steam and debris to set back your terraforming effort a hundred years or more. You will be too busy evacuating the planet to attack us again. If you are wise, you'll start evacuating now."

The image winked off.

Creator! Favia drooped against a tabletop. That hadn't even been an if-then ultimatum. It had been a pronouncement. A declaration. All around her, people stood openmouthed. No Antaran had predicted this planetary savagery.

She pressed toward the terminal that had caught Boaden's attention. Over its transmitter hovered a warship's image.

Stasia edged through the crowd toward her mother. "It's huge," Stasia exclaimed. "That must be one of their new ones. What can we do?"

Boaden had already hustled to another terminal, where he stood talking to a small uniformed image over its projector, the head of Antar's

Miatrixan reinforcements. Boaden sounded angry. Justifiably, in her opinion—

"Mother!" Stasia exclaimed.

Favia turned around. Stasia pointed at the warship's image. The projectech had shrunk it in order to display outer-system space behind it, all the way back to Antar Gate.

Five more ships had emerged. Favia didn't recognize their configuration.

Boaden sped back across the room. Favia and the others scurried aside to let him pass. "Kocab," he exclaimed. "Kocab came though! They're Kocaban cruisers."

"What can they do against that?" Stasia pointed at the big Tdegan ship.

Boaden shook his head. "According to Emlin's specs, the new Tdegans can cover their aft quadrant but only against one or two attackers. It'll have to turn and defend itself. It'll be depending on its fighters till then."

Favia gazed at the big ship's image as Boaden sent the Kocabans a message. Coded, she assumed. Several minutes later, the projectech punched in a series of calculations and announced, "Yes. It's turning. It's going to try wiping them out before it comes for us."

"But it hasn't changed course." Stasia scowled. "It's still headed our way."

Could that be? Favia turned to Boaden.

"That's right," the tech said. "It's not decelerating. Only rotating. As it comes."

Her heart seemed to fall toward her stomach.

Minutes turned to hours. The projectech line-fed that terminal's image into the overhead projector. Favia ordered more chairs. Planetary delegates, family members, and estate staff sat down again, craning their necks to watch overhead images. Maybe people ate and drank in other rooms, but no one in the nerve center moved. Their doom or their deliverance would be determined within hours. If Tdega targeted Mare Novus, any Antarans who survived must scatter to other planets. That would overburden food production systems. Or else they must crawl to Tdega as refugees.

That had probably been Gamal Casimir's plan all along. The empaths could not run to Tdega, though. The paranoid Casimirs would surely try to wipe them out.

Far into the night, the image changed. "Tdega now firing on the Kocabans," an Outwatch officer announced. Silence fell again.

Favia sat beside her daughter, who winced periodically. Finally, Favia asked, "What's wrong?"

Stasia shook her head. "People are afraid," she whispered. "Every now and then I synch with someone. Then I wish I hadn't."

Stasia must have learned to synch simply by observing other empaths, although she'd steadfastly refused to be trained. "Your Uncle Alcotte could help you with that." Favia glanced aside. Alcotte stood next to Boaden.

"If we live through this," Stasia said, "I think it's time I let him."

Deeply touched, Favia reached for her daughter's hand.

Someone close to the overhead terminal gave a shout. "What's that?"

Three more ships appeared through Antar Gate. Another pair trailed the three.

Boaden peered at them for a moment and cried, "Vatsya! And the Tdegan is broadside to them. It's helpless and it knows it. It's going to accelerate out of this approach vector. I guarantee."

Joyful shouts echoed off the walls.

⸻

The battle for Antar took two days, as military ships hundreds of klicks apart decelerated and maneuvered into firing positions. Favia watched Boaden's prediction come true: the big Tdegan newcomer reabsorbed six of its eight surviving fighters and then poured on speed that impressed even Boaden. One Kocaban defender, caught between the Tdegan ship and the Gate, was destroyed as the big war wagon sped away. The other defenders scattered and let it go.

The next evening at dinner, after everyone slept a few hours, Boaden summed up the action. "Gamal Casimir probably ordered that captain to protect his ship at all costs. It's their newest and best."

"But what now?" Favia asked softly. "It'll be back, won't it?"

"I think so," he muttered. His face had gone gray. "But we've won a respite. We'll regroup and prepare a new defense—and send off a Gate message to your husband."

"Thank you," she said. Maybe carrying the Head Regent's load had finally shown Boaden just how well Filip had served.

Bring him back safely, she prayed, *and soon!*

29

The *Woodman* passed through Antar and Sunsis Gates without being challenged. This baffled Filip. Despite wartime conditions, the Sunsis system was taking no steps to defend itself.

He kept the other representatives informed of the triads' successes and failures, and the systems council continued to discuss terms to offer the Chaethe. Captain Hardette's scantechs identified two barges full of refined metal pellets in orbit over Sunsis A, probably bound for Tdega. That suggested a new strategy: to blockade Sunsis Gate as Admiral Lalande had blockaded Ilzar, but this time to keep Sunsisans inside. That would slow but not stop the spread of infestation, since Chaethe had already been encountered at Antar and Tdega.

Meanwhile, two young Outwatchers practiced operating the scanner that would identify infested individuals.

At four days until ETA, Filip called all the empaths together. Nine of them made the *Woodman's* galley feel psychically crowded. According to Vananda, Karine had slid toward clinical paranoia. Convinced she would not live to stand trial, she'd stopped cooperating with treatment.

Filip took one of five seats at the small table anchored to the deck near the galley's serving station. Vananda sat at another, alone and self-sufficient. Joao, wearing the serenity of long experience, stood beside china-fair Lyova. Rena sat at a third table with young Kenji, whose short, blond hair was twice as long as her red aureole, and they were chaperoned by Qu and Bord. Dark, intelligent Bord also had shown signs of being drawn to the vivacious Rena, but although she sat between them, her side glances and leftward lean told Filip she was with Kenji.

Interesting.

Karine stood against the far bulkhead, crossing her arms across her chest. She had contributed nothing—yet—to this or any other recent strategy session.

Soft sounds surrounded the narrow galley: the engines' quiet thrum as deceleration began, ticks and whishing noises from life support, and a barely perceptible vibration that Captain Hardette attributed to the ship's gravidic system. Since launch, Hardette's crew had steadily decreased power to the gravidics. Sunsis A had only eighty percent of Antar's gravity, and if all they could do to prepare for Sunsis was adjust to its gravity, at least they could do that.

Qu, nexus specialist for Filip's triad, was speaking to the others. "We would be honored to attempt the first contact, if none of you object. If anything goes wrong, you will be able to adjust the other triad's strategy."

Filip eyed Qu and Vananda. He'd never doubted the dedication of either. Qu had served two terms on the Pawson town council, assisting his wife, the mayor. Their twin sons had just been accepted to enter Nuris University, two years ahead of their age mates. Vananda had introduced Filip to Favia, guided her only child into public service, and aided the Order in more ways than Filip could count.

At such a time, it was good to remember those things.

Vananda nodded. "We agree. The honor of first contact should be yours, Filip."

Qu, then, would attempt to touch the alien minds first. If Filip's triad failed, Vananda would try the next synch.

Filip shifted his weight on the hard galley stool. "We've covered strategies to follow first contact. A final option should be considered. If we come to a crisis—if first contact proves fatal, for example—" Tam Vandam's death had been discussed and half a dozen explanations suggested. "Those who remain might enter full enmeshment as an offensive or defensive posture. May we discuss that?"

Karine pushed off her bulkhead. "That's a permanent condition." Her tone scolded everyone present. "It's unforgivable. I dealt with a pair of full enmeshment victims years ago. Only one regained enough independence to function, and that was marginal."

Vananda spoke calmly. "Don't you expect to die anyway, Karine?"

Karine scowled.

Qu and Lyova eyed Vananda. Filip assumed they were synching with her, listening for explanation.

"By combining our strengths," Vananda said, "we might survive an attack long enough to turn aside our attackers' intentions. Then we might force them to listen."

Karine flattened her hands and made a pushing gesture, and though her tone was hostile, Filip was glad she had finally entered the discussion. "You're taking this out of order," she said. "The risks of infestation and mind control are incredible. You're living in an imaginary world."

"What are you driving at?" Filip asked softly.

"I have been thinking for several days." Karine glared down at them. "We were wrong to try this mission. We're the last people the Concord should have sent. One of us, carrying a parasite, could bring down the Concord. An infested empath could monitor other humans and arrange for their infestation."

Filip felt Kenji and Rena start to reflect Karine's fear. "What are you suggesting?" Filip kept his words calm. He must not let her affect the young people. Their courage boosted the whole team's morale. If he pushed her to explain, maybe she would betray herself.

Karine leaned against a ventilator, and a puff of air momentarily inflated her brown culottes. "It would be better to sterilize every Concord planet than to let the Chaethe spread. The Devastators were right."

"Karine." Vananda squinted and compressed her lips. "You can't mean that."

"I do. We can't destroy all Concord planets, but we have this ship. It would be easy to land at the Sunsis colony without decelerating—"

"No!" "Never!" Kenji and Rena objected simultaneously.

You were right, Filip thought at Vananda. Karine's paranoia accused the entire universe of hostile intent, with herself as its primary target. He wondered whether she'd developed such self-centeredness as a counseling defense. And where was her faith?

Rena and Kenji no longer looked frightened. Karine's overstep had affected them just as he'd hoped. He had a solid team of eight again. He smacked the tabletop several times with an open hand and finally got order.

"Karine," he said, "we are discussing the possibility of deliberate enmeshment. Not planetary destruction." He caught her angry stare and listened hard. Her fear throbbed like a raw wound. She was a flawed tool, useless to the mission. He'd misjudged her, hoping she could be won.

"I will not even consider it," she said.

Qu raised a hand with his thumb tucked into his palm. The gesture looked like a benediction. Perhaps he meant it personally, or as the blessing of Antar's previous Regency families on the mission. "If enmeshment is our best defense, of course we must use it."

By counting empty ration packets, Llyn estimated that their ship had passed Tdega Gate—but when she remembered the spinning sphere, nothing—not even life or death—seemed worth worrying about. Infinity existed. Eternal love. She'd seen proof. And as Elna Metylene had begun, Jahn continued explaining the sect.

She'd sat close to him, swimming tandem in shared thought, listening and learning and teaching each other. Whatever happened at Sunsis, she had known joy that she'd ever dreamed could exist.

As days passed, she also adapted to an odd new plane of existence, overloaded by two sets of senses and two centers of thought. Once, she'd been an emotional monotone. Now whenever Jahn dozed, she felt sleepy. And whenever thinking of Sunsis frightened her, he comforted without being asked. She would have been content, locked in this cabin, if only they hadn't been headed for Sunsis.

There'd been another surprise, too. Ever since they'd meshed, as Jahn called it, her craving to touch him had become controllable. The emotional link calmed her desires. Somewhat.

She wished he felt the same. Perhaps men were simply different. She'd caught sensations from him—which he quickly stifled, exactly as she stuffed down her fear—that she found deeply flattering but uncomfortably provocative. Close confinement plainly was weakening his resolve to stay chaste and alert.

He lay on the deck next to the bulkhead, rubbing his eyes. The scabs had vanished, but dark circles had aged his face. So had his full beard. He looked nothing like her urbane tutor, Jahn Korsakov—neither Tdegan nor Antaran, but like a primitive prisoner—and he looked exhausted. He'd slept only three hours at a stretch since they boarded, unable to lie still any longer than that. He said his bones still vibrated.

He was listening for Gamal Casimir again, tracking him to different parts of the ship. Casimir would be informed as soon as Tdega attacked Antar, Jahn insisted. According to Jahn's finger-counting and the number of empty ration packets, that news could arrive today.

Llyn lay on the lower bunk, watching this wild man who had become the other half of her awareness. He yawned—

Then he caught his breath, fully alert. "He's hearing something?" Llyn guessed aloud.

"Sh."

She shut her eyes. She felt Jahn strain to catch some distant perception.

Abruptly, she peeked. A smile stretched out on his face. She felt his excitement without trying to listen, but she didn't catch the meaning. "Yes?"

"He's angry," Jahn whispered. "Reinforcements reached Antar in time."

Filip watched a yellow-brown planet resolve and grow in *Woodman's* viewport. Two pale swirl patterns of cloud cover fascinated him. Three hundred years ago, Antar might have had this much open sky, plus oceans. So much of Sunsis A's imported water had been boiled away that it was now largely desert again.

Boaden's news of the aborted second attack on Antar had reached him two days ago. Boaden now meant to make Antar an armed camp. Filip might disagree, but it was no longer his place to defend Antar. He had his own mission: to approach a hostile alien race, negotiate peace, and if possible, to survive.

"It looks dry," he said softly.

"Hot, too," a slightly familiar voice remarked behind him.

Filip reclined his chair. Captain Hardette's scantech sat nearby, checking several rows of sensors. The command cabin had three seating tiers in a straight line, all nine seats capable of reclining, beneath a low row of narrow bars of light.

"Habitable only at the poles." Or so Filip had heard. He glanced up at Captain Hardette in the top seating row. The Captain seemed pre-occupied with a display that hung in midair in front of him, probably calculating how to grapple those pellet barges, return to the Gate, and unload them.

Filip turned back to the viewscreen. As Sunsis A grew closer and clearer, a pale green area appeared at its south pole. Weed prairies stretched north from a band of symmetrical hills clearly designed to precipitate as much water as possible. The darkest green region south of the hills hardly looked large enough to support civilization.

He wondered how long ago the Chaethe had returned to human-settled space, and why—and whether the Chaethe were full-circle telepaths, with the gift of sending as well as the empaths' gift of receiving, to facilitate living inside other creatures' nervous systems. Maybe they had finally defeated the Devastators. Maybe they had *absorbed* the Devastators.

Tomorrow, he probably would know all those answers.

He glanced at another screen. A Tdegan ship had come in through Sunsis Gate two days behind them, but by Captain Hardette's estimate, it would arrive at Sunsis less than three hours later than this ship. The comm officer had intercepted a standard signal: declare your purpose. Filip had ordered the comm officer to reply, *Flag of truce.*

That had ended the exchange. The Tdegan ship was larger than this one and probably carried weapons. If Filip's mission had been less urgent, or if the Concord's representatives had come to Sunsis for different reasons, he might have ordered Captain Hardette to set the *Woodman* into a sling orbit, seize those barges, and blockade the Gate. Immediately.

He swiveled his chair toward the comm officer and said, "Try the colony."

The communications man opened a line. "Sunsis A South, Sunsis A South. This is Antaran Consular RLD-4, incoming."

Static.

"Give them another hour," Filip said. "I'll be back then." He pushed out of his seat and trudged up the cockpit steps, exchanging nods with

Captain Hardette as he passed the third-row command chair. Bubbles hissed through Hardette's shoulder-balanced prosthesis. Filip wondered how long ago he had stopped hearing at that frequency.

Several empaths had gathered in the galley. Qu Yung sat alone with his eyes closed, probably meditating. The three nexus specialists were together: Kenji, Rena, and the triad-orphaned Joao. Kenji clasped Rena's hand on the tabletop.

All four turned around as the hatch shut behind Filip.

Sensitized to Qu, Filip felt him come alert and listen closely. "The Tdegan ship is still out there," Filip said, "and still on approach. But they're not talking, and neither is Sunsis yet. If we get no response, we'll land tomorrow. There's no reason to wait. Are the others in their cabins?"

Joao smoothed his silver hair. "Yes. I think—"

The hatch at the galley's other end slid aside. Karine paced through, and Filip synched for a moment. She felt cold and angry. Thought bubbles from a fatalistic undercurrent popped through her stream of thought. Plainly, she was convinced she'd die soon.

Sometimes he longed for the old days, before this trip, when his empathy had not been trained to such an intense, precise pitch.

Vananda followed Karine, holding both hands deep in the pockets of an embroidered vest that hung to her hips. Her faint smile looked like her sister's.

How he missed Favia!

He addressed Karine. "Will you help us? We all need you."

Karine's neatly combed hair brushed the line of her uptilted chin. "You need *someone* competent."

"We need full cooperation."

"I intend to cooperate."

"Thank you—"

A panel on a galley bulkhead squawked. "Salbari?" That was Captain Hardette's voice. "We're getting a signal from the south colony."

Filip listened around the cabin. Rena felt eager. Joao, reluctantly determined. Karine, dull and blank.

"I'm on my way." Filip stood up.

The cockpit hatch remained open. He walked through and stepped down to the observer's seat. He thought he felt one of the other empaths follow him. "What are they saying?" he asked.

The communications officer touched his control bar. "Sunsis A South, please repeat."

A female voice answered. Her voice reverberated from sound panels on several bulkheads. "Antaran Consular RLD-4, this is Sunsis A South. We will transmit an approach vector as soon as you request it."

The comm officer touched a different spot on his control bar. An unintelligible burst rang through the cabin. "Got it," the pilot announced.

Captain Hardette straightened. "Set course."

Filip swiveled around and asked, "May I transmit?"

Hardette nodded. The comm officer reached over Filip's shoulder to touch another spot on his control bar. He mouthed, "Go ahead."

"Sunsis A South," Filip said, "we wish to land and speak with you in person. We are unarmed and traveling under a flag of truce. We particularly wish to communicate with any of you who might speak for the Chaethe civilization."

Silence.

Filip glanced back over his shoulder. Vananda stood framed in the open hatch, clutching the fronts of her embroidered vest.

"She's probably passing that message to someone in authority," Filip told her. "It'll take a—"

"Antaran Consular RLD-4," the voice returned. "We acknowledge you are unarmed, also request truce and desire to communicate. How many of you will require housing while we speak?"

That sounded promising. Captain Hardette's Cruxan crew would stay shipboard, ready to launch if the primary mission failed. Nine empaths, five planetary representatives, and ten of the Outwatchers would debark. Filip worried that he might not have brought enough Outwatch personnel to guard his delegation and the *Woodman*. "There are twenty-four in our embassy."

"We acknowledge twenty-four," the voice said.

"We have also been monitoring a Tdegan ship." Filip glanced at the screen, where the Tdegan ship still loomed. "Can you tell us its intent?"

"It has come to negotiate as well."

The *Woodman* decelerated for the rest of that day and part of the next. The unseen controller's coordinates guided Captain Hardette's pilot through a deceleration orbit and then over the circumpolar band of hills. From this close, they definitely looked too regular to be natural. "Weather control?" the comm officer asked.

"Yes." Filip pointed. "The settlements will be just inside those hills."

The polar plain showed pale green up close, patchworked with darker squares and irrigation canals. Just inside the hills, Sunsis A South looked like a normal colony, with crop fields and hydroponics domes that surrounded a large industrial complex. Filip stared hard at that complex, guessing at one reason Tdega had chosen to take Sunsis out of the Concord with it. Metals!

"No vehicles on the roads," the scantech announced.

None? That seemed odd.

Their course took them back out over the hills to a broad, sandy field. Near it, an enormous, new-looking building reflected brilliant sunshine.

As the *Woodman* touched down at the edge of the plain, Filip sat strapped in at the observer's post. The thrumming engines fell silent for the first time in days.

"Antaran Consular RLD-4," the controller's voice said, "please wait on board. Someone will come out to guide you."

"Acknowledge, wait on board." Filip stood. "Captain, would you join me in the galley?"

Captain Hardette nodded.

The other four system representatives waited there, along with Lieutenant Yelenich of the Outwatch. They'd been told to expect external temperatures even warmer than Antar's, but dry. Dio Liion wore her long green gown, and to Filip's surprise, her hair flowed loose over her shoulders. The Miatrixan delegate had dressed in flowing black. Vatsya's young Defense Force Major wore a green-and-gold uniform, and Senator Igrim's white dress tunic matched Filip's. "Lieutenant, your people are ready?" Filip asked the Outwatch man.

Lieutenant Yelenich nodded. His blue-gray uniform strained at its midsection. Apparently, he had gained weight underway. "Our scan crew is ready," he said. "Shields and helmets are issued. Did everyone receive a helmet last night?"

Dio Liion shrugged. "I can't knot my hair under it, but it will fit."

That explained the long, loose hair over her shoulders. Filip had also helped Captain Hardette adjust his new headgear to accommodate the neck prosthesis.

Lieutenant Yelenich took a step forward. "Two of my people will stand with each representative—including you, Regent Salbari, if you change your mind."

Filip shook his head. He needed freedom to see and move. Straightening a bloodstone on his collar, he asked, "Are there any other questions?" Every possible question must have been discussed seven times. "Any last orders, Senator Igrim?"

The elder statesman stood slowly. Filip had seen Igrim's medical records. Nearly crippled by joint degeneration, the Kocaban Senator also had a heart problem, and not long to live.

"Thank you all," Igrim said in a solemn voice. "Thank you particularly, Regent Salbari. Your people and their efforts will be in our prayers. May our Creator deal kindly with us all."

Permission to emerge came half an hour after the *Woodman* landed. Every person debarking carried a minimal survival or overnight kit in an Outwatch pack belt. Filip stood with Qu and Rena as the crew lowered the boarding ramp and equalized cabin pressure. Qu looked serene, but Rena turned her helmet over, around, over, around. Designed for wear on muggy Antar, it was a series of opaque brown strips that would cover the nose, ears, and most of the back of the head. Antaran surgeons had insisted that there was no need for eye protection, so the helmets remained open for vision and ventilation over most of the face.

The main hatch slid aside. An oven-warm blast blew through Filip's hair and fluttered his culottes. A man with olive skin stood below on sandy ground. He walked toward the ramp.

Do not desert us now, Filip prayed, maintaining his self-control like a shield.

Qu and Rena donned their helmets. Carrying his own, Filip walked down to meet the Sunsisan. His footsteps clanged on the ramp.

The scanner operators walked with him, sweeping their instrument slowly around. Turning to Filip, the lead tech shook her head. "It's impossible to get a reading," she said. "It's overloading."

They probably were all carriers, even the man below them. "Thank you," Filip said. "Take it back on board." He beckoned to Rena and Qu and turned around. "Good day," he said. "My name is Filip Salbari. I greet you on behalf of Antar's Regency families. Do you speak for the Chaethe civilization?"

The olive-skinned man wore a loose, thin white shirt and Tdegan-style trousers. He shook his head ruefully. One of his cheeks twitched. "They are gentle masters, but they will not talk to you. Not like you probably want to talk."

"You and I are human." Filip spoke sympathetically. "We belong to a sentient race that should be respected, not exploited. What is your name?"

"I am Malukulu."

"Thank you for greeting us, Gen Malukulu. Do you understand what I said?"

"Now is not the time. The need is great. Come down."

Filip hesitated. "Wait one minute while I tell my people to follow us." Filip turned around. Qu and Rena stood behind him, helmeted but recognizable. Two helmeted Outwatch soldiers carried long, curving body shields and stood with them. Filip had tried lifting one of those shields. He was glad he didn't have to carry it.

Bord, Kenji, and Vananda waited at the top of the ramp, holding their helmets against their hips.

"Have them all come down," Malukulu called. "All twenty-four, please. We will accommodate you." He gestured with an open hand toward the large building. "Nothing fancy, but adequate."

To the right of the new building, a road threaded a gap in the weather-control hills. Pedestrians streamed through it. A larger group of people stood outside the shining metal building. Long pants, short pants, sarongs, and culottes were all in sight. The Sunsisans tended toward tanned skin and long, muscular bodies.

"Wait one moment," Filip said to Malukulu. He walked halfway back up the ramp. Behind Bord and Kenji stood the other three empaths—no longer a triad—and the formally dressed representatives with their Outwatch escorts, all hanging back in the off-loading area.

"What do you think?" he asked Vananda.

She gazed out at the crowd and crossed her arms over her vest. Virtually all the Sunsisans had turned to stare at the *Woodman*. "I think we should try it," she said, "and I think we should try immediately. Before the Tdegans arrive."

"I agree. Igrim." Filip addressed the Senator. "Don't let your group step off the ramp unless we succeed. If we don't, back up and close the hatch. Lock it and launch."

Urban Igrim nodded.

Filip walked back down to rejoin his partners. "Rena," he murmured, "if bringing one or two more into your nexus will help Qu, signal Joao."

Rena seized and gripped his hand. He hoped Stasia, who wasn't much younger, might be thinking of him today. Praying, perhaps.

The hot breeze lifted hair alongside his face again. He turned back to their Sunsisan escort. "We're ready," he said.

"Come with me," Malukulu said. Filip synched momentarily. He heard an undulating frequency alongside Malukulu's disconcerting hunger, and an odd tone in his voice. "We are pleased that you have come. We only wish there were more of you."

30

Filip followed Malukulu's long strides toward a sandy, open square in front of the metal building. Its broad doors gave it the appearance of a barn or a hangar, not a hostel. The deep sand made walking difficult.

Malukulu halted near the center of the square. The parade that had followed them formed a semicircle: Rena and Qu, together with Vananda, Bord, and Kenji—all helmeted—stood around Filip and the Sunsisan. Karine, Joao, Lyova, and their Outwatch bodyguards stayed several meters back. Sunsisans also gathered at the foot of the *Woodman's* ramp. One Sunsisan pointed at Captain Hardette's prosthesis. Others made welcoming motions.

The representatives remained on the ramp. Meanwhile, Outwatch personnel interspersed themselves among the empaths.

Malukulu sidled away from the group.

Disquieted, Filip raised his voice. "We have come to establish communications between the Concord and the Chaethe civilization."

"—ation." His voice echoed off the huge building's broad door.

"Will someone speak for that race?" he asked.

A stooped, gray-haired woman walked forward. Her loose pink dress was covered with enormous white flowers, and dull pain flickered across her wrinkled forehead. "I am Winnow. We are glad you are here. Thank you for coming. But why are the others holding back? And aren't there more of you? We were told to expect twenty-four."

Of course they'd counted. Filip approached the stooped Sunsisan woman. "I am Filip Salbari," he said softly. "The others will join us soon. Will you speak for the Chaethe?"

Winnow shook her head. "Not yet." She turned toward the large metal doors. "Come in, Filip Salbari. Welcome."

He shut his eyes. The hot breeze rustled his hair and flapped his formal black culottes. He felt Qu and Rena step closer. He reached into Rena's mind, steadying Qu as Qu tried synching with Winnow.

No, not with Winnow. Qu must synch with the weird, undulating frequency behind hers. "I wish to speak with your Chaethe partner, Winnow." Qu spoke softly, obviously focused on the contact he must attempt. "Your Chaethe partner—"

Filip sensed Joao and Lyova standing ready to support them. Rena's strength pulsed and grew as the triad reached amplification resonance. If this attempt succeeded, there would still be a world of misunderstandings to settle.

Through Rena, Filip sensed a change in Qu's inner frequency. For one moment, Filip thought he heard thousands of babbling voices.

Then they shrieked. The scream blasted through Filip's mind, momentarily blinding and stunning him. He dropped his helmet and fell off synch.

Qu crumpled and fell on his face without trying to protect it.

Rena dove toward the sand, a streak in Filip's blurred vision. "Qu?" she cried. "Lyova, Joao—help!"

Joao rushed forward, each step digging a pit in the sand.

Winnow stepped closer to Filip. "What did you do?" she cried. "It hurt, it hurt."

Filip tried to synch with Qu. He heard no mental activity. Joao crouched and seized Qu's wrist. He bent toward Qu's chest and shook him by his shoulders.

Qu did not move. Filip's throat constricted. Joao tore open the survival kit on his belt.

Rena stared up at Filip. Her upper lip curled in horror. *No pulse,* she mouthed.

"We can't panic," Filip murmured. He glanced from Winnow down to Qu, up to Winnow.

Joao ripped the backing off all three of his stimulant patches, a full resuscitation dose for heart failure. He slapped them onto Qu's neck and bent over his chest.

Filip's Outwatch guard pushed forward. "Let me," she ordered. Filip stepped back. The Outwatcher knelt beside Qu, first breathing for him and then pounding his chest. Joao remained at Qu's side, clutching his hand. Time seemed to stop. The Sunsisans stood staring.

The Outwatcher rocked onto her heels and stood.

She shook her head.

Filip exhaled shakily and covered his eyes. Qu was dead without a mark, like Tam Vandam.

Stall them, Filip thought at Joao, hoping Joao remained synched. *Give me another minute. I have to think.* He felt muzzy. The hot breeze seemed to push through his ear into his skull. Had Winnow's Chaethe parasite killed Qu? Or did other empaths—besides Tam Vandam—have the deadly ability to kill themselves or each other?

Still crouching, Joao repeated the motions of looking for a pulse. He clasped Qu's wrist again. He examined the throat patches.

Winnow held her head in both hands, threading bony fingers through her iron-gray hair.

Filip eyed Vananda, who would synch for her triad as Qu had synched for his. Brown curls escaped between her helmet's protective brown strips. He mustn't ask her to risk this.

Joao rotated Qu's helmet to cover his face.

"No!" Winnow cried. "He can't be dead! We need every one of you. What happened?"

"I don't know." Filip disliked the way his voice quivered. A bitter thought tugged at the back of his mind. Rena, Tam Vandam's replacement, had established that nexus. Had Rena killed Qu by establishing too strong a resonance? They were experimenting on deadly ground.

Bord, Vananda, and Kenji drew together, plainly preparing to make their attempt. He didn't know if he should let them.

Rena pushed up to her feet, hands trembling at her sides. "What are you thinking?" she demanded. "What happened?"

What was she picking up from his stray thoughts? He didn't trust himself to answer steadily. He stepped closer to the other triad, and Rena followed him. "Kenji," Filip said, "can you decrease your back-feeding to Vananda? There might be a danger—"

Rena flung both hands toward her mouth, clapping her helmet. "Did I—"

"Kenji," Filip repeated softly, "do you understand?" He turned to his almost-sister, Antar's strongest living listener. "Do you understand the risk? If you're not willing—"

"We are ready to try." Vananda laid a hand on young Kenji's shoulder. "Do your best," she told him. "I can partially mute feed-back if I know I may have to. But that means you and Bord will catch more of it."

It had to be tried. At least they knew the danger. Around them Sunsisans milled, speaking in low murmurs.

Steeling himself, Filip faced Winnow again. "We must communicate with the Chaethe civilization," he said. Listening to Vananda, he sensed her triad preparing.

"They don't want to talk with you." Winnow rubbed her head. "Especially not if it means losing more of you. Follow me. Please hurry."

Vananda opened her hand and then her mind. She lunged forward.

She fell limp in the sand. Through his synch touch, Filip heard another shriek. This one drove him to his knees. Bord and Kenji toppled, too.

Aghast, Filip eyed the triad. His vision blurred. Their inner frequencies fluctuated wildly, but all three were alive.

He blinked and rocked back. Sunsisan pedestrians focused out of the blur, closing a circle around his people and the spaceship. Many of the Sunsisans held farm implements, as if they had been called from the fields. Those tools could double as weapons, and the Sunsisans looked—and felt, he affirmed a moment later—frightened. Their parasites were losing potential carriers. Lyova, Rena, Karine, Joao, and himself remained: five, plus their Outwatch guard, against several hundred.

His Outwatch guard strode toward the fallen group.

"We need you on watch," Filip ordered her. "These three aren't dead."

Rena knelt beside Kenji. "He's alive," she affirmed, near tears. "But something's terribly wrong. What are we doing?"

And they'd barely begun to love each other. "Do you want to stay with him?"

Rena scrambled to her feet, so full of pain that Filip synched only momentarily. "No," she said, her voice harsh. "I can't help him except by helping you."

Filip touched her shoulder and beckoned to Lyova. "No more synch attempts." After coming this far, after training themselves as thoroughly as possible, they had only one defense left. He caught his Outwatch guard's glance once more. "Hold them back."

She glanced side to side and nodded.

Filip turned to his partners. "One dead, three unconscious. We must try the enmeshment." And why hadn't whatever killed Qu stunned Filip or Rena? Had Qu absorbed the full blast, protecting them?

Joao clasped his hands. "We are ready. Give the word."

Karine would not enmesh, which left only four. Maybe enmeshed, they could neutralize whatever had killed or stunned the others, whether inner terror or overwhelming alien frequencies.

"Do any of you speak for the Chaethe civilization?" Filip called at the ring of Sunsisan farmers.

No one answered. A gust of breeze whipped through the circle, bending but not breaking the eerie silence.

"Give up, Filip."

He looked over his shoulder. Karine stood with arms crossed, anger darkening her face inside her helmet. She cradled a needler inside one elbow, to his surprise. Had she brought it aboard, only pretending to cooperate—or had she stolen it from the Outwatch? "Keep us from being consumed." Terror and scorn sharpened her voice. "Tell the Outwatch to fire on us."

Furious, he turned his back on her.

His Outwatch guard raised an eyebrow and nodded.

"Be ready to stun her," Filip whispered. "Don't let her shoot us in the back."

The guard nodded again.

Lyova, Rena, and Joao stepped closer. "We will enmesh, then," he said. "Lyova, when it's done, synch for us. Rena, you are our nexus—"

"No," she pleaded, shaking. "I can't control well enough. Look at Qu. I—"

Heart-wrung for her, he turned to Joao. "Joao, stabilize Rena's nexus. I know she can do this."

Joao nodded. Rena composed her face, but her lips quivered.

Filip shut his eyes to concentrate. He must aim for full synchrony with all these friends, going deeper than any empath ought to go.

Someone tugged his tunic. He opened his eyes.

Winnow stood behind him. "Come with me," she said in an odd voice. "We want to accommodate you."

"Wait." Filip glanced up. A deep rumble sounded overhead. Had the Tdegans arrived? Were they out of time?

Rena squeezed his hand. He shut his eyes again. He'd prepared himself spiritually, but he dreaded this. Even if they survived, they would finish their lives institutionalized.

But if this was the only road forward for humanity, he must walk it.

"No more distractions," he whispered. He drifted deeper, listening hard. The others' presences felt raw against his own.

Winnow tugged again. He ignored her and started to alter his inner frequency.

"Filip!" Karine was shouting in his ear. "They're landing, you idiot!"

He broke off and looked up. A midsized shuttle dropped out of the dusty sky, creating the roar he'd been trying to block. Sunsisan humans sprinted away, smiling and calling to each other.

Filip dropped Rena's and Joao's hands and shouted, "Stay together." Outwatch people carrying Vananda, Qu, Bord, and Kenji struggled away from the landing area, leaving round footprints. Filip followed.

He hoped someone had picked up his helmet. They must not give up, but they must deal with Tdega first.

As Gamal's shuttle landed, he briefed his shuttle crew as to the reason they'd come to Sunsis. Naturally, their first reaction was horror. He assured them that he meant to deliver his prisoners and then leave.

It was true. But they all were his prisoners: Antarans and Tdegans, spies, troops, and shuttle crew—and he meant to give every one of them to the Chaethe. He, Bellik, and Zavijavah could fly the shuttle. They would return to the orbiting transport. Bellik had disabled ship-to-ground communications, assuring Gamal it would take days for the transport's crew to diagnose his falsified glitch. By then, Gamal would be back on board—with or without his newly infested Chaethe carriers. No word of infestation could return to Tdega. Not yet.

The crew opened the hatch. Gamal almost wilted in the hot, dry air, but his heels bounced on the deck. Even after backing off shipboard gravity, he was a lightweight here. An oily hint of industry scented the air that filtered into his helmet. He wished he'd worn cooler clothing.

He had Zavijavah's promise that he would return to Tdega alive and unhurt. Zavijavah stood behind him in the hatchway, looking around and stroking his mustache. Gamal wondered whether Rider recognized the place.

Several troops off-loaded the electromagnet. He had warned them not to wear metal planetside, and he'd issued them nonmetallic slug rifles with appropriate cartridges. The electromagnet would give him the upper hand, a final threat in case Zavijavah tried to betray him. He had told Zavijavah that its purpose was to deflect flying spores, but he also remembered its other effect.

He held the only remote control.

"This way," Gamal murmured to Zavijavah and Bellik, who headed the squadron of soldiers. Two guarded the prisoners—several Tdegan political anarchists, the Antaran transport's crew—and three spies: the Antaran Ambassador, Jahn Emlin, and his former daughter, Llyn Torfinn. He had ordered ten other soldiers to spread out behind the group of Antarans as soon as they got close enough. Gamal couldn't tell how far away they were.

It was a short walk to the ring of Sunsisans enclosing the Antarans in their culottes. Still, the sand, the heat, and Gamal's heavier-world equilibrium made slow going. He felt wonderfully strong here, but his legs kept pushing him too far forward, making him wobble to compensate. By the time he stepped through the ring, he felt sweaty. He recognized Jal Malukulu, head of the Sunsis A South Colony, from c-net transmissions between Sunsis and his ship.

Malukulu walked to meet him. Gamal glanced at the Antarans—nearly all of them wore inadequate-looking helmets, and about half were Outwatchers carrying body shields—as he clasped Malukulu's hand. He'd asked Malukulu not to communicate officially with the Antarans.

Malukulu had promised to cooperate, though the Antarans had arrived first.

Good man.

"Welcome," Malukulu said.

"We're honored to meet you. My heir, Bellik Casimir."

Malukulu offered Bellik the handclasp between equals. A faint fog showed inside Bellik's helmet. Gamal hoped his wasn't fogging, too. He would like to try his transmitter, but that could wait until Zavijavah's need was relieved and he'd made his offering. Then, if ever, the Chaethe would think kindly toward him.

He gestured the escort soldiers forward. Llyn and Jahn stared all around and stayed close to each other. His surveillance crew hadn't reported what he wanted to hear, but they clung to each other like lovers. "Jal Malukulu, this is my daughter, Luene. She is spoken for." He would call her his daughter today.

Malukulu nodded without offering his hand. Llyn kept her hands down. Her slightly stunned expression reminded Gamal of the unearthly poise that had struck him the first time he'd seen her as an adult.

Gamal inclined his head toward Jahn Emlin. "And this is an Antaran spy. Have Gen Zavijavah take him first, to make sure he can do it properly."

"Are you ready?" Malukulu asked Zavijavah—or was he speaking to Rider?

For the first time in months, Osun Zavijavah smiled broadly.

As the Tdegan party had walked from its shuttle toward the Sunsisan circle, Filip had led Rena and Joao toward the spot where the Tdegans would pass. Lyova remained with the stunned triad, digging through her Outwatch pack belt for her own first-aid kit.

At almost the moment Filip spotted Gamal Casimir among the queued men, he recognized the small, slender young woman with shoulder-length black hair.

"That's Llyn!" Rena exclaimed.

"Yes," he murmured. So Casimir had brought her here. Filip should have refused to send her to Tdega. Could that young man beside her be

Jahn? The beard altered his appearance—but yes, it was Jahn, plainly a prisoner, probably exposed as a spy. He must have tried and failed to escape with his young students. Where was Alun Casimir?

The Antaran Ambassador walked behind Llyn and Jahn, escorted by red-coated Tdegan Security. Despite his fears on behalf of the young people, Filip clenched his hands. By presenting the Ambassador for infestation, Casimir was symbolically offering all of Antar.

Malukulu greeted Casimir, who had brought his nephew Bellik—Filip remembered him from the c-net transmissions—and a smaller, fair-skinned man wearing brown plainclothes, enormous dark glasses, and a drooping mustache. Appalled to hear Malukulu speak familiarly with Casimir when he had refused to talk with the Antarans, Filip realized that this colony had indeed allied with Tdega. Here at least, secession was genuine.

He must speak to Casimir.

"Be ready to defend yourselves," he murmured to Joao. He touched Rena's shoulder and tried to comfort her. Then he took back his helmet from the Outwatcher who'd picked it up. He stepped out of the group.

As he walked, he glanced aside at Karine. Llyn hadn't looked toward her yet, but Karine had obviously spotted Llyn. She stood staring, possibly synching.

He avoided looking at Jahn.

Although distracted by the heat and low gravity, Jahn had instantly recognized his Uncle Filip and Granduncle Joao. An instant later, Lyova Waverly's name popped into his mind. He spotted an Outwatcher standing guard over Lyova, who knelt beside four prone bodies. Only one face was covered. Next to that man lay a woman wearing a vest like Jahn's mother wore for special occasions.

His mother? Was it?

Possibly. Uncle Filip walked with a team of empaths. Naturally, he would have brought Granduncle Joao—Grandfather Athis Pallaton's brother—and probably Jahn's mother, who was Antar's strongest surviving listener.

But why was Mother lying so still?

Jahn's shocked grief rocked Llyn's balance. She caught a glance from Filip Salbari as he walked toward the Casimirs. That calmed her. If Regent Salbari was here, then all was well.

Regent Salbari looked at her again. As if he had been synching with her, he raised an eyebrow and shook his head.

Maybe all was not well. Was he ill? Caught in a double web of grief and relief, she spun blindly. Jahn kept staring at the fair-skinned, matronly woman who knelt by the— No, he was staring *at* the prone bodies. Somebody lying there must be precious to him. She wondered what was keeping him from sprinting over.

Then she spotted Rena Tourelle with Regent Salbari. She flicked a hand to greet Rena.

Beyond Regent Salbari stood a helmeted woman with Karine Torfinn's no-nonsense stance, Karine Torfinn's chin-length brown hair, and Karine Torfinn's way of staring.

Karine. She *would* be here.

And she would be synching. Llyn drew up straight and shot thoughts like needler charges. *I have forgiven you. Whatever happens here to either of us, I will see it with my own eyes, not yours—and with Jahn, not with you. I have outgrown you. I am free.*

Then she seized Jahn's hands and tried to comfort him, just as seeing Regent Salbari had comforted her.

Jahn gave her a weak smile. "He's not the Creator, Llyn." His whisper sounded faintly amused.

She pressed his hand between both of hers.

"Who is the woman?" she whispered.

"My mother. She's only stunned, but Lyova doesn't know why. She's trying to revive her."

His mother. What about hers?

She looked at Karine again. Karine's facial twitch frightened her. She didn't look sane. And she held her hands oddly, as if she were hiding something.

As that thought flitted through Llyn's mind, Karine tucked a hand deeper into the crook of her other elbow.

"Jahn," Llyn whispered. "Does she have a needler?"

Jahn turned to eye Karine. Llyn felt the answer. He didn't need to speak.

She wondered why she felt so steady. She stood surrounded by people whose lives were not their own, such as Osun Zavijavah. They meant to make her one of them. Sunsis A had far less gravity than Tdega, too. That ought to make her feel lightheaded, if nothing else did. But she stood steadily, anchored to Jahn and that spinning sphere. Nothing else seemed worth worrying about.

Her thin shift smelled musty after seventeen days. The hot breeze warmed her clothing, her bare arms and legs.

Gamal's black-shirted escorts let a pair of Antarans approach. The helmetless man had long, graying blond hair. Could it be—

Wonderful! Gamal beckoned Filip Salbari forward. Years ago, Salbari had told him that he wasn't a particularly strong empath. Still, Gamal was willing to bet Salbari felt Gamal's delight now. Once infested, this Regent would carry Chaethe spores back to Antar's upper circles. Salbari walked with an odd-looking female. Between the strips that constituted her helmet, her red hair was far shorter than his own.

Salbari halted in front of him, trying to look stern in a pair of long black culottes and a white tunic. "Regent Casimir," he said softly, "what are you doing?"

Gamal hadn't forgotten that Salbari could load his voice with persuasive overtones. "I am finalizing a treaty with my new allies," Gamal said. "Do not interfere."

"You have imprisoned an Ambassador of the Antar system. That is an act of war."

"I also hold your nephew as a hostage." Gamal let himself smile. "Do you think whimpering for reinforcements ends a war?" He turned to the colony head. "Jal Malukulu, this man is Filip Salbari, formerly Antar's highest planetary Regent and the chief of our oppressors. Treat him accordingly."

"Jal Malukulu and I have met," Salbari said. "Gen Malukulu, forgive the sharp words between Regent Casimir and myself. Our systems are involved in armed conflict."

"I hope it can be stopped soon." Jal Malukulu's voice took on the atonal lilt Gamal had heard so often in Zavijavah's. "Armed conflict wastes so many lives."

"I agree." Salbari turned to Malukulu. "I came to Sunsis not because I am still a Regent, but because I am the head of an Order that hopes to communicate with—"

Salbari—head of the Empath Order? The whole mutant lot of them? Gamal didn't hear Salbari's next several sentences. This was a coup, then. Salbari must not escape. Gamal caught Zavijavah's attention, signaling until he felt sure Zavijavah had spotted him through the dark glasses. *Did you hear that? Do you want him?* he mouthed.

Zavijavah smiled for an instant and then winced. All color drained out of his pale face. Was Rider wailing?

No! Rider probably wanted Salbari for itself! Not for one of its off-spring, but it surely meant to abandon Zavijavah. To take another host and let Zavijavah die.

Well, that was all right. Gamal could train another Security Chief. With Antar subdued, the Chaethe would want power over the Concord. And they loved sensory enhancements. They would enjoy inhabiting empaths. Gamal mentally dismissed Osun Zavijavah from his service.

"... on behalf of Concord humanity," Salbari finished.

Gamal nudged him. "You're surrounded by armed men," he said blandly. "Including myself."

"That doesn't surprise me." Salbari still held his inadequate-looking helmet, probably made from inferior Antaran plastics, against a hip. "We carry no weapons. Only shields."

"That doesn't surprise *me.*"

Malukulu blinked rapidly and spoke. "Thank you for your gifts, Regent Casimir. The new people are confusing. They shrink from fighting but try to speak."

"What?" Bellik finally stepped forward. He had stood at Gamal's shoulder, gloating while Salbari talked himself out. Now that Gamal thought for a moment, he knew what Salbari had tried. Salbari had no helmet transmitter, though. He could only listen. After Salbari was infested and under Gamal's orders, Gamal would command the complete circle of telepathy!—*if* his transmitter worked.

"They are mutants," Gamal told Malukulu's Rider. "They are not members of our race."

Salbari interrupted. "That's not—"

"Keep quiet." Gamal glared.

"Let me speak—"

Malukulu pointed at Filip Salbari. "You," he said. "Speak."

Filip drew a deep breath. At last, he felt certain the Chaethe were listening. "We are normal in almost every respect," he told Jal Malukulu. Synched with Casimir, he had discovered plans within plans—but challenging Casimir's imperial hopes must wait. "And we want to speak with you. The empath mutation occurred when a do-not-express gene on the human chromosome was destroyed," he said. "The ability to listen empathically is latent in all humans. It was suppressed before our race left its home world. Those of us who follow ancient religious persuasions believe we know why ..."

Osun Zavijavah stared at Salbari, driven to full attention, but he was not listening. Sweat dripped off his face and trickled down his sides and chest. Salbari could have been reciting grocery orders for all he knew or cared. Although Rider was stroking almost continuously, Zavijavah ignored the illegitimate pleasuring. The false delight.

Rider meant to abandon him. It wanted Filip Salbari's body. To a parasite, Salbari's sensory enhancement would seem even more wonderful than a seer's, and his position as Head of the Order was further enticement. Zavijavah would be forced to walk into the liberation facility, but he would be carried out.

And Casimir wanted it that way! Casimir had experimented on him for years, using him like an animal. Now Casimir would let Rider kill him instead of reproducing normally, as he'd been promised.

All around, Sunsisans clutched farm weapons, and Casimir commanded two squads of troops. Yet between Zavijavah's fatalistic certainty and Rider's lewd stroking, he felt queerly relieved. His slavery was over. Soon he could rest.

There was one thing he would like to do first. He mustn't think about it, though. Rider would try to stop him.

"This interests us," said Malukulu—or the alien who spoke through him, as Gamal realized from the lilt in his voice. "I will speak. We honor telepathy. It is one of the Two."

"Two what?" Gamal stepped closer.

"Two—" Malukulu's face contorted. The Chaethe had to be trying to express a concept for which Malukulu had no words. "The Two," he repeated. "The Two are forbidden."

"What about intelligence?" Salbari asked. "Doesn't that matter? We mean you no harm, yet you harm us."

What was Salbari talking about?

"Harm?" Malukulu laughed. "Humans think they are intelligent. We have layers and depths of thought. Thought and intelligence. Your most advanced technology is throwaway primitivism—except weaponry, which you, Filip Salbari, seem to disapprove. We have fought a long war."

"With the Devastators?" Salbari asked.

"They tried to destroy us. We had barely made the change then. We needed to take bodies who could fight for us."

Gamal didn't understand all that, but he saw a point that needed to be made. "Now, you know we can fight, and fight well."

"You took intelligent hosts who helped you escape the Devastators?" Salbari broke in.

Malukulu inhaled, expanding his brown chest inside his thin white shirt. "We want a safe place. We need intelligent allies. Sociable, too."

"Sociable?" Confused again, Gamal glanced at the liberation building, then at Bellik, then Zavijavah. His Security Chief seemed intent on Filip Salbari.

Rightfully so.

An old woman in a flowered dress that hung loose from her shoulders, who had stood with the Antaran delegation—maybe their own greeter—stepped up beside Malukulu. She answered, "Sociable, because hosts must reproduce. Chaethe multiply."

Gamal nudged Salbari. "They also don't like to occupy anyone who *looks* infested. The one Zavijavah carries abandoned a host that it'd accidentally disfigured. They can liberate correctly here." He pointed at the facility. "You won't look any different. Nor will you, my dear," he told the short-haired woman. Standing close to her, he wished he had his depth perception back.

"And you?" That sneer destroyed her appeal.

"I am their contact person. They need me as I am."

Salbari's hands twitched. Maybe he finally realized he would not escape. "You spoke of the Two." Salbari faced Malukulu. "The Two are forbidden. What did you mean?"

Gamal touched the right flap of his sweaty tunic, where he had hidden his needler. "I think that's enough," he told Salbari. "You're not in charge here. This is a Hegemony world."

The woman extended both arms to Salbari in a pushing gesture. "Your people could not break through. For a little while, we hoped that you would. So we beg you to aid us in this other way. Come." She beckoned with brown hands, smiling warmly. A dozen colorfully dressed Sunsisans near the mammoth door stepped aside. Others walked forward, blocking escape in other directions. "And please, call the others on board your ship. They must join us."

Bellik bumped Gamal's elbow and murmured, "I think it's time to step out of formation."

Gamal addressed the woman. "Some of us will not enter."

"But you must. That is why you came here. We need you all."

Gamal pointed at the soldiers who'd remained close to the Tdegan shuttle. "That machine is a powerful electromagnet. Think of the effect it would have on individuals with iron inside their skulls. I have the remote in my pocket. Unless you let me and Commander Bellik remain outside, I will turn it on."

After a moment, she spoke wistfully. "We lose two of you?"

"We will finish these talks after you do what you need to do. You must be in pain." Trying to sound sympathetic, he stepped closer to Malukulu.

He murmured, "If you let us two stay here, I will order my soldiers to lay down their weapons and join you, too."

Malukulu glanced around the half circle of troops. "Twenty more. Twenty for two. Yes. How will you control them?"

Gamal shrugged. "I won't. You will. Their weapons are dud-loaded."

Salbari's horrified knit-brow expression delighted him. Today, the pacifist disapproved of disarming people.

"But you may have nineteen. I will keep one with Bellik and myself. He is armed." Gamal smiled at Filip, who soon would speak for his old friend Rider. "We'll discuss this at length," Gamal said. "In a few hours."

Salbari finally put on his helmet. It made his head look like a sliced pumpkin with hair sticking out the bottom. Gamal didn't see a lockdown collar on it.

The old woman grasped Salbari's upper arm. "I think you'd rather remove that," she said, using an unmistakably human tone of voice. "They can penetrate the spinal column. That would cripple you—and they would leave you as soon as they could, and then you would die. But they need to reproduce now. They'll only do it that way if they have to."

Stunned, Gamal glared at Zavijavah. "You never told me that."

"It never told me," Zavijavah answered through clenched teeth.

Salbari's red-haired junior partner stepped away from him and unexpectedly waved her arms. "Tdegan soldiers," she shouted, "you've been lied to! Gamal Casimir gave you unloaded weapons! Ask why he really brought you here!"

31

At first, Filip didn't detect any reaction to Rena's shout. Then a Tdegan soldier safed his weapon. He eyed the loading chamber, removed a cartridge, and rolled it between his fingers.

Rena stepped closer to Casimir. Instantly suspicious of her intent, Filip synched with her. He sensed a flash of memory that included Tam Vandam and three non-empaths. She lunged. Her helmet bounced against Casimir's.

"Rena, no!" He seized her arm. With her other hand, she grabbed Casimir's helmet collar. She held on with the painless strength of youth. Casimir flailed his arms, tried to back away, and stumbled against Osun Zavijavah.

Filip tugged Rena toward nexus, trying to calm her. Her inner frequency only intensified. She was empathically stronger than he. He couldn't save her—or Casimir—that way. He dropped off synch and opened his eyes.

Osun Zavijavah lunged forward and slid his hands inside Casimir's transparent helmet collar. To Filip's shock, Zavijavah clutched, working his fingers against Casimir's throat. Probing for the airway.

Filip shouted at the Tdegan troops. "Get him off!"

Two black-suited soldiers jumped forward and seized Zavijavah. Zavijavah flung back his head. He squeezed his eyes shut, clamping both hands over his ears.

Filip clutched Rena's shoulder. "Rena, no! Not that way."

"Let me go," she sputtered, but at least he had broken her lethal concentration. "He's evil. Even his friend wants him dead. If we don't shut him down, he'll destroy everyone."

Gamal Casimir slowly turned circles in the sand, blinking and waving both hands in front of his face. Rena had done *something* to him. Stunned him, maybe.

Bellik must have realized the same thing. He seized Gamal's left elbow. "Malukulu," he cried, "get two of your people. This man has been mentally injured, but he'll survive. You need bodies. Take his." Bellik grappled Gamal's helmet and tried to wrench it off. It didn't budge.

Bellik hated him, too? His nephew, his heir?

Two brawny men wearing short pants and sandals sprinted forward. "This is locked on," Bellik said shortly. "Take him that other way."

"Wait," Filip cried. "He'll recover. Don't—"

"Are you certain?" Bellik narrowed his eyes. He glanced at the fallen triad. "Recover? I'm not sure they will."

"No." Filip had to speak truth. "But I will not give up my people's lives."

"Get him out of our sight," Bellik ordered, "before I kill him myself."

The Sunsisans clutched Gamal Casimir by both elbows and led him toward the huge building. Bellik lowered his voice and fumed, "Disarming my troops." His helmet fogged.

"You didn't know?" Filip asked.

Bellik worked his left hand. "No. And he would have given me to the aliens sooner or later, too. I'll be kinder to him than he would have been to me."

Briefly synching, Filip realized Bellik's ambition ran as deep as Gamal's. Apparently, the poisonous power-mongering infected that whole family.

"But the parasite will leave him as quickly as it can find another—" Between strips of his helmet, Filip saw something move behind Bellik. The Tdegan who had been checking his weapon aimed it at the trio stumbling toward the huge building. He fired. After a loud report, nothing else happened.

"She was right," the soldier shouted. "These are dummy loads!"

Gamal Casimir struggled against the Sunsisans. None of his troops moved to help him.

"Good riddance," Rena muttered.

Filip hesitated. Not even Gamal Casimir deserved to be invaded and crippled by an alien parasite, but every human here would enter those doors unless he kept the Chaethe talking. Unless he brought them to a different agreement. He could not order the Outwatch to abandon his colleagues and defend Gamal Casimir. He must make it clear he shared Casimir's risk, though.

***

Llyn had rushed forward when the confusion broke out. She couldn't guess what Rena had done to her father—she'd never seen his facial muscles go slack like that—but if walking Gamal Casimir to the infestation building wasn't justice, she didn't know the meaning of the word.

To her astonishment, Regent Salbari reached for his helmet clasps, released them, and pulled it off again. "Please, Winnow," he said to the Sunsisan woman. "You sensed our effort to speak mind to mind. You said telepathy was one of the Two."

"But only one." Winnow shook her head. "You did not complete the circle."

The legendary circle of listening and speaking: did these beings have the same concept?

Regent Salbari spoke again, but Llyn could tell he was only stalling. "We want to communicate from our natural state. Give us a little more time. Let us try to find a way."

"Have you ever been in pain?" The woman frowned. "You want it to end."

Llyn's newly doubled memory thrust up the image of Jahn, chained by his ankle somewhere in the Residence while Gamal had him tortured. She shuddered.

"I understand," Regent Salbari began, "but—"

Llyn caught motion at the edge of her vision. She spun to look. Karine was lunging toward Casimir's troops. "Shoot everyone—shoot everyone!" she cried. She dashed at Regent Salbari, brandishing her needler.

"Down!" Rena flung herself against Llyn and dropped with her. Prone on the sand, Llyn couldn't follow the scuffle, but half a minute later, Jahn was backing away and Regent Salbari held Karine's hand weapon.

Rena helped Llyn stand and brushed sand off her shift.

Karine had seized Regent Salbari's helmet. She thrust it at Llyn. "Put it on! If he's stupid enough to take it off here, of all places—"

"Don't you have more important things to do?" Llyn cried. Her own voice sounded harsh. Several brightly dressed Sunsisans hurried up behind Karine. "Look at them!" Llyn said. "Are you going to help Regent Salbari or hinder him?" In that moment, she realized that her father had taken the electromagnet's remote switch with him into the building. They were defenseless.

"Gen Malukulu, Gen'n Winnow." Even now, Regent Salbari maintained a serene tone of voice. "Please control them. There's still time to talk."

Karine pushed Regent Salbari's helmet at Llyn again, whispering, "Take it, you ungrateful infant."

Llyn turned away from Karine, grabbed Jahn's hand, and held tightly. Out in the Outwatch circle, she spotted Lieutenant Metyline, who would rather die than suffer—and who was ready to make it happen, to face eternity and the Creator. Uncanny calm settled over Llyn. "Regent Salbari," she said softly, "let me try talking with them."

Karine grabbed Llyn's shoulder. "No! You're not capable! It killed Qu Yung." She glared at Jahn. "And your mother's dying from trying it—"

Llyn felt Jahn resist the urge to strike her. "Be quiet," he snapped.

Regent Salbari took a step toward Llyn. "You're not afraid." She heard surprise in his voice.

"I was," she said, "and I will be again. But not now. I've had to adjust to two universes." She glared at Karine. "Maybe I could understand these people. I want to try."

"You'll need a synch specialist." Karine seized Llyn's free hand at the wrist and slid her hand up Llyn's arm. "Salbari, I'll assist my charge. I'm willing to die with her—"

Regent Salbari grabbed Karine's hand and flung it off. "Get back," he said. Llyn had never seen such a fierce look in his eyes.

Karine backed two steps away.

"Go. Stand with the group." Regent Salbari beckoned to the Antaran

Ambassador. The tall, gray-haired man strode out of the Tdegan escort group and laid a hand on Karine's shoulder.

Karine glowered at him, at Salbari, at Jahn. She pointed at Llyn, spearing the air with one finger. "You are the most deceitful, ungrateful—"

"Enough," Llyn shouted. She would not tolerate any more verbal abuse. Right or wrong, she made her own choices now. And she was grateful for many things. But not for this. Not now.

"Hold her down if you have to," Regent Salbari ordered the Ambassador. Karine backed away with him.

Regent Salbari leaned close to Llyn. "She's ill," he murmured. "She loves you, but even her love is sick."

"I know." She nodded. "And I know that the Sunsisans aren't as terrified as we are. I hear it in their voices."

"Really?"

She nodded again. "They're afraid—they're in pain—but it's different from what I've heard in Gen Zavijavah." And it was. She couldn't guess why, but there was a different tone when they spoke.

Regent Salbari caught the Sunsisan pair's attention again. "This woman is Llyn Torfinn. She—"

"She was introduced to us as Luene Casimir." Winnow straightened her thin shoulders.

"That is also her name," Regent Salbari said. "She has lived on two Concord worlds and inside another reality. She has earned the right to speak."

The Sunsisans, Malukulu and Winnow, bent their heads together, talking and gesturing.

Regent Salbari beckoned Jahn closer. "What has happened between you and Llyn?"

Her cheeks warmed. She felt oddly embarrassed. Jahn stepped in, making such a tight triangle that his elbow touched her arm. "I'm not sure. It's not painful, like they say enmeshment is. It's a communion, like … No. It's not like anything."

"Could you listen and hold a nexus? Simultaneously?"

Jahn eyed the Sunsisans. "Nexus should be easy. We're almost there already."

Regent Salbari raised his eyebrows.

"I could try," Jahn said. Llyn sensed his fear. And his willingness. "I will try."

Regent Salbari studied Llyn with warm eyes. "Whatever happened between you two, it is good. May we all survive to learn what it is."

Jahn had been watching Salbari for hand signals. Now, he caught "listen deeply." He synched to catch Salbari's message. He respected Salbari, but he'd never envisioned the man as a leader in life-and-death crisis.

A shaped thought slid into his mind from outside: *Qu died trying what you're about to attempt. Your mother is alive but stunned, and I don't know if she will recover. Nor the others. Are you willing, knowing that's the risk?*

How could he succeed where his mother, a fully trained, mature talent, had failed?

Llyn echoed his alarm but quickly regained her resolve. She would not be content until she tried this.

We are willing, he formed plain words.

Try Winnow. She seemed willing to give information. He heard Salbari's gratitude in those words. *If any of us survive, you will be honored. If you are killed, I will try to assist Llyn. If we fail, the others will enmesh. They will attempt a unison effort.*

Jahn understood. He took Llyn's hand. "Are you ready?"

Warm wind tossed her dark hair around her shoulders. She looked small and delicate, with just two qualifications to face an alien race: her past and her courage.

She nodded.

He quieted his mind and listened for the Sunsisan's inner frequency. Again he felt two phenomena. Winnow, the human, was alert and afraid and in pain. The other sensation was a high-pitched, warbling whine superimposed over her frequency.

He pitched his own inner frequency to the warble. Gently, he gathered Llyn deeper into nexus, synchronizing their shared frequency onto an oscillating rhythm that approached but did not achieve the alien vibrato. This was like trying to block synch, but much more precise.

I don't think I can, he admitted to her.

Let me.

But you can't—

He was wrong. She could. And she did. He felt her imagine a clipped height and an irregular downslope, entering the oscillation. He matched it. She deepened its trough, and he matched that.

Thousands of voices shrieked inside his head. Her optimism surged—cautiously. *Can you hold that?* She seemed to be modulating the vibrato, like a transmitter superimposing information onto a radio wave, even controlling its volume. Where had she learned to do that?

Abruptly, he knew. *I can. I will,* he answered.

Laying down control of a nexus might kill him, but that was a better fate than Gamal Casimir faced. He hid that fear from Llyn and backed down. She seized and held the frequency.

He did not die. He wasn't even stunned.

She'd done it.

He quieted all thought and effort, except what it took to support their shared inner frequency. It now was a wild—but controlled—oscillation.

Llyn, too, felt initial contact as a babble of shrieking voices, but an instant later, it focused. Geometric imagery appeared where the stark Sunsisan landscape had vanished. She knew this music. This mindscape had other inhabitants!

Turning back to Jahn once more before plunging forward, she formed a thought. *Are you all right?*

In his perception, the shrieking had faded to a frightening but nonlethal babble. He was hearing simultaneous, unintelligible speeches where she perceived bitter but familiar song. He didn't seem to be in danger.

She stopped clutching his perception. She let herself float. Voices sang and spoke, not with words, but with seventeen-tone chords and harmonies.

She plunged into midstream. A thousand bright images floated alongside her, wafting through space unmarked by grid lines, rushing ahead of the current, urging her to greater speeds, and it felt wrong. Wrong!

The Chaethe were trying to draw her too deep, too quickly! Was this what they'd done to Jahn's mother, or was it a second defense against outsiders who survived to make contact?

She sang herself away from them using Jahn's simple melody.

Abruptly, the multitude swirled back toward her, quieting. She felt spotlighted, as if Tdega's stars had all stopped twinkling to watch her.

She had never set words to this tonality. She wasn't even sure it was possible. {Is this …} she began, and as if she perceived the words with some sense other than hearing, they flicked at the edge of her mind.

Silence waited.

{Is this … how you give voice?} Her thought translated oddly, but the tonality sounded natural.

A burst of joyous color erupted around her. {You speak!} A rose-colored entity whirled toward her. It sparkled like an oval jewel.

Llyn tried again. {I am learning,} she answered softly. The rose-colored jewel drew closer. {I desire to sing with you. Is this how you … you do it?}

{What are you?} The rosy oval whizzed past so quickly that she thought for a moment she'd been run through.

{My …} There was no term for "name." {I am Llyn. I am human. We have wanted to communicate with you for many weeks.}

A brilliant, amethyst-purple shape moved toward her—or had it grown larger? It projected a deep, resonant bass. {We dance at many levels, Llyn Human. Vocal speech uses symbiont tissues. It survives, it survives from our early civilization. We use it to control the symbionts. Your race commands tamed creatures. You understand.}

Llyn formed mental pictures of Alun's dog, Bear, and the clinic dedo, Squeak. Trying to show the bass entity these images, she found herself singing a melody she could not consciously follow. She tried to control it. It faltered. She tried releasing herself to sing instinctively again, but once she had choked, that was difficult.

The brilliant shape quivered. {Yes,} it sang. {Like those animals.}

The rosy jewel swooped closer, beckoning her to dance as the green geometric had done so long ago. This time, Llyn understood, it was not only permissible but imperative to join in.

The jewel led her in a slow, solemn sweep that orbited the brilliant amethyst-purple shape. Slowly, Llyn realized that the rosy oval wanted her to orbit in a position opposite its own, forming a balance.

Once Llyn took that place, thousands of shapes swooped into other orbits.

Together they created a sphere.

Erratic modulations shivering through the nexus meant nothing to Jahn. Only the sense of Llyn's presence—which flitted from one emotion to the next, deep in some incomprehensible experience and obviously communicating with *something*—assured him that his efforts were successful.

He slid into a marginal trance and maintained his inner frequency at the oscillating alien rhythm. If he let it falter, he might lose Llyn. Whatever she was doing, however and wherever she was doing it, she must do it herself.

Yet obviously, she had them talking.

{Listen now,} the brilliant amethyst nucleus boomed. Llyn made a supreme effort to concentrate. A succession of geometric dancers slipped into her orbit. Each briefly took up a satellite orbit around her. As they danced, they flooded her with information.

{We nearly went extinct …}

{Silent, silent forever,} chorused the multitude.

Llyn felt their grief and fear. {Silent,} she wept with them.

{Our bodies had begun to die …}

Through the matrix, superimposed onto her mind's eye, appeared an image of small but noble creatures with long, nimble fingers. The Chaethe originally had bodies! But when plague struck—a plague that destroyed nervous systems—many died before one Chaethe, forever honored in memory, created a way to encase their neural clusters in metal and use other species as symbionts. Other species had larger bodies and accessible skull openings. A tragically small minority survived the change to free parasitism. The new Chaethe learned to accelerate their own reproductive cycles to suit shorter-lived symbionts—but they had not been made that way.

Then, alas, they tried to take the Devastators. That race had a hive mind and resisted parasitism with terrible, perfectly coordinated violence. That disaster hardened the Chaethe multitude to a new way of thinking. Parasites by necessity now, and communicating telepathically with their hosts, their new ethical requirements would exclude very few species from infestation.

Surely, they longed to be re-bodied. But the universe was filled with marginally intelligent life for their use.

The stream skipped ahead. {We meant to colonize fertile Tdega ...}

{Tdega, Tdega,} chorused the multitude.

{Tdega!} Llyn agreed. The lush, beautiful planet was unlike any other Concord world. Of course they would want to settle there. Somehow her partners had danced all that information into a sense she did not know she could use. Was this how Tdegan honeybees beat out messages?

Vibrating contentment, her current partner shot out of orbit. Another geometric took its place. The music became modal, with a longing tone color. {One of us entered a Tdegan. Our brother had never learned to sing harmony. It was faulty.}

{Faulty,} chorused the multitude. {Flawed, broken.}

{How sad,} Llyn sang back. The brilliant nucleus reverberated a somber basso, underscoring her response.

Two smaller presences jumped into orbit with her partner, creating a tiny lunar system around Planet Llyn. She found herself dancing—absorbing information—too quickly and in too complex a way to comprehend. This time, she simply let it happen. Once they danced away from her, she understood that this canta—this multitude—was a research team that had been dispatched to the Concord cluster. Its mission was to see whether humankind should be officially approached. Because they suspected—

That train of thought cut off abruptly, and Llyn could not tell whether they were deliberately hiding something from her, or whether they were simply returning to topic. The defective Chaethe, sang others who surrounded her partners, had ridden its new symbiont back to Tdega. It had refused to wait for official colonization of the new, fertile world.

Rider? Gen Zavijavah's Chaethe parasite was defective, an outcast?

Yes, indeed. It had also stolen one of the colony's prized physical possessions, an artificial-reality unit built by previous symbionts to Chaethe specifications. Isolated in a small, non-multitudinous spore group, with this apparatus the research team had hoped to re-create inner space in a way that even other creatures might experience. The unit could train a Chaethe's descendants—the spores released into new symbionts—to impress within a canta.

Her inner world! Llyn swiftly shifted her orbit to ask a question. {Canta? You used that term before. What is a canta?}

All the Chaethe shivered gleefully, creating a vast rippling laugh. {This is a canta. We are a canta. A choral multitude. Our joy and our strength.}

So they lived as interlocking awarenesses. Less than a thousand—maybe ten thousand—apparently seemed lonely to them. This must have been another reason, besides adapting to those second symbionts, to learn to reproduce so quickly and so young. Too young, maybe.

Struck by another realization, Llyn responded. {So you don't often communicate with your carrying creatures because that would mean leaving this dance!}

{Of course, of course, of course …} She felt their joy.

{Of course,} Llyn thought on, {you would want this for your children.}

{Yes, yes, yes …}

A shape wafted toward her. It was green and covered with glistening spikes, and to her shock, each spike had its own voice. Again she found herself too deep in simultaneous speeches to understand immediately.

But she understood—something. Gamal Casimir had been the multitude's first target in the Concord, as the most powerful human on a lush, desirable world. At first, the multitude feared their defective songmate would try to penetrate the man—or liberate one of its descendants into him—before they made him a true canta member's symbiont. Then came an even greater disaster: Casimir stole the AR unit for his own purposes. The defective Chaethe willfully and reprehensibly left its first Tdegan carrier, and Casimir would not allow it access to the AR. Unable to reimpress with the canta, it became an increasingly dangerous renegade, rebellious and ambitious, lost to the dance.

Zavijavah. Unquestionably.

{Why, why then, did it bring more humans here?} Llyn asked. {Here for your canta.}

{That was the work of Gamal Casimir Human. Our symbionts here are not like him.}

Llyn keened her grief, harmonizing with all her partners. In a silent corner of her mind, she tried to absorb all that information. Might Jahn be following the song, if not the dance? The renegade Chaethe—it had stolen the AR unit from these others. Her father had stolen it again. Jahn had explained how Casimir sent her to Antar. Now, she knew how her mind had been reshaped: and where, and why, and by whom. No mysteries remained. {Gamal Casimir Human's body,} she wept, {it was the father of my body. But not of my mind. That is my own.}

The brilliant nucleus boomed out a new melody. {He betrayed his own species, as well. He attacked Ilzar Sphere and Antar Sphere. The act of a beast, an animal.}

They'd wondered whether humans could fight the Devastators. Her father had twisted that concern to fit his own aims—and so, now, the aliens wondered whether humans were nothing but another inferior, amoral animal species.

Drawn deeply into the aliens' multiple sphere of view, Llyn slowed her own orbit using a burst of control music. {I feel shame,} she sang, relieved that a term for that concept existed. {Grief, on behalf of my species. Most of us see Gamal Casimir Human as a renegade, faulty like the dancer who left you. Those two formed a … a partnership, a duet.}

The harmonizing presences fell silent. She felt utterly alone.

She sang on without accompaniment. {My people fear you,} she grieved. {It is hard for us—like death, like silence—to be ruled by others. It causes pain like … like this silence. You should not …} Trying to think of a way to express infestation that would not offend them, she dropped several beats. {You should not use us,} she sang as she regained the rhythm. {Please understand how we feel.}

Another flood of information came through their dance, not their song: their culture was based on nuances of tonality too alien for Llyn to grasp. Even this dance barely approached their actual existence. This was recreation. This was a level where they could meet less gifted civilizations. But they did not live here.

Chaethe minds must be truly alien. {But there is too much pain,} she protested.

{What humans call pain is little compared with our danger sense. To us, physical pain is parallel to …}

Uncontrolled by Llyn, her memory rewound and fast-forwarded. At last, they went on.

{… To the human taste sense. If something tastes terrible, a human simply spits it away. Danger sense is purer than your pain. We never use it to control a symbiont. Spore pain is part of life, as when …}

Again, the eerie feeling of having her mind turned out and shaken.

{As at the time of birth. It is briefly unpleasant and soon forgotten. Symbionts dread pain, but there is so little compared with the benefits we bring them. If the Sunsisans' pain seems bitter, tell your people—beg your people—to help them by yielding to us.}

Benefits? Llyn had caught that word. Now she recoiled. She had thought she'd been getting somewhere. Now she understood how limited her diplomatic powers were. She spun in place, exhausted. {I am not accustomed to this dancing,} she sang. {I am not strong in this music. I must rest a moment.}

Abruptly, the canta started streaming again. As before, it tried to pull her deeper. They did not want her returning to consciousness.

The rosy oval whizzed back into orbit around her. {Please do not fear us. We will make you welcome.}

{You will destroy me!} Llyn sang.

The rosy song turned bittersweet. {You learned to weaken us—}

To weaken them?

Other shapes whisked the oval out of orbit. Llyn braked with another burst of control music. Weaken them? She struggled to recall anything she had done that had affected them. Back in the AR, she had listened for other shapes' control melodies. Muting them had made them disappear. But these were real intelligences, not programmed ones—and there were too many of them for her to mute individually.

The canta paused in its rush downstream. It created another orbit. Presences danced around her like electrons, complex orbitals forming rings, lobes, and clouds.

She tried not to see it. She tried to focus her eyes on the Sunsisan landscape. It had to be here—right here, in her line of sight. Her mind was overloading with strange senses.

Help! she cried. *Jahn, let me out!*

She felt herself lifted and shaken. The world turned bright and hot. She stood against Jahn, enclosed by his arms. A hot breeze flapped her shift against her calves.

She peeled away from him. He grunted, as if he were waking up. Sweat gleamed on his forehead.

Regent Salbari, Bellik Casimir, Rena, and the two Sunsisans stood close by. Osun Zavijavah sat in the sand several meters away, rubbing his temples. Behind him, Tdegan soldiers stood in a cluster. They held their weapons like clubs.

So Zavijavah's Chaethe was a defective outcast. Had it deceived her father into calling it an Ambassador?

"Are you all right?" Regent Salbari whispered. "You've been in a trance for almost an hour, and none of the Sunsisans have moved." He looked side to side.

So did she. The Antaran Outwatchers sat in a second circle between Llyn's nucleus and the outer orbital of Sunsisans. The similarity to what she'd just escaped struck her. Humans and Chaethe did share some concepts and images.

Was it enough?

Once Jahn's eyes cleared, she sank down with him to sit and rest. Regent Salbari's circle joined them. "Did you follow any of that?" she asked Jahn.

He rubbed his beard with both hands. He shook his head.

"Let me show you." She shut her eyes and slipped into easy accord. It took several minutes—and his help—to recall the dance for him.

"Incredible," he whispered. He turned and locked eyes with Regent Salbari.

Regent Salbari's concerned expression softened. Slowly, he smiled. Llyn wondered whether Rena was making a nexus for the other empaths.

Winnow and Malukulu sat cross-legged, expressionless. Bellik disdainfully brushed sand off his black pant legs. Events were leaving him behind, stranded like a rock at the edge of a stream. "Luene," he demanded while the empaths communicated, "what happened? Did you talk to the Chaethe? What did they tell you?"

Abruptly, she pitied her queued cousin. Antar detested him, and the Chaethe interpreted his—and her father's—actions as bestial. What was happening to her father, or had it already been done? She winced, sympathizing. He'd been misled by a renegade, but he'd gone along. Willingly.

"The Chaethe don't speak," she told him. "They sing. And they dance."

"Like an e-net show inside your skull?"

She grimaced. He was too full of himself to understand an alien viewpoint. "In an inner world," she said.

"Hah." Bellik smirked. "Training you worked, then."

Yes. Maybe better than he or her father would have liked. They were not going to like the outcome. Did she dare hope that?

Bellik grasped Regent Salbari's shoulder. "Did she tell you why she was able to communicate?"

Regent Salbari nodded, his expression somber. "They have little respect for your uncle, Commander Casimir."

Bellik thrust his chin forward. "Why?"

"For attacking human worlds."

Bellik raised his head. "They wanted to know we could fight. A military leader sometimes makes difficult decisions." Bellik pointed at Llyn. "Explain how Tdega trained you to translate."

"He knows," Llyn murmured.

Gray-blond hair blew into Regent Salbari's face as he spoke. "Gamal guessed right about communicating with them, but he tried doing it for greed and power."

"And to save humanity," Bellik insisted.

Rena had also pulled off her helmet. "But only Tdegan humanity." She glared.

Llyn flicked her thumbs against each other. She couldn't remember how she had weakened the canta. It had to be something simple. She reviewed all the techniques she'd used for controlling unpleasant images—

Was that why she'd lived when the other children died? Because she'd learned to protect herself? "Regent Salbari," she said, "if I could keep the Chaethe from taking me too deep, I might serve as a translator. You should speak with them. I haven't begun to convince them."

"You should rest." Regent Salbari shook his head. Sunlight glinted off the triangular garnet on his collar.

She managed a smile. Perhaps others had seen the jewel-drop imagery. She must ask.

Later.

Winnow twisted her hands in the lap of her loose flowered dress. "They're stirred up," she mumbled. "Please don't stop."

That, Llyn realized, had been the voice of Winnow, the human. Wrung with pity, Llyn touched Jahn's arm. "Can you?"

Jahn took her hand between both of his. "They tried to trap you," he said. "They don't want to give us up as hosts. Be careful."

32

Llyn drew a deep breath. "Now," she murmured to Jahn. She pressed through his presence ...

And plunged into a current flowing hard and violently inward—a whirlpool, not an orbit. They had been waiting to seize her. She braced herself. Gathering courage, she sang a control phrase at them.

They shrank and drew away.

Then it was as she'd hoped! Letting another species approach them officially, with control music, gave that species power over them.

She sang again, an old melody that had eliminated disagreeable objects from her own inner world. The Chaethe diminished again—but there were thousands of them, and this time, although the geometric objects shrank, they drew closer and more of them appeared. She wouldn't surprise them again that way. The current whirled faster. At its center spun a vortex of incomprehensible depth. That had to be the gate to their deeper plane of existence. If she fell through, she might never escape with her sanity. She clutched at the fabric of space-time, trying to stop her slide. It didn't help. Every revolution swept her closer.

She'd meant to save her inside-out gesture for her last need. Evidently, the need had already come. She emptied herself once more—

And emerged into silence. Here, too—to her shock and wonder— spun the image of incredible speed and brilliance. It continued to shed thousands of garnet shards each second. Now, she saw that its powerful gravity also exerted an inexorable pull. Every shard returned to it.

{It's you,} Llyn sang in a whisper. She had not expected to find this in Chaethe inner space. {Or are you another?}

{It is I.} Three chords leaped from the spinning center, fortissimo but bearable.

{Have I died?} she asked.

It seemed to sparkle. {Far from that.}

As before, she found it impossible to feel afraid in this serene, mirthful presence—except for a reverential fear that was almost joy. She still couldn't discern its shape, though. It spun too rapidly. {What are you?} she asked.

Again, it answered incomprehensibly: {I exist.}

Maybe it was simply incomprehensible by nature. Or maybe it was everything.

{I am not worthy to ask you questions,} she began—

{I can impart worth. I have paid its full price, and I have called you. You must ask, though. Then stand and receive it.}

{Regent Salbari said one day I would know my real value. I still don't—and I don't understand.}

{Acceptance often comes before understanding. Sometimes it takes years. Sometimes a lifetime.}

She quivered. The entity fascinated her. Apparently, she could find it from any inner world. {Then I ask. I have tried to find my worth for a long time. I know now it is not mine for pleasing Karine. It is not mine for being Gamal Casimir's daughter. It did not come from joining with Jahn.}

The great whirling orb sang again. {All you have endured has refined your mind's eye to see ever more clearly. You lack only one thing.} It seemed to slow. For an instant, she saw three distinct segments. From one of them spattered a garnet shower. More droplets—or jewels—tingled their way through her, mingling with her soul's substance.

She sang herself small, a gesture of worship. Fear and pain and questions would wait. This time, the change felt far deeper. Before, she'd been called. Now, having received the gift, she was also received. She would gladly stay in that posture forever.

Another garnet shower stung and roused her. {You have found peace. Now go. Give it to the Chaethe. And to your people.}

{Me? Are they our allies now?}

{They still mean you harm.}

Her singing voice squeaked. {I'm too small. And it's too late—}

{It is never too late for the living.}

{They will attack me again. Will you save me?}

{You will defend yourself. Remember your struggles. All of them.}

Time seemed to wait as she thought this through. All of her struggles? {I don't understand. But I am willing.}

{Then take peace with you.} One more garnet shower suffused her.

She turned right-side out again.

The whirlpool spun as if she'd never left. Uncountable shapes and colors spun around her and kept her in the strongest current. Maybe the minutes she'd spent at the center counted against eternity, not time.

Then she remembered her very first reaction inside this mindscape. She anchored herself to a relative location on the whirlpool. She focused on the deep peace that still reverberated in her soul. Then she sang Jahn's song. Its simple, twelve-tone melody and human words seemed irrelevant to Chaethe inner life, but to her, they meant love, power, and discovery.

The whirlpool slowed. Its amethyst core focused again. The Chaethe universe shuddered. It would have terrified her if she had not just returned from the source.

Did she dare call it the Creator?

Another melody jumped into her mind: her own song, her gift from the true composer, which she'd been given on that long-ago afternoon when she attended the University choral concert. She remembered it note for note! She didn't understand why these songs increased her power and diminished the Chaethe, but plainly, they did. Some part of their tone-based culture obviously shrank from this music.

And she must weaken them—temporarily, at least. They must not incite their Sunsisan hosts to attack the Tdegans or Antarans.

So she sang. Gradually, the spinning shapes froze in positions that took their coordinates from Llyn. The sphere became an unmoving formation around her.

{We want you as allies, not as enemies,} she sang.

Out of the sphere plunged her rosy jewel. It shimmered submissively, obviously afraid of her.

She didn't want that either. She needed Salbari.

{Wait for me,} she commanded. {I wish to introduce another of our leaders to you. A stronger, better one than Gamal Casimir.}

{You are not a leader?} Her rose-colored partner sang in a small voice. {You were liberated from a leader.}

Liberated? Abruptly, she remembered that was their reproductive idiom. {I dance my own dance,} she sang back in harmony with the rose-colored entity. {But I choose to serve others.}

Orbits shifted. The brilliant, massive amethyst object fragmented. Its thousands of shards vibrated individually. Their harmonies reminded her of a choral anthem. {Life's goal is perfection, perfection in order to serve perfectly.}

Another concept they shared—with some humans, anyway. She shook herself hard. *Jahn? Jahn?* she repeated. *Get Regent Salbari into nexus. Hurry!*

Reality shifted again. She sat cross-legged, slumping across Jahn's lap. Jahn spoke in a low, urgent voice to Regent Salbari, who gripped his hand. Bellik leaned close, tilting his head, plainly trying to listen. Llyn faintly saw the inner world, superimposed over the Sunsisan landscape. They did not occupy the same space, except in her mind. This had not happened before. Was she in danger?

She blinked at Bellik, who flushed and said, "I demand to be included. You would not be communicating with that race without the education your father gave you." His helmet fogged as he spoke.

"I owe him nothing," she realized aloud. "Did you hear what he told me? He said, 'You are not my daughter. You are Llyn Torfinn, the creation of an empath.' He disowned me, Bellik. He can't have it both ways, and neither can you."

"But I didn't—"

"My father gave me away, and you never had a claim. I owe you nothing."

She turned her head. Regent Salbari sat watching her, keeping his face bland but wearing smile lines around his eyes.

Jahn nudged her, his touch warm and real. "We'll try it."

She eased back into accord. The inner world focused again. Hundreds of glimmering shapes wove slowly around her, surrounding her like a multicolored, multifaceted hollow globe. Some traveled at one tempo, others more quickly or slowly, but all of their tempi fit a new rhythm of rhythms, a new posture of receiving and listening.

They did fear her. She wondered if fear might make them attack her again.

A new, intense point of light circled close to her. She saw it as a glowing bloodstone and heard it sing with Regent Salbari's voice. {She speaks truth. We want you for allies.} His singing voice had a rich timbre, but he sang only one note.

The Chaethe did not respond. On a hunch, she repeated his words, setting them to melody.

A chorus responded, singing in the tenor range. {New voice, listen. You have a translator, translator. Yet your world is not strange to us. We know it through symbiont senses. We know now that your people can sing with us. Do not sing against us.}

Llyn tried to sing softly aside to Regent Salbari, but she composed her lyrics with exquisite caution. {I've found a stronger control music than theirs.} She hoped that made sense to him.

Another voice sang to Regent Salbari. {Your servant's music masters ours. Yours must be even more powerful.}

It sounded like an obeisance. Llyn felt her first thrill of fear since leaving the innermost Sphere. If they learned otherwise, might they attack Regent Salbari?

He sang again. {We want you as allies. Llyn, repeat only that. Nothing more.}

She set those words to melody.

The cloud shimmered.

{Now this,} he sang to her. {They must bind themselves by whatever promise they hold sacred to stop using our bodies. If they will do that, we will do everything in our power to protect them from the Devastators.}

{But,} Llyn began.

{Quickly, Llyn.}

So she translated.

The amethyst chorus that had assembled when the center fragmented formed a pair of broad rings encircling Llyn and Regent Salbari. {Here is wisdom, wisdom in numbers,} they sang. {You who still suffer physical need, hear them.}

Llyn stared at the glimmering rings, which now plainly showed as separate from the multitude. Were those Chaethe who had died, or Chaethe at their next stage of metamorphosis? They were truly alien, and this felt like proof.

Still, she didn't have to understand. She had to obey. To accept, and to translate. She listened for a response from the rest of them.

The spiked image swooped into position across from Llyn and Regent Salbari. {Your race has met both moral conditions for equality. One is the ability to listen and sing to us.}

Telepathy, one of the Two? But the empaths only had half of that circle.

Apparently, she provided the other half, though she did not understand how. If the Chaethe destroyed her, humankind's hope for freedom from infestation died, too.

Now she was truly afraid. She was the weak link in a chain that must hold two civilizations together—and if she broke, catastrophe could follow.

Their answer confirmed her guess and her fears. {The other is mastery of our language, and you are plainly a master,} its spines sang in chorus.

{Those are the Two,} sang the amethyst rings.

The multitude broke orbit and danced wildly in all directions around her and Regent Salbari, blurring the sphere so utterly that it encased the rings like an outer shell. Truly frightened, she clung to Salbari.

Wait. She must not fear. She must remember the innermost and its blood-red shards.

Gripping that thought, she relaxed. If she stood her ground beside Regent Salbari, she was safe. They seemed to think Regent Salbari also knew how to weaken them, since she looked to him as a leader. She must not let them learn the truth, not until she taught someone else to sing control music!

Dancing wildly, they probably could not hear her. Again she sang at Regent Salbari, pianissimo and monotone. {Since I can translate, they seem to assume you can, too. Maybe all humans will be able to, given proper training.}

{Will they let us try?} the other monotone returned, gentle-voiced.

{This is the moment of decision,} she answered.

The multitude slowed. Its wild harmonies calmed. For an instant, she glimpsed huge shapes behind them: a landscape, perhaps, illuminated by thousands more of the creatures.

{Will they declare us ineligible for infestation?} Regent Salbari asked her.

{We will be your allies, your allies.} Llyn sang it loudly. {We will sing with you, and dance the Great Dance, but you must not live inside our bodies anymore.}

{Hear this,} Regent Salbari sang. {We lived on these worlds for four hundred years before the Devastators tried to destroy us.}

Llyn translated.

{They ruined our worlds. They killed thousands of us. All out of fear of your people.}

Llyn set that to melody, a grim minor tune.

{Fear, hate, and evil often sing harmony,} answered the amethyst rings.

{Tell them I understand and deeply agree.}

Llyn complied.

The rings danced and spun.

From the shell came an alto chorus. {We have fought the Devastators for centuries longer. Your people sing infant rhymes and call it civilization.}

{But we are children of the innermost Sphere, as you are,} Regent Salbari answered through Llyn. {We are your siblings, not your prey. Your canta is a research team, sent to approach us. Now you know you may no longer use our bodies.}

{We require bodies. You may be a people of faith,} the rings answered, {and perhaps you aim at civilization. But you are obviously not there yet.}

{You are deeply correct,} Regent Salbari answered. {In many ways. But we are the innermost's children.}

The canta began whirling again. {Sunsis colony is happy. It is safe. We meet our symbionts' physical needs and protect them from harm. That is why we banned dangerous vehicles.}

All those pedestrians, and those primitive farm implements. This explained it.

{Sunsis colony is not happy,} Regent Salbari challenged them. {You sense that. Do not pretend you do not. Spore pain may be joyful for you, but for us it is terrible. You may not use our bodies.}

{Symbiosis is natural for you. Your bodies teem with tiny Riders. Some harm and kill you. Others cause worse pain than we do.}

{We have no natural partners who tamper with our will or our freedom. You may not use our bodies. You must find others.} Llyn translated. She waited.

{A species in test can be used as symbionts for a trial time,} sang the amethyst rings.

{How long?}

{Less than four hundred of your years.}

{Unacceptable. You may no longer use our bodies.}

The shell's song came softly this time. {We must have bodies. Without them, the canta will die. You must respect us as your siblings, too.}

They admitted weakness—they confessed their need—framed as a request among family members! Negotiations might follow, but at this moment, this precise moment, the war ended.

Llyn had no time to exult, though.

{Have you no law,} Regent Salbari was asking, {forbidding you to change other civilizations?}

{That would be meaningless. We must enter. We must interfere, or we die.}

For the first time in Regent Salbari's presence, Llyn's rosy partner sprang back out of the shell. {Llyn Human, Translator, you sang of other creatures. What are these things you called dogs? What are dedoes?}

Llyn's mind created two terrible images: poor Squeak with metal spores in his head, and Bear passing them on to her puppies as she licked their ears clean. {No!} she protested.

{Llyn!} Regent Salbari's monotone reprimanded her. {Translate. Do not negotiate.}

I serve a greater ... {I apologize, apologize,} she sang. {I spoke out of turn. My Regent will describe them to you.} Inwardly, she cringed.

{Dogs are not right for you,} he insisted, {but dedoes are creatures that our race created. They have little intelligence. Their human creator thought that keeping intelligent animals was slavery. Your using our bodies, even kindly according to your own understanding, also is slavery.}

The shell hummed softly and drew closer.

{Their human creator did not trust humans to take adequate care of them. So she bred them without any pain sense.}

The humming grew louder.

{They breed more rapidly than humans. They can bear three and four in a litter, two or three times a year.}

{Do they have clever hands like yours?}

{No,} Regent Salbari admitted, {but we could translate your wishes if you took their bodies. We could offer our own hands in treaty. But we will not allow the rest of our bodies to be used.} He hammered that concept like the chorus of a song. It was the obvious way to negotiate with this race.

{You would translate? Do they have outer-world voices, so we could speak?}

Regent Salbari hesitated. Llyn held her breath. {No, but the people of my kind, those who can hear mindsong, we will serve as translators. I am head of that kind. I can promise on behalf of us all.}

{You will give us these dedoes?}

Llyn trembled again. This seemed like buying one people's peace at the expense of another's. She hated the idea … and yet dedoes had little intelligence to subvert, and no pain sense. Without loving ownership, they could not survive.

And would she rather see Squeak infested, or Jahn?

It was good to be bodied. Surely, the Chaethe hadn't forgotten. At some level, they must remember.

{Maybe in time,} Regent Salbari said, and she relayed to the canta, {we could breed creatures to suit you even better. I can promise my people's efforts in that respect also. But you may no longer use our bodies.}

{No more.} The lyrics resounded around her, two incredibly loud chords that must have shaken Sunsis A to its molten core.

{That is your promise?} Regent Salbari asked.

{No more.} The chords repeated. {By the innermost Sphere—by its speed and its power—no more, if you meet the conditions you promised.}

{Then we pledge …} Regent Salbari repeated the promises he had already made. Llyn translated.

Then she broke into the formalities. {What about Gamal Casimir? Is it too late for him?}

The amethyst rings fragmented into hundreds of small moons. {Too late,} they sang. {Before the promise was made, his body was breached. He is the last. No more, no more.}

{We two will leave this song for a time,} Regent Salbari sang. {We must tell our people what we have promised you, and what you promised us. There will be more to sing and say. There are humans whose bodies cannot be made whole again.}

{They cannot live now, cannot live without us,} the canta confessed.

{We will negotiate on their behalf.} As soon as Llyn relayed that promise, Regent Salbari's presence winked out.

The rosy oval pulled Llyn away from the dance's center. {Stay with us,} it sang. {We have much to learn from each other. You are happy here. Your melodies show your contentment here. Why must you live in the unreal world?}

{It is real. Real to us, as the Creator made our senses.}

Intense beams of light shot from all directions toward a single point. The rings coalesced, collapsed, and formed the brilliant amethyst center again. {Come inside,} it sang. {Come in. Let us reason together.}

Her guide kept spinning around her. {We would welcome you, welcome you. We would never distress you. You would be honored, honored.}

But this was not her world. Jahn lived elsewhere. {Please guide me out.}

A cloud of alto voices surrounded her, singing, {Be your people's Ambassador to our canta! Live with us, stay with us, dance alongside.}

{Yes, yes, yes.} It echoed around her, but the voices seemed to sing discordantly. One note held, clashing with other melodies. She wafted toward it.

A glimmering gold polyhedron spun in place. {We chose him years ago,} the canta sang around it. {We wanted Gamal Casimir Human. Now he is the last. Thus he is honored.}

{He is *damaged*,} sang the gold polyhedron, maintaining its discord. This singer took no pleasure in its new symbiont, her father. {He would not cooperate, as he made others cooperate. The helmet could not be removed, so his spine is affected, and he was already blind in one eye.}

{He is still honored,} the canta insisted. {Llyn Human, we honor you, too.}

{I must rest. I must think.} Chilled, Llyn sang softly. Her new perception of Jahn's unending closeness had somehow faded. He could not dance inside the canta. Even Regent Salbari, with years of training and experience beyond Jahn's, had needed Jahn's help to enter and Llyn's help to sing. She also pitied the polyhedron, who had been selected to take Gamal Casimir's body but was forced to cripple it. She had never realized he was partially blind.

And she was exhausted.

Jahn? she cried silently. *I need you. Help me out! Can you hear me?*

The canta waited.

No answer came.

Jahn could not live this way. He was human.

Was she?

Karine had thought her soul had been altered. What if those AR years did change her at soul level?

And she and Jahn might never escape whatever they had done to each other's souls—like impressing within a canta, or so she guessed. Even if she returned to physical reality, it would be to a new kind of existence. How many more adjustments could she survive?

Deep down, the certainty rose. Created human, she remained human.

{I love a man of my kind,} she sang toward the center. {We are usually happier in pairs.}

{Llyn, Llyn.} A chorus of voices beckoned. {We honor you as the first who came to us. We will make you a gift. We are sorry, are sorry, that evil came from our renegade. He and his spore descendants deliberately destroyed symbionts. That is evil among us. We will destroy him, and keep Gamal Casimir Human. Tell your Regent.}

{But he has suffered so much already.}

{A renegade deserves to—}

{No, no. His host, Osun Zavijavah,} she sang. {He has already suffered.}

There was a moment's silence. {The renegade means to leave him anyway, to kill him and seize your Salbari Regent. We must destroy him quickly.}

Llyn wished Regent Salbari had not left the inner world. {If you can force him—your renegade—to destroy himself, can you force him to destroy the parts of Osun Zavijavah that feel pain—first?}

{We can do that.}

To Llyn's surprise, it felt right to pity Gen Zavijavah.

33

Karine sat cross-legged, aching for the danger her child faced. As minutes dragged, she became increasingly certain Llyn would not recover from the seizure that laid her out, blank-eyed, in Jahn Emlin's arms.

Karine glanced at the deadly doors where Gamal Casimir had entered, then over her shoulder at the Sunsisans. She would let those shabby farmers club her to death with their shovels and hoes rather than walk into that building.

Suddenly Salbari beckoned—to Rena. The redheaded girl scooted forward, grinding sand into her culottes' knees. She and Salbari stared at each other for a moment before Rena crabwalked back to Karine. "He wants you to see this. He's so proud of Llyn."

Karine jumped into synch, desperate for information. Rena passed on a third-generation image of Llyn's inner vision. The colors and shapes looked sickeningly familiar. Karine had struggled to train Llyn out of that environment, to make her forget it. Now, according to Rena, they must all hope Llyn remembered it well enough to survive inside.

Should she have nurtured Llyn's unusual skills?

No! Years of habit and deep conviction throttled those thoughts. Llyn had disobeyed her. If the aliens devoured Llyn, only Llyn was to blame. Llyn and Filip.

How could she rescue Llyn now?

The multitude pushed Llyn toward a spot in the darkness that they alone illuminated. She thought it might be the place where she'd entered—and at that spot, Jahn's presence seemed close. Warm.

Exhausted, she sang herself through.

The Chaethe must have helped her this time. Immediately, her outer senses focused. "Jahn," she breathed. "Regent Salbari."

They both turned to her. Beyond them sat a blur of other people. Past that group stood Osun Zavijavah. Alone. His dark mustache deepened his frown.

If only she could help him—

"What is it?" Regent Salbari whispered.

She whispered back. "They're going to destroy their renegade. They promised me Gen Zavijavah won't suffer—"

Abruptly, Zavijavah collapsed without a sound. His forehead seemed to be swelling. Darkening.

Llyn shut her eyes. Shouts surrounded her, but she curled forward and ignored them. Warm arms enfolded her.

It would feel so good to sleep.

Rena's shout startled her. "Casimir—he's back!"

Llyn straightened. Rena stood pointing at the huge building. Two Sunsisan farmers emerged. One carried a limp human in a Tdegan dress uniform. It had to be her father. He was bleeding at the back of his neck.

She shut her eyes again. She relaxed into Jahn's embrace.

But shuffling noises roused her, and she opened them again. Two farmers stood beside Bellik, and her father had been laid in Bellik's lap. He made no attempt to cooperate. Obviously, he had no body control below his shoulders. His wide, fear-red eyes flicked left and right.

Her heart went out to him.

"Regent Casimir." Regent Salbari spoke as firmly as he'd addressed the Chaethe multitude. "The Concord will gladly receive Tdega, if you wish you rejoin us."

"Yes." Her father grunted the word. "That's for myself. Not for *it*. Bellik, give him my hand."

Bellik lifted her father's hand off his leg and extended it to Regent Salbari. Palm up. Submissive.

Regent Salbari grasped it. He did not turn the handclasp. "There must be reparations."

Bellik cleared his throat. Llyn thought his eyes looked frightened. "Nuris University. Rebuilt," Bellik said.

"And food templates," Regent Salbari prompted.

Llyn held her breath.

Bellik offered his own hand this time. She doubted Bellik would go on cooperating this willingly, but for now, he plainly saw the wisdom.

Llyn shut her eyes. Without even needing Jahn's help this time, she escaped back to the inner world, where revulsion darkened the shapes she saw. {Must it be so terrible, so terrible?} she sang. {Did Gen Zavijavah have to die? Will the new Rider kill my father that same way? And …} A new thought struck her. {Did the renegade infest other humans on Tdega?}

The basses answered, their notes ponderous and slow. {We—do—not—know.}

But the rosy oval reappeared. {We could find them. Take some of us to Tdega Sphere. We will reimpress the poor renegade's children. We will bring them back into the canta.}

{Have any of your people been to Tdega?} Llyn asked. {Those inside the canta?}

The multitude vibrated again, singing laughter like grace notes. {Our people have had a presence at Tdega Sphere for centuries, Llyn Human Singer. We set an automated space station in orbit around its red sun centuries ago.}

The so-called Devastator artifact was *Chaethe?* Llyn trembled. {You set it there?}

{We did, we did, we did.} She heard amusement and pride, but also an odd hesitancy. They felt embarrassed to tell her.

Another group sang. {We meant to defend Tdega, once we colonized it. We still could defend Tdega from other races. Tdega is safe, it is safe from Devastator beasts!}

{The war station was already programmed to destroy incoming weapons,} sang the basses. {So it survived the Devastators' purge. As did Tdega Sphere. We saved it for you. For us. We saved Tdega for all humans, and for Chaethe.}

{Thank you,} she exclaimed, flabbergasted. {Excuse me, but this is important news, and I must tell my people.}

She found the entry point without help, but she emerged gasping this time, all temptation gone. If she had chosen to join the canta permanently, this body of hers would have become bedridden, as helpless as she'd been in a float tank.

Then she must live here, in the outer world. Besides, Jahn lived here. "Regent Salbari," she exclaimed.

He turned toward her.

"They put the artifact into orbit at Tdega. It's not a Devastator artifact at all!"

"They what?"

It would take too much effort to explain. "Synch with me, sir. I'll show you."

What had awed Llyn terrified Filip. Evidently, humankind had lived with a Chaethe-controlled robotic presence for two centuries. If it could destroy Devastator warships, it could be turned against humankind. All the Chaethe would need was time to arm it.

They must leave. Soon. There was more negotiating to do, as soon as Llyn regained her strength.

Abruptly, Karine waved both hands. "Llyn," she cried. "Tell them I still have the AR unit."

Llyn shook her head, looking as confused as Filip felt.

"The AR machine." Karine's eyes had gone wide. "It's in crates. In the clinic basement."

"Yes!" Llyn exclaimed, and she collapsed in Jahn's lap again, looking paler than ever. She was slipping. Filip must not let her—or Jahn—continue much longer. The afternoon had gone on too long. Sunsis A's solar day lasted fifty hours, or so he'd been told.

Burgin Hardette, Senator Igrim, and Dio Liion suggested demands they must make of the Chaethe. Gamal Casimir volunteered the fact that the Chaethe could be thwarted by electromagnets or ethanol.

Then the talk turned to hosts for the Chaethe. "Are there enough dedoes to go around?" Dio Liion asked.

"Of course not." Captain Hardette stepped forward. "This is going to be a rough transition."

"They need more bodies right now." Gamal Casimir's voice sounded weak. "Otherwise, these hosts will start to die. Humans can't carry four spores. It will kill them."

"He is right." Jal Malukulu still sat with the central group. "Sunsis A North is sparsely populated. Those of us they've taken can stay here. The ones who take dedoes can move up north." He held himself straighter than before, Filip noticed. With more dignity.

"Why not here?" Senator Igrim asked.

Malukulu spread his hands. "Our human children's human children will be born free. We must protect them."

Bellik cleared his throat. "We have range animals that are normally slaughtered at two years. If the Chaethe are desperate for temporary bodies, we can ship in several thousand within twenty days. Those will suffice while the dedoes breed, won't they? Infest them young—when we brand them and dock their tails—and then simply don't slaughter. Let the Chaethe do it for us, when they leave the creatures for your dedoes."

Filip's throat constricted. The little meat Antarans ate was tissue-cloned. Still, he would support almost any step that did not crack open the door for more human infestation.

And the talks went on, and eventually he forbade Llyn to go back inside. But to his surprise, she struggled to her feet, helped by Jahn. In an oddly modulated voice that sounded like Chaethe music, she asked, "How many empaths could learn, could learn the Chaethe language if they tried to teach us? The more translators they can find, the sooner they can leave our systems. The transducer helmet will help. We must build more of them."

Joao raised a finger.

"Me," Rena called.

Karine stared at her feet.

"Llyn," Filip called, "we will commit ourselves to every empath available and willing. Llyn, are you here?"

She glanced at him. She looked up into the sky and sang something he did not understand.

Karine scrambled to her feet, and this time, he found himself empathizing with her.

"Llyn," he said. "Llyn, listen to me." He synched with Jahn. Llyn turned her head past him, cocking an ear to listen. "We can teach Chaethe language to other empaths," he told her. "We can offer facilities on Sunsis and Antar. But you must teach us. You're going too deep, for too long. Come back. Come out and rest, Llyn. Can you hear me? You're in danger."

His monotone rasped like dry sticks scraping compared to the canta's sweet music. {There will be many of us to sing for you,} she told the multitude. {But I am tired. I must rest.} She thought of Jahn, waiting. Of Regent Salbari, and even Karine.

She was human, not Chaethe. {I'll return when I can,} she sang wearily. She wafted toward the entry point ... and through, with a wrench that nauseated her. Hot wind made her even dizzier. "I'm done," she muttered to Jahn. He severed the connection, and grief stabbed her like long metal spores, like knives, like all the pain she ever had known.

But she belonged with Jahn. Surely the Creator wanted her here in this world, where she'd been born. Human.

Someone stepped in front of her. She looked up into Regent Salbari's solemn eyes. "Thank you," he said. "Rest. Lie down, both of you. We will have peace in the Concord, thanks to you."

"There's so much left to sing. I mean, to say." Darkness unraveled the edges of her vision.

Strong arms lowered her onto the sand.

"I'm all right," Jahn insisted.

Uncle Joao supported his shoulders. "You must be half dead. She certainly is."

Jahn glanced down at Llyn, who was already asleep and going deeper by the moment—but it was only sleep. Sweet, normal sleep. Her drowsiness beat at him.

Then he remembered. "Where's Mother?" he exclaimed, shaking free.

He stumbled over to Lyova Waverly and the group she guarded, lying near the outer circle. Sunsisans turned to each other in clusters, dropping their farming tools. Some shook their heads.

His mother lay with her curls askew, breathing slowly. "Can you synch with her?" he asked Lyova. "Is she—"

"She seems stunned. I don't think she hears when I try to wake her up."

Jahn knelt and fingered the white stimulant patch on his mother's throat.

"It should have worked by now," Lyova said, caution in her voice.

He stretched into synch. The last time he'd seen his mother, he had been slower and weaker. His abilities had grown.

And she was the Order's strongest listener. Imitating Llyn's inner song, he tried to project. Maybe she would hear. Maybe she would recognize him, if he came close enough. {Mother,} he called. {Mother, it's done. It's over. We've won.} His weary eyes watered. {Mother, Llyn made peace with the Chaethe. Mother,} he repeated.

At the deepest level of synchrony, her inner frequency quivered. It accelerated. Her eyes twitched.

They opened.

"Vananda!" Uncle Joao cried.

The next time Llyn saw Karine, a long Sunsisan night and a day and another long night had passed. Gate-relay communiqués had returned from all eight Concord worlds. In a concrete house on the edge of Sunsis A South's main settlement, treaty terms were being modified.

In a smaller house, Karine stood in front of a gray wall. Sunlight streamed in her eastern window. "You are not listening," she insisted. "There is still hope you may recover from enmeshment. You must avoid Jahn Emlin. I have an extra bed. I need you here. I don't feel well."

"Let me try this again, Karine." Llyn pitied her. She tucked her hands into the pockets of a billowy summer dress, Winnow's gift. Llyn now knew that Winnow's Chaethe symbiont portrayed itself as a rose-colored oval. They were becoming friends. All three of them. "I came to tell you this. I have forgiven you again, and you need to know why. You humiliated me in front of Regent Salbari and half the population of this town."

"When did I—"

"With Regent Salbari's helmet." It was a relief to tell Karine so, but she doubted Karine would understand. "I also came to say good-bye. Karine, I love you. I want the best for you. That's why I will support Regent Salbari's criminal abuse charges."

Karine clenched both fists. "I have offered to assist the diplomatic effort. That charge is ridiculous."

"You are helping." Llyn had to agree. "And everyone is grateful. But your heart and habits have not changed. You are a worthy, valuable person. And when you're better, you can be—"

"I am not sick. Do you—" For one moment, Karine's expression softened. Llyn heard pain and hope as she asked, "Do you think I am?"

Not long ago, Llyn would've rather lied than hurt Karine. She tried to answer gently. "When I have gone, you will only find someone else to control unless you let Herva Metyline treat you. They tell me her clinic isn't as comfortable as yours, which is high praise to you. And I promise I'll come see you often—"

"Get out!" Karine thrust a hand toward the door.

Although the words stung, Llyn smiled. She'd resisted manipulation—and it worked! It did not hurt to turn and walk out.

She emerged onto the front porch, where Rena and Jahn stood waiting with Karine's Outwatch guard. "That's over." Llyn sighed.

Jahn touched her hand. She reached down into nexus and was comforted.

Across a rectangular table, Filip watched Gamal Casimir. Besides the six worlds that had not seceded, Tdega was represented by the Casimirs, and Sunsis by Jal Malukulu, who gave his symbiont access to these talks. Sunsis B had also sent a representative. An Ilzaran envoy would arrive within a week.

Gamal had been furnished with a small personal transport. Servomotors that he controlled with his chin operated a right-arm brace. He extended that hand, asking Senator Igrim for the right to speak. Bellik sat near the wall behind him. In the five days—Concord time—since they landed, Bellik had thwarted two more attempts on Gamal's life.

Gamal's symbiont, an honorable canta member, had pledged its cooperation, but there could be little rehabilitation.

Urban Igrim acknowledged Gamal, who jerked his chin against the control surface. His arm sank onto the table. "I have heard from my constituents, too," Gamal said. "My son, Siah, says that the Tdegan Board will refit Sunsis A North for Chaethe-dedo symbionts and a few human facilitators. We will build a satellite campus for Nuris University there." He cleared his throat, took two rattling breaths, and went on. "I am asked to offer my services as Regent for that campus. Bellik will assist me."

It would be a fitting exile. Filip kept his hands folded on the table, thankful to have use of them. Back on Tdega, Llyn's brother Siah—who had exiled himself when Gamal attacked Nuris University—had taken up functional headship of Tdega, as well as the care of old Head Regent Donson.

Senator Urban Igrim addressed Filip. "Sir, you resigned the Head Regency, but I believe you have the authority to accept that application."

"Yes," Filip said. "Welcome to Nuris University, Regent Casimir." It felt good to say that.

Gamal's face twitched.

Humans stood to learn prodigious amounts from the Chaethe, who had parasitized three other spacefaring races. Nuris University soon would be the greatest information repository known to any species.

Except perhaps the Devastators.

The balance point of this new alliance was a chilling understanding. The Devastators were still out there, who asked no questions before boiling whole worlds' oceans away. They might not return for ten human lifetimes, but someday, the Human-Chaethe alliance would face them. If the Chaethe could convince them that they no longer menaced the Devastator hive, a threat to all sentient races might end.

In peace, not war.

In the meantime, Nuris University's surviving geneticists would go to work designing a new symbiont species. The Chaethe requested the ability to enunciate words, of course. Comfortable sporulation would be an equally high priority. In a best-case scenario, something like their original bodies might be developed.

Senator Igrim's chair at the head of this table was padded and reclined for his comfort. "Forgive me for not standing to speak," he said. "Even in this pleasant heat, my joints are no younger than they were yesterday."

Representatives murmured assent.

Vananda sat beside Filip, still looking pale and moving slowly. The Chaethe still were insisting they had not deliberately attacked her, nor Qu—and so synching with Chaethe was left to Llyn and Jahn, until other empaths learned to master the hazardous modulated vibrato of that alien inner frequency.

"I spent several hours this morning with the canta," Senator Igrim said, "assisted by young Gen'n Torfinn and Gen Emlin. Regent Salbari's proposal that Nuris and Bkellan Universities fund research into limiting Chaethe reproduction is tentatively approved. They still need to dance through the idea ten or twenty times."

Several representatives applauded. Some turned to smile at Filip. He bowed his head and exhaled thanks. He'd been afraid that the concept would offend the Chaethe. "According to Gen'n Torfinn," Filip explained, "most of the canta already hails our proposal as a breakthrough."

"I can't believe they never thought of it," Dio Liion said. As soon as the need for helmets had obviously ended, she'd reknotted her hair.

Senator Igrim shrugged. "It is an alien mindset, and this unbalance is evidently a side effect of turning themselves into parasites. They are unhappy in communities less than a thousand, and greater numbers add to their pleasure. They see now that this would help them live peaceably among other people, spending more time doing what they enjoy. And they even have offered, if we succeed in those aims, to seek out other cantas and proselytize them."

"Other cantas?" Captain Hardette repeated. "There are more of them?"

Filip raised an eyebrow. What had Hardette expected?

"Of course there are," Senator Igrim said. "And four other spacefaring races."

A warm breeze blew back Llyn's hair. She looked up into Jahn's beardless face. His auburn hair had grown in, and to her amusement, his eyebrows were dark red. "Regent Salbari says this enmeshment is permanent, then?" she asked.

He nodded. "But acceptable. The question is, is it acceptable to you? Karine is right. You could probably learn to cope—alone—if you never saw me again."

But they'd walked together to life's very edge. "I don't want to cope without you," she said. "I love you. It's just that I feel too immature to make a lifetime commitment. I'm free, but I'm awfully young."

"Remember what I said about the learning curve." He circled her waist with an arm.

"I do." She nodded. "But—"

"Salbari is willing and qualified to perform the rite."

"But he needs me. He's doing better at synching, but I'm still involved in those treaty talks."

"I know that. And they know about us. You admitted that the Chaethe are anxious to see us … didn't they call it 'finishing our song'? You also told them we tend to be happier as couples."

She clasped her hands behind his neck and pressed her shoulders against his body. Never in any of her lives had anything felt better.

It was good to be human, and they loved each other. They worked well together. They shared their deepest beliefs. If they meant to build something totally new, those sounded like good foundations.

She tipped back her head and said, "Let's talk to Regent Salbari."

34

Two years had passed since the Tdegan War. Llyn had spent so much time among empaths that she almost felt like one of them.

After all, she was almost *part* of one of them.

The new Nuris City and University domes stood 150K northwest of their former site, where a magma plume still crept upward underground. Llyn sat in a recently built faculty lounge and stared at its two-meter i-net screen. Jahn pressed a leg against hers. His deep satisfaction reinforced her own.

Immediately after they had returned to Antar, the Order had awarded him a second collar garnet, like Regent Salbari's—marking him as an honored elder statesman, though he wasn't even thirty. His grandfather would have been proud.

She and Jahn had worked through deep, unsettling problems that were typical of enmeshment victims—which they were—and of her deep, unchanged need to please others. With Regent Salbari's help, they had established personal thought-privacy zones. Now she could retreat into herself when this world baffled her, and when Jahn caught her unconsciously piggybacking his thoughts and feelings, he threw her off.

But gently.

Karine's son, Niklo, sat on another couch in the University's faculty lounge, wearing a pale-blue lab uniform. With Karine removed from the clinic and barred from practicing, Niklo had gone into psi medicine after all. He was already a brilliant intern here at NU, promising to surpass his mother. In three more years, the Torfinn-Reece Clinic would be his by default. For now, Elroy and Tamsina were keeping it open.

Clinician Herva Metyline had reported to Llyn yesterday. True to form, Karine was bitterly fighting to control that clinic where she now was a resident patient. No release date had been set, no freedom offered, until she stopped trying to seize other people's responsibilities.

"There it goes," Jahn exclaimed. Llyn eyed the monitor. Along one edge of the big screen, data represented velocity relative to Tdega Gate. At the image's center hung a blue-gray sphere that bristled with antennae, the very satellite that had menaced—and ironically had protected—Tdega for two centuries. The image did not change, but numbers along that margin began to shift. The satellite had steered off its orbital vector and headed toward deep space.

"Yes," Llyn exclaimed. The craft was crewed by Sunsisan humans and guided by Chaethe commanders. Jahn's close friend Kai Oldion had helped design components that made the launch possible, and here on Antar, Chaethe and humans now studied each other as fellow sentients. Llyn served as a full professor.

Jahn served the Order.

A familiar black-and-white dedo rubbed Jahn's legs and edged forward to snuggle the couch. Jahn stroked Squeak absently. Many of Squeak's progeny now served as hosts for mature Chaethe. Several had lived on campus with Llyn and Jahn as she labored to teach empaths the melodious Chaethe language. Stasia was one of her star students. The Chaethe had taken well to dedoes, and empaths—so quick with inner frequencies, so slow with seventeen-tone music—were also learning to understand a purred, howled new language. Even the Casimirs' ultrahigh frequency transmitter was proving useful when modulated at certain wavelengths.

Dedoes didn't seem to mind their Chaethe symbionts. Naturally, they experienced no discomfort. They sat purring for hours, perhaps absorbed in the Chaethe inner dance.

Squeak sat down next to Niklo, still purring. Other dedoes seemed so happy with their symbionts that Llyn almost felt guilty about keeping him Chaethe-free.

Almost.

"There won't be much more to see." Jahn rubbed his leg against hers.

"They're under way, but we won't see any real change in position for two or three days. It'll take that long to build up speed."

"I know. But I wanted to see the first numbers shift."

Most of the aliens were headed to another star system, fulfilling another term of the Sunsis Treaty. They carried away two genetic break-throughs: hundreds of newly bred Dancer pups, and their own extended reproductive cycle. Only a few ambassadors would remain in the Concord.

Squeak jumped into her lap, still purring.

She had made an AR appointment for this evening—not to escape, but to pay a regular visit. She had joined the empaths' worship community. Occasionally, though, she returned to the innermost and emerged refreshed. Whole. She'd brought Jahn inside that sanctum before they left Sunsis, and together, they had asked a blessing on their marriage. Haltingly trying to use inner song, Jahn sang himself small and worshipped.

And the garnet droplets showered them both.

AUTHOR'S NOTE

"The Deer's Cry," basis for the anthem in chapter three, is credited to Patrick of Ireland. It is also known by other names, including "Patrick's Breastplate." I first encountered it in *1000 Years of Irish Poetry,* ed. Kathleen Hoagland (Devin-Adair Company, 1947). The full text can be found on numerous websites.

ACKNOWLEDGMENTS

To Ron and Janet Benrey, Chris Blackmore, Ken Bruwelheide, Gary Bummer, Carwin Dover, Bob and Carol Flaherty, Steve Gillett, William Gillin, Anne Groell, Karen Hancock, Barbara Keremedjiev, Tana Kradolfer, Steve Laube, Martha Millard, Robert S. McGee, Cheryl Moore-Gough, Kerry Nietz, Jerry Oltion, Janna Silverstein, Chris Sorensen Sims, Mark Tyers, Gayla Wiedenheft, Ed Willett, and others I've forgotten or never knew by name:

You contributed, knowingly or unknowingly, to this book. The best words on these pages belong to you. Mistakes, inconsistencies, incongruities, and weak wordings are mine.

> *I consider that our present sufferings are not worth comparing with the glory that will be revealed in us. …And we know that in all things God works for the good of those who love him, who have been called according to his purpose.*
>
> *Romans 8:18, 28 (NIV)*

ABOUT THE AUTHOR

Kathy Tyers published her first science fiction novel in 1987 and has been writing ever since. She's published ten novels, including two authorized novels for the Star Wars expanded universe—*The Truce at Bakura* and *Balance Point*—and her original science fiction series *Firebird*.

She has also published a travel book, co-authored a book with classical guitarist Christopher Parkening, and recently published the writing reference *Writing Deep Viewpoint: Invite Your Readers Into the Story*. If she isn't writing, she might be teaching a flute lesson, mentoring a hopeful new author, or battling weeds in her vegetable garden. Kathy lives in Montana with her husband William Gillin.

Visit her website: *www.KathyTyers.com*

Travel the
Firebird Universe
with Kathy Tyers

Available Now!

Firebird
Fusion Fire
Crown of Fire
Wind and Shadow
Daystar

www.enclavepublishing.com